The Blood Stiller

by

Minerva Taylor

TELEMACHUS PRESS

This book is a work of fiction. Names, characters, places and incidents are either the product of the author's imagination or are used fictitiously. Any resemblance to actual persons, living or dead, or to actual events or locales is entirely coincidental.

THE BLOOD STILLER

The publisher does not have any control over and does not assume any responsibility for author or third-party websites or their content.

Cover designed by Telemachus Press, LLC

Cover art:
Copyright © iStockphoto/771714/tacojim
Copyright © Thinkstock/136326964/iStock

Published by Telemachus Press, LLC
http://www.telemachuspress.com

Visit the author website:
http://www.thebloodstiller.com

ISBN: 978-1-939337-95-5 (eBook)
ISBN: 978-1-939337-96-2 (Paperback)

Version 2016.04.04

Printed in the United States of America

10 9 8 7 6 5 4 3 2 1

Map of St. Petersburg

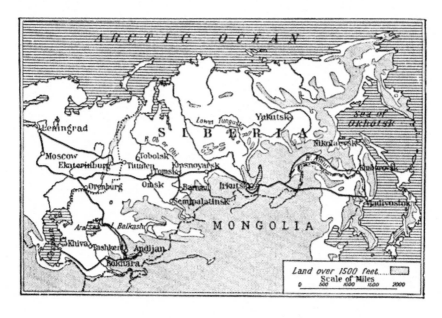

Map of Trans-Siberian Railway

We live without power of law,
like flocks of ravens they come and sweep over the land.

Alexander Pushkin, *The Brother Robbers*

The Blood Stiller

In March 1917 against the background of WWI, Russia, fighting on the side of the Allies, exploded into revolution, toppling the Tsarist government. Tsar Nicholas II was forced to abdicate his throne and was imprisoned with his family in Siberia. In October of that year, Lenin and his Bolsheviks wrested power from the temporary Provisional Government. Fierce resistance to the new Bolshevik regime led the country into a bloody civil war between the Reds, the Bolsheviks, and the Whites, the Tsarists and others who opposed them.

PROLOGUE

PRINCE VASILY ALEXANDROVICH Dolgorukov, the Tsar's aide, and once Marshall of the Imperial Court, hastens through a deserted field. His worn leather boots sink in to the cracks of the barren soil and his shabby officer's coat swings behind him. He glances quickly at his pocket watch hanging from his vest. It is 9 a.m. and the air is still cool, not yet surrendered to the blast of noonday heat. He clutches a battered Vuitton suitcase in his right hand and looks as though he could be catching a train to Paris as he surveys the limitless blue sky, broken only by a copse of fir trees in the distance.

The prince does not know the name of the stocky man pointing a rifle at him with such purpose. No words have been exchanged between them. His bulky captor, squeezed into a leather coat ripped from one of his earlier victims, is an enthusiastic member of the Cheka, the Bolshevik secret police. He communicates by viciously jamming the rifle into the prince's back.

Dolgorukov staggers in half comic steps to keep from falling. The Cheka thug lets out a loud guffaw, his thick lips opening like a gash in his lumpy face. Shivering, the prince tightens his grip on the suitcase. It is a luxury item, he muses, like the nobility; neither stands up well to violent wear and tear. Both are useless in this squalid new world.

In spite of the recent hardships of captivity, Dolgorukov has kept his good looks. Fair, well built, with fine features set off by a thick well-trimmed moustache, he once graced the drawing rooms of St. Petersburg and Paris. He marvels at chance, which brought him to this torturous march to the edge of a deserted field.

After he left Tobolsk in April with the Tsar's party, he had nursed the slight hope that Commissar Yakovlev was aiding in their escape. But the man from Moscow had delivered them to the hostile Bolsheviks at Ekaterinburg.

At the Ekaterinburg train station the local Soviet guards separated him from the Tsar and Tsarina and bundled him off to prison. They had not even permitted him to say a last farewell.

During his last days in the cells, he heard that the White Army in Siberia was advancing on Ekaterinburg. The prince still believes they might take the city and rescue the Tsar, if he is by some miracle still alive. There are grim rumors to the contrary. To his relief, the guards, always drunk and unpredictable, had not bothered to search the suitcase. Today before dawn they had told him he was leaving and to take his baggage with him, as though he were being set free. Like all the Cheka reports, his death will be recorded; shot while attempting to escape.

And now, even though he still carries the charge entrusted to him by the Tsar, it has all come to nothing. As he and his escort reach the middle of the field, a line from Pushkin's poem *The Brother Robbers* comes to him. *We live without power of law; like flocks of ravens they come and sweep over the land.* The prince stands silently at attention feeling the cold steel press against his scalp. As though bidden by his last thoughts, dark birds fly up and scatter at the sudden violent noise.

The stocky executioner impeded by his tight leather coat, sweats and grunts in frustration as he struggles to remove the suitcase from the dead prince's iron grip. He viciously kicks the body.

With the eagerness of a crow feeding on carrion, he strips the prince's pocket watch and the medals hidden underneath his shirt, and scavenges down to the leather boots. He places one foot on Dolgorukov's stomach and viciously pulls the leg upright. A second rifle shot, a popping noise from the direction of the trees, stops his exertions. A faint expression of surprise floats over his brutal face and he sinks down.

A large wild-haired creature with a rifle, his rags flapping about him, crawls swiftly out of the wood toward the two bodies. Tears flow like rivulets through the dirt on his face, seeping into a bushy beard. This beggar looks nothing like the idealized picture of the White Army's spy, the Bogatyr.

"Too late, too late, old friend," he murmurs, hovering near the prince. The Bogatyr knows now there is an informer, a traitor among them. He rips the coat off the executioner's corpse and covers what is left of the prince's distinguished features. In a graceful swift movement, the Bogatyr pulls out his knife from his belt, and hacks the suitcase away from the stiffening fingers. Then he disappears into the trees.

Chapter 1

Rural Ohio, USA: 2000

I IMAGINE MYSELF from afar, a tiny figure hidden in an old land-scape photograph. The wide vista shows a pale sky, scoured after a hard rain, fringed below by a vast expanse of trees, dark with moisture.

Near the bottom of the picture, dwarfed by the massive forest, a trail like a piece of thread frays away from the minute country road through the trees and winds past abandoned fields to the cabin, dropped in the middle of the clearing like a child's forgotten toy box.

Sheltered on the porch, I am barely visible, a slight blur. But I know a closer look through the telescopic lens of the killer's rifle would bring me into focus. I am sitting on the top step holding a shotgun with a black dog beside me. Although it is quiet after the violent afternoon storm with only sounds of the forest to break the silence, my head thunders with verses from long ago.

> *The old Cossack, Ilya of Murom,*
> *Set out on his good steed*
> *Past the city of Chernigov.*

> *Under Chernigov, the troops were quite black*
> *Quite black, like black crows.*

He urged his heroic steed
Into the midst of that mighty host.

He fixed a tempered arrow,
And drew his silken bow-strings;
He shot at Nightingale the Robber
Putting out his right eye from its socket.
Nightingale fell to the damp earth.

Like a boot on the damp earth, the lines from the old Russian *Byliny* are stamped forever on my mind. The poems echo inside my head, singing the deeds of those ancient heroes, the *Bogatyrs*. The words hammer at me, beating out their dark measure with the death chorus of cicadas massed on the screen door. They allow me no rest while I keep watch for the killers in the long twilight.

The lyrics pound on, conjuring up the last Russian hero, the spy, the Bogatyr. His ghost flits through the trees in front of me. I see him ragged and exhausted, struggling on in the vast Siberian plain, burdened with the secret.

Out in the fields beyond the porch the Russian émigrés, survivors from a violent fairy tale, seem to dance out from the lines of the *Byliny*. The women float by in faded gowns; the men in frayed uniforms sagging with medals from the Tsarist past. It is not surprising that their stories enthralled someone like me who wanted to escape my own life. I was caught in the web of their fantastic plot.

If not for my extensive archive, I would find my own role in this sinister narrative hard to believe. But then the alarming e-mail messages convince me of the dangerous truth of my story. I touch the cold steel of the shotgun. Conscious of my fear, the dog stirs and lays his head against me. I try to stop shivering even though the late summer nights have not yet surrendered to the autumn chill.

It is dangerous to keep the archive active, but I must fulfill my promise to Madame A and her family. And I cannot let the murderers triumph. But most important, I think of Katya and my need to explain my actions to her. The dog moans in his dream, in forewarning perhaps of what is to come.

Fear winks at me like the fireflies drifting in the growing darkness. Every evening, I scan the skyline above the woods in the distance and the derelict fields to the left and right but there is only the blank sky and the silhouettes of lush trees.

Since the messages, I have begun to reorganize all the archive files, collating, reviewing, cross-referencing and copying them on discs and memory sticks. It has taken time to go through the massive amount of material collected since 1970 and still I do not have all the answers. I regard these records as a series of vignettes, small scenes that seem to have little connection, but eventually create a larger canvas of the tragedy. Each day I shift through the files and reflect on my own part in the narrative.

Like an innocent wandering in the forest I was ignorant of the dangerous snare of the past when Madame Feodosia Petrovna Antonova came into my life, and I became one of the hunted.

New York: 1970

On that evening, I was pacing in my bare feet through the long hall of my new Manhattan apartment. I began in the living room and stumbled through the study, bedroom and kitchen, all only ten feet wide. I passed the two closets in the kitchen, one of which held a bathtub, the other a toilet with a chain pull.

"Bastard!" I cursed him as violently as I knew how before trekking away from the cold tiles of the kitchen to the soft carpet of the bedroom and back into the small study and living room. More than once I had asked myself what I was doing here. It seemed as though I had been dropped in a stranger's apartment in a foreign country.

Only a few weeks ago I had been standing on the sidewalk at 82nd Street and 2nd Avenue outside this drab brownstone building.

"It's a railroad apartment, probably built for workers in the 1890's," Ms. Stonor, the real estate agent said, checking the time on her diamond watch. She was very attractive with smooth dark hair flicking in the cold wind.

"You're lucky; you're the first one here." Her large gold bracelets jangled as she glanced at the watch again.

"And"—she emphasized the 'and'—"you're on the ground floor, good neighborhood. Yorkville is coming up. Lots of light from the big window." She pointed with a long red manicured nail to the ground floor window of the narrow building facing the street.

I had glanced briefly at the inside of the apartment and stopped listening as she droned on about the rent and the amenities. At some point during her monologue, I vaguely remembered interrupting the haze of words to say I would take it. Slightly crazed, momentarily forgetting why I was there, I had become focused on the desperate wish to trade places with Ms. Stonor.

This desire to change identities had become all encompassing in the few minutes I had known her. I was unreasonably jealous of her poise and her well-groomed appearance. Her neatly tailored Chanel suit, Halston coat, and Italian shoes made me feel as though I had spent the day on the farm digging up potatoes. I watched her step into the cab, hailed with an authoritative lift of her arm and envied the fact that she obviously had somewhere to go while I merely existed on the edge of nothing.

My nothing existence became even more apparent after the movers had put down the last of my possessions in the shabby apartment. This unusual place like a long hall symbolized my failure, and I couldn't bring myself to unpack the boxes and luggage containing everything I grabbed before fleeing my former 5th Avenue residence.

"Damn, damn," I screamed, stumbling over the boxes again, wandering in a mist of anger and wild frantic grief. It wasn't like me to be at the mercy of my feelings. They came like gusts of wind without warning, like one of the tornadoes that swept through the small Ohio towns in the spring.

This lack of restraint was uncharacteristic and shameful. My family and the people in my small town rarely indulged their emotions. Many of them were descended from pioneers who cleared the land of forest and worked the fields in spite of ever threatening illness and death.

I was five years old when my mother died, and I clearly remember that my father was dry-eyed throughout the funeral. After it was over, he put on his work clothes, took the dog and his tractor out to his fields and didn't return for two days. I sensed his grief never abated, but he rarely spoke of my mother, as though her memory was too sacred to mention in common conversation.

My unhinged state had led Abigail, my only friend in the city, to recommend an appointment with her analyst. I had refused; the suggestion was insulting. No one where I came from ever went to a shrink unless they were declared insane, but it did seem possible I was borderline. In the study, more like a closet with a window facing the dark stairwell, I looked in the mirror and pushed my long hair, tangled in frizzy wet strings away from my face.

Had I really been featured in Vogue last year? How had the journalist described me? 'Attractive young woman married to a scion of the Digby's entertains in her 5th Avenue apartment.' It was a fantasy, never to last.

Snippets of gossip in Women's Wear Daily had awarded me celebrity status without any accomplishments of my own except marrying a wealthy Digby. After the break-up, I had cut every magazine picture of that smiling, poised society woman into shreds.

I reached the end of the line, the kitchen, and admitted to myself as I did every few minutes that I was a twenty-six year old failure and an impulsive fool. I, who once had prided myself on being a cool self-possessed intellectual, had lost my way.

I had begun to pace out of the kitchen when the doorbell seemed to buzz right through my spinal cord. Switching off the light, I pressed my head against the door, trembling as I listened, focusing on the four locks, totally feeble if a killer lurked, waiting to break through the door.

Short heavy breathing came from the other side. My legs turned rubbery, and I held my breath, terrified. Only an axe murderer in a balaclava would ring a doorbell at 2 a.m. in Manhattan. A hesitant knock shortly followed. I looked through the peephole, but could make out only the open door across the grimy hall and a section of peeling brown paint.

"Who is it?" My voice quavered.

"It is I, your next door neighbor. Madame Feodosia Petrovna Antonova."

"I can't see you?"

"I am not tall enough for you to see me. But it is all right. I don't wish to disturb you. If you are frightened, I shall return tomorrow."

The muffled voice was thick with a European accent.

I left the chain hooked, but kept the door ajar, and looked out through the crack. A small figure stood in the dark hall. My fear evaporated; I opened the door wide and snapped on the light. A tiny woman stepped onto the threshold.

She pushed back fine grey hair straying out of her chignon and burst into speech. "I apologize. It is an unusual time to make a first call upon a neighbor. I no longer keep calling cards to let the hostess know in advance as I did long ago in Russia. I am Madame Feodosia Petrovna Antonova," she repeated. "You may call me Madame A for short. But I explain. Russians like to use a patronym, their father's name, after the first. Mine is Petrovna. It is the custom. I have heard you walking about all this week, just as I do every night. I thought we fellow insomniacs might become acquainted."

Her wrinkled face was transformed by a most charming smile as she wrapped the light blue robe around her wisp of a body. The ornate robe, rather stiff with gold braid lent her a hieratic appearance, like a figure floating in the background of an icon or in a Chagall painting.

"Please come in." I tried to keep the reluctance out of my voice.

"I'm sorry. I haven't introduced myself. Christina Gartner." For the first time since the divorce I used my maiden name.

I was one of a long line of Christinas from my pioneer great great grandmother to my own grandmother, who took care of me after my mother died. I was an only child, the last Christina, I thought, now that I was divorced.

Madame Antonova tottered in on Minnie Mouse shoes, black wedgie pumps from the thirties, with her stockings sagging around them.

"Forgive me. I am 'en dishabille'. It is the hour," she said with dignity as though caught out in a fancy drawing room. I could not help staring in amazement, thinking she might well be a hallucination brought on by my mental state.

She fumbled with an ivory comb, attempting to catch the recalcitrant hair. Her slanted youthful eyes, like sapphires, shot off vivid golden lights and seemed out of place in the tiny wrinkled face, the color of old leather upholstery, made distinctive by high cheek bones and a narrow pointed nose.

Her sharp glance swept over the kitchen, and she spoke in a rush of accented words. "At my age sleep evades me, and I try not to wake Anna Georgievna, my daughter who is not well and must rise early for work. But it surprises me that you are up and about at this hour. Young beauties like you are either asleep or dancing at a disco." She let out a hearty belly laugh, surprising for her size.

The mention of a nightclub was like dropping corrosive acid on my heart. Lawrence would be at one of those places tonight. I stood awkwardly in front of this strange woman, knowing I looked ravaged. She must have heard my wild shouting.

"Is something wrong? Forgive me for asking," Madame A said, discreetly struggling with her comb.

"Oh, no!" I stepped back in alarm, pulling Lawrence's robe with his athletic crest tight around me. He'd given it to me the first time we were together, and even though everything was over between us, I couldn't bear to part with this fragment of what might have been. I controlled myself. Bawling like a calf, my dad always said, was weak and ridiculous and didn't get you anywhere.

The sudden break up of my marriage had been a great shock, leaving me stunned, almost zombie like. I had shown no emotion when Pinky, Lawrence's new lover, had come to support him while he told me the sordid details. I could still see them holding hands, sitting opposite me on the couch. Cloudy fragments of these details, a glimpse of high strappy heels, red pouty lips and outrageous spiky hair with purple streaks hovered, threatening to break over me. Madame Antonova silently patted me on the hand as we stood in the middle of the kitchen.

"Will you stay for some tea?" I choked out the words.

"That would be lovely," she said, her little face wreathed in a smile. I led her around the boxes to a chair at the table between the two shuttered windows and slipped an unpacked box under her feet, which didn't quite reach the floor. The shutters blocked out a back garden of dull concrete and weeds. A cat screeched in the dark.

"No one uses the back garden except for stray cats. It would make a lovely retreat, but the landlords won't permit it. Mrs. Vacek upstairs throws scalding water on the cats." Madame A stabbed her finger toward the ceiling. "She's barbaric, just like the Bolsheviks. I find it most disagreeable." She spoke in a burst of perfect academic English with her unusual cadence; her little feet tapped restlessly on the box.

"That is terrible," I said, "I haven't noticed. I've only been here a week."

Madame A was quick to add. "I beg of you. Do not get the wrong impression. This is a lovely building in spite of its shabbiness. Everyone is very pleasant, except for Mrs. Vacek. Have you met Jack?"

"No, who's Jack?" I said without a spark of interest.

"He's a young detective, or do they say cop, who lives upstairs." She paused, frowning slightly. "I was surprised that the Stranksy family moved away on such short notice. They had lived here for many years. But it was a welcome change. Jack moved into their apartment only a few weeks ago, and has been exceedingly kind to us. Annushka, my daughter and I call him *Le Sauvage Noble*, the noble savage; a term, as you know, coined in the Eighteenth Century."

She considered, tilting her head. "But perhaps meeting him might not be possible. He travels much of the time. And I see that you may not be staying long."

I looked around at my messy apartment. A half-eaten carton of Chinese food from two days ago festered on the kitchen counter, along with an empty bottle of wine. Unpacked boxes and clothes were scattered around as though a small tornado actually had hit the apartment.

"I haven't had the time to unpack," I said as an excuse. "I may be going home to live with my dad and concentrate on my PhD."

When I met Lawrence I was writing my doctoral thesis on Martha Washington and her influence on President Washington's government policies. My advisor, Professor Enid Langdon had been very impressed. She said it was a seminal work, certain to be published and might lead to a professorship in The Women's Studies Department at San Diego State. But that was another lifetime. I tossed it all away to marry Lawrence. The irony of my situation did not escape me.

"So," Madame A pronounced emphatically, examining me with her sharp eyes. "You are what they call in the Western movies, *Hors-la-loi*, outside the law, a desperado hiding out."

I nodded, amused at her accurate turn of phrase. I was an outlaw on the run from my former life, I thought, searching through the clutter until I found the kettle bought earlier that week, still in the Bloomingdale's bag. Abigail had forced me out to lunch and to shop. At her urging I had been extravagant and bought a lot of things to rehabilitate myself, in Abigail's words.

It meant little to me that I was a rich divorcee. Lawrence had insisted on a large settlement, uncharacteristic for a man discarding a wife. Outraged at his betrayal, I initially resisted this attempt to buy me off, but Abigail's urging and my practical midwestern upbringing led to my accepting the agreement.

Sometimes I trembled at the amount I was worth, but rationalized that if I hadn't met Lawrence, I would have finished my thesis and have a job teaching at university, my heart unbroken, and my ego intact. Perhaps I would have been published and invited on panels with women's liberation leaders like Gloria Steinem and Kate Millet. In retrospect, I was puzzled at my eagerness to compromise my beliefs and throw away my life for him. But there it was; I couldn't seem to recover my old self, a stranger to me.

"Have you made the acquaintance of any other residents in the building?" Madame Antonova said.

I shook my head. It would have been rude of me to say I wasn't interested in meeting the neighbors. I filled the kettle and experimented for the first time with the gas burner. It flared up, nearly setting my hair on fire.

"As I mentioned, the Vacek's live above you, and Jack Reilly, our *Sauvage Noble*, above us. It is, I must confess, a small building compared to the one we inhabited overlooking the Neva River in St. Petersburg."

Oblivious to my struggle with the leaping gas burner threatening to torch the kitchen, she went on, "Two brothers named Sanford live on the top floor on our side; Mr. and Mrs. Murphy and their daughter Agnes occupy your side. I am on speaking acquaintance with all of them, but in the short time I have known Jack, he is the most congenial. We have already become friends."

After opening three more shopping bags, I found an herb tea, which the clerk at the health store claimed was very calming to the nerves. Since the break up, I hadn't bothered with my herbal remedies or vitamins, abandoning my brewers yeast, acidophilus yoghurt, desiccated liver and egg yolk mixtures for large quantities of wine, drunk, most times, right from the bottle.

"Sorry I don't have sugar." I said.

Madame Antonova's face lit up with pleasure at the mug placed before her. She clasped her small crooked hands together in delight, exclaiming, "How lovely to try something new!"

Her gratitude would have seemed highly exaggerated in anyone else, but I assumed it was very Russian. And everything about her seemed unreal, unconnected to the present.

"C'est bon," she said after a small sip, setting her mug down as though it were precious china and looking at me with sympathy.

"What has happened to you my child?"

My characteristic reserve cracked and emotion flooded through me. Later, I found it hard to understand why I trusted her and opened up to her. I hardly ever showed my feelings, and never to strangers.

"Divorce," I said, my voice flat, "after only two years. I was so trusting and stupid I didn't suspect anything was wrong, at least not until near the end."

Madame Antonova said. "I also am divorced, so know what you are speaking of. Was it an affair?"

I nodded. I couldn't tell Madame Antonova everything. Her toes would curl up in her wedgies from the shock. Still, it was a relief to be able to confide some of my distress. Even with Abigail, my only friend from Lawrence's crowd, I had kept my anguish to myself.

I went on thinking aloud. "It's just that I hate being such a fool. Everyone seemed to know what Lawrence was up to except for his grandfather and me. We met at university." My synopsis became very disjointed. "He used me."

Madame Antonova fidgeted and broke in, "I understand. A year after my marriage to the famed Dr. Georgi Sergeievich Antonov, he acquired two very young mistresses, ballerinas, of course. This was the custom among aristocrats and even for the young Tsar. But Georgi Sergeievich was only a well known professor who took on airs and prided himself on his aristocratic friends, among them the Grand Duke Nicholas Romanov."

Her voice had an edge of bitterness. "I discovered his affairs in 1904 when I was eighteen, pregnant with Sergei. I realized Georgi was a terrible little man with pretensions and no heart. But what did it matter? Life as we knew it ended with the Russian Revolution."

"But wasn't that in the early 1900's?" I said, getting control of myself.

"1917, to be exact. I am about to turn eighty-five, but it seems like yesterday to me," she said.

I was an American history major and knew very little about the Russian Revolution; only that the Bolsheviks took over the country and executed the Tsar and his family. It was hard to connect something that happened so long ago with Madame Antonova perched like a sparrow in my kitchen.

"My troubles could never match such a catastrophe," I said.

"No, that is true, and you are young." She leaned across the table. "And you are very beautiful. You will find happiness again. You remind me of Mathilde Kschessinskaya, the Tsar's mistress, the star ballerina who danced at the Mariinsky Theatre. I saw her many times. Krasavitca! Beautiful! She escaped from the Bolsheviks and married the Tsar's cousin, Grand Duke Andrew. With your lovely figure you certainly could be a dancer. But more, even more." Her eyes grew bright with enthusiasm. "You remind me of Countess Marina Michailevna Blevtova, a great friend of mine, a poetess, and an intellectual."

I had no idea who these beautiful people were from over fifty years ago but liked the comparisons. Although I had been called attractive, I wasn't a great beauty. This was blatant flattery, and I certainly needed it in my present condition. Madame A possessed a singular charm that was hard to resist.

She reached over and clasped my hand. Her own was like a tiny autumn leaf, so small and dry it hardly grazed my skin. "I do hope you decide to stay for a time. I have enjoyed living here for many years. It is very convenient, near to the Metropolitan Museum where I once worked. But it is the rooms that endear me."

She turned and looked down the long apartment, her eyes narrowing as though peering into a dark tunnel. "These rooms are like a railroad car. They remind me of travelling to Finland in the summers before the revolution, and then crossing the Urals into Siberia, fleeing from the Bolsheviks. I try not to think of the escape, only the trains that carried me to safety. But still, I shudder at the thought of the Cheka, the secret police who hunted me. I still feel their poisonous breath on my back." Her eyes grew wide with some remembered terror.

Before I could ask what she meant, there was a loud knock at the door and a hysterical cry. "Mamasha, Mamasha."

Madame A nimbly jumped off her chair, "Oh dear, it's my Annushka."

I opened the door to a short plump doughy looking woman with a bad perm.

"Please, is my mother here?" Her round face with its snub nose was distorted with fear.

"Yes, yes, I am here, my darling. Be calm." Madame A soothed her as though she were a small child.

"Mamasha, how could you? I woke up and you were gone. I thought they had come to take us away." Her voice quavered on the edge of hysteria. "You know they always come at night."

Madame A interrupted. "I'm sorry, my darling Annushka. Our new neighbor invited me for tea, so gracious at this late hour. But we mustn't forget our manners. May I present my daughter, Anna Georgievna Antonova. Anna, this is Christina Gartner."

Anna was silent, regarding me with suspicion. Then she spoke like her mother in the same dramatic rush of accented English. "It was very kind of you to have Mother to tea. She does spend so much time alone while I am working. And she has trouble sleeping." Taking Anna by the arm and patting her, Madame A said. "See everything is fine, my dear wonderful darling Annushka."

Then turning to me she said, "I wish you could also meet my artistic son Sergei Georgievich."

Anna frowned and said something sharp in Russian. Her face crumpled in agony and she hurried out.

"You must excuse my Annushka. She is not well. It is my fault that I frightened her this evening. She views her life as a tragedy. It is all to do with her terrible childhood. Sometimes she blames me and darling Sergei Georgievich for the revolution, for everything."

She raised her arms in the air despairingly.

"Thank you for your gracious hospitality. Perhaps we can meet again soon." She gave a little bow and then as if she had made a decision about me, said, "Yes, you must come for breakfast tomorrow morning. It is an order."

She hesitated at the door. "Sometimes I close my eyes in bed and the apartment sways back and forth, and I am again on a train, returning to the past. Even when I was fleeing I often felt safe and snug. Many important events of my life took place on trains."

That night I lay in bed, my mind full of my neighbor's intriguing conversation. Had she really travelled through Siberia to escape the revolution? I nodded off thinking it seemed hardly possible, so far away in distance and time. Then to my surprise, inspired by the romance of her words, I felt the rocking of the train, heard the click of the wheels on the track and rushed through a strange landscape, passing great forests of fir trees covered in snow.

The next morning for the first time since the divorce, I did not wake up thinking of Lawrence's betrayal. A strange scene from my dream remained with me. I recalled that it was from an old newsreel of the Russian Revolution I had seen at the Museum of Modern Art Film Studio along with two of Eisenstein's films, *The Battleship Potemkin* and *October.*

The newsreel had been more dramatic than the Eisenstein films, made by the great director in 1925, because it was real footage of the revolution, shot on the streets of St. Petersburg in 1917 by an unknown cameraman.

The old flickering images of women in long slim coats and hats, men in odd-looking jackets and smocks seemed strangely formal as they ran in panic through the streets. Harmless looking puffs of smoke hung in the air like soiled cotton candy, and then a body would fall to the ground in comic strip fashion. Antique cars with rifles bristling from the windows careened through the streets with men in costume drama hats hanging like Keystone Cops on the running boards. Was Madame Antonova on the streets of St. Petersburg that day? I remembered she had invited me to morning tea. Intrigued, I pulled on my clothes and knocked on her door.

Chapter 2

New York: 1970

"HOW CAN I explain the catastrophe that befell our world? I think of an incident shortly before the revolution, while I was visiting my parents in the Caucasus. One evening I was returning from a concert in a small open carriage, escorted by my father's Cossack officers." Madame A's voice took on a dreamy quality.

"It was a narrow dirt road cut through a deep forest. As the horses sped along, my sable wrap caught on a tree branch and flew out of the carriage. We retraced our trail to search for the fur, but it was as though the terrain had changed completely, and we could not find it. It seemed to have slipped away into darkness, like our lives after the revolution." She sighed and leaned her head to the side as though to ward off the worst of blows.

We sat in her dimly lit kitchen, our folding chairs drawn up to an old card table, one side stacked with the clean china the Antonovas used every day. In marked contrast to the cluttered room, the breakfast table was shielded on one side by a grand silver samovar that frequently gave off steam, hissing like an offended duchess. At the opposite end of the table two sets of battered mahogany shelves held old sepia photographs in polished art nouveau silver frames.

A wintry light gleamed through the back window, shadowed by snow slowly dropping in huge silent flakes. I felt safe and snug; Madame A's past sheltered me like a warm soft blanket.

Since the divorce some part of me had withered and died, leaving me a shell of my former self. Or as my grandmother would say, the stuffing was knocked out of me. Initially, I fought to overcome this puzzling indifference to life around me and tried to revive my academic career by finishing my thesis. I found my long forgotten stacks of notes on Martha Washington scattered in cardboard boxes where I had carelessly tossed them two years ago, believing they were irrelevant to my new life with Lawrence.

After several attempts to sort through the notes, years of work which now seemed dry meaningless scribbles written by a stranger, a rough sharp feeling of anger and hurt cut through me. In a fury, I wrapped all my scholarly phrases in a plastic bag and threw them in the trash. At this point I had reached an impasse, and wanted to escape from any reminder of my former life. In my self imposed isolation time stretched out before me and I had fallen with ease into a daily ritual with my neighbor.

As soon as Anna left for her office, there would be a short ring on my doorbell, and Madame A would greet me 'a la Russe', kissing my left cheek, then right, then left again, as I stepped across the threshold into her past.

Even though we were separated by huge gaps in age, nationality and experience, there was a surprising bond between us, a shared understanding of life. Perhaps it was my self-imposed exile, my disillusionment and longing for what I called BL, life Before Lawrence, which made me sympathetic to her enormous loss.

In those first meetings Madame A told the story of her journey from a luxurious St. Petersburg apartment to this humble kitchen in Manhattan. Her steps toward exile began shortly after Lenin and his Bolsheviks seized control of the Russian government in the October 1917 Revolution.

"Lenin used terror against his opponents to keep him and his minority party in power. He became a dictator." A shudder passed through her small body. "Even before he seized power he encouraged his thugs to murder anyone opposed to him, excusing the worst brutality with the phrase, 'the end justifies the means.' That little bon mot really meant it was perfectly acceptable to torture and kill opponents to reach a Marxist paradise."

She picked up a large sharp knife and efficiently cut the bread into thick neat slices.

"At first the murderous intent of the Bolsheviks seemed unreal. We intellectuals were naïve and couldn't believe that some of those revolutionaries we had partied with a few months earlier and had regarded as friends, some even lovers, actually planned to kill us, to eliminate the entire upper and middle classes. I still wonder how they could do such evil things."

As though to banish these thoughts, she rearranged the cracked Sevres china plates, the pots of jam and butter on the table in an orderly fashion and poured out tea.

"We knew it was time to get out after my dear friend Leonid Tolshin, a well known liberal who strongly opposed Lenin's terrorism, was found dead of knife wounds inside his apartment. The beasts slashed out his eyes." Her voice trembled.

"The country was in chaos, lawless, which suited the Bolsheviks. The Leather Coats knocked at your door, took you away in the dead of night. There was no safe place." Whirling her head, she seemed to listen for the knock, but after a few tense moments recovered and moved her chair closer to the table, staring in melancholy at the room crammed with the detritus of exile.

"We never unpacked our bags, believing every day the Bolshevik gangster government would fall and we would return," she said.

My thoughts strayed to my own scattered bags and boxes, still lying where they had been dropped as I followed her gaze.

The room, lit by a bare bulb hanging from the ceiling, was an wilderness of clutter: burnt out pots and pans, a cracked chandelier that once had covered the ceiling light, worn out appliances, stacks of magazines in French and several broken dishes. A small path on the cracked lino floor cleared the way to the 1930's sink, stove and refrigerator and then meandered on to the tiny bathroom. Several battered suitcases with intriguing labels in Chinese and Russian were stacked near the door, ready for an immediate flight to a place of safety.

"We didn't think to change anything, and dreamed only of returning home. Some of our friends, lured by Bolshevik lies, did go back, but found no paradise and were murdered or imprisoned in the Gulag. Poor trusting fools. The Leather Coats still hunt us down." Her voice lowered to a whisper as though they might be listening at her door.

Her often-repeated terror and hatred of the Bolshevik secret police, for which she had various names, among them the Cheka and the Leather Coats, seemed highly exaggerated. At the time I assumed her fear was imagined, a delusion brought about by the trauma of her past.

In the following days I gratefully settled into this refuge from my former life. Madame A's many photos and personal accounts of the revolution fascinated me and acted as a balm to my pain. In fact, her stories became more vivid and real to me than life outside on 82nd Street.

Then one morning some two weeks after we met, I noticed the photograph, which led to a disturbing experience that still bewilders me. I began to think that Abigail was right in suggesting I needed a session with her psychiatrist.

Chapter 3

New York: 1970

MY FIRST STEPS into that dark forest of Madame A's past occurred that morning at breakfast when I glimpsed the compelling face partially hidden in one of the photographs on her crammed top shelf. It was the first time I had noticed this picture.

Madame A placed the photograph on the table. "It is Gregori Efimevich Rasputin and my husband Georgi."

The two men pose in front of a large building with a curved door in art nouveau style. Georgi, dark, very plump, and rather short, encased like a sausage in a dark suit, fades into the background beside his companion.

Rasputin dominates. He wears a long black robe, tied at the waist with a rope. His beard hangs down onto his chest, and his lank hair, parted in the middle, falls to his shoulders. His face, with a large nose and wide thin mouth partially hidden under a moustache, is coarse and fairly unremarkable, but his mesmerizing eyes seem to possess a separate identity, as though existing outside the photograph.

Madame A tapped at the scrawl at the bottom edge of the photo. "That is Rasputin's signature."

"Wasn't he called the mad monk?" I said, noting the strange light in his eyes. The few things I had read about him seemed really bizarre and hokey.

Madame A sighed. "That was vile slander, but there were differing opinions about him even among my intellectual friends. Religious mystics, particularly aristocratic society women became his devout followers. Many skeptics thought he was a depraved fraud."

"Did you actually know him?" I couldn't disguise my skepticism.

"I met him only once when he arrived at our flat to see Georgi, his acquaintance and business partner. At the time he was in great favor at the Tsar's court."

A guilty look swept her sharp features. "I kept this snapshot in spite of Georgi's fear. It was taken in 1916, two days before Rasputin's murder."

She hesitated, as though debating whether or not to continue.

"After his death, Georgi was frantic to eliminate all evidence of their friendship. Of course, this was impossible. The Okhrana, the Tsar's secret police who guarded Rasputin's life and also spied on him, were aware of their association.

"It was dangerous to have connections to the Holy One. After his murder, the secret police targeted his friends. They wanted to both discredit him and pin the killing on someone other than the guilty members of the Royal family. The Okhrana's leaks to the press before and after his death were scandalous." A momentary look of anger passed over her face.

"Before he was killed Petersburg was rife with rumors that Rasputin frequented nightclubs, like Yar, in a drunken stupor, bragging about his relationship with the Tsarina. There was talk that he used cocaine and other drugs. Once it was reported they found him in a club's private rooms, engaging in unorthodox sexual acts, sandwiched between a man and a woman."

I was repelled by her last remark, which somehow reminded me of Lawrence's embarrassing behavior.

She seemed oblivious to my discomfort and went on. "Tsarina Alexandra Feodorovna almost certainly received Okhrana reports of Rasputin's drunkenness and orgies, but truly believed in his holiness. She worshipped him because she believed he had the ability to stop the hemorrhaging of the Tsarevich Alexei, the heir to the throne. The poor child suffered from hemophilia, inherited from Alexandra."

She shook her head sadly.

"It was a tragedy. The Tsarina was a granddaughter of Queen Victoria, the original carrier of the defective gene. Poor Alexandra was completely devastated and blamed herself for the Tsarevich's incurable affliction. She was very religious, but turned to mystics and quacks, anyone who could help."

"Wasn't there a scandal involving Rasputin and the Tsarina?" I said, thinking his bad reputation lingered on. There was even a rock song describing him as lover of the Russian Queen.

Her eyes snapped with anger.

"They were never lovers. Nor did he molest her daughters, the Grand Duchesses, as rumored. The Tsarina desperately wanted her son to be healed and to inherit the throne and was devoted to Rasputin because he gave her hope. The accusations of an affair were very unjust but understandable, because the public were kept ignorant of the Tsarevich's illness and Rasputin's ability to relieve his suffering."

She took a drink of tea, reflecting. "Keeping the illness secret gave ammunition to opponents of the Tsar who accused Rasputin of controlling the government through his influence with the Tsarina. The left wing press printed lewd cartoons of Alexandra Feodorovna and Rasputin that fomented the people's hatred of the Romanovs."

"But was it true? Was he really able to stop the Tsarevich from bleeding?" I said, thinking that rational people could not believe that nonsense. She dipped her spoon into the honey and slowly stirred it into her tea before answering.

"There was no medical explanation for Rasputin's ability to stop the bleeding; some thought that he used drugs and hypnotism to help Alexei. Others concluded that Madame Vyrubova, a close friend of the Tsarina, informed Rasputin when the bleeding was abating. Then he would appear and pray over the boy as though he had affected the cure. And of course, the Tsarina had become a religious mystic and believed his powers came directly from God."

I looked down at the photograph. The subject's arresting eyes, flecked with an eerie white light like over exposed film, seemed focused directly on me. It struck me as a weird reversal, as if I was the inanimate subject in the photograph, and he was examining me. Disconcerted, I looked away into the cluttered room, studying the labels on the old suitcases.

"But there is another explanation." Her voice was barely audible. "Through the ages in Siberia there existed blood stillers, healers who could stop the bleeding of injured people and animals. This healing skill came to the Siberian peasants long ago from the Altai shaman, the ancient priests of the nomadic horse tribes of the steppes. When the Bolsheviks took over, shamans were forbidden to practice on order of death and forced into hiding. The healing secrets vanished."

A shadow passed over her normally kind face, and she seemed lost in reverie for a few moments. Then she said something in Russian under her breath, picked up my cup, poured the cold tea in the sink and filled me another from the boiling samovar. Her voice came at me from out of the steam.

"It is called *Zagovarivatt' Krov,* this secret skill to control the flow of blood." The words sounded outlandish in this small kitchen in New York, and a slight tremor of uneasiness passed through me. "It is said that Rasputin used the shamans' ancient healing to stop the Tsarevich's hemorrhaging. Believers called him the Blood Stiller."

I was drawn back to the photograph. I knew it was my imagination, but his eyes held me, trapping me inside their blinding intensity. I struggled to listen to Madame A but her voice grew faint.

For a moment, the room faded into a blank frightening whiteness. In the flash of light I saw a small boy lying in bed, screaming and writhing in pain. There is a melon size bulge in his lower abdomen where blood, bursting through ripped vessels, masses. A middle-aged woman, her fine features strained and white in anguish, sits beside the suffering boy, wiping his forehead.

The bearded man dressed in a white robe, looms like a shadow in the doorway before he enters. The distraught woman kneels before him kissing his hands and he blesses her. He leans over the bed and touches the screaming child with his rough hand. His eyes hold those of the sufferer, and he bends to the waist, his long greasy hair dragging over the bedcover. He whispers to the boy. The boy grows quiet and smiles. A dark phantom, he stands motionless by the bed while the boy sleeps.

Chapter 4

Rural Ohio: 2000

FROM THE PORCH I watch the fog slowly roll in and curl around
the trees, gradually covering the forest in a gray blankness. Over the years I
have tried to erase all of the invasive visions and dreams from those first
days with Madame A, but they remain to haunt and mystify me. I am not a
true believer in the supernatural and still wonder at my gradual acceptance
of Madame A's words, my susceptibility to Rasputin and his mysterious
power, his lingering influence.

New York: 1970

Two days after I saw the photograph of Rasputin, I made an effort to pull
myself together and accepted Abigail's invitation to lunch at the Four
Seasons Restaurant. It was a brilliant winter day, and I took the long walk
from my apartment down Park Avenue. But even the dazzling bright sunshine could not dispel the sad eerie image of the sick boy and the dark
shadow of his healer still lurking in the back of my mind. It was preposter-
ous. I thought of myself as a rational person and yet had no logical explanation for what had taken place.

That next morning at breakfast Madame A did not mention Rasputin.
In fact, she never spoke of him again. She had fussed over me, looking

concerned, asking what had happened, was I all right? I had left so suddenly. Embarrassed, I claimed I had a touch of the flu, realizing how absurd the image would seem to her.

As I drew near the restaurant, I considered telling Abigail about this strange episode, but knew I could never find the words to describe it without seeming unbalanced. She only would accuse me of becoming an eccentric like my neighbor.

When Ab dropped by last Saturday I introduced her to Madame A and they had taken an immediate dislike to each other. Hostility filled the air and after a few minutes, Madame A had made a quick exit.

"She's weird," Abigail said watching her close the door.

"No, she's not. She's foreign and old and maybe a little jealous."

"It's something more than that," Abigail persisted. "Can't you see through her? She's sly and very controlling. She's using you. To tell you the truth, you're acting weird yourself. Why do you want to sit here every day listening to her made up stories and running errands for her like some kind of servant or social worker?"

I didn't see it that way, but still Abigail's comments did upset me. Just ahead, the Seagram's building, an elegant bronze sliver, rose up against the blue sky and Abigail was waving to me in front of the restaurant's 52nd Street entrance. We checked our coats, stopping for a moment to admire Picasso's famous screen Le Tricorne and then made our way to the Grill Room.

Abigail loved coming here, claiming that it was like dining in a work of art, whispering that 'everyone who is anyone' lunches here.

"This is our own power lunch," she said, smiling and waving to well-dressed movers and shakers as we were led to our table. Most of the city's big deals—real estate, financial and political—were brokered in this room.

Spectacular looking in a close fitting low cut black dress accentuated with a simple string of large pearls, Ab tossed her silky hair and threw a kiss across the room to Jackie Kennedy sitting in the far corner with her sister Lee Radziwill and Truman Capote.

I knew she was well connected, but still was amazed that she would be on throwing kisses terms with Jackie Kennedy.

"She came to the last show at the gallery," she said, noting my look of surprise. "Great for business."

Abigail ordered champagne and before she picked up the menu, looked critically at me. I was wearing a dark green suit and had pulled my hair back off my face. As an afterthought I had scribbled on some lipstick as I hurried out the door.

"That color really suits you, but frankly Christina you don't look well. You need to get out more." Translated from Abigail language, that meant I should go out with her to a single's bar, pick up a stranger and have wild sex with him. She was certain that my hatred of men was due to sexual frustration, something I suspected she had read in a pop-psych book.

I nodded and stared at the menu, and for an instant, glimpsed the suffering boy's face on the page; his screams of pain an undercurrent in the elegant room.

After we ordered Ab turned to me with a look of purpose. "Now, as I've said before, you have to get over it." She launched into her usual lecture about starting a new life, which again meant having a lot of sex with strangers and working for her at the gallery, but I didn't hear much of it.

The waiter floated toward us with plates of food; suddenly the boy's face rose in a cloud in front of me. The wall murals swirled in blobs of color.

Abigail broke in, "Are you ok? You look like you've seen a ghost."

"I'm fine." I smiled weakly at her apt cliché and tried to drink some champagne, but my stomach lurched and I put down the glass.

Abigail's voice was distant, as she chattered on about her boyfriend Slade until I suddenly heard, sharp and clear. "I take it you agree then to going out with Slade's brother Mike. You'll love him. He's even more of a dream than Slade. It could be a very long delicious evening." She sighed.

"They're partners in their father's brokerage firm. The night we met in the bar, we discovered our families are great friends, have known each other for ages. I'll arrange a double date, something casual, maybe PJ Clarkes. How about this coming Saturday night?"

"I'm sorry. I'm just not ready to date." I said, alarmed at the idea. Slade was rude and coarse and the few times I had met him, seemed on the edge of violence. I couldn't understand why Abigail found him attractive. There had to be more of an incentive than going out with Slade's brother for me to 'get on with my life'. Besides, I didn't want to be fixed up with anyone or at the unimaginable worst, sleep with Slade's brother. Feeling woozy again, I slid back in my chair.

I don't know how many minutes passed with Ab anxiously staring at me before I admitted to not feeling well. She grabbed the check and tried to hail a cab for me, but they all whizzed by.

"Never mind," I said, "a walk might make me feel better. Thanks for the lunch and trying to help me out of my misery."

She hugged me when we parted and said she would call soon. I crossed Park and walked up Lexington Avenue, still looking for a cab, puzzled at my behavior and agitated with Madame A's talk of visions and wandering holy men; it reminded me of the holy rollers and other religious sects back home, who practiced snake handling and speaking in tongues.

Dodging the crowds rushing out of the subway, I focused again on this strange peasant in the photograph who claimed to have healing power from God and remembered some of the shocking things my neighbor had told me about him, explaining his dual nature.

Frantically searching for a cab, I continued toward Bloomingdale's on the narrow crowded sidewalk, passing tattoo shops, massage parlors, manicure studios and cheap leather shops. I could hear Madame A's voice through the rumble of trucks and cars, their horns honking.

"The man was married, had children. And yet."

Her words, completely out of character, now seemed to emerge from the steam floating up from holes in the pavement

"He went to the *banya*, the Russian baths with aristocratic women who were his disciples and practiced his resistance to sins of the flesh by ordering them to wash and fondle him."

In the glinting rays of the sun, I felt a dizzying rush of blood and stopped in front of a Bloomingdale's window displaying mannequins dressed in polo shirts and shorts for the coming season in the Hamptons. I blinked in the brightness; the glass shimmered like a mirage in waves of water, and I saw for an instant a flickering image of a young woman. She is naked and her hair falls below her waist as she walks in a trance into the baths where the man is waiting. She leans toward his lower body and washes him. He caresses her breasts with rough calloused hands. She follows his eyes as they step deep into the steaming water and slide together.

"You are free. There is only good in being with one possessed by the Holy Spirit. Believe." His reedy high voice echoed inside my head.

The image faded to the woman's back covered in bloody welts. Gasping, I quickly turned away, bumping into an indignant woman next to me, apologized and hurried toward 82nd Street. A smell of decay from the gutter pursued me as I pushed through the crowds, stumbling over an old man begging in a doorway, running the twenty blocks, stopping only to catch my breath, until I reached my apartment.

Exhausted, my head drumming, I threw off my coat and lay down on the bed, sinking into a deep sleep.

The next afternoon, after an unsuccessful trip to the library to find information on Rasputin, I took a cab downtown to the Strand Book Shop at Broadway and 12th Street to continue the search. Rising panic over these rampant images of the past forced me into action and I turned to research, believing that correct information about this man would stop this invasion of my psyche.

As I left the cab, I tried to dismiss the thought that Madame A could have had anything to do with these mental aberrations, mysterious scenes of the past. And yet was it merely coincidence that I spotted the photograph that morning? Was it just idle conversation about Rasputin? A tiny doubt crept in.

After two hours of searching through what Abigail called the eight miles of books on the Strand's shelves, I discovered an intriguing old book, little more than a pamphlet squeezed between two volumes of Russian history.

In the cab back to my apartment, I caught a glimpse of myself in the mirror and was barely recognizable in my stocking cap, my face white and haunted. Was Abigail right? I had been furious when she asked how long it had been since I had slept with someone. As though I couldn't live without a man. As though it was the answer to everything. Was I going crazy? Could looking at a photograph after being dumped by Lawrence make me irrational, cause me to hallucinate, do this to me?

I was more like my rational self again after I made some tea and sat at the kitchen table with the book, which I believed to be a primary source.

Rasputin: A Stranniki. An Apologia was engraved in large letters on the brown cover. It had obviously seen hard times. The cover and binding were coming apart and there were dark foxing stains on its frayed yellow pages.

It seemed unusual that both publisher and author were anonymous and that the author had chosen to write in English. A stamp on the inside cover showed that the book was purchased in 1917 from Watkins, the English bookstore in St. Petersburg. This would have been shortly after Rasputin's murder. The opening page read:

> *This book is the most authoritative and truthful account of Rasputin, compared to all the scurrilous attacks on the Holy Man. The Russian Orthodox Church has always sanctioned the tradition of wandering holy men called Stranniki who receive prophetic and healing powers directly from God. Rasputin was one of the chosen Holy Stranniki.*

The name *Stranniki* seemed to harken back to some obscure medieval time, and it was incredible that in the twentieth century, Russians still had faith in miracles and prophets.

> *Rasputin, a Siberian peasant, became a drunkard wastrel, thief and outcast from his village. Although he had a wife and children, he began a life of aimless wandering. His life changed dramatically when he visited the monastery at Verkhoturye and was struck by a vision of the Virgin Mary, who commanded him to wander in quest of God.*

> *Thereafter, by his good deeds and mysterious power from God, he soon was well known as a Stranniki and healer, eventually becoming a favorite among the mystical devotees in the aristocracy and the powerful bishops in St. Petersburg. His mysterious ability to heal led to an introduction to the Tsarina, who was searching for a miracle cure for her son's illness.*

The book cited several eyewitness reports of Rasputin healing many afflicted, with exact place and date, but to my disappointment, there was no description of his healing methods.

The following pages attempted to explain Rasputin's dual nature: his lecherous and drunken behavior, which contrasted with his spiritualism and performance of holy miracles. This contradiction came from his association with the Khlysts who greatly influenced his thinking. His first contact with them seems to have been while he was staying at Verkhotury Monastery, which sheltered the bizarre sect, outlawed by both church and state. I was skeptical that there could be any philosophical justification for this sex-crazed man who used religion to seduce women, but fascinated, read on.

Khlyst, which means whip, is the name outsiders give to the sect, known for their brutal beatings of members for purification. Their major tenet is that through sin one will be saved. The sect, known to its members as The Believers, live in communities called Arks. Each Ark is led by a man and woman believed to have the spirit of the Mother of God and Christ within them.

Members must abstain from sex, except for the ceremonies on 'rejoicing days', when they whip themselves into sexual frenzy by dancing and whirling and end with intercourse between with all members. Children born after this rejoicing period are believed to have the Holy Spirit within them.

For a moment, the woman's bloody back flashed before me. If this was true, Rasputin's followers could have been beaten like the Khlysts. I began to shiver.

The main defense for Rasputin's seductions was the Khlyst belief that through sin one can be saved. A flimsy excuse. There were pages describing the shocking behavior of fashionable Petersburg women who obeyed his orders to lick his feet and wash his body to show humility and belief.

That night I dreamed that the young woman from the banya was standing in the corridor of a train as it dashed through the Siberian forests. A light revealed a shadowy figure approaching from the opposite end of the car. As they passed in the rocking corridor his eyes bored into her. He beckoned to her whispering. She moved toward him and he was upon her, rocking the car.

My cries of passion woke me. I was shaking, aroused, in a sweat that soaked my sheets, with the hoarse whisper 'believe' still buzzing in my head. I stumbled to the kitchen and poured a glass of wine and sat trembling, unable to sleep. I tried to be reasonable, to convince myself that the dream was directly related to reading the book and my conversations with Madame A, but I sensed this was about me in some deep frightening way. Just before the dream ended, the woman had turned toward me. The face was mine.

Chapter 5

Rural Ohio: 2000

LOOKING BACK IT seems my mind had been out of control, as though exposure to Rasputin's photograph had infected me with those disturbing images of the past. The recurring dream, which kept me awake many nights, gradually faded into some obscure corner in my mind. As time went by, I concluded that my neighbor's description of the blood stiller was only an interesting story that played on my overworked imagination.

The photograph never again appeared on Madame A's shelf and because of the embarrassing nature of what I called episodes I never mentioned it. Some time later, the Rasputin Book disappeared from my apartment. It was as though they had never existed, as though I had imagined them.

To counter my still remaining doubts, I continue to substantiate the facts of my story by removing a piece of evidence from the Finland File, stored in the cabin's sitting room. This room and the adjoining bedroom contain my archive of the last thirty years, arranged in order in metal file cases. I study this photograph for a moment under the light, and then return to the darkness of the porch.

Relieved that the sliver of light can no longer be seen from the field or woods in front of the house, I sit back on the step and run my hand over the dog's soft fur. It is difficult to construct the past in the small amount of time left to me. Even with extensive documentation I struggle to get at the entire truth of Madame A's story. In the dark sky I can see her quite plainly at breakfast thirty years ago in New York City, showing me the Finland photograph of the Druzhina. Then, the subjects had seemed charming, faded historical figures, and nothing in their expressions suggested that their actions long ago would become so dangerous to me.

New York: 1970

"There." Madame A held a large silver framed photograph up to the light. "Everyone I loved was there that day. It was July 1917, our last summer at the dacha in Finland."

The samovar hissed, fogging up her kitchen windows, enclosing us in our tiny ramshackle outpost of pre-revolutionary Russia. While she served the tea I studied the picture, arranged like a formal painting, grainy and soft focused on the edges.

"Georgi took the photograph. He was known for his expertise and was often asked by officials to document government works. I have never begrudged his interest. After all, these are the only records I have of my vanished world."

The four, who look as though they had wandered off the set of a Chekhov play, pose on a sunlit wooden porch behind a large oval table set with teacups and a samovar. Sleek, elegant and young, they exude an air of prosperity and wellbeing, unaware of the hardships ahead. Three vigorous men surround Madame A, a delicate fine boned young woman with large inquisitive eyes. Madame A's brother Andrei, an army officer, stands directly behind her and towers over the group. He has a rough flat-cheeked face with a hooked nose and a wide smile, partly hidden by a large curling moustache.

To her right is Peter Von Krantz, once an aide de camp to the Tsar and still dressed in a military uniform. Peter, blond and well built, with fine handsome features stares confidently at the camera as he holds Madame A's right hand, almost caressing it. Prince Dimitri Sherbov, from an old noble family, stands to her left. He has a haunting melancholy look and turns his sharp hawk-like profile to gaze down at Madame A.

"They were very different, but blood brothers, devoted to each other. My father General Brislov owned a mansion in the Caucasus near the Black Sea between Sochi and Sukhumi, not far from his old *stanitsa*, the Cossack village where he grew up. Grandfather was the *Ataman*, the chieftain of the village." Madame A sipped her tea, staring at the photo as though willing the three subjects to life.

"Dimitri and Peter, whose families had estates nearby, were our play-mates. We four were inseparable and spent hours playing games related to the legends of *the Bogatyrs*. Similar to the Knights of the Round Table, these warriors were true historical figures."

"Papa was the first to call us the *Druzhina*, outriders of the most famous Bogatyr, Ilya of Murom, whose *bylina* dates to 13th Century Kiev. This was not because we conquered the Tatars like the Bogatyr, but created chaos among the three households with our mischief." She laughed heartily, and then growing serious said, "We *Druzhina* stayed together until the end of the revolution, but then …"

She stopped and put a spoonful of jam into her tea and then mine. We both stirred and sipped. It seemed natural, as though I had always drunk tea the Russian way.

"That summer was idyllic, but we all knew, even the children, that we were poised on the brink. I have named this photograph 'Avant Le Deluge'. In this case it means just before the Bolshevik Coup swept us all away that October.

"We had left Petersburg earlier than usual and luckily escaped the July Days, the failed uprising. Radical soldiers stormed the Provisional Government headquarters in the Tauride Palace, determined to take over, shouting Lenin's slogan, 'All Power to the Soviets'," she said.

"Kerensky's provisional government put down the revolt, jailed Trotsky and other socialist leaders and issued a warrant for Lenin's arrest on suspicion of being a German spy. We knew he was in the pay of the Germans."

Her eyes shot off sparks of excitement.

"Imagine: as we sat on our porch drinking tea, Lenin was hiding from the police nearby at his friend Bonch-Bruevich's dacha in Neivola. It was a tragedy that he escaped. If he had been caught, I am sure the revolution would have failed."

She looked again with longing at the photograph.

"It was a delightful surprise to see my brother, Peter and Dimitri together that summer. They had been travelling incognito, in and out of Russia for some time on a mission for the Tsar," she whispered dramatically.

"What was the mission?" I readied myself for an interesting story.

There was a long silence.

"I should never have spoken of it," she said in a sharp tone. "It is something that must be buried forever." Her features suddenly dissolved into a wild hunted expression.

"But surely it can't matter now!" I tried to keep the exasperation out of my voice. I couldn't understand the importance of her secrecy. It seemed ridiculous.

"You are wrong. It is very dangerous. Lives would be at risk. You must never reveal what I told you. I was foolish to tell you." Her voice was harsh with fright.

An uncomfortable silence descended on us. I waited for her to speak, but her face had gone blank as though she had shut down the present. Outside the kitchen windows, black snow clouds formed, pitching us into darkness and for a moment the kitchen seemed a foreign frightening place. I jumped up and hurried toward the door, mumbling a thank you, but she didn't seem to notice.

That night I woke from a deep sleep to whispering movements in the back garden. I sat half-awake in fright for a few moments and then crept into the kitchen and opened a crack in one of the shutters. It was only the cats prowling the back garden. My imagination was getting the better of me. They stared at me with wide eyes, hissing as though I was the intruder.

Chapter 6

New York: 1970

I ABSENTLY HUMMED, *Monday, Monday,* my favorite Mama's and Papa's song, in my off-key monotone, as I walked in the blizzard up 2nd Avenue toward 82nd Street. This morning I had bought bread for breakfast at Orwashers on 3rd Avenue and 78th Street. Their ovens ran all night to produce delicious dark pumpernickel that Madame A insisted tasted like that of Filippov's, the court baker.

Sitting at the breakfast table she said, "The Governor of Moscow claimed he found a cockroach in Filippov's bread. In those days one didn't want the wrath of the governor over one's head. Furious, he demanded an explanation. Thus, Filippov invented raisin bread to prove him wrong." She laughed heartily, but the story made me queasy.

It was early and the deserted streets, laden with mounds of snow lent the city a pristine benevolent air, a contrast to how hard and indifferent it had seemed the night I discovered Lawrence's hidden closet in the bedroom. Reeling from its shocking contents, I had walked along under 5th Avenue's cold glittering lights and stopped outside the Pierre Hotel. In the glitzy bar a group of well-dressed young professionals gathered in front of the huge window facing the street, talking and laughing, their drinks gleaming in the light. I felt an aching loneliness, knowing their glamour was from another world, now out of my reach.

But today I had slipped inside a snow globe like a toy figure in a bubble of the past. When the blizzards began earlier this week, Madame A announced that the heavy snow reminded her of winter in St. Petersburg.

I ducked against the wind blowing in fits and starts, whirling the snow, obscuring the street ahead. Through the dense curtain of snowflakes I imagined gliding in a horse drawn sleigh to the shops along Morskaya and Nevski, lights sparkling in ice and snow. I could see the *dvorniks*, the house porters, sweeping and shoveling the snow on Petersburg streets.

"Can't stop that day," I sang, back to reality, stepping over a pile of dog crap steaming in the white snow and empty cigarette boxes and beer cans exposed by the wind. Paper and rags were caught like victims on the wire fence of the huge vacant lot. I turned the corner onto 2nd Avenue and stopped singing.

Just ahead a tall figure, vivid against the snow, was marching toward me at a fast pace, the warmth from his body melting the heavy flakes falling on him. His wild long hair, flecked with snow, hung to his waist. His tall upright body was poured into tight grey Dr. Denton long johns, over which he wore black lace women's panties with red bows.

Unreasonable panic seized me and I tried to escape over the piles of snow to the other side of the street, but it was too late. He goose-stepped directly toward me, his silver heeled shoes sloshing into the drifts of snow and out again. As he dashed by, his fists moving up and down, his wild eyes fastened upon me for a long frightening moment.

He marched on, his foam-flecked mouth screaming, "Worthless bitch!" and disappeared around the corner of 1st Avenue.

I was unnerved but amused by this unlikely apparition and his insult. A man wearing women's underwear in that peculiar manner would be subject to arrest in any city other than New York. After I left the Digby apartment and my sheltered existence, with a car and driver to take me everywhere, I felt vulnerable, a bit frightened.

Like the crazed marcher, the city's abrupt violence and insanity came at me every time I stepped outside my door, waiting around any street corner. Two days ago I saw body bags outside an apartment building on 83rd Street. Tibor, the super, said they were drug killings.

Abigail, a fount of clichés, always said, "New York keeps you on your toes."

In spite of the craziness, I was staying on and had called my Dad, explaining that I needed space and time to get over the break-up. But in truth I couldn't face the sympathetic looks and the gossip of people back home.

And I was fascinated, almost spellbound by Madame Antonova's past, her tales of Russia before the revolution. What did it matter if her stories were incomplete or possibly exaggerated or that she was vague about her life after the revolution? Later, I realized she was an expert at revealing only what she wanted me to know.

I slowly picked my way through the large white snowdrifts along 2nd Avenue, thinking back to her puzzling fear and demand for secrecy over some mission for the Tsar that took place over seventy years ago. She had been traumatized by the murders of her friends and family, but I had begun to suspect there was something more buried in her past that frightened and silenced her.

I slowed, stepping over a patch of ice. Her suggestion that Rasputin could be a blood stiller, actually possessing the power to heal, was truly bizarre. It surprised me that one of the Russian intelligentsia could fall for something so superstitious and medieval. I avoided thinking about what neurosis had caused my own weird visions of the man. There were other mysterious incidents involving my neighbor, and my rational explanation for all of them was that she was merely eccentric, like many of her friends.

But I couldn't discount the envelope; it remained a vague nebulous warning. One morning Madame A reached into her robe and with trembling hands brought out a letter-size envelope.

"You are the one person in this world other than my dear children that I trust completely. I give this only to you. If something happens to me, you must open this. It will save Sergei and Annushka. Will you help me?" she begged.

"Yes, but nothing will happen!"

She raised her head; a cloud had drifted over her sapphire eyes, shutting out their brilliance.

"That is not a certainty. I am a very old woman and could die soon. Sergei is a genius, an artist, but impractical. What I give to you will protect him. Promise me you will do this," she said.

I promised, reluctantly clutching the envelope. The scene seemed unreal, melodramatic with Madame A drifting in and out of Russian and broken English as though she had forgotten both languages in her distress.

"And I beg of you. Tell no one, that I have given you this."

"I won't tell anyone," I said. This seemed crazy.

"You are an angel, a granddaughter to me."

She grasped my hands and kissed them and hurried to the door.

"I must go before Annushka wakes and calls for me."

The instructions on the envelope, written in an old-fashioned beautiful stylized script read *'To be opened in the event of my death.'* It was signed, notarized, and dated February 7, 1970. I was tempted to open it, but thought she might soon want it returned.

A sudden fear seized me, and I looked around wildly for a hiding place. I picked up a pair of leather boots from the closet, removed the insole from the right one, folded the letter underneath, and glued back the insole. I was mystified as to how this hiding place had come to me. Maybe it was some obscure recollection of a scene in a spy movie.

There was something disturbing about the request. What she had said afterward had seemed to verge on paranoia, but at times I wasn't so sure.

"You will occasionally read of a so-called accidental death or disappearance of a prominent Russian émigré. I am thinking of General Miller who was kidnapped and sent back to Russia to be tortured. I think there will be more murders now." I didn't ask her what she meant by now.

I tried to brush aside my misgivings and came out of my reverie a block from 82nd Street. The snow had stopped, leaving the sky a sharp blue, the air bitterly cold and clear as though one could take a stick and poke through its brilliance, shattering it like glass.

Coming toward me, from uptown, a man strode with purpose, his large bulk in dark shadow against the brightness of the sky and snow. As he drew closer, I saw that he was bundled up against the cold and carried a briefcase. He had an old fashioned air, accentuated by his lumbering posture and his long heavy trench coat.

An odd thrill passed through me, a presentiment that I would see him again. I stopped for a moment to watch him as he looked around intently and turned the corner some distance in front of me. When I reached 82nd

Street, Louis the green grocer and his workers were shoveling snow and waved, moving daubs of color in the white landscape.

In the narrow hall, smelling of boiling cabbage from the Vacek's apartment, I took out my mailbox key, turned toward the boxes opposite my door and jumped back in surprise. A trembling figure huddled against the wall.

Chapter 7

New York: 1970

MADAME A WAS flattened against her door like a small crushed bird.

"What is it?" I rushed toward her

She grabbed me tightly. "I have an unwelcome visitor. A rat." she said.

"Oh my God." I could hear my voice rising hysterically.

"I left the window open last night. Fresh air is good for one. This morning after my own darling Annushka departed he was there on the sill, staring at me, so brazen and bold. I attempted to frighten him by throwing pans, but he bared his teeth at me."

She squinted. "He looks at me with vicious little red eyes. I have named him Lenin during our standoff."

She tried to joke to overcome her distress, but failed and rubbed her eyes and cried out, "I cannot bear it. Memories of my last days in Russia. Rats everywhere, covering the fields, in the railroad cars."

Then she managed to compose herself and looked upstairs as if to heaven.

"Jack is coming to the rescue. It is my luck that le sauvage noble has just arrived home. He will confront le rat." She heaved a sigh.

"I hope so," I said. "Is it still there?"

"Oh yes, I looked in a minute ago," she said.

I hated and feared rats. At the farm, the cats had kept them out of the barn, but once I accidentally cornered one who flew at me in attack. I could still see his teeth, his moist eyes. It had taken hours for my dad to get me out of the locked bathroom.

We crouched together, waiting for rescue. I heard heavy steps on the stairs, and when I looked up I felt dizzy, as though I had stepped off a fairground ride. It didn't seem possible, but Jack Reilly was the man who had been walking toward me on the street. His huge shoulders were slightly bent forward as if anticipating some trouble ahead. Close-up, he resembled a retired athlete, hard and muscular with a slight thickness around his middle. His face blurred the moment I saw the glint of cold steel in his gloved hand. A gun! This was unreal. He looked like a hit man from the movies.

He barely nodded to us before entering the apartment. We cowered against the wall and heard claws scraping the kitchen floor, some rustling, a small pop and then silence. He paused in the doorway, and then came toward us, carrying a plastic garbage bag with the small bulk at the bottom.

"He's gone. You'd better keep your windows shut from now on. I'm surprised he escaped the cats," he said.

"Le rat est mort," Madame A solemnly announced to the hall. "Thank you, thank you, mon cher sauvage."

He dropped the bag with a sickening thump, pulled off his gloves and put out his hand.

"Jack Reilly, your upstairs neighbor." His accent was tough New York.

"Thanks for helping us." I limply shook his outstretched hand. "Madame A has told me so much about you." Still shocked by the sight of the gun, and feeling sick every time I glanced at the bag, I couldn't think of anything better to say.

He wasn't handsome, but possessed a reckless dangerous look and an air of authority. He had high cheekbones, rather thin lips and his nose was too big with an artificial crook in it, likely the result of a fight. His thick sandy hair, fairly long with sideburns, was the latest hairstyle, worn by men who thought they were studs; the kind Abigail picked up in singles bars.

"I'm Christina Gartner," I said, acutely aware that my hair was in pigtails, and my nose almost certainly gleamed from the cold, like a bright red

Christmas bulb. I was wearing a shabby old ski jacket, but at least had removed my stocking cap.

He laughed, looking me over, his eyes fixed on my braids.

"Where did you come from?"

His laugh enraged me, made me a comic figure, a reminder of how Lawrence had made a fool of me. I fumed in silence.

"You're not from New York. I bet you're a farm girl."

I was furious in that way I am when my feelings are precarious and felt a slow curl of panic in my stomach.

"Why did you have to use a gun?" I said.

"Well, I could have hacked it to death with a machete. At least I had a silencer. Are you feeling sorry for le rat?" He held me with his eyes.

I supposed he meant that to be funny, but I didn't see the humor.

"It makes me wonder what you do to humans."

"Don't ask." He laughed again, his dark eyes intent on me

Under his studied gaze I felt transparent and injured as though wherever his eyes glanced they left bruises on my skin. The slow warmth of desire burned through me. I couldn't continue to look directly at him so examined the peeling paint on the wall behind his head.

"I am so glad that the two of you have met even if we had to kill le rat to do so." Madame A, whom I had momentarily forgotten, had rescued the pumpernickel from the floor and wrapped her blanket tightly around her.

"Yeah, me too." He turned to me. "Maybe we should get together for a drink."

"Perhaps," I said, but thought never, even though I had to admit I wanted to. He wasn't my type and I knew it would be taking a risk to have anything to do with him.

Madame A was retreating into her room, carefully looking around before entering. "Thank you again, dear Jack. Darling Christina, I will see you later."

"See you around." He reached out and gave a little jerk to one of my braids.

I closed the door to my apartment and could still hear his laugh. Disgusted that I should care how I appeared to a virtual stranger, I rushed to the bedroom mirror and became even more depressed. I could be labeled homespun, like the farm housewife in *American Gothic*. All I needed was a pitchfork.

Jack Reilly might have been Madame A's le sauvage noble, but there was an air of danger and mystery about him that contradicted her description. She told me he was a cop, and travelled frequently, but she hadn't known where he went. He struck me as someone who enjoyed collecting women like notches in his belt, and it seemed out of character for him to befriend an elderly Russian woman and her daughter.

I shivered thinking how his dark brown eyes had, to use an Abigail cliché undressed me and sized me up, affirming that I was a Miss Rah Rah redneck. The mocking phrase came from some of Lawrence's crowd who regarded me as a nobody, totally boring, wholesome to the core and truly out of place married to Lawrence. How could this humiliation have happened to me? I still remained surprised and bewildered by my sad journey to this flat; it was almost as though it had been travelled by a stranger, not a strong advocate of women's rights, a PhD candidate with a promising career ahead of her.

Dad always said I was practical, had common sense, but I lost that attribute the day I fell in love with Lawrence, the only romantic impetuous thing I ever did in my life. I remember my father quoting an old saying, "If it is too good to be true, it probably isn't true." It still taunted me. At the time it didn't occur to me to ask why Lawrence would want to marry me. I believed that he loved me.

Every detail of our meeting came back with painful clarity. I was deep into my work on my thesis and was buying books at Long's for the summer term at Ohio State. This great looking guy stood beside me, introduced himself and gave me a lift to the dorm in his Porsche. Lawrence, a recent Harvard grad, explained that he was taking an advanced accounting course to prepare to run the family business, his grandfather's idea.

I was mesmerized, in a kind of hypnotic ecstasy. I can't quite describe the feeling, but I believed it was love. My few former boyfriends paled beside Lawrence. I admit now that the whole idyllic package, the handsome husband, the gracious living, and the excitement of New York dazzled me.

Soon after we met he took me to meet his grandfather who lived on the Digby estate southwest of Columbus. When he was three, Lawrence's parents had been killed in a car accident on the Riviera, and his grandfather, a widower, had raised him.

Gramps, an older version of Lawrence with gray hair and the same clear blue eyes, dressed in a plaid shirt and khakis, walked slowly using a cane to meet us at the front door. Lawrence said he had been ill for over a year. From his appearance it would be hard to guess he controlled a corporate empire unless you noticed the hard, no nonsense look in his eyes.

Before lunch Gramps took me for a walk around the estate, called The Farm.

As we passed beautiful manicured country gardens Gramps said, "Digby's have lived on this land since 1790. The first Digby fought in the Revolutionary War and received a land grant as payment. We were poor as church mice when we came but went into canned foods during the American Civil War and prospered."

We had reached the top of a small hill in a sweeping green carpet of grass and I looked at the rolling fields, fenced in for miles. Near us racehorses grazed, and in the distance there was an airstrip and landing pad for a private jet and helicopter.

We walked down to the old stone farmhouse by the river, framed by huge sycamore trees. The original homestead had been artfully restored, retaining that rural atmosphere but adding all the creature comforts. A huge rough looking original fireplace dominated the room, furnished with old chests and comfortable couches and chairs. Old portraits of the family hung on the walls and I later discovered that Abigail's gallery had supplied many of the early American primitive paintings. I loved the house and it seemed to me that a perfect life lay ahead.

Lawrence wanted to live in New York, but Gramps remained firm that the head of the company must live at The Farm. I knew they had many arguments about it. But when we became engaged, Gramps changed his mind and agreed under 'certain conditions' that we could spend part of the year in the city. Lawrence would be promoted to company head and take over the New York office.

Gramps was too old-fashioned to discuss the terms of his deal with me, and Lawrence by design never mentioned it. I discovered later the condition was that I was to get pregnant the first year of marriage.

There was a small wedding at The Farm. The only guests were my Dad, Gramps and a few people who worked for the Digby's and had known Lawrence all his life. Dad, who looked ill at ease in his old suit, didn't say one way or the other whether he approved.

We flew to the city in Gramp's jet and moved into the Digby's 5th Avenue apartment across from the Metropolitan Museum, as far away from The Farm in every way possible.

I stood in front of the mirror, my thoughts rolling on. He had picked me to impress Gramps and not, as I had believed, because I was attractive, sexy and intelligent. I was chosen only because I was naïve and easily manipulated. How he must have laughed to himself. I was like the prize cow, a wholesome type of farm stock approved by the old man.

Chapter 8

Rural Ohio: 2000

I STIR RESTLESSLY on the porch step, fear driving my rapid pulse. They are close to finding me.

Earlier today the photograph appeared without warning on my computer screen. The picture of Madame A walking with me was taken in early spring, 1970 on 82nd Street outside the apartment building. For long moments I stood trembling, unable to move, unable to turn off the computer. The rush of adrenalin made it difficult to think back, but I was certain we had never posed for anyone.

After I was able to control the paralyzing fear, I forced myself to look in the mirror hanging in the kitchen to the left of the sink and saw a stranger. I felt relief. No one would recognize me from that old photograph on the screen.

When I first went into hiding I cut my long hair and dyed it black. As the years passed and I became more secure, I reverted back to my own light color, now streaked with grey. My straight regular features have coarsened with age.

My youth has been wasted in all these years of hiding, and there is so much to regret, but I always will be thankful for having Abigail Townsend as a faithful friend who saved my life. I long for her to be here now, to calm me, to make me laugh, to say my fear is ridiculous; that it's all nonsense.

She is a central figure in my story. I think back to the year I met her in New York.

New York: 1970

My newly installed phone rang, driving me out of my reverie into the kitchen. It was Abigail.

"Hi. Let's go out tonight." Her voice was cheerful, full of energy.

"No, I can't. Can we make it next week?" I was not interested in going to a bar.

"Why are you so snappy?"

"Sorry, one of the neighbors I just met is really irritating."

I didn't go into the rat killing. That would bring on another harangue from Ab that I should move in with her.

"He thinks he's a stud." She caught the bitterness in my voice and sighed.

"You've turned into a confirmed man hater. I'll forgive you if you don't read any more issues of Ms. Magazine or join a women's group. All right, next week just for dinner. Is it ok if I give your phone number to Sam? He said he had to see you, that it was important."

I flushed with embarrassment and reluctantly agreed. I had been avoiding Samuel Westerby, but his law firm handled the Digby Corporation's affairs and this meeting might be related to the stock I received in the divorce settlement.

"He wants to know more of the gory details of the break-up," I said, cringing at my behavior at our last meeting.

"Don't be so paranoid. He's attracted to you, has been since he met you. He's told me many times. Call you tomorrow," she said.

I was relieved that she seemed not to have heard of my drunken night with him. At least Sam was discreet.

"I'll call you. I'm really sorry I was rude, Ab."

Abigail was the only one of Lawrence's crowd who had remained my friend after the divorce. She was the daughter of J.P. Townsend III whose pharmaceutical empire circled the globe. Townsend's Ltd. recently had built a factory in China.

Lawrence and I had been living in New York only a few weeks when she invited me for lunch at her loft above her gallery in Soho. I had never been in a Soho loft and that day, as I rode up in the creaky elevator, was amazed to discover that spacious apartments, and artists' studios existed inside these huge iron-fronted factory buildings.

"My great-great grandfather, Old Jed, started the family business by selling his patent medicine, Townsend's Elixir," Abigail explained as we sat in her large kitchen.

"Townsend's Elixir was guaranteed to cure everything from rheumatism to impotency. It was a bizarre potion of blackberry juice, chamomile, some other stuff, including cow piss and the most important ingredient, morphine."

Her eyes sparkled with mischief. She served me a salad and bread from the oven.

"My illustrious ancestor also ran gambling games to supplement his income. Can you imagine? Jed travelled through the Midwest in a painted wagon. It doubled as living quarters and the stage for his medicine show starring several Shawnees, among them his wife, my great-great grandmother, Little Swan."

We finished our lunch and moved for coffee to the spacious drawing room with huge windows overlooking Spring Street. I noticed a Rauschenberg and works from other well-known Pop artists hanging on the cream walls above the couches.

Abigail was in her bare feet, her manicured toenails painted a bright red. She looked beautiful in a tight t-shirt and hot pants, a vivid contrast to my beige skirt and blouse, which I had thought suitable for lunch with a prominent socialite. I was so bland I was in danger of disappearing against the cream walls, and wondered why a sophisticated New Yorker would be interested in someone who looked like she spent her days picking corn.

She curled her long bare legs up on one of the white leather couches.

"My father would like to forget that Old Jed started the business with a medicine show, but I won't let him. It's such a gas. He goes apoplectic when I tell people that Jed was run out of most small towns in the Midwest."

She opened a drawer in the coffee table, took out some pot, and slowly rolled a joint. I stared aghast at this unexpected turn in the get acquainted lunch.

"Have some." She held it out to me.

"No thanks," I said, stiff with disapproval, imagining our imminent arrest and at the same time realizing I sounded like a Victorian spinster.

She took a few puffs, amused at my reaction. Abigail was a striking beauty and a daredevil. She liked to think of herself as a bad girl, and went out of her way to do things that were not 'socially acceptable'. After graduating from university, she became a Playboy Bunny, not a good career move, but fun. Even before I met her, I had heard about her wild reputation. There were rumors of her creative sex with pairs of men picked up at bars and some kind of toe worshipping ceremony. I didn't believe any of it, but Ab seemed to like the notoriety and did nothing to discourage the gossip.

"Guess I'm like Old Jed in personality, but I look like my great-great grandmother," she said, finished with the joint, her successful attempt to shock me.

Later we descended in the massive elevator to the gallery entrance, passing her staff installing a show of primitive American painting and sculpture.

"Isn't it amazing?" She pointed to the large oil painting of her great-great grandmother hanging in the entrance to the gallery, named in her honor. Abigail could have been a clone of her ancestor. She had inherited Little Swan's dark hair, classical features, large black eyes, smooth dark skin and long legs.

"My Auntie Beatrice always claimed that an itinerant artist travelling in the Midwest painted this for Old Jed in exchange for some of the elixir, but my research indicates it might have been George Catlin," she said, reflecting for a moment.

"Owning an art gallery in Soho," Abigail's arm swept toward one of the large off white rooms hung with early American primitive paintings, "is not much different from peddling Townsend's Elixir. Just like Old Jed, I run the best show in town."

Her parties were legendary. The Little Swan Gallery exhibitions featured Folk Art, Pop Art, and Abstract Expressionism. Along with Andy Warhol's factory, it was the 'in' place for the beautiful people.

"The trick is to persuade a society figure or museum director to buy some of the works. Then you're on your way," she said with a laugh.

After my divorce, I had refused her repeated offers of a job, knowing I would have to associate with Lawrence and his friends who frequented the gallery. Abigail said the offer was open if ever I changed my mind.

When I saw her last I had asked her not to give my address to Lawrence or any of his cronies. "The bastard still thinks we can be friends," I had said.

"I won't, but some wonder why you're avoiding them."

"Ab, let's be truthful. With the exception of Samuel all of them thought I was a hick. I wonder why you have anything to do with me."

"Don't be silly. I knew we were going to be friends when we first met. You have a big chip on your shoulder. They're not so bad. You're too sensitive."

"I just need time to sort things out," I said. "Besides, my neighbor intrigues me. She led a fascinating life and tells interesting stories."

"I'm asking again. How do you know she's telling the truth?" Abigail said.

"That's terrible for you to say. I know she is. She has so many photographs of the people she talks about, and almost all of them are signed with personal messages. Why would she let me take notes on her story?" I was indignant at the accusation.

"You're going to write a book about this woman?" Her eyebrows went up registering surprise.

"Maybe. It's a great story so far." I was slightly embarrassed at my half lie. It had only been a half-hearted attempt to take notes, an excuse. In the end I did not write anything and my notes would be filed in the archive.

"Be honest with yourself, Chris. You're using this as an escape. Stop wallowing in self-pity. It's crazy. Why would you be so involved with an old woman and a past that has nothing to do with your life? It's history. Irrelevant, for God's sake."

"That's exactly the point," I said.

But what Abigail said was true. I was in a rut, content to travel every day back to Madame A's Russian past. And at night, when I slipped into my railroad car and to bed, I escaped to some outpost safe from hurt and humiliation.

Chapter 9

New York: 1970

AFTER MY LAST conversation with Abigail, I didn't dare tell her that I had offered to accompany Madame A to her doctor's appointment. It would have meant another lecture on having a life.

Dr. Samuelson's vast office on 79th Street, once a railroad baron's mansion, evoked a turn of the century atmosphere that suited his patients.

In the dark circular lobby, Madame A was greeted with dramatic cries in Russian and French by at least a dozen acquaintances, all waiting their turn to climb the large curving staircase to the examination room. The exiles, wearing faded Paris designer pieces and uniforms from the early twentieth century, seemed to have stepped from an old Movietone News reel. Madame A's feet were clad in elegant leather ankle high galoshes, straight from a French WWII movie. And she was wrapped in the hooded sable coat brought out of Russia which she claimed was the 'only garment that can keep a real Russian warm.' Her soft gloves were French 'from Cabassue's in Petersburg' she said, wiggling her fingers.

The émigrés possessed a curious vitality, as though surviving the horrors of the revolution had given them new life. They were still fighting the revolution, and the room fizzed with their heated arguments and discussions. Some paced the hall while others argued and gossiped on the large Empire leather sofas.

In the midst of the hubbub Madame A pointed out a surviving member of Admiral Kolchak's staff and one of the last Tsar's bodyguards. I was amazed that the frail man in the corner whom everyone snubbed was Kerensky, the head of the first government after the revolution. He had escaped after the Bolsheviks took over; some claimed dressed like a woman, and ironically ended up sitting with his enemies in a doctor's waiting room in New York.

"And over there," she whispered, "two Trotskyites are still plotting to take over the Russian government."

But even the violently opposed Social Revolutionaries and Monarchists agreed on the skill of Dr. Samuelson. 'Our Niki,' Madame A called him, was an émigré's son and a man with infinite patience in dealing with the crotchety elderly Russians who flocked to him.

We took seats on a recently vacated sofa. Above us on the dark paneled walls hung Russian landscape paintings and portraits of the Doctor's family by the famous artists, Serov and Repin. Niki's father had cut the canvases from their frames, rolled them up and carried them with him when fleeing Russia.

Directly in front of us an enormous man in a shabby pink military coat elaborately decorated with tattered gold braid stood with his back to the room staring at a large oil painting entitled *The Bogatyrs* which depicted the heroic figures as medieval knights.

Before I could ask, Madame A said, "That is Hasim. He was a member of the famous Tekintsky Regiment and a loyal aide to my dearest brother. That is all that is left of his uniform, poor man. He wears it to places where there are Russians who will recognize it."

Hasim turned around as though he might have heard and limped toward us. He was very dark with carefully trimmed grey hair and a large moustache. In spite of his limp, he carried himself like a soldier. His fierce looking eyes, the same color as Madame A's, crinkled good-naturedly as he smiled and swept up to us, curving his huge body low to kiss Madame A's hand. They exchanged greetings.

"Madame," he said, looking concerned, "Are you ill?"

"No, Hasim Ivanovich, I am only here for my check up."

"I praise God that you are well. I myself have come for pills for an old war wound in the leg, but it doesn't do much good."

"That I deeply regret. May I introduce Christina Gartner?" She held out her hand toward me.

Hasim smiled, showing huge yellow teeth and bowed.

"I am charmed. Forgive me for not noticing you. I was admiring this painting of our noble heroes," he said. "It takes me back to the days of the civil war when I fought alongside our own Bogatyr, the great spy and warrior; may he be blessed in heaven." The old man crossed himself.

"But Madame, it is fortunate that we meet and a coincidence. I planned to visit you this week. I have an important message. Decisions must be made."

He leaned toward her and whispered. I caught only a few words in English, "The one designated by blood?" He seemed to be asking her a question.

Madame A had looked startled at his words, then displeased and very upset. I could see she was struggling to control her anger. She glanced over at me, but I continued to study the paintings, pretending I had not heard. Then she said something quick and hard in Russian, and Hasim's long face dissolved in hurt, the features running together. He whispered, "No longer. I cannot."

Their conversation continued in a stream of vehement whispered Russian until I was jolted by a phrase I understood. *"Zagovarivatt Krov."*

Hasim bowed and left quickly, and we waited in silence until Madame A was called upstairs to the examining room.

As we rode home I wanted to ask her about the conversation with Hasim, but she was too distressed and angry. I was sure I was not mistaken. *Zagovarivatt Krov* described Rasputin's skill in stopping the flow of blood and healing the Tsarevich. But whom was Hasim whispering about? Who was the one designated by blood and what did this have to do with my neighbor? Was it just gossip?

Finally I said, "Is something wrong? Can I help?"

"No, it is betrayal, just as in the revolution. You can trust no one."

Chapter 10

New York: 1970

THAT EVENING, I sat at a table near the piano in the Sign of the
Dove restaurant, nervously twisting my napkin, thinking that meeting
Samuel Westerby here was a bad mistake. I had accepted his invitation because he claimed he had something important to discuss with me. But how
could I face Sam after that night at the gallery? It was masochistic to return
to this restaurant, a romantic old coaching inn where Lawrence and I had
spent many evenings. Even after two years the waiter recognized me and
nodded, causing a rush of memories of my brief marriage.

I could see Lawrence leaning across the table, his smile dazzling, telling
a hilarious joke, his irresistible laugh filling the restaurant, filling my heart. I
mourned him as though he were dead, even though the man I idolized had
existed only in my imagination. He had been laughing at me, mocking me.
It was this real Lawrence, the nasty bastard that I had to deal with. He recently claimed through his lawyers that he wanted to be friends and had the
nerve to accuse me of being vindictive and unforgiving. I took a big swallow of water and my chest heaved, the anger returning. He dumped me
when Gramp's died, before the funeral. I felt bitter and mean.

"Christina, great to see you." Samuel Westerby IV leaned his well-
groomed head over and kissed me lightly on the cheek. He smelled like
soap. I blushed. Vague images of that drunken night with him flashed in
front of me.

Pristine in his Brooks Brothers suit, Sam sat down and the waiter, instantly hovering, brought the wine list. He was handsome, blond, and patrician. He had all the confidence of the rich, well born, and highly educated, but even without these advantages, he would have been a success.

He gazed at me, keen with admiration. "You look terrific. I like your hair that way."

"Thank you," I said, trying to smile.

My hair was gathered up in a chignon with wisps of curls around my ears in a style similar to that worn by Madame A in her old photographs. When I had dressed in the cashmere Halston mini, clipped on the diamond earrings, my engagement present from Gramps, and shrugged on the sable coat, a wedding present from him, Madame A, who had come to my door, clapped her hands together.

"You look a snow queen, like a Romanov princess."

She was prone to exaggeration, but I knew that I looked unusually attractive tonight. Two men at the bar had turned to watch me as I walked into the restaurant.

Sam studied the wine list and ordered a Meursault.

His square even features contracted in an earnest smile. "It's been nearly a year since I've seen you."

"Yes, at Abigail's gallery party." I said.

Detailed scenes of my night with him, obscured until now in a kind of comforting alcoholic blackness, suddenly beamed at me as though a voyeur with a flashlight had searched them out. I was ripping off my clothes, pulling him down on top of me like the star of a porno movie.

I burst out. "What happened after the party, I'm so sorry. I can't remember everything, but know I was disgraceful. I wasn't myself. I was so angry and so drunk."

"Don't," he said, taking my hand, "Let's not talk about it. I only hope you don't think I took advantage of you."

I looked down to avoid his eyes. The excruciating memory of his hands on my breasts and my standing over him in some absurd position swept over me.

"What have you been doing since? I mean, I know it's been difficult, but you seemed to have completely dropped out," he said.

"Did you mean since we had our one night stand?" I said, a little too loud, bewildered at my growing anger. "I did drop from sight in your little world, but there is life beyond the social columns of Vogue and WWD. I have no social credentials in your world. You were all Lawrence's friends, not mine."

He started to protest, but I broke in, "Why didn't someone tell me, rather than watch me make a fool of myself?"

Sam blushed, having flashbacks of his own. He probably wanted a sensational repeat performance from me.

"I didn't know much about Lawrence's private life. He deliberately kept it from me." Then he blurted out, "What are you going to do? Stay in the city, I hope."

"For a while," I said.

"Abigail's worried about you, says your on your way to becoming a recluse. She thinks you're too involved with your Russian neighbors, that they're weird. I hope you don't mind, but she asked me to find out about them. My family knows many of the prominent émigrés but haven't heard of the Antonovas."

I caught my breath, not believing it. They had been talking about me, discussing my personal life. It was humiliating, even though I knew they meant well.

"And so what does that mean?"

He took my hand again. "Are you sure it's safe? After all, this is New York."

I laughed, thinking of tiny Madame A and her odd Annushka. There was some mystery about them, but I was positive they were harmless eccentrics.

"Abigail definitely has double standards. Are you certain everyone she invites to her gallery parties is safe? What about that guy she's dating now, that Slade? Talk about weird. He dresses up in military uniforms ordered from catalogues and imagines he's in some Special Forces unit. The last time I went to the gallery, he was wearing a Nazi uniform and marching up and down Spring Street. At first glance I thought the postmen had new outfits." I had warmed to the subject, to overcome my embarrassment and anger at being treated like a wayward schoolgirl or a case for a social worker.

"That is weird," he conceded, watching the waiter uncork the wine. He looked sorry he had brought up the subject.

"Abigail doesn't like Madame A because she's old, poor, and foreign, not among the more social of the émigrés. What possible danger could there be?"

I didn't mention the arguments I had heard in the Antonova apartment or Madame A's conversation with Hasim, and didn't even consider telling him about my strange dreams and visions of Rasputin. These incidents were puzzling, but as the days passed uneventfully I remained convinced there were innocent explanations for all of them, and although it was a stretch, even for the envelope she had asked me to hide,

"Abigail says Madame Antonova's niece has a Russian boyfriend who works for the Soviet delegation at the UN. Most of the Russians attached to the UN are connected to the KGB," he said.

"You can't mean spies." His comment was so ridiculous I laughed out loud. The idea of spies in any form was alien to me, the stuff of movies. And the thought of Madame A being involved in espionage was hilarious.

"We are in the middle of the cold war, it's not a laughing matter. I know for a fact the Russian delegation is full of them," he repeated. "My friends say it's just difficult to prove."

Offended, he turned to the wine and sniffed the cork, then whirled a small amount around in his glass, sniffed several times and took a sip, discreetly gargling as though it were mouthwash before he swallowed. He called it chewing. The waiter stood poised with the bottle in mid-flight until Sam nodded, and then he poured.

"You'll like that Meursault; it's a good year," Sam said, wanting to change the subject.

He was so nice, but there was an enormous gulf between us symbolized by the Meursault. At home the drink was hard cider or beer. I had never tasted wine until I met Lawrence and his friends. We raised our glasses.

In the silence that followed he took a large drink and said, "I know what you do is none of my business, but I care what happens to you."

I cleared my throat, but my voice still came out a little shrill. "That's very kind, but I am really all right. I have postponed getting my doctorate, but have been working on a project that interests me. I'm taking notes on Madame Antonova's life story and hope it can be published."

This wasn't completely true, but at least it explained what appeared to be an unhealthy obsession with my neighbor, and showed that I was doing something with my life.

He looked dubious. "I'm only worried about you. Not trying to pry. Shall we order?"

"Just a salad for me," I said.

"Surely that's not all." He was disappointed, perhaps sensing this would be a short evening.

When the salad arrived, I had no appetite and barely touched it.

Sam anxiously watched me push the food around my plate.

"I'd like to see you as often as you'll let me," he said, taking a deep breath.

I thought how kind and considerate he was, remembering that he had seemed worried about me that night when he took me home, and I turned into a sex maniac. Afterward, Sam had wanted to stay with me to comfort me, but I insisted that he leave.

He went on, "I'm in a difficult spot. Lawrence called. He wants to see you. He begged me to talk to you."

"So that's why you asked me to dinner! After all, the Digby Corporation is your client." I was having trouble controlling my anger.

"That's not true. I planned to take you to dinner before Lawrence asked me to deliver his message."

"Just what is that message?" I snapped.

"He wanted me to tell you he does care about you in his own way and would like to be friends. There is something else I need to discuss with you." He looked sheepish. "He's interested in buying your Digby stock. There is some clause in your settlement about price that he would like to negotiate."

"All of this is very good for the Digby Corporation and Lawrence, but maybe not for me. Why would I ever want to even speak to him again, let alone be his friend or negotiate a contract?" I jumped up from the table and rushed past the two men at the bar, who were watching with interest.

I scrambled for my coat at the checkroom and somehow managed to get through the door, knowing I was creating a scene, but didn't care. I guess I really had been thinking that Sam was interested in having sex with me, but to my humiliation it was business all along. This dinner was all about Lawrence.

Samuel followed me into the street, his face a picture of bewilderment.

"Please Christina, I don't approve of Lawrence's behavior. I'm just delivering his message. I rarely see him and only on business since he resigned from the Racquet Club. He called me to try to explain that night at the party but I refused to accept his excuses. It was cruel, what he did to you."

"He's still your client." I ran from him, slipping on the pavement in my heels and hailed a cab.

"At least let me take you home." Sam was running beside me.

"No, thank you" I said, getting into the cab.

"Please, can I call you?" He held my arm, his eyes pleading.

To get away, I nodded yes, and he let go. I slammed the cab door. Scenes from the party engulfed me. Lawrence was stoned, pointing and laughing at me, calling me horrible names. As he came toward me, the crowd was silent, parting the way for him. I did not recognize the person with him, and it took me a few moments to realize that Lawrence was holding hands with a man in a dress, his face made up, his lips and cheeks garish with color. It was Pinky, his new lover.

Chapter 11

New York: 1970

THE CAB STREAKED up 1st Avenue. A homeless man, rags wrapped around his feet, his hair tangled like a huge bramble bush, pushed a shopping cart piled high with his belongings into the street just as we approached the traffic light. The cabbie slammed on the brakes. Oblivious to our sudden stop the man labored across the road. The driver, his face obscured in the darkness, cursed under his breath.

Painful scenes hounded me as the cab raced uptown. In the dark of the backseat, Pinky's image rose before me in a cloud of expensive perfume, punk hairdo, lipstick and polished nails. He perched on the arm of the sofa like an exotic parrot, holding hands with a Lawrence I didn't recognize. Lawrence was playing out one of his fantasies, kitted out for Wagon Train in a white leather cowboy suit. He did not remove his ten gallon hat, nor did he apologize for his behavior.

Instead he crossed his white boots, and he and Pinky agreed without my saying a word that it all could be worked out. I studied the pattern of studs on the boots, stifling the urge to laugh hysterically. It was all too crazy. Lawrence said it was best for the Digby Corporation that we stay married and suggested that Pinky live with us. I would get used to it, he said.

During this surreal conversation I could only stare at Pinky with a mixture of hostility and fascination. It was strange though; I couldn't really hate this person who had come between Lawrence and me. He seemed rather likeable, and later I realized he had nothing to do with Lawrence's deception.

Soon after this I had run into Pinky at Bloomingdale's lunch counter. It was hard to tell he wasn't a woman until you looked at his large wrists and feet. When tears came to my eyes, he reached out with his big knuckled hands in white lace gloves and patted me on the shoulder. Then we sat down and talked, and I learned it was entirely Lawrence's plan. Pinky claimed he hadn't known Lawrence was married until that night.

The cab jerked to a stop at the corner in front of speeding traffic and blaring horns. After paying the fare to the muttering driver, I stepped out and was nearly overrun by a pack of dogs sniffing my fur coat and jumping around amid frantic attempts by a plump middle-aged woman to get them under control. She wore a waxed jacket and green Wellington boots. Her red stocking cap was perched on a mop of curls, and she seemed to float along on a raft of dogs, leashes extended in different directions.

"I'm terribly sorry." She finally was able to rein them in. Her English accent was only mildly surprising. She looked as though she'd walked right out of the English countryside onto the New York streets.

"I believe I've seen you in the neighborhood. You do live on the block." She studied me with little sharp eyes, disconcertingly like her terriers.

"Yes, I'm Christina Gartner."

"Violet Springsmith." She shook hands vigorously.

The dogs swarmed. "Sit, now sit," she ordered.

And miraculously they did, examining me with keen excited eyes. "May I introduce Chaucer, Dickens, Shakespeare, and Eliot, for George, not T.S."?

Two large poodles, a furry looking mutt, and a cairn terrier all snuffled around. The cairn, Eliot, licked my hand, and the touch of his cold nose and soft fur soothed me.

"I suppose it seems an affectation to give them writers' names, but they are my favorites." She patted each of the furry heads.

"I like the names. Do you mind if I walk along with you?" I said, on impulse.

"I would love company. We always take our evening constitutional this way."

Guided along by the dogs, we rushed around the block, through dirty melting snow past the rundown boarding houses fronted with overflowing garbage cans, the rubbish strewn vacant lot, the grocery store, stopping suddenly when the dogs wanted to sniff. It was fun and I didn't care that my feet were wet from the slush.

"You're in the apartment across from Madame Feodosia Petrovna Antonova." She studied me with little curious eyes.

"Yes," I said, surprised. "Do you know Madame Antonova?"

"She and Anna always have been good friends of mine. They give me scraps for my dogs. I worry a bit about the two of them. Madame Antonova is getting frail, and Anna doesn't seem to be well, although one can't always tell. She has a gloomy personality," she said as we headed back, the dogs leading the way.

At my door, I petted the dogs and shook hands again with Ms. Springsmith, feeling less desolate, even cheerful.

"I am at home a great deal of the time, keeping track of my investments, clipping coupons as they say here, and taking care of these terrible creatures. Come to me for tea some afternoon soon."

My mood changed abruptly when I stepped into the hall. One of the lights had burned out and the remaining bare bulb gave the place the grainy menacing look of film noir. It passed through my mind that in the movies people always are murdered in halls like this. I saw the large figure hunched on the stairs in front of me and shrieked.

"Don't worry. It's your neighbor, Jack." He stood up and came toward me. Relieved, I stepped forward under the light.

"Oh, sorry I screamed. But you scared me. Well, good night."

I tried to rush past, but he stepped in front of me.

"You look good all dressed up." His voice was low, almost a growl. "It's too early to be home. What happened? Was your evening at The Sign of the Dove a failure?"

His stare was menacing, filled with an unreasonable anger.

"It's none of your business. Please let me by." I was trembling.

"Of course, Mademoiselle," he said, but he still blocked my way. "A classy babe like you doesn't belong in this building. This place isn't grand enough for you. What are you doing here, slumming with your fancy friends?"

I shrank against the wall, but he kept coming toward me.

"What do you do for a living? From the looks of those earrings you could have robbed Cartier or maybe you're just a high class hooker." He reached out and touched the earrings. He was so close I could feel his breath on me. "Bet you and your friends were out partying while poor slobs were dying in Nam."

"Get away from me," I said, in a half sob. "I'll call the police."

I pushed at him, alarmed at how solid he was. It was like trying to move a refrigerator.

He laughed, "I am the police."

"I'm going to report you," I shouted. Furious at the insults and frightened, I managed to slip past him.

I swung the bolts on the door, shaking, tears in my eyes, my heart thumping wildly. Why did he care what I was doing here? It seemed an attempt to bully me, to frighten me away. Maybe he was just another nut job. New York was full of them. A sudden rush of fear overtook my anger. How did he know I was at The Sign of the Dove?

Chapter 12

New York: 1970

I SAT UP all night, afraid that the savage would try to break in. He knew I was at the Sign of the Dove. He had been following me, but it was no use to report him. No one would take my word against his.

The next morning, feeling ragged, I was still thinking about calling the police when Madame A rang my doorbell.

"Christina, I have brought a friend to see you."

Surprised because we never met on weekends, I opened the door. A red mist of anger descended on me. Jack stood next to her, gripping a bunch of yellow roses, looking extremely uncomfortable.

Madame A spoke quickly, her little hands moving in supplication. "Please, Listen to Jack. I am so fond of both of you. It would be distressing to me if you were not on amicable terms."

Jack towered above us. "Sorry about last night. No excuses. It was just wrong."

I was silent with fury. Looking contrite he awkwardly thrust the flowers at me, but it all seemed forced and calculated. He wasn't the type to beg forgiveness. Compared to Lawrence and Samuel, he was rough, as though he had weathered conditions in some terrible place.

"Come in," I said, slamming the flowers on the counter. I was crazy to let him in, but curiosity had overcome my anger, and I was sure he wouldn't do anything in my neighbor's presence.

It was comic to see tiny Madame A push him into the room.

"Anna is home today and not feeling good so I must go. But dear Jack, I know, would be grateful for a cup of your wonderful coffee. It smells delicious."

Before I could open my mouth to protest she was gone.

He sat at the table, silent and rather subdued, although the air around him seemed charged with a primitive kind of energy. As he raised his cup I noticed a jagged scar that began on the back of his hand, ran up his wrist and disappeared into his shirt sleeve.

"I'm sorry," he mumbled, "I know you just let me in to please her."

"Yes." I forced myself to stare him in the face. "Just like you brought your flowers and so-called apology."

He turned red. "That's not the case." His voice was low, and in spite of the antagonism, there was an indefinable sense of intimacy between us.

"I asked her to come with me, coward that I am. I apologize again for scaring you. I'm not very good with women," he said in an abject tone.

"Oh, you gave me the impression you were a stud," I said.

He ignored my sarcasm.

"It's no excuse, but I just had a bad night. Too much booze." He studied the pattern on the tablecloth.

His remark surprised me. I didn't believe that he was drunk. When he had come close enough to touch my earrings, threatening me, his breath had not smelled of alcohol, and he seemed in control.

"I want you to leave," I said, furious again, remembering his demeaning insults.

"I'll go." He hesitated as though he were going to say something else, but changed his mind, then reached down and gently brushed my cheek. A fleeting expression of vulnerability, almost sadness crossed his hard features.

I felt myself caving into desire. Then he was kissing me hard, and pulling me down on the kitchen floor. He cradled me with one arm and unbuttoned my blouse and jeans. I held out my hand saying no, but my halfhearted protest died against his body. His hands and tongue travelled over me, and I felt myself open to him. We were gripped in a fierce surge of passion, and I was robbed of any reason. I do remember crying out, and then lying limp on the floor, stunned and uncomprehending, until he helped me to my feet and held me.

In the doorway he turned and said, "You're too soft for the city. It's dangerous for someone as fragile as you. Go home. That would be best. If ever you have any trouble, call me." I saw again the fleeting expression of sadness in his eyes.

At breakfast the following Monday, Madame A said in her peculiar phrasing, "You must excuse Jack. I know you are angry beyond belief, but he suffers greatly. He was very upset that he behaved so badly." She buttered her bread, dripping honey over it with deliberation.

"What did he tell you?" I said, embarrassed, hoping she hadn't heard us. I couldn't understand why I had slept with him. Abigail's blunt question surfaced. 'How long has it been since a man has even touched you?'

Madame A waved her hand dismissively, "Oh, that he was unbearably rude and wanted to apologize."

"It's ok." Flushed, suffused with the heat of passion, I couldn't look at her directly and changed the subject. "But there is one thing that puzzles me. He knew I had been at the Sign of the Dove. Was he following me?"

"I did mention that you were meeting someone there, but I don't believe he followed you. I hope you won't be angry with me." She nervously rattled her cup against the saucer.

"What kind of cop is he?" I asked, still trying to hide my blazing face.

"Jack is a type of detective, a plain cloth man. Is that how one says it? He once told us that he has a special position, something in connection with the secret service."

"What else do you know about him?" I tried to mask my interest, but kept feeling the pressure of his arms around me.

"He was severely wounded in Vietnam, the only survivor of his platoon, and spent a very long time in the hospital. I don't think he has recovered from his war experiences. He has never said this directly, but I sense it.

"Perhaps the reason he behaved so badly is that he thinks you are from that group of young people who oppose the war. He has great resentment against those who protest and are hostile to the veterans," she said.

"That's ridiculous. He doesn't know anything about me."

The war had seemed very remote this past year. A few months ago I had read that the government had bombed Cambodia and that National Guardsman shot students protesting at Kent State. There were reports that some veterans were being treated with hostility by anti-war protestors, but I didn't believe Jack had threatened me for that reason. In spite of the sex his behavior the night before was puzzling.

Madame A seemed far away in thought, looking out of the kitchen window at the cats sleeping in the gray morning.

She said slowly, "I understand Jack and the horrible things he went through. One can only know if one has suffered through a war. It is so hard to accept the death of loved ones. Even among those who survive, the more sensitive never recover. It is no wonder that he is sometimes rude."

She smiled in her charming way and said, "I know he is what is called a rough diamond, but you have forgiven him."

Chapter 13

Rural Ohio: 2000

I AM RESTING in the cool twilight after my return from the city. It is always a difficult trip. Yesterday I removed the heavy branches placed across the trail to hide the Cherokee and worried all night that the jeep would stall or that its license plate had been traced.

This afternoon when I drove back down the trail the dog rushed out to greet me, growling and leaping around the car, grateful that I had not abandoned him. He senses that each time I go out into the world I may not return. Today I withdrew all my money from the bank, still with the hope that the killers have not traced me.

Several days ago I changed my e-mail provider and address, but still cannot bring myself to turn on the computer, knowing there will be a message of death from cyber space.

I put my supplies and groceries away and paced restlessly around the kitchen table, glancing at the blank screen. The material piled next to it contains documents purchased from my most recent source. He identifies himself as Boris, an ex KGB agent with access to that organization's archives. I have not yet filed this material in its proper place because it is so painful to examine again.

I finally open the folder and stare down at the three black and white mug shots scanned from a KGB file, dated July 15, 1971. There is a note from Boris: 'I thought this would interest you.' A jolt of pity and fear goes through me when I remember.

The woman's face and upper torso are taken in full front and left and right profiles. Her torn prison smock barely covers her breasts. Her head is shaven and bruises, which show black in the photo, cover her face and neck, suggesting blood vessels have burst throughout her body. Her large eyes are saturated in pain, ominous reminders of what will occur after she stops posing. There is no name, only the note from Boris and a number underneath the photograph.

New York: 1970

Sunday, midmorning, I heard a commotion in the street. I rushed to the living room window and peered through the slats of the shutter. A tall elegant woman in furs emerged from a chauffeured car, struggling with two magnificent Borzois, snapping and snarling at Violet Springsmith's dogs. The driver of the large black car jumped out to take the dogs, followed by a square, stocky well-dressed man.

The woman disappeared from view and I heard the hall bell, followed by loud cries and sudden eruptions of Russian. It had to be Zoe, the adored niece, orphaned daughter of Madame A's brother Andrei. Madame A had told me their tragic story. When Andrei's cavalry regiment was posted near Baku on the Caspian Sea, he fell in love with a beautiful Azeri girl, named Almas, which means diamond. Her family was strict Muslims and threatened to kill her if she married outside her religion. The lovers fled into the Caucasus Mountains.

Almas' father, an important tribal chieftain, and her four brothers went after them. In a standoff at the cave where the lovers had hidden, Andrei killed her father and one brother. It was a great scandal and caused unrest in the region. The family wanted revenge, either money in recompense or Andrei's death. He escaped to Petersburg and was forced to resign from his regiment.

His reputation was restored before WWI when he risked his life in service for the Tsar. The couple escaped after the Whites were defeated, and then tragically after WWII they were tracked down by Cheka agents and shot, leaving the baby Zoe an orphan.

Out on the street the well-dressed man was arguing with Ms. Springsmith. I figured he must be Nicolae, the boyfriend, when suddenly he turned and I shrank back. His protruding blue eyes under the white eyebrows and low forehead seemed to look straight at me through the shutter. His elaborate blond coiffure, like a cherub's in an eighteenth century French painting presented a strange contrast to the psychopathic blankness of his face. I thought of going out to help Ms. Springsmith, but something about the conversation made me hesitate.

Ms. Springsmith looked like she had been ducked in hot water. Her gray curls tossed indignantly as she quickly turned her back on Nicolae and hurried with her dogs toward 1st Avenue. I was chilled that he might have seen me and was afraid to open the shutters further, even after he returned to the car with the Borzois.

An hour or so later Madame A brought Zoe to my door. Her face was as beautiful as her figure; perhaps as Madame A claimed, she resembled her mother Almas. Her large slanted eyes grew darker with dislike of me, and I caught the subtle odor of her expensive perfume as she reluctantly shook my hand. She carried herself like a haughty Russian aristocrat and wasn't the poor rescued orphan I had imagined.

"I'm so glad to finally meet you," I stuttered. "Madame Antonova talks about you a lot."

"Really, does she?" Zoë turned to her aunt who looked slightly embarrassed.

"Oh Zoe, you know how proud I am of you."

"Yes, I know," she said impatiently, "I'm sorry I can't stay. Nicolae has an important meeting."

Madame A looked sad. "I hoped you would stay for tea, but perhaps another time. Oh dear, Annushka is calling. Excuse me. Oh! Darling Zoe, you dropped your glove in the kitchen, let me retrieve it."

As soon as Madame A was out of earshot, Zoe hissed at me, "Who the hell are you?"

"What do you mean?" I was startled by her hostility

"You can't be who you claim to be. Why would you want to help a poor old woman and her sick daughter?" She looked with disgust through the open door at my kitchen. "Who are you?" she asked again, "Why would you live in such a pit? You must expect there is something for you in all this."

I stepped back, bewildered by her attack.

"Anna is seriously ill, I want you to stay away from them. I will handle everything. They are my family. Do you understand? Stay out of it. You won't get your hands on their valuables." She put on a smile when Madame A reappeared, holding out an expensive leather glove.

"Thank you Auntie. I was just expressing my appreciation to, uh …?"

"Christina," I supplied, still stunned.

"Yes, Christina, for taking care of you," she said.

"She is an angel. My other angel," Madame A said.

"Is Anna ill? I didn't know." Madame A fidgeted, obviously distressed and nervous. She seemed about to tell me something.

"It is her weak heart. Come Auntie." Zoe turned in the hall, and started in surprise.

"Oh Nicolae, I didn't see you."

He had emerged silently out of the darkness of the hall, nodded and went inside Madame A's apartment. In spite of his well-tailored suit Zoë's boyfriend was sinister, more like a gangster than a UN diplomat.

She pushed Madame A across the hall and inside her apartment.

I crept over to Madame A's door to listen. Nicolae's guttural Russian went on for a few moments.

Zoe said, "What are you telling her?"

Then she began screaming in Russian.

Madame A pleaded. "Zoe, that's not true. I am telling her nothing. We are just friends. Isn't that so Annushka?" Anna did not answer.

I rushed back to my apartment and heard the door slam, followed by the heavy tread of Nicolae and the click of Zoë's high heels down the hall. What was Madame A accused of telling me?

And the scene in the street only added to the mystery. I had the impression that Ms. Springsmith and Nicolae had encountered each other before. It seemed incongruous but from the few words that floated back to me through the window, I thought Ms. Springsmith was speaking Russian.

Chapter 14

New York: 1970

THE NEXT DAY I bumped into Jack in the hall. He was wearing his heavy coat and standing in front of my door, holding a set of keys. He looked surprised, almost embarrassed.

My stomach turned over in a rush of wild emotion, like riding over rapids in a flimsy boat. He had made no effort to see me since he made love to me. What had I been thinking? What had come over me to let myself open to such dire humiliation? I didn't want to talk to him but he blocked my way.

"Did you want something?" I tried to keep my voice on an even keel, determined to show I didn't care.

"No, I was just going out." He tucked the keys in his pocket and put his hand on my shoulder. It seemed to burn through my sweater to my skin, and I moved away.

"Are you all right?" He seemed at a loss at what to say.

"Fine," I said, hoping he wouldn't notice my trembling.

"Got to go." He was so distant, so cold, like Lawrence. It was surprising how much it hurt. That day I wandered aimlessly in the cold rain around Yorkville, my new neighborhood; its small enclaves of charming old brownstones and rundown rooming houses were tucked like a crazy quilt between modern high-rises and specialty shops.

Once the preserve of German and Irish immigrants, the area still exuded a mysterious European air. Hungarians, who fled after their revolt against the Communists in 1956 and Czechs who arrived after the Communist crack down on the Prague Spring in 1968, added to its atmosphere.

After browsing in Paprika, the Hungarian store on 81st Street, which sold old-fashioned cookware and spices, I stopped at the corner stand to buy vegetables for dinner and Ms. Springsmith's rosy face appeared over the bin of tomatoes, her dogs clustering around her. Since the night we met I had joined her and the dogs a few times on her evening walks.

"Christina, You must have tea with me." She led me across the street to her brownstone mansion. I wanted to escape to my reading but she insisted. There was a steeliness about the woman masked by her friendly manner.

A frail man in a dark suit and white shirt opened the door. His long rather dismal face broke into a smile as he took my raincoat, Ms. Springsmith's waxed jacket, and the plaid raincoats of the four dogs. They trotted briskly into the large luxurious drawing room overlooking the rainy street and jumped onto expensive antique chairs, protected by tatty blankets.

"Please sit down." Ms. Springsmith pointed to a wing-backed chair near the crackling fire in the large sitting room, then plumped down on a great carved hall bench and pulled off high green rubber wellies, replacing them with incongruous looking Moroccan style slippers. She made a futile attempt to smooth down the reddish gray curls like brillo pads framing her florid cheeks. The dogs watched her with bright expectant eyes.

The butler, a little unsteady on his feet, waited at the hall door.

"Will the young lady have tea, or some other beverage, Madame?"

"Tea, please," I said, admiring the oil paintings which hung around the paneled room. One over the mantelpiece featured an elegantly dressed, plump young woman with towering powdered hair. She possessed the same little round blue eyes, snub nose, and florid coloring as my hostess.

"Ancestors," Ms. Springsmith said. "That was the first Lady Violet, painted by Gainsborough. She was fortunate that ample women were in fashion then. By the by, I take the liberty of calling you Christina. Love

America for the informality. Is that all right?" she said, not giving me the chance to answer.

"And you must call me Violet, even though that one, a Countess, would roll over in her grave." She looked up critically at the 18th. Century likeness.

"It's terribly jolly to have a new neighbor. And I am so glad we ran into each other today," she continued.

The butler staggered in with a heavy tray bearing a huge silver tea pot and a smaller one with water, a mound of small sandwiches and pastries and placed it on a round mahogany tea table between the two chairs.

"Thank you, Stedman. Tell cook it looks delicious," she said.

Stedman gave a good poke to the large fire and as he left, she whispered, "I didn't really want a butler, but he begged to come with me."

She strode around the table in her slippers and her expensive green tweed suit, poured the tea, passed small cucumber sandwiches and then sat on the other side of the table.

"When Pater died, I decided to come live in Mater's house."

She had an annoying affectation of using the Latin for mother and father, a hangover from boarding school days and Latin class.

"Mater died years ago. She had the money and Pater, the family tree. But his aristocratic family was just too much for her. Too much buggering. It wasn't a happy marriage. So here I am." She threw her short plump arms up in the air. "No longer Lady Violet Springsmith, just plain old Violet. Now tell me about you." Her small eyes bored into me.

I was nervous that she would ask embarrassing questions, but she didn't look like a gossip column reader so probably hadn't seen the worst articles about me.

"I've recently gone through a divorce and am trying to decide what I want to do with my life," I said, putting two tiny sandwiches on my plate.

"You're better off." She shook her head, her curls bouncing, "I've never had much truck with men. Filthy, unpredictable creatures. Even Pater, to whom I was devoted, put me off a bit. Of course, he was saved from much foolishness by having the discipline of the military. Dogs are more faithful and have better morals."

She bit viciously into her sandwich.

I stifled the urge to laugh.

"I understand you have got to know your neighbors quite well," she said.

"Not so much Anna, but Madame A and I meet often."

"Anna's always been a hard one to get to know. I hear you go for breakfast most mornings. Terribly kind of you to give the old woman company." She picked up another sandwich.

"It's not a question of kindness. I enjoy being with her and don't really think of her as old. She is charming and her stories are fascinating,"

Ms. Springsmith's wide brow furrowed. "She's a dear, but you ought to take her stories with the proverbial grain of salt."

"Do you mean she's not telling the truth?" I put down my teacup, thinking Abigail had said the same.

"Not exactly," she said slowly. "It's just that she tends to be vague and has a vivid imagination. Quite frankly all of these Russians are a bit eccentric and do color the past. They indulge in *vranye,* a kind of creative lying, either to tell a good story or to make them in some way unique or heroic. Of course Russians understand this and accept it, but others like you might take this *vranye* literally."

She passed the plate of sandwiches, taking another two for herself. "Some of these émigrés have rather sordid or undistinguished pasts so they claim all kinds of deeds and pedigrees, sometimes just for attention; other times it can be lucrative."

Springsmith went on, "I'm a bit worried about the poor dears'."

"Why?" I waited for the answer while she stirred her tea, frowned, and added more hot water.

"Short on money. Feodosia has a small pension, and there is Anna's salary, but that's hardly enough to support them and take care of Sergei."

It seemed odd that she knew so much about the Antonova's affairs. I couldn't imagine my neighbor confiding in her.

"Madame A told me Sergei was an artist," I said.

She nodded, curls bobbing. "He is some kind of artist, but he doesn't sell much of his work and needs economic support."

Madame A often spoke of Sergei in adoring terms, but never gave me the opportunity to ask specific questions about him. All I knew was that he was a kind of genius and had been traumatized by the revolution, and was too nervous to live in a city.

"I have never met Sergei, although I know he lives on the Jersey shore. Feodosia visits him only a couple of times a year," she said, silent for a moment, ruminating.

"Of course Feodosia is frail and it is difficult for her to travel, but I believe she manages four trips a year. Besides Sergei she visits a friend in the Midwest for a few days. I am not sure exactly where, but it is one of those insignificant states, like Ohio or Iowa, all much the same in mediocrity," she said, drawing her plump body up in haughty disdain.

I bristled at her snobbery but said nothing.

"Anna never visits her brother. She never goes anywhere. It's always work and home every day since I've known her," she said.

Although Anna had studied architecture at NYU and was top in her class, she seemed even more rooted in the past than Madame A. She spoke with a heavy accent and curiously resembled the worn Russian women in newspaper photos, sweeping the streets or standing in line for food.

She didn't appear to have any friends or a life other than her job and taking care of her mother. Madame A had once said, sadly that there had never been a serious man in her daughter's life, and even when she was young, Annushka had been afraid of men, and had no desire to marry.

Ms. Springsmith said, "Anna resents Sergei. I know she contributes to his support because she doesn't want to worry her mother. But still, he must have income from other sources."

She leaned toward me, her curls bobbing. "Between you and me, I'm positive Madame A has some valuables that she brought out of Russia. Has she ever mentioned them?"

"No," I said, surprised at this claim. "What could they be?"

"I am not at liberty to tell you, but am convinced they are worth a lot of money." Her voice grew conspiratorial. "Perhaps you can persuade her to sell some of them to make her life easier. Recently, I offered to be the agent for a slight fee, but she said it was none of my business. I had never seen her so angry. Absolutely furious. I was terribly hurt by her reaction. She had been a friend for years, always had treats for my dogs. I was merely trying to help; quite unlike that niece of hers, Zoe who does nothing for her."

"I met Zoe this past Sunday," I said.

"Ungrateful child. Madame A and Anna worked tirelessly to get that orphaned girl out of Eastern Europe. Then they educated her, and what do they receive in return? Nothing."

She jumped up, and said, "Time for treats."

The dogs were on the alert.

"Zoe seems to be doing ok financially," I said.

"Ha!" Ms. Springsmith spat out in disgust as she threw each of the dogs a chocolate biscuit.

"They put her through Brearly and Vassar. Mind you, the girl's intelligent enough, but a man trap. Her money comes from the boyfriend Nicolae. Who knows where he gets it."

She threw the dogs more biscuits, and continued, "Before Nicolae she was supported by a series of boyfriends. A fitting description of her could never be uttered in a drawing room. This latest boyfriend Nicolae seems to be more lasting, unpleasant little rodent that he is. But she does nothing for the Antonova's. Every time that hussy turns up in that big car, courtesy of the UN, Madame A and Anna are upset for days after."

She sat down again and refreshed her tea.

"From my front window I saw you speaking to Nicolae. I also met him that day," I said.

She furiously stirred her tea. "This past Sunday?"

"Yes, I heard the commotion and thought maybe there was some problem between the Borzois and your dogs. By the way, I'm really impressed that you speak Russian."

"Russian," she hooted, "hardly. No dear, totally wrong. I wish I did. I'm hopeless at languages. Barely passed French after studying it for seven years. Now I remember. The beastly man was very rude about the dogs. Told me to keep them away. In my own neighborhood, mind you. The cheek of him. Shaky, especially took offence."

"Zoe told me that Anna needs an operation."

"So it is serious. I know she hasn't been well. Something must be done to help them. It would be in their interest if you could encourage Madame A to sell some of her treasures," she persisted.

It had never occurred to me that my neighbor, who seemed on the edge of poverty, might have valuable objects. I thought about the contents of the envelope I was keeping for her, but then Madame A claimed that every piece of her jewelry had been sold or bartered to flee Russia, and that the only valuables she managed to save were her photographs.

I left with the distinct impression that Ms. Springsmith had asked me to tea to discover what I knew about Madame A's treasures.

Chapter 15

Rural Ohio: 2000

THE FULL AUTUMN moon illuminates the night sky and in the faint shapes of clouds passing briefly over its surface, I see the émigrés clustered together. Their Russian chatter returns to me in the rustle of the dry leaves and takes me back to a scene in General Turev's ballroom. How could I know that I was meeting some of the major characters in my own dark tale at the celebration of Russian Easter?

New York: 1970

I had been invited to Russia Easter after coming upon Anna on one of the folding chairs in the middle of the Antonova's kitchen, savagely beating a mixture in a large bowl.

"*Pashka* is a cheese cake, but Anna Georgievna Antonova's also adds ingredients of almonds, chocolate and hard labor," Madame A joked. "She has been beating it all morning for the Easter celebration at General Turev's. He is awaiting you. You will come."

Easter in St Petersburg came to life at General Turev's mansion on the Upper West Side, next door to the famous Dakota building., I wore a traditional old white linen dress with high neck and puffed sleeves taken from

Madame A's trunk, and once owned by her dear friend Natasha who died in Harbin from typhus.

As we swept up the grand staircase with chamber music floating around us, General Turev, tall and dignified in his Tsarist uniform plastered with medals, met us at the top. His clipped gray hair surrounded a wide forehead, large nose, and thin mouth; his military appearance was rendered more distinctive by a patch worn over one eye. I envisioned him commanding his troops from horseback.

General Turev's memoirs *My Life Struggle for the Monarchy*, published and translated into English in 1923, had become part of my source material on the Russian Revolution. In 1919 when the White Army was in retreat in Siberia, Turev's train was taken by the Reds and during their captivity, his wife was killed. The general escaped to the Caucasus, and commanded a Cossack regiment until the White Army was finally defeated and evacuated from the Crimean ports in 1922.

"My dear Sasha Gregorievich," Madame A said.

"Dearest Feodosia Petrovna Antonova." The general hugged her exuberantly and they kissed *a la Russe*, bobbing left, right, left. Then he turned to Anna.

"My little Annushka, you look lovely." He sighed with regret. "My Paul is now in charge of the Double Eagle office in Paris converting many to our cause. A new generation has become dedicated to overthrowing the corrupt Soviet government. If only he had been able to come today. I always hoped the two of you would marry."

Anna looked almost girlish and laughed. She had none of the sparkle of Madame A, but her coarse features, framed by greying tightly curled black hair, were lightened by a lovely smile and her dark eyes glistened with life. It was curious, but nothing more had been said about her illness and pending operation.

"And you have brought your lovely American neighbor. You must be Christina. I'm honored that you are attending." He bowed and kissed my hand.

We followed him through grand mahogany carved doors into an immense ballroom, crowded with guests, their conversations a buzz of

Russian and French. The women were dressed in the traditional white gowns and the men, like Turev wore old Tsarist uniforms. Madame A, who stayed close to me, nodded and bowed to a lovely woman wearing old cracked leather ball shoes and an expensive gown, shabby with age.

She whispered, "The Countess Varvara, once the belle of Petersburg. Her family lost everything in the revolution, but to General Turev, that doesn't mean a thing. What counts with him is who one was in Russia before the revolution and how loyal one is to the Tsar's memory. He makes an exception for me."

The general reappeared at my elbow.

"Christina, you must have some of our traditional Russian food," He lead me to a large table filled with delicacies and handed me a plate. *"Zakuskie,"* he said. "That, you know, is caviar and *blini,* the small pancakes. Come try some."

"I see you are good friends with dear Feodosia Petrovna," he said. "We met in Siberia during the civil war. Ah, she was a young woman then."

He went on. "She possessed lovely hair and eyes, an elegant figure and always was as fashionable as it was possible to be during that time. And she was so accomplished. She rode a horse like her Cossack ancestors, better than most of my men, and used her excellent French translating for our White Army. But it was her irresistible charm that set her apart. She could persuade anyone to do anything she wanted. All the men were in love with her even though she was married with two children and without her husband." He spoke as though he too had been in love with her.

Nodding approval at my empty plate, the general filled it up again and continued. "It was said that soon after the Bolsheviks came to power, her ex-husband Georgi Sergeievich Antonov abandoned Feodosia and the children and fled to Siberia with his mistress. But of course, I have only heard this from others, since I did not know her then."

Madame A had described Georgi returning home in a panicked state and searching frantically for something in his photographic room, then leaving without any explanation. She suspected he was running from someone powerful in the new Bolshevik government.

"She mentioned that once. It must have been terrible to have to cope alone with two children," I said between bites. Madame A had said she and the children met only once with Georgi when they first arrived in the United States and never saw him again. The general moved closer to me, combating the noise in the room.

"It seems very strange that after obtaining a professorship at Princeton in the late twenties, Georgi Sergeievich Antonov disappeared without a trace. Again, this is hearsay. I never met the man, but this remains a mystery to the émigré circle. But then Feodosia doesn't dwell on the dark parts of her past. That is how she is able to survive. How many of us survive."

He took a small glass of vodka from a tray and downed it. "She perhaps hasn't told you all she suffered. Dear Feodosia and the children lived on the train in a car near us when the White forces in Siberia were winning and advancing toward St. Petersburg. Then Sergei became ill, and she and the children left the train for a long period. When they returned she was a different woman. I cannot explain, but she had lost much of her vivacity and seemed frightened and secretive. She kept to herself much of the time after that."

He frowned. "I never discovered what happened to her during that time or where she had gone. Perhaps she has told you of this?"

"No, nothing about it." This seemed an odd question since they were old friends and I had known her for only a short time.

He thought for a moment, and looking intently at me said, "Does she ever speak of me?"

"She told me you gave her the wonderful silver samovar, and has described you just as you appear in the history books, a hero with a distinguished military record during the civil war."

He smiled. "Too much flattery for an old man."

"She does disagree with you on the Monarchist issue,"

"She thinks I am deluded in my mission to destroy the Bolsheviks and restore the Monarchy. But I think she soon will change her mind."

A tone of excitement crept into his voice.

"The Soviet Regime is very unstable, about to disintegrate. There is a great chance that we will prevail, we will return. Our organization is a threat to them. That is why their secret police shadow us."

He did not expect me to answer, but nodded across the room to someone who had just arrived. "I must greet some of my other guests. Please excuse me."

Dinner was announced and we all filed into the grand dining room, lit by blazing candles. At the dining table, laden with heavy silver and imperial plate, the guests stood at the general's command while he proposed a toast to Russia and the late Tsar, tears streaming down his face. Others at the table wept as well and saluted Turev as the *Vozhd*, the leader of Russia in exile.

I was seated between General Turev and General Kosloff, a bald powerfully built man, with an oriental appearance set off by a drooping moustache. His uniform had been mended so many times there was no material left without a patch. He was very congenial and talkative and kindly translated for me.

He ate the first course of salmon in the hurried concentrated way of the hungry and then turned to me. "Why Turev wants to return to Russia when he has such a good life, God only knows. Some of us who are nearly beggars have reason, but we are not crazy enough to go back to that hell." He smiled, showing a glittering row of gold teeth.

"It is a half-baked idea, but I admit that in the past year his monarchist group The Double Eagle has gained more support. This is a mystery to me. If we did go back to our country, we would immediately retrace our steps and come back here. The Bolshies have destroyed the old Russia and put something monstrous in its place." He frowned stroking his moustache.

After we finished the dessert course, which featured Anna's pashka, General Turev leaned across to Kosloff and said, "You must be following the latest in the Anna Anderson case."

"Yes, it is a very interesting outcome," Kosloff said, and lowered his voice to explain to me. "Anna Anderson claims to be the Grand Duchess Anastasia, the Tsar's youngest daughter. It has been in all the newspapers. She supposedly escaped from the Ipatiev House the night the other members of the family were murdered. Although the claim seems doubtful, she is the right age and bears a resemblance to the Grand Duchess. It would be difficult to prove at this late date. The last photographs of the family were taken in 1918 when the Grand Duchess Anastasia was seventeen."

"Nonsense," Madame A, sitting on the other side of Kosloff, overheard the conversation and interrupted. "She is just another impostor."

Her voice took on a surprising hardness, "They all were shot. We all know this. No one escaped."

The atmosphere had become tense; everyone had stopped eating. The table was in uproar, with much shouting and arguing in Russian.

Later in the evening while the music played for dancing, Madame A and I sat with the two generals in a small alcove in the ballroom. Anna had gone to sit at another table with the Countess Varvara an old friend of her mother's. The argument about Anna Anderson continued and Kosloff spoke in English for my benefit.

"Now Feodosia Petrovna, be reasonable. This Anna Anderson has lost her case, but it has not been proven that she is an impostor. Only that there is not enough proof that she is the Grand Duchess Anastasia."

"But why would she go to court after all these years?" I asked.

Kosloff answered, "Money. This court defeat prevents her from claiming any Romanov money or property."

"There is none. What money existed, most of it in Germany, was eaten up by their inflation." Madame A said.

Kosloff argued. "Because of the imminent war and the threat of revolution, I know the Tsar had devised exigency plans to pass on his wealth and power to the next generations. In fact, vast quantities of land and natural resources could still be claimed by those who possess certain documents."

"That is not true," Madame A said. "It has been proven not to be true."

It was odd that she seemed so upset. I also was surprised by her detailed knowledge of the case.

"If this Anna Anderson had won her case, it could have been very dangerous for her," Turev broke in. "The Russian government has no legal claim on émigré money or property, but there are many instances in which an émigré dies in suspicious circumstances or in other words, is murdered by the Soviets, who then invent an heir to claim the property. There is one such case in the Swiss Courts at the moment."

"This discussion is pointless." Madame A waved a dismissive hand.

"Feodosia, please. This is not so," General Turev said, rising to his feet. Red-faced, he staggered drunkenly, then controlling his anger, fell into his chair. "I was with the White Army in Ekaterinburg on July 25 when they captured the city from the Bolsheviks. This was nine days after the family's supposed execution. After we interrogated all of those suspected of any involvement in the murders, it still seemed plausible that some of the Romanov family could have survived. If true, a survivor would have a claim to the throne and any family fortune which could be found."

"Ridiculous, a fairy tale," Madame A said, "The Sokolov investigation proved the family was murdered. The evidence is there for all to see."

"What is the Sokolov investigation?" I asked Kosloff.

He leaned over and whispered as the argument went on.

"Sokolov was the White government's official investigator of the Romanov murders. After the Whites were defeated, he left Russia with the evidence, but he continued to gather information and published his report in 1924 in Paris. He remains the final authority for most émigrés."

General Turev said, "How do you explain that the bodies were never found? In fact, the murders could be a fiction."

"But why would anyone do that?" I asked, totally intrigued.

"I believe there are three reasons that the murders could have been a fiction. The Bolsheviks deliberately could have confused the issue and kept the family alive, holding them for ransom in a secret deal with the Germans." Kosloff drank another glass of vodka.

"But then Whites who opposed restoring the monarchy could have perpetuated the story that the family were all dead. My own thinking is the story of their deaths was circulated to protect any member of the Tsar's family who might be still alive. It would be very dangerous even now for any of the family who survived to come forward." His comments silenced Madame A.

"What does it matter? There is no way to change Russia's government," Kosloff said in a weary voice, "We must stop living in the past."

"Ah, my dear friend, you should be more optimistic," Turev said. "Conditions are terrible in the Soviet Union, according to my secret intelligence reports. People are desperate to escape from that miserable country and its satellites. Every day there are shootings of escapees along the Berlin Wall. It is only a matter of time until something happens."

"What would that be?" Kosloff challenged.

"We will just have to be patient a while longer."

It was puzzling that these émigrés could not agree over main events in their history and became so angry at each other. It was so far in the past, I didn't see how it could matter so much.

General Turev's claim that something would happen in Russia to lead to the return of the monarchists did seem like *vranye,* the boasting that Ms. Springsmith had mentioned, not to be taken seriously. How would Turev, who left Russia at the end of the civil war, know what was going on there now?

The next morning at breakfast we discussed the party in detail. The argument about the Romanovs intrigued me. I didn't realize then that the conversation was significant to what happened later.

"The party was wonderful, like stepping into St Petersburg of the past," I said, thinking it had been fabulous grown-up make believe. "Thanks for loaning me the dress."

"You must have it. It fits you beautifully. It is a copy of the dresses the Grand Duchesses wore the last summer their father was on the throne. The poor little girls had done no harm," she said.

"Isn't it interesting," I said, taking the opportunity to bring up the subject, "that General Turev still claims there might have been survivors?"

"There is absolutely no evidence that any of the family was spared." Her voice was cold and filled with scorn.

"Evil opportunists concoct these stories to make money instead of doing honest work."

"Is it possible to read that Sokolov report?" I said timidly. I seemed to have touched some hidden anger or fear in her.

"You could, dear Christina, but the report consists of seven volumes and has only been published in French and Russian. Some years ago I read and summarized it for General Turev and other émigrés. The general chose not to believe Sokolov's conclusions, and I suspect he destroyed my summary."

"What were Sokolov's conclusions?" I dared to ask, busying myself spreading honey on my bread.

"The Tsar, Tsarina, Tsarevich, and the four Grand Duchesses along with their servants were murdered on the night of the 16th, or in the early hours of 17 July, 1918. In the middle of the night they were awakened and told that they would be moved to a new location to protect them. They were taken down to the basement of the Ipatiev house and lined up as if for a photograph. Then eleven men under the command of Cheka Commissar Yurovsky fired on them. The Grand Duchesses had sewn jewels into their corsets so some of the bullets did not penetrate; the killers bayoneted those still alive to finish them off."

I shivered at her graphic description. For a moment the kitchen seemed to echo with shots and frantic cries.

"I am sure it was not a pretty sight." Her voice was dry and cold. "The bodies were stripped of all clothes and jewelry, loaded onto a truck, and taken to a forest outside Ekaterinburg. There they were destroyed by acid and grenades and buried in an area near the Four Brothers Mine."

"But how could Sokolov conclude that there were no survivors if the bodies were never found?" I said, knowing I was risking her anger.

"It is true that the bodies have not yet been found, but the authorities are searching the wrong locations. And there was enough detailed evidence at the mine to indicate the family was dead: including the false teeth belonging to Dr. Botkin, their physician, jewelry, belt buckles and other possessions. And of course, none of the family ever reappeared.

"This has encouraged many opportunists, like this Anna Anderson, to falsely claim to be a member of the family." I noticed that she was shaking slightly. "It is a subject I do not wish to discuss again."

Chapter 16

New York: 1970

THE NEXT MORNING I awoke from a nightmare, my arms held out in the air, screaming. I was running beside a moving train, begging the man watching to help me up to safety. For an instant I recognized his smiling face but it faded into blankness in the morning light. I could not shake off the floating remnants of terror and unable to go back to sleep, dressed and went out for the newspaper.

I had tucked the *Times* under my arm, and was unlocking the hall door when Jack came down the stairs. I tried to hurry by without having to talk to him, but it was too late to escape. In the days that followed our sexual encounter I had continued my solitary existence, the only break in my routine an occasional dinner with Abigail or Samuel. Abigail did coax me out to Warhol's factory for a party, which I didn't enjoy. I felt removed, on a different level, as though watching the guests from afar.

Jack did not call me or try in any way to get in touch with me. I made the flimsy excuse that he had been travelling. His silence was humiliating and I tried to convince myself that I never wanted to see him again. There was no doubt I had been used. Why would he be different?

This morning he was wearing jeans, denim shirt, and tweed sport jacket and could have been a young executive in casual clothes, but his watchful eyes betrayed him. Instinctively I drew away; he put out his arm to trap me against the wall.

"Hey, you're still angry with me, aren't you? I really am sorry for that night." His one arm was poised over my head and he came close, lightly touching me. He gently held my arm, and my body bent toward him, like a plant to light.

"'It's ok." My voice was artificially loud and cheery, like a doll whose voice box had gone wrong. The feelings churning inside me were unbearable. I tried to give the impression that making love on my kitchen floor meant as little to me as it did to him, but tears started in my eyes. In panic I shrugged off his arm, and raced past him down the hall to the back door.

Tears ran down my cheeks. I am sure he noticed. I threw off my coat and wiped my face then sat down at the kitchen table and opened the paper, gazing blindly at the print. The article in the lower left column of the front page made me forget my hurt for a moment.

Count Anatole Von Grubov Burial

Count Anatole Von Grubov, a prominent leader of the Russian monarchist organization, the Double Eagle, was buried yesterday in Paris. White Russians who fled their country during the revolution gathered at the Orthodox cemetery at St. Genevieve Des Bois, south of Paris, to say farewell.

Count Anatole left Russia in early 1918 after Kerensky's Provisional Government fell to the Bolsheviks. He became a social and political leader of the Russian émigrés in Paris and an influential member of the Double Eagle, an organization dedicated to overthrowing the Communist government and restoring the Romanov Dynasty. Several other prominent members of the group have been kidnapped or murdered by Russian agents, but the count managed to survive to age 87. (See accompanying article, p.2)

I rushed over to Madame A even though it was early and she didn't read newspapers, even Russian ones, declaring she'd lived through a lifetime of bad news and didn't need more.

She opened the door, blinking in the dim light of the hallway and smiled broadly, kissing me in the Russian fashion.

"Sorry I'm early," I noticed she had just begun to set the table for our breakfast.

"Have you seen this?" I handed her the paper.

Plucking her reading glasses from her robe pocket, she read the article intently, and then turned to the accompanying one on page 2. Her eyes widened, drained of their softness.

"I'm so sorry. I thought he might be a friend of yours and you would want to know," I said, feeling uneasy.

She seemed unaware that I had spoken. When she glanced away from the page, she looked stunned as though someone had given her a hard blow. Almost in slow motion she removed her glasses, folded them, and tucked them away in her robe. Her usual charming expression had turned stony cold, her eyes from sapphire to black. The change was startling. In an instant, she became another person, staring at me as though I was a stranger.

A gust of anger swept over her and she threw the newspaper on the floor.

"What is it?" I said, picking it up. "Can I help?"

"I don't wish to speak of this ever. Please go now."

I was startled by her words and hardly dared to admit to myself how hurt I was. But what could this mean? Why would she be so upset and angry with me? Maybe she wasn't feeling well I reasoned as I returned to my apartment.

I couldn't believe her abrupt dismissal was final and waited every day for her to knock on my door, saying it all was a mistake. I tried to find logical reasons for her behavior and recalled an argument that erupted from the Antonova's apartment late last Wednesday night. Zoe's voice was raised along with Anna's and Madame A's. They spoke mainly in Russian, so the few English phrases stood out with clarity.

Zoe said, "Look at the photograph. I am sure."

Then Anna's voice, "They lie about everything. It is dangerous. Do not believe it."

Madame A said, "It's a fake. Please. Do not do it."

There was more shouting mainly in Russian, then silence, quick footsteps down the hall and the sound of the front door closing.

I waited for her to demand the return of the envelope she had asked me to keep and the books I had borrowed, but there was silence from the other side of the hall. When her knock didn't come, an unreasonable sinking depression overtook me.

Lost, adrift without her companionship that had eased the pain of my divorce and Jack's rejection I roamed the streets in the afternoon, sat at coffee shops, or wandered through the rooms of the Metropolitan Museum.

One late afternoon I was leaving the museum when I saw General Kosloff, bundled up in an odd looking cape, sitting on a bench near the entrance watching the street as though contemplating a military maneuver.

"Christina," he said, as I approached. "You look so unhappy. I cannot think why. It is spring. Look at the lovely trees, the daffodils."

Chapter 17

New York: 1970

IN THE RAW spring sunshine General Kosloff surveyed the street before he marched through the doors of the L&K, the Hungarian restaurant across the street from my apartment.

Although he had been reluctant, I had persuaded him to have lunch after our meeting by the museum, thinking he might have some insight into my neighbor's strange behavior. I sensed it was his poverty that held him back. On the pretext of giving me a history lesson on General Kolchak's Siberian campaign, he finally agreed.

He wore the same ancient threadbare uniform and an odd-looking sheepskin cape, a Cossack *shuba*, draped around his shoulders, but was scrupulously clean and carried himself like a military man.

General Kosloff was even more squarely and powerfully built than I remembered from the Easter dinner. When he saw me, his wide face flat like a plate, cracked into a smile.

"My dear Christina, it is a great pleasure to see you." He bowed and kissed my hand.

"General Kosloff, I am so glad you could come."

"Please, you must call me Kosloff."

He held out my chair for me before shrugging off his cape and sat down across the table, consulting the menu in a businesslike manner.

He quickly made his choice, and nodded with approval at the restaurant with its pressed tin ceiling and long communal tables, crowded with Hungarian men in thirties suits who always met at lunch time.

"This reminds me of an old café I used to frequent in Budapest when I was a young officer visiting my uncle."

Kosloff ordered in Hungarian and the waiter, a small middle-aged man with birdlike features and slicked back hair beamed at hearing his mother tongue and bustled off, returning quickly with two water glasses and a bottle of Bulls Blood.

Kosloff downed half a glass of the wine before asking, "How is Feodosia Petrovna? I intended to call on her after our lunch, but received no answer when I telephoned."

"I haven't seen her for a few days," I said, embarrassed, not willing to admit she was angry with me. "I know Anna is not well so didn't want to disturb them."

"Anna Georgievna is one of the casualties of the revolution. I fear our Annushka saw and experienced too much brutality as a child to ever be well or happy."

"Do you mean she was hurt physically?"

"We won't go into that now," he said flatly.

"Madame A was very upset by the death of Count Von Grubov. Have you heard?" I said.

"Yes, the whole Russian community knows of course." He pointed to the newspaper, *Novoe Russkoe Slovo, New Russian Word*, on the table beside him. "I was not personally acquainted, but admired his attempt during the twenties to drive out the Bolsheviks and restore the monarchy. It was of course, futile."

"But why would she be so distressed?" I said, thinking that was an understatement.

For a moment he looked startled, then shrugged. "Perhaps my memory fails me, but long ago in Petersburg I recall reading about a literary evening at the Count's. Feodosia and her well-known husband Georgi attended. The Antonova's were his friends, part of that group of intellectuals." The waiter brought huge plates of goulash and noodles and Kosloff dropped the conversation. He had to restrain himself from gobbling the food, as though it had been a long time since his last meal.

By the time Kosloff polished off two orders of apple strudel, the restaurant had emptied except for two elderly customers sitting near the kitchen. He quickly surveyed the street outside before bringing out an ancient leather folder, an oblong roll, from an old army pouch and placed it on the table.

He regarded the cracked dark brown case with reverence and pointed with a stubby finger to the admiral's gold initials stamped in Cyrillic on the edge of the leather roll. When the last two customers had left he released the brass buckles and unrolled the maps. His accent became thicker and his voice shook with emotion.

"Admiral Alexander Vasilevich Kolchak's maps of the Siberian Campaign, when he was the Supreme Ruler of all the Russia's. The Supreme Ruler presented them to me before the Reds transferred him to the Republic of Irtysh."

"What do you mean, the Republic of Irtysh? Wasn't he executed?" I said.

"Yes, my dear; it is a typical Russian joke, concocted out of grim necessity. These days it is known as black humor. Admiral Kolchak's government was located in Omsk on the Irtysh River. After the admiral was shot and crammed through a hole under the ice, the joke became a euphemism for anyone meeting his end in the same way."

He broke into a ferocious smile, revealing again flashes of gold. He seemed all of a piece, like a chunky wooden carving.

"Admiral Kolchak and I used these maps during the campaign which lasted little more than a year before disaster struck." His thick hands attempted to smooth out the creases. "The Siberian action was different from any other war. Imagine a landmass two and a half times the size of the United States with huge areas of unpopulated land, often sub zero in winter. The Siberian Railway, completed only a few years before the revolution, was the most efficient way to travel these distances. The only towns were those at the railway stations, and in between were vast stretches of wilderness." He pointed out the railway stations on the map.

"Snow drifted in the winds. One moment the ground would be nearly bare, and the next step might plunge you into a drift over your head." His voice seemed far away.

The restaurant faded before my eyes to a great sweep of beautiful, yet treacherous white expanse.

"Troops were transferred to the battle field by train, and most of their actions involved taking towns along the railway. Picture it. A train races along the tracks, then jerks to a halt. The doors of the cars burst open, in wilderness and troops on horses fly out to attack the enemy. Whichever side captured the most stations and rolling railway stock controlled Siberia. There were, of course, the inevitable instances of sabotage, blowing up trains." He filled his empty wine glass before continuing.

"There were few rules in this war between the Reds and the Whites. Both sides committed unspeakable atrocities. The veneer of civilization was stripped away. It was possible to murder without consequence even if the act had nothing to do with the war. I make no excuses for myself. It loosened the beast in me just to survive."

He took a photograph from his pocket and surreptitiously handed it to me. I gasped and placed it on the table. In the yellowed photo, marked *White Army Headquarters in Siberia*, a group of ragged smiling Cossack troops pose with severed heads, some still with eyes open, lined up like soccer balls in orderly rows.

"Heads of the enemy Red troops," he said in a quick rough voice. "It might interest you to know that these men were under the command of General Turev, but one must understand the circumstances."

I drew in my breath, not believing him. It was inconceivable to me that General Turev could have anything to do with this atrocity.

"You must remember. It was sometimes difficult to control the savagery of men who had lost family members."

"How did you come to fight in Siberia?" I said, wincing at the photograph.

"Like other officers I was given the choice of joining the Red Army or imprisonment and eventually death. I hated the Reds and escaped to Siberia, joining the White Army and the Czech regiments.

"I didn't realize that Czechs were involved in the civil war. What were they doing in Russia?" I called the waiter over and ordered another bottle of wine.

"The Czechs were former Russian prisoners of war who had deserted the Austro-Hungarians, enemies of the Allies, and were travelling across Siberia to Vladivostok to return by ship and join the Allied troops against Germany and Austro-Hungary. They hoped to be part of an independent Czechoslovakia after the war. Then a curious event took place. I have never been sure it wasn't orchestrated," he said, stopping to reflect.

"The Czechs, living in railway cars at the tracks at Chelyabinsk, had a dust up with Hungarian troops, repatriated by the Treaty of Brest-Litvosk, who were in adjacent cars. As the Hungarian train was pulling away, one of their men threw a piece of iron, and hit a Czech soldier. The Czechs stormed the train and killed the guilty Hungarian. The local government jailed those responsible for the soldier's death.

"Trotsky, the Red War Commissar, ordered that all the Czechs be disarmed before they were allowed to move on. Suspicious of the Bolshevik's, the Czech's refused, freed their men, and captured the town. Their leader Captain Gadja and his regiments began a military campaign, controlling great sections of the Trans-Siberian Railway and joining the Whites. They became a major force in the struggle against the Reds. I joined them in the advance toward Ekaterinburg where the Bolsheviks imprisoned the Imperial family."

He pointed to the map with a stubby finger.

"After we drove the Reds from Ekaterinburg and discovered the family had disappeared from Ipatiev House, contrary rumors circulated; that they were all dead; that they had been rescued. Gadja, now a general in the White Army, did not totally believe the story that all were executed and ordered an independent investigation.

"Madame A is positive they all were massacred and refuses to even discuss it with me, although she knows I'm fascinated," I said. The conversation had taken a strange turn.

"It probably always will remain a mystery," he said.

"But there seem to have been many attempts to rescue the family," I mused.

"Yes, of course, but most were clumsy and doomed to failure."

He was silent for a moment, as though searching for the right words. "There was something I discovered when I was in Ekaterinburg." He seemed to think better of continuing, the habit of keeping secrets still with him.

"As I mentioned before, the family's survival was extremely important. Any number of groups might have wanted them under their control for political purposes or financial gain."

"So what happened? What did you find out?"

He didn't answer my question directly. "In Perm we captured several guards from Ipatiev House who were accused of participating in the massacre." His eyes slanted like tiny cuts. "From experience I know prisoners will confess to anything under interrogation."

To my disappointment he didn't finish the story. He seemed uneasy, glancing around the restaurant toward the door. Jumping up, he went over to the big windows and anxiously looked up and down the busy street, then quickly folded up the map case and threw on his cape.

"My dear, it has been a delight, but I must go. Thank you for the lunch," he said, taking my hand and bowing. I realized I had not learned anything about Madame A's past and before I could make another date for lunch, he was gone.

Chapter 18

New York: 1970

ABIGAIL KEPT NAGGING at me to get over it and get on with my life. I finally decided to take her advice and accepted her job offer. I was meeting her that night around the corner from The Little Swan Gallery at the Spring Street Bar, a Soho hangout for uptown people, artists and gallery owners. Abigail had assured me that Lawrence was out of town, vacationing in Morocco with Pinky.

"Not that you should mind any longer," she said. "You'll have to get used to the idea of running into him at the gallery." I didn't care as much; my strong feelings over the divorce were slowly receding and I was confident I could handle facing up to Lawrence.

Perhaps it was the gory photograph of the severed heads spread out on the ground in front of smiling Cossack troops that made me want to be less involved with Madame A and her eccentric friends. I recalled Kosloff's remark, "My dear Christina, no matter how romantically people write and speak about the civil war; believe me, it was no picnic." Still, I just couldn't believe that the charming and civilized General Turev had ordered those savage beheadings. And then I was uneasy about hiding the envelope for Madame A. Was this her eccentric whim or was she threatened in some way?

Earlier today she had asked me to breakfast and apologized for her behavior, giving the excuse that she was upset about Annushka, who was going into the hospital the next day for her heart operation. I was immediately sorry for her and put my arm around her and felt with a shock that she was a wisp of skin and bone.

While I showered and dressed, I thought about Kosloff and his reluctance to discuss Madame A's past or to go further with his story on the Romanov executions. It seemed to me that these émigrés only revealed facts about their lives during the revolution when it put them in a good light. And then it was difficult to know who was telling the truth.

I glanced in the mirror, satisfied that my jeans and suede jacket seemed right for Soho, and was outside locking the door when loud voices drifted out from the Antonovas'. I stood in the hallway listening, in shock.

"Calm down, please Annushka. Your heart!" Madame A pleaded over a deluge of Russian. "Don't worry, my darling, she is good. I trust her. I must. It will be all right. Please Annushka, come back to bed. I have told her nothing."

Madame A's words, 'I have told her nothing' rang in my ears, drowning out the clamor of the Spring Street Bar. Stung by the cold tone of my neighbor's voice, I resisted Abigail's attempts to interest me in her friend Ed Blanton, a self styled poet, whom I immediately disliked. Ed was lanky, with long greasy hair and sideburns, and could be considered handsome in a fatuous way. He fancied himself a Marxist and wore a cap and pea coat like Lenin's, and was known to spend more time in bars than at his desk writing poetry. One of Abigail's faults was that she tolerated, even encouraged poseurs like him.

The place was packed like it was every Friday night. I was sitting with Abigail and her boyfriend Slade Maxwell in a booth, looking out on the wide street lined with iron-faced warehouses, converted into lofts and galleries. Slade, dressed in one of his military uniforms, a replica of Mussolini's black shirts, nodded an unenthusiastic greeting. His stubby little boy face under the short military haircut was marred by a permanent scowl, and he looked ready for violence every time another man spoke to Abigail.

"I don't like that creep. Don't you have anything to do with him," Slade said, after Ed gave up on me and moved on to another table.

"But he's a friend. And I thought he and Christina might have something in common," Abigail said. She seemed timid, unsure of herself.

"He looks like a fairy. One of those fairies who pretend they're studs. Women fall for that." He sneered and called the waitress over, ordering another drink.

Abigail's hands shook as she lifted her wine glass. Attempting to steer the subject to more neutral ground, she turned to me, "I'm glad you're coming to work for me. We'll have great fun. When can you start?"

"Whenever you want me," I said.

"Don't try that shit with me. Changing the subject." Slade's face turned a deep volcanic red. He grabbed Abigail's arm.

"Let's go. I'm tired of this fucking place."

"No." Abigail jerked away from him, sudden tears in her eyes, "I'm not ready; I'm supposed to meet up with some customers. Maybe you should go on."

After that I excused myself and went to the ladies room.

When I returned to the booth, Slade was gripping Abigail's arm and pulling it viciously behind her back. No one sitting nearby noticed that she was gasping in pain. When he saw me, he released her. "I'm not finished with you, you cunt." He jumped up and pushed his way out through the crowd.

Abigail's voice choked on a sob, "Thanks. You came back in time."

"Are you OK? Has he ever hit you before?"

Her tears spilled over; crying was a rarity for her.

"I'm all right, but I'm really scared. What a mistake." She cowered in her seat, her mascara running in lines down her face like black soot.

"I always thought he was crazy. Whatever did you see in him?" I said, wondering at my credentials for dispensing advice about men.

She didn't answer. "I have to get away from him, get out of the city for a while. I'll go out to Long Island. I have a house there he doesn't know about. Could you come with me?" Still crying, she rubbed her arm and sank farther back in the booth.

"When will you leave?" I motioned for the waiter to bring the check.

"As soon as I can arrange for someone to look after the gallery. But I'm going even if I have to close it. Maybe I'm being selfish but please, would you come with me? You might want to get out of the city for a week as well." She took deep breaths between sobs.

I had never seen Abigail like this. She was so frightened, so vulnerable. "Yes, I'll come with you. Let me check to see if he's out there."

When it was all clear, we ran around the corner to Ab's gallery. She unlocked her door and rushed inside. I managed to hail a cab uptown.

Settling into the taxi I searched the empty street. We had escaped Slade, but I was still worried over his threats. I would go with Ab to Long Island, even though I felt somewhat responsible for Madame A.

I went back over my neighbor's puzzling behavior, knowing her argument with Anna this evening had been over giving me that cursed envelope.

I was skeptical that Anna's illness had brought about the change in her. Madame A had known about Anna's hospital tests the day the obituary appeared, but still calmly prepared our breakfast. The cab crossed Houston leaving the high warehouses behind, and wove through tiny Greenwich Village streets. She had seemed angry, but looking back, I believed it was more fear than anger. Something in the Von Grubov articles had frightened her.

I rushed into my apartment and sorted through the pile of newspapers stacked by the door. I found the article on page 2.

There was an interview in the top left hand column entitled *The Box of the Harpuiai*, with the sub-heading, *The Count's Missing Treasure*.

I crept out to the hall and listened at the Antonovas' door, thinking Madame A might be awake and pacing the floor, but there was no sound. I hung up my coat, and because I was cutting out wine, made a pot of herbal tea before sitting down at the kitchen table to read the article.

For years, art dealers and museum curators believed that Count Von Grubov owned a priceless carved ivory casket, never catalogued with his collection. Dating from the 4th Century the casket belonged to Helena, the mother of the Byzantine Emperor Constantine. This rare object is known as the Box of the Harpuiai, Greek for the Harpies, the Snatchers, who carried off the souls of the dead. Carved with these mythical creatures and other scenes from the legend of Jason and the Golden Fleece, the box is a much earlier version of the exquisite 10th Century Veroli Casket now in the Victoria and Albert Museum in London.

Always secretive about his collection, some of it said to be of dubious origin, Von Grubov recently ended speculation about the casket by announcing that it was not in his possession after early 1918. In an interview with the New York Times a few months before his death, the Count disclosed that he had smuggled the casket to the late Tsar Nicholas II while the ruler and his family were imprisoned in Tobolsk, Siberia and that the Tsar may have bartered it in an attempt to rescue his family. The casket disappeared without a trace after the Romanov family was murdered in 1918.

The count explained that he had not mentioned the casket previously, but was now willing to reveal what he knew because the information could no longer harm anyone. "I did not, of course, give the casket to the Tsar in person, but to a young man whose identity was not known to me," he said. "I assumed that it still was in the possession of the Tsar when he was taken from Tobolsk to Ekaterinburg. No one knows what happened to it after that. After I escaped to Paris and heard reports of the Tsar's death, I received an urgent message from someone called the Bogatyr claiming he had been given the casket. He asked me to contact the underground opposition to aid in moving it out of Siberia. I did not act on this information because I suspected it was a Bolshevik trick to incriminate me. This man may very well have been the last person to possess the casket."

Maybe I wasn't thinking straight after the terrible end to the evening, but I couldn't find anything in the articles that might have frightened Madame A.

The only connection I could make to her was the White agent named for the legendary hero, the Bogatyr. I remembered the story of her childhood friends pretending to be the Druzhina, the outriders of the Bogatyr.

Still puzzled over her reaction, I clipped out the two articles and put them in my handbag, then undressed and fell into bed. I lay awake for a long time.

Three tiny dots like insects crawl on a vast white sheet of snow. A strange background noise, a wild keening, follows the moving figures until they are upon me. A ragged, frost-covered woman and two bone-thin children with haunted eyes gesture to me to follow them.

I woke from the nightmare shaking and clutching at the blanket, and stared at the bedside clock. It was 3 am. The fog of sleep lifted when I heard heavy footsteps tramping down the hallway. The Antonovas' door opened and the wailing which had penetrated my dream grew louder. The sound was coming from Anna.

Madame A tried to sooth her. "Annushka, it will be all right. I promise you. No one is going to hurt you."

A man's voice gave an order in Russian.

In a low trembling voice, Anna said, "They will put us in the cellar like before. They will hurt me. This time I will kill myself."

She switched to Russian, and I only understood the word Harbin.

"No Annushka," Madame A said, "it is the hospital to make you better."

Anna began whimpering piteously, pleading in a way that could be understood even in a foreign tongue.

I opened the door a crack and saw the small huddled retreating backs of Anna and Madame A marshaled along by Nicolae and his bodyguard.

Chapter 19

Rural Ohio: 2000

THIS MORNING AS the light crept over the fields I again read General Kosloff's memoirs and filed them away. His past is even more mysterious in light of the terrible events that drove me underground. When I manage a few minutes sleep in my upright position, watching, waiting for the killers, the same nightmares from thirty years ago return.

New York: 1970

During the next four days there were no messages from Madame A. Each morning I would make coffee and, opening the shutters to a gray rainy dawn, ask myself questions. Where had they gone? Why did Nicolae and his bodyguard come for them before dawn? Was that why Anna was so frightened?

I thought of General Kosloff who had known Madame A in Siberia. He might have some idea of what frightened the Antonovas. I dialed the payphone number he had given me and after several rings was about to give up when he answered, out of breath, and agreed to meet me again at the L&K.

It was a lovely spring day, but Kosloff wore his heavy shuba and carried a plastic shopping bag stuffed with books and papers. The waiter greeted him like an old friend and they chatted in Hungarian for a few minutes. The Hungarian men who were daily customers sat near the back by the kitchen, but it was past lunchtime and there was no one else in the restaurant.

After the waiter brought the wine and took our orders of Chicken Paprika, I said, "Anna has been taken to the hospital for an operation."

"Yes, heart trouble, isn't it?" I was not surprised that he knew. The émigré network worked faster than broadcast news. "She was never healthy. I hope it goes well. I will call in when she returns home if I think it is safe."

"But she was crying and frightened."

"Unfortunately, Annushka is always frightened."

He emptied his glass and sat in deep thought a few minutes, then reached down in the bag and removed a number of books. Dust flew everywhere, covering his face in a cloud. The Cossack general erupted in explosive laughter, his body shaking.

"I am not a good housekeeper," he said, coughing. He grinned in his savage way and lowered his gravelly voice.

"These are for you. I have heard you have a penchant for historical research. You might find them of interest. I have included my unpublished memoir along with other documents and books because I am struggling to loosen the grip of the past. I believe in the old Georgian saying, '*who remembers the past, let him lose his eyes*'."

I gingerly slipped his book of dusty fragile memoirs from the pile and opened the first faded page. At the top was a quotation from Lenin.

'*The revolution does not need historians.*'

"Did Lenin really say that?" I looked up. His round face had darkened, like a cloud over the moon.

"Indeed. The Bolshevik government sentenced Grand Duke Michael Romanov, a respected historian to death. Maxim Gorky, the writer, pleaded with Lenin to save him, citing his scholarship. That quotation was Lenin's answer to Gorky. The Grand Duke was shot." We sat in silence for a moment.

"Do you have another copy?" His book seemed to be disintegrating as I spoke.

"Yes, I have hidden it. I did not have the heart to completely give up my small remnant of the past. I am not so naïve. They would want to destroy it, to remove all evidence of their murders," he said, looking up eagerly as the waiter served our food.

After quickly eating his chicken paprika and side order of cabbage, Kosloff stared at me with narrowed eyes. "I suspect you invited me here as before because you want me to tell you all I know about Feodosia."

I nodded, embarrassed that he had seen through me, but at least he was good-natured about it and seemed ready to talk.

"Both Feodosia and my own past must be understood within the background of the revolution and civil war and our association with Admiral Kolchak, whom we both revered. In November 1918 Kolchak took over as Supreme Ruler in Siberia and the Allies began sending men and supplies to support us. I was in command of an undercover unit, delivering messages and orders from Kolchak's *Stavka*, military headquarters, across enemy lines to Allies and other White strongholds in the South and West of Siberia. I once sneaked back across the Urals into Moscow."

"It must have been really dangerous." I called the waiter over and ordered more wine.

"Yes, and exciting, although it came to nothing. I was in disguise, often as a ragged peasant, and sometimes as a Red commissar in a leather coat. It was hard going because I couldn't always travel on enemy rail."

He smiled, his mouth turned up in his broad face. "We were always in danger because there were enemy spies and desperados among the many roaming partisan groups. You could be killed by a starving beggar for a crust of bread, by a Bolshevik spy or for that matter, by a sudden blizzard, burying you in the snow."

He had finished his tea and poured more wine, as though fortifying himself for one of his journeys.

"I met Feodosia in Omsk the late summer of 1919. She was working in Kolchak's office, writing telegraph dispatches in French to our Allies. We became friends almost at once. Her husband had fled the Bolsheviks and there were rumors that she had been living with a White officer, but he was no longer in Omsk.

"Feodosia Petrovna travelled in the best circles and was a good friend of the admiral's mistress, Madame Timireva. In the end this friendship brought her nothing but trouble." he said, rummaging in his bag and bringing out a photograph.

Kolchak in uniform and the women in elegant riding clothes sit stiffly on a bench reviewing some ragged looking troops parading in the distance. They seem forlorn isolated figures in the vast landscape. Madame Timireva is beautiful with soulful dark eyes. Kolchak, a small lean man with a stern ascetic face, gazes with a gloomy expression at the soldiers, and seems to be expressing unhappiness at their inadequacy. Madame A is turned slightly as though in adoration of the historic couple.

"Our futures looked grim, so people took love and pleasure where they could find it. I can't deny I myself, at times, was indiscreet. Many ladies of ill repute circulated in Omsk," he said, his eyes darting like little sparks in the broad face. "Beauty was the great currency, enabling woman to survive. And you must remember, Feodosia was an attractive young woman, I guess about your age, and was travelling without her husband.

"There was a curious twist to our acquaintance. Thinking back over those days, I realized I had met one of her lovers while on a mission. It was soon after we went into Ekaterinburg."

"Was it the same man she lived with in Omsk?" I said, intrigued.

Kosloff spoke slowly, staring up at the patterns on the tin ceiling, "I can't be certain, as my encounter was earlier, before I met Feodosia, but he spoke of her as his mistress. Feodosia never mentioned her lovers; she was very discreet about her private life."

"What did this man look like?" I said.

Kosloff fidgeted. "I remember only the frank conversation. He was dressed in rags, and I would never be able to identify him."

He looked grave. "Soon after Feodosia and I met, Kolchak's White Army was in retreat across Siberia. I greatly admired Kolchak, but he made many errors in judgment that led to his downfall. Like so many others we were at the mercy of these mistakes. Many on his general staff were corrupt, feathering their nests with supplies meant for the front. My major criticism is that he allowed the corruption or, to be lenient, didn't seem aware of it.

He also made enemies of Ataman Semenov and General Gadja, the Czech commander. Both could have come to our aid."

He reached in his pocket and pulled out a torn map and traced the hatched lines of the Siberian Railway from Omsk to Vladivostok, pointing to a place called Chita on the Manchurian border, midway along Lake Baikal.

"Ataman Semenov, a Cossack leader opposed to the Bolsheviks, controlled this section of railroad; pity to anyone who tried to pass Chita without his permission."

Kosloff took another drink of wine and said, "Semenov had a ferocious reputation. Often said to burn enemies at the stake. Of course, he did nothing to contradict the stories. It was crucial to the White Army that they be able to send supplies through Semenov's territory. He often cut off supplies to Kolchak's troops and demanded bribes.

"I myself had several encounters with the Ataman," he said. "He did a great service to me through his influence and connections, and it is possible he helped Feodosia Petrovna."

I looked out the window at the traffic on 2nd Avenue, but saw only trains moving in a vast empty wilderness.

"When the Bolsheviks took control of Siberia, Semenov, with Japanese support, escaped into Manchuria. He often wrote to me complaining he lived in complete boredom."

Kosloff held out a dirty brown stained envelope.

"In this letter, he claimed he helped Madame A to escape from Harbin; a fact she never chose to tell me. But then, it might not be true." For an instant I pictured the trunks with old Harbin labels stacked in her kitchen.

Kosloff went silent for a few moments, and then roared with laughter.

"Semenov was relieved of boredom at the end of World War II, when Dairen was captured by Soviet troops. He was taken back to Moscow, tortured and hanged like a piece of meat."

I shivered, and took a large drink of Bulls Blood. These émigré stories nearly always led to some inconceivably terrible death. Kosloff went on, sifting through his memories.

"Gadja, the Czech leader, was dismissed by Kolchak after only two months as commander." He shook his giant head. "Kolchak's treatment of the Czechs cost him his life and endangered ours."

He emptied the rest of the wine into his glass before continuing.

"We left Omsk on the admiral's train only hours before the Reds arrived. It was November, bitterly cold and snowing. Feodosia, the children and I were quartered in the staff cars and seldom saw Kolchak and his mistress together although the admiral would appear to receive cables. Feodosia and I were completely loyal to the couple. She was indispensable, in charge of the secret telegraphs in French sent to General Janin, head of Allied Forces and to the Czechs, imploring them to let our train through and to give Kolchak protection. They ignored the telegrams.

"Both rail lines were heading east to flee the Reds and became clogged. The Czechs put us on the slow track and we were stalled for days. The number of trains carrying the admiral's government and staff also delayed us. There were six trains and a seventh carried the government gold reserve, estimated to take up twenty-nine freight cars.

"Alongside the train, on the *trakt*, the old Siberian road that followed the rail lines, it was pure hell."

The general had tears in his eyes and had difficulty speaking. The waiter brought another bottle and left it at his elbow.

"The road was crammed with refugees and retreating soldiers in indescribable distress, with no one to help them. Some crawled with lice; others wore the gray face of typhus and were shunned. Covered in frost and snow, wearing rags, we at first thought they were wolves. I cannot forget their faces raised up to us as they stepped over frozen remains of corpses, horses, and those about to die, begging us to take them on, but there was no room."

He grabbed the bottle of wine, poured another glass, drank it down, and poured another.

"It is no wonder Feodosia never speaks of this time. We stayed on the train through hostile territory. The Czechs removed Kolchak from the train and put him in a second-class car. He was their prisoner. His mistress and several of us stayed with him, although sympathetic Czech officers warned us to try to save ourselves. Madame A and the children left the train with two officers." He shook his head.

"I was heartbroken when news came a few days later that she and the children had been shot by the Cheka. When we reached Irkutsk, the revolutionary government arrested Kolchak. Madame Timireva accompanied him to prison. I slipped off the train in disguise and tried to organize the admiral's escape, but it couldn't be done. You know from my black joke that after they shot him, they pushed his body under the ice into the Ushakovka River. I escaped to Chita, and Semenov saved me, took me to Harbin near the border in Manchuria."

"So that was the last you saw of Madame A until New York," I said. The waiter cleared our plates and brought us tea.

"Indeed no. I walked into the Hotel Moderne in Harbin, and to my surprise and great happiness, Feodosia, wearing an elegant travelling outfit, was sitting at a table with a stranger. He was dressed in civilian clothes and looked to me like a speculator or adventurer. She introduced him as Victor Matsev. I believe it was an alias. He was an aristocrat with fine handsome features and fine manners, the opposite of someone like me, but he was a cold bastard. His expression told me he was not to be trusted. She was afraid and wouldn't tell me how she had made it there with the children." He drained his glass once more.

"She said they were going back to St. Petersburg. I protested, telling her it was suicide. Matsev was hostile, claimed he had friends in government and Feodosia would be safe. He threatened to have me arrested if I became involved. Feodosia sat with her head down, not looking at me. She told me to go. I was afraid for her, and using my sources, found where she was living, but when I called, the landlady said she and the children had left days ago.

"After that I worked as a bodyguard for Chang Tso-lin, the Chinese warlord who ruled Manchuria, until I earned enough to buy passage to the United States."

His face broke into a smile. "Feodosia and I, by some miracle, met here at General Turev's. You understand, we were never lovers, but very close friends because of all we had been through together." He rose quickly and pulled his cape around him.

"I should not have told you all this but I couldn't help myself. The wine makes me talk too much."

I stopped him before he left the restaurant, still wanting some reassurance.

"I know this is probably ridiculous, but I am a little worried about Madame A and Anna. They have been gone four days and there has been no word. I would have thought Zoe or Nicolae would inform some of their friends about Anna's condition. Have you had heard anything?"

Kosloff's flushed face turned ashen. "I did not know Nicolae was involved. That is most unfortunate," he said.

Chapter 20

New York: 1970

I WOULD HAVE reason to remember Kosloff's parting statement.
On the following Monday Madame A appeared at my door.

"My Annushka is dead."

She looked shrunken like a wizened corn doll and leaned against the
doorframe for support. I was stunned.

"It was too late to save her. They say she died of heart failure after the
operation." Her voice trembled. "I stepped out of the room for a moment
and when I returned she was gone. Zoe was with her. I take comfort that
she wasn't alone."

I gently led her into the kitchen and onto a chair. She sat lost in
thought for a moment, then raised her head, her eyes milky with tears.

"You know Annushka feared going away from home. I regret that her
last hours were so filled with needless terror," she said.

"But why was she so afraid? Nothing seems to have happened to her
since you left Russia."

Madame A didn't answer. She stared at the cats outside my window.

"Perhaps if she hadn't felt abandoned by her father, poor child, things
might have been different. We buried her in a lovely old cemetery in upstate
New York. Only Zoe, the priest and I were there. I cannot bear to tell
Sergei just yet. He is all I have left in the world." She sighed, and put her
hands to her head.

"Too much has happened in the past weeks. I must think of what I am to do. It is urgent." She burst out, "He cannot look after himself. He's a dreamer, an artist. I must see to him."

She dropped her hands and whispered, "The envelope, do you still have it?"

"Yes, don't worry. It's hidden. I will follow your instructions, but they won't be necessary, I'm sure," I said.

"You have not spoken of this to anyone? Not Ms. Springsmith."

I shook my head, mystified. There would be no reason for me to tell Ms. Springsmith.

"You will help me when the time comes?"

"I promise," I said, irritated at her insistence, not knowing what she could mean. I felt even more apprehensive and wished I hadn't become so involved with the Antonovas.

Later, I was buying groceries for Madame A and ran into Ms. Springsmith and her dogs. As they swarmed to greet me I told her about Anna's death.

"Do you know if she was conscious at the end? Did she have any last words?" She leaned close to me, her little eyes inquisitive.

"I have no idea. You would have to ask Madame A." I was offended by her cold manner.

"What will the old girl do now? She can't support herself and Sergei without Anna. Did she say anything else to you?"

"No," I said, thinking that lack of money could have brought on Madame A's worry about Sergei.

"I'll go to see her. It's possible she will now sell some of those treasures she denies she has, either at auction or at A La Vieille Russie. All Russians of note sell their valuables there. Let us go my beauties. Come for tea soon, Christina," she said, moving in the wake of the dogs.

As I entered the building, Jack was leaving Madame A's apartment.

"The old lady told me you were out shopping for her." He took the heavy bags.

"Thanks," I said, not meeting his eyes. He did have some virtues, even if he screwed every woman in sight.

"She is unique, a grand person," he said, "but she seems lost and confused now that Anna is gone. Do you know what she'll do?" His arm brushed against me as we walked.

I shook my head, flustered at the contact.

"Will you let me know if she needs my help? I won't be around for a few days. Have to go out of town again," he said.

I nodded, wondering where he was going and what kind of cop would travel so much. I followed him into the kitchen and he put the groceries on the table.

"Thank you, my darlings." Madame A was wearing her blue robe and sat among the jumble of objects from the past, her photographs her only companions.

Back in the hall Jack suddenly reached out and pulled me to him and fiercely kissed me. I found myself melting into his body, my lips lingering, kissing him back. I trembled all over. I was crazy for letting him touch me, but never wanted him to let go. It only lasted a moment before he said goodbye.

That evening the hall was filled with sounds of Russian as a number of émigrés including General Turev came to pay their respects, but Kosloff, her great friend, had not come. I tried to reach him that night, but he did not answer the pay phone.

Anna's death marked the end of our tranquil breakfasts. My neighbor no longer told stories of her idyllic life in Russia. Shortly after her return we were walking past the vacant alley, and she cried out, pointing to the wire fence encircling the lot.

"Please, let us cross to the other side." She shielded her eyes.

Still shaking with fear when we returned home, she said, "All of the memory has returned. I am unable to sleep. I see everywhere the corpses strung up along the fence, the fingers still laced in the wire as the train went by."

At times she seemed ready to tell me what was troubling her, then would abruptly turn away in silence.

I tried to raise her spirits, but in the following weeks she remained traumatized and obsessively preoccupied with her papers and documents.

When I called on her, I would find her slumped in her chair, glasses perched on her nose, leafing through papers. She had no stories for the photographs I asked about, nor would she leave her apartment unless I insisted. During these forced walks she started at every street corner and constantly looked over her shoulder, convinced that someone was following her. On our return she would resume her position in her chair and close her eyes, dismissing me. At night I would hear her scurrying around, opening drawers and ripping and cutting papers. I wondered what would happen to her.

Chapter 21

New York: 1970

"MY DARLING CHRISTINA, my troubles may be over,"
Madame A announced.

She was wearing an elegant black dress and her hair was in a neat bun.
Revived and full of life, she beckoned me to the table. I sat down, stunned
at this sudden change in her mood.

"Yesterday afternoon, when I was at the lowest point since times in
the revolution, I received the most surprising call. Such wonderful luck! It
was dear Vladimir Georgievich Antonov."

"Georgi's brother?" I was still trying to adjust to her amazing
transformation.

"No, he is the half-brother of my poor deceased Annushka and dear
Sergei. He is Georgi's son by his second wife, Nadya."

"You didn't tell me Georgi had another son." I noticed that she had
straightened and dusted the photographs.

"I confess it was a pleasant surprise. Georgi wasn't fond of children
even his own. He vanished from our lives after the divorce. Once
Annushka attempted to find him, but he had retired early from Princeton,
leaving no forwarding address. Even his close colleagues had no idea where
he'd gone. Annushka was very bitter at his desertion." She nodded vehe-
mently to confirm this.

"And now this miracle. It was as if I had prayed to the miraculous Icon of the Virgin of Kazan just as the Tsar always did before Russian troops went into battle. This son of Georgi exists, and he has telephoned me."

She clasped her hands together and twirled like a young girl to the samovar. She poured out the tea and sat down, moving a pile of pans and dishes next to her.

"But how did he find you?"

"Vladimir had read in the newspaper of poor Annushka's sudden death. The dear boy was very sympathetic so I found myself telling him all my problems."

I sliced the dark bread in thick uneven chunks, thinking it was unusual for her to confide in a stranger, particularly a Russian and over the telephone. She always was suspicious of Russians she didn't know.

I also was a bit jealous, as I had believed my special qualities had led her to confide in me. But General Turev had suggested that her charm was turned on to anyone who might be of use to her. I didn't want to dampen her happiness, but this Vladimir's call seemed very coincidental.

"Cheri, you seem suspicious. Why?"

"It just seems sudden for him to contact you, after all these years. Why now?"

"Annushka's death prompted the telephone call. He thought I might need help.

"Vladimir told me that Georgi died some years ago on a farm in upstate New York, and he continued to live there with his mother Nadya until his marriage a few years ago. He now has a small boy of his own, a child of three named for Sergei. Georgi had told Vladimir that he had a half brother. But the most wonderful news. He wants to help Sergei and me. He will save us."

We fell silent for a few moments. Madame A had regained her appetite and eagerly ate her bread, buttered another slice and dripped it with honey.

I wondered how she could assess Vladimir's character from a telephone conversation.

"But why does he suddenly want to help. It doesn't seem logical," I said.

"He said that toward the end of his life Georgi felt remorse over abandoning Sergei and Annushka. Vladimir wishes to make amends to Sergei and me. He and Larissa, his wife, are coming to meet me soon. And then, if all goes well, we might live together as a family."

"But you don't know these people. You can't go off with them."

She was offended. "I am always very careful. Believe me. Vladimir knows so much about me, small details of my past in Russia that only Georgi could have told him. And of course, I immediately contacted General Turev who has investigated and found Vladimir to be genuine, the person he claims to be. I trust him totally."

"I'll give you the money to help Sergei," I said.

"Ah, that is kind of you, but this would be from family. After all, he is Sergei's half-brother. Don't worry. I promise not to make any decisions to live with them until we meet and see how we get along."

Filled with a frenetic gaiety, she seemed to forget I was there.

"We are speaking on the telephone again tonight."

"I wanted to let you know I'm going to Long Island with Abigail for a week. I'll get some groceries for you before I leave." I gave her Abigail's number in Quogue.

She didn't seem to be listening.

"Vladimir lives in a nice suburban home with a large garden and many trees, in New Jersey, and says I would be most welcome. Perhaps it will re-mind me of our dacha in beautiful Finland." She sighed happily.

Then suddenly conscious again of my presence, she said, "But please, will you keep the envelope? I know I have no right to ask this of you."

"Of course, I will." Rising to go, I hugged her frail little body. It was as though my time with her had ended.

Chapter 22

New York: 1970

THE NEXT DAY Abigail and I fled New York in fear for our lives. Early that morning I was packing the last things in my suitcase when she appeared at my door like some wild apparition, a weird smile on her face, her hair a mess.

"Slade is in the basement of my apartment building." She spoke quickly, out of breath. "He broke in. I think he hit the super and knocked him out. He called me from the basement phone, said he was coming after me. I climbed out on the fire escape and ran down the five floors to where my car was parked."

Somehow she had managed to drive to my place before collapsing. She dropped to the floor, trembling and crying. I helped her into her new Jaguar and climbed into the driver's seat with no protest from her although I had no experience on New York highways.

As we hit the Long Island Expressway and sped toward the Hamptons, she stared straight ahead at the stream of cars, repeating, "He'll kill me. After that night in the bar the judge put a restraining order on him, but that doesn't mean he can't kill me."

It was a raw day, even for early April when we arrived in Quogue. Most of the houses were closed for the winter, and the small resort seemed ghostly in the mist as if inhabited by shadow creatures. A lone seagull swooped around high hedges and crabbed dark branches of enormous trees brooded along the wide main street. Abigail's house, large and shuttered with a wandering porch, was one of several enthroned on wide lawns like abandoned grand dowagers.

We stood on the porch while she struggled with shaking hands to put the key in the lock. The front door creaked open and the cold house exuded an unpleasant musty odor, as though indignant to be occupied by humans before late spring. We turned on the heat, put down our suitcases, found some sheets and made up beds in the two rooms near to the upstairs bathrooms and the kitchen downstairs.

Abigail was quiet after her outbursts on the highway. Fear had drained her face of its usual vibrant color. Even when we drove through the deserted village to the A & P in Westhampton and bought enough gourmet food to stock a deli, she remained tight-lipped and tense. When she did make an attempt to be cheerful, her laughter was forced and rough as though coming from a stranger.

We stacked the groceries on the kitchen table, filled the refrigerator and then drove across the inlet drawbridge to the beach. The flat golden expanse, framed by long grass and fantastic modern houses, ribboned the sea for miles. Bending our bodies against the wind, we walked quickly on the sand that sprawled into the blue grey sky; our footprints, like phantoms, slowly erased by the rolling waves.

This walk became part of a routine we followed every day that week. We slept late and after eating a large breakfast would read or bicycle around the empty streets. In the afternoon after lunch we jogged on the beach. I tried to calm Abigail who alternated between reasonable discussions of what she would do next about Slade and sudden fits of terror. These moods left her white and shaking, but diminished like the waves at low tide, as the week wore on.

Tonight was our last and Abigail had sufficiently recovered to cook her special Chicken Provençal. We were finishing our dinner wine before a crackling fire in the old fashioned drawing room. Abigail's Auntie Beatrice who bequeathed her the house had been a talented decorator, furnishing the room with oriental rugs, fine antiques and lovely faded chintz covered sofa and chairs. I remember thinking the décor seemed a cheery façade, not quite camouflaging the house's forbidding New England character.

Abigail had stretched out her long slender body on the flowered sofa. Her vivid paint box color had returned in contrast to her wraithlike appearance a week ago. I was about to say that the week had been good for both of us when she became slightly morose, and pulling up her sweater, showed me the various fading bruises inflicted by Slade.

"Why couldn't he be normal?" she moaned.

I turned away repelled, wishing she hadn't shared that with me. She often made me uncomfortable.

"But Ab, what could you expect? You met him in a singles bar. Those places breed crazies. If they're not crazy, they just want to get laid. They're not interested in a long term relationship." I spoke frankly. The wine had made me reckless.

"Exactly like me," she said defensively, "Anyway, what's wrong with a good fuck?"

I visibly jerked at her language just as she expected. Abigail called herself truly liberated and relished using four letter words when she wanted to shock or make a point. She never failed to be amused at my reaction, knowing my strict upbringing insured I never became used to it.

"I'm probably safe here. Slade doesn't know I own this place. He thinks I summer in Southampton." She jumped up from the sofa and closed the curtains on the empty rain filled street.

"I always thought he was slightly off the wall, wearing those military outfits." I really meant he was a psychopath, but toned it down.

Abigail plopped back down on the couch, ignoring my comment.

"I guess I've got to use more judgment, but I can't resist the thrill of meeting some fantastic looking stranger." She grinned, her mood changing, and cocked her head thoughtfully. "It's that great unknown out there. And some night I'm going to meet the right man. Really Chris, why don't you come with me once in a while? You're so prissy; you could use a little loosening up."

"I just don't like it," I said, stung at the word prissy, but relieved that she didn't know about my recent erotic dreams, the wild night with Samuel or my equally brief but passionate encounter with Jack on my kitchen floor. My behavior still surprised me. "There is something sinister about those places," I said, "You're kidding yourself if you think it's safe.

How many other Slade's are out there? I'd rather stay home with a good book."

I immediately regretted those words. It wasn't totally true, but it seemed to show that all her earlier hurtful remarks about my life being as exciting as a librarian's had some relevance. Indeed, it was prescient of my future existence.

Abigail wasn't the type to learn from experience. Like a child she always felt she could do anything she wanted without consequence. She would be out to the clubs the minute we returned to the city.

"Looking back, Slade and I had great sex. I didn't mind when he first got rough. It was exciting, and he seemed almost to be joking until he turned really nasty." She looked thoughtful.

I wondered at her sanity. How she could have great sex with that violent flake who dressed up like a storm trooper in military costumes? How did she get past that? And now he wanted to kill her. I tried not to think about what had gone on between them in the bedroom. Whips, chains? It was beyond me.

Scrunching down in the comfortable chair, I stared into the fire, my disgust and incomprehension fading as my thoughts returned to Madame A. I had telephoned her again today but there was no answer. I was probably worrying over nothing. General Turev had checked on Vladimir Georgievich Antonov and said he was all right.

His sudden appearance was unusual, but then so many of the Russian refugees had eccentric lives and strange stories. I imagined Vladimir's father, the rotund panicked Georgi, in the chaotic Petersburg rail station. Georgi, nervously patting down his hair, flashes his Provisional Government pass. He takes Nadya by the arm, rushing along to his private railway car, silently pressing money into the guard's hand, fleeing from the Bolsheviks with his mistress and a pile of luggage.

Could this Vladimir have been conceived during that journey? That was a romantic idea, but I didn't think it was possible. Madame A hadn't mentioned her new friend's age, but did say he had a small child. If Vladimir had been born nine months after that train to Siberia, he would be much older. I tried to picture this Vladimir, tall with light hair, resembling the photographs of the young Sergei, his half-brother.

Abigail, still musing on sex, her favorite topic, broke the silence.

"I suppose I shouldn't ask, but what was it like, sex with Lawrence? I never told you, but every girl who knew him wanted to jump in bed with him. We all were jealous of you."

I cringed at this unexpected question and hardly knew what to answer since he had been a total fake.

I tried sarcasm. "Well, the earth didn't move, if that's what you mean."

In retrospect our lovemaking seemed very dry, a little like slipping a folded letter into an envelope. Blinkered by romantic notions, I didn't have enough experience to judge Lawrence, to realize that he was only going through the motions. I couldn't share these images with Ab. It was too humiliating.

"It hardly seems real anymore," I said.

Abigail raised her eyebrows. "It wasn't that long ago. I thought you were in love and still heartbroken."

I had slowly distanced myself from that painful period of my life. In truth, Lawrence now seemed very far away, like a tiny indistinguishable blob in a landscape painting.

She waited expectantly.

"There wasn't much sex," I confessed, already wishing I hadn't. "In the first few months it was all right, but after that, Lawrence had seemed half-hearted, not very interested, although I never dreamed at the time there was anything wrong. I thought he was just sensitive to my feelings and was worried about his new job at Digby Corporation."

I had been a pathetic figure exactly opposite from a champion of women's liberation, clad in my seductive black nightgown waiting for him to come home, wanting him to be the man I married. When he did occasionally pop in for a change of clothes, I humiliated myself by begging him to stay.

"He was very cold to me toward the end, like a stranger. I blamed myself. I still do, and I guess all of you knew," I said.

"You're wrong about that. None of us did know. We thought he married you because he was in love. We never dreamed he would be living with that grotesque Pinky."

"It's not Pinky's fault. I don't think he understands that Lawrence is a fraud, although I'm sure he'll soon discover it." Bitterness had crept into my voice. My astonishment at Lawrence's sudden coldness, his lack of interest in me swept over me like the sudden draft that blew through the house. And like an idiot I had become involved with Jack who treated me in the same indifferent way.

"Maybe you'll return to normal when you start working at the gallery and stop spending your spare time with your Russian neighbor." Abigail said.

Ab just didn't like Madame A and when I asked her to give a reason, she only would say 'bad vibes'.

"You know, something odd happened to her just before I left."

Abigail clapped her hands to the side of her head and moaned, "Do I want to hear? Oh, go ahead."

Her interest grew after I told her about Madame A's surprise call from Vladimir. She stared off into space a few minutes, then said, "That's weird, the timing especially. Have any of her friends heard of this Vladimir?"

"She said General Turev had checked and found him to be legitimate. Vladimir claims his father died some years ago and that he and his father felt guilty over the abandonment of Madame A and the children."

"Don't know if I believe that. I've known a lot of émigrés through family connections and you never can tell about the wilder ones. They don't seem to know what the truth is and are always squabbling about irrelevant things that happened in the past."

Abigail yawned and stretched. "It will probably all be explained and you'll meet this Vladimir when you get back. Do you mind if we call it a night? I haven't slept much this week, but tonight I think I can."

It was surprising how quickly she had recovered from her fear of Slade. She had drifted into a false sense of security and didn't believe he would carry out his threat to kill her. I wasn't so sure. After she went to bed I checked the locks on the front and back door, turned on the porch lights, remembering the man I'd seen on the beach that afternoon.

Abigail had tired of jogging and returned early to the car. I continued running, and didn't notice the two figures standing in the dunes until I was nearly upon them. One wore a leather motorcycle suit and helmet and had parked his Harley nearby. The other, dressed in a boxy looking shiny suit and black shoes, looked out of place on the windswept beach. I came close enough to be nauseated by his strong cologne, which reeked of rotting lilies. His blunt features under the short black crew cut were hard and impassive and his small grey eyes held mine for a moment when I nervously said hello. He didn't acknowledge my greeting, staring through me at the sea; his fleshy hands like slabs of meat were fingering worry beads. My heart pounding, I had raced back to the car. I didn't mention the encounter to Abigail; there was no need to scare her.

I pulled back the curtain and the dark windows of the house across the street stared at me like square unblinking eyes. I jerked back; Slade and the thugs he hung out with could have followed us. Panicked, I rushed through the cold hall to the large kitchen with windows facing the back garden. For a moment I thought I glimpsed a smear of a white face pressed against the window. Averting my eyes, afraid of what I would see, I madly rummaged through a drawer, crashing through utensils until I found a butcher's knife. Hurrying upstairs, turning on lights as I went to the bedroom, I laid the knife on the nightstand within my reach.

That evening the bedroom, decorated in brown plaid with nautical pictures on the wall, evoked a heart breaking melancholy. An old wooden model of a sailboat, surrounded by shells and stones collected from the beach was displayed on the chest opposite the bed. On the wall above the chest hung a framed photograph of a boy with blond hair and a wide smile, standing on the deck of a small sailing dinghy in front of the Shinnecock Yacht Club. Auntie Beatrice's son Richard had been killed in a sailing accident years ago. This was his room, untouched from that tragic day he died at sea.

I quickly put on my pajamas and climbed into bed but couldn't sleep and browsed through the stack of books I'd brought with me to continue my research. Most of them were accounts of the imprisonment and execution of the Tsar and his family, which had fascinated me since I heard the arguments at Russian Easter.

I had bought two books on the Romanov family and borrowed some from the library. General Kosloff also had given me several folders and documents about the Romanovs. I knew Madame A would never loan me any material on the subject. Her vehement refusal to discuss the Romanov deaths drove my curiosity. I could hear her now.

"Believe me Cherie, most of what is written about the family is untrue and only for profit. The Bolshevik Cheka was very thorough. None of the poor family escaped. Lenin and his Central Committee specialized in lies and half-truths, deliberately creating a mystery about the Romanov deaths. One must never ever believe the Communists. They lie. They lie."

She had stopped for a moment, as though considering something. "The Tsar and his family were innocents. Their murders were a signal to even the most liberal that an evil force had been loosed in Russia. Casual indifferent murder had become part of Russian life."

She lowered her voice to a hoarse whisper, with her familiar refrain, "The leather coats are *besy*, bestial creatures from hell."

Her whispered '*besy*' hung in the air above me. I sat upright in bed, my muscles aching with tension. Slade and his friends were bestial creatures from hell. They wouldn't hesitate to kill, would enjoy it.

I took the thin soiled book from the pile General Kosloff had given me, grabbed a bunch of tissues from the box on the bed stand, and scrubbed off the thick greasy layer of dust. Dark blood soaked stains and the word *Murder*, crudely hacked with a knife gradually appeared across the battered brown cover. After a nervous glance at the butcher's knife, I opened the book and found that it was a photograph album. The contents filled me with horror.

Chapter 23

New York: 1970

THE NEXT DAY we drove back to the city. I was exhausted and preoccupied, unable to think about anything except the bizarre murder album of the Romanovs that had so frightened me last night.

There was no doubt that one or more of the Romanovs had taken the snapshots. Was it possible that a member of the Tsar's family or a retainer had pasted in the photos and written those chilling summaries? But the album continued after the reported murders. If the entire family and their servants had been killed, who had created this macabre record? Was it the truth or had someone tampered with the original? And why had the last photograph been removed?

The Rolling Stones blared from the radio, another sign that Abigail seemed unconcerned about Slade's death threats. Blissfully unaware that he might have been stalking outside the house last night, she raced along the highway in the Jaguar, snapping her fingers to 'Jumpin' Jack Flash'.

"Would you mind turning that down?" I said.

She immediately lowered the volume and looked at me with a worried expression.

"What's wrong Christina? Look, I'm sorry I shouldn't have asked you about Lawrence last night."

"I'm just tired. I didn't get much sleep. Don't worry; it was ok to talk about him. This week was fun. Thanks for asking me."

She clicked off the radio, and we drove the rest of the way in silence. For a few moments I felt guilty for spoiling her fun, but then my thoughts returned to the album. I couldn't figure out why Kosloff had given it to me. Did he think of it as just another faded historical document that I would appreciate as a researcher? He claimed he had found it in Siberia but was vague about the exact location.

I stared out the window at the cars passing in a background of clear blue sky, but saw only the faces in the photographs; the dark stains on the album cover, the bloody boot print on the last crumpled page. I was relieved when Abigail dropped me at my apartment late that afternoon.

Before I left the car I said, "Are you going to be all right? Do you want to stay with me?" We both knew Slade was still out there.

"Thanks. I'll be ok. The bastard's due in court this Tuesday. He wouldn't dare come near me." But the fear in her eyes reflected my own vague uneasiness.

I was worried about Madame A. I had tried to telephone her several times, but there had been no answer and when I last called the line was dead. I put my bags down inside my apartment and immediately went across the hall and knocked.

The door opened slowly and I reeled back in shock. Tibor the super, in his worn leather jacket, gripped a vacuum hose and smiled at me. I remember my numb fear and surprise, as though my body had received a huge shot of Novocain.

"What are you doing here? Where is Madame A?" I shouted.

He smirked self-consciously and shrugged his large shoulders, which filled the doorway.

"I clean for landlord. Old lady gone. Gone," he repeated, smiling.

"But where?" My voice was shrill, high with incredulity.

"Don't know, Ok?" he said, in an attempt to please. His smile grew vacant, frightened at my hysterical questions.

"Maybe Thursday, men came with van. Move old lady's things. They ask me to clean up. They pay me good," he said.

Still unable to grasp what had happened, I said, "Let me in."

Wary of me, he quickly stood back from the door and scratched his head. "The men are foreign, very nice, pay me good."

This did not sound like a move to Vladimir's family.

"How many men?" I said, wanting to shake Tibor out of this complacency.

"Maybe four." He answered slowly, "Very generous."

I seemed to float in slow motion through the rooms, searching for some trace of Madame A, some memento, a note, but there was nothing. Tibor was still half-heartedly going over a spotlessly clean floor. The sun was going down and the meager light lent a strange haunting air to the empty rooms. Shutting out the vacuum's roar, I closed my eyes for a moment and then opened them, hoping the clutter in the kitchen would reappear, along with the samovar, the silver framed photos, the untidy bookcases in the living room and tiny Madame A presiding over all. But everything magical had gone. Only the draperies still hung, mocking the empty room. I went back to Tibor who was vacuuming the kitchen.

"How did she seem?" I said.

He looked up, puzzled. "Huh?"

"Was she frightened?"

He turned off the vacuum, frowning, "I didn't see old lady much. They very good though."

"Where did she go? Did she leave an address?"

He shook his head slowly. I gave up and went back to my apartment and sat on the bed, paralyzed with indecision. What to do, what to do, the phrase ran through my head like a pop song. It just wasn't like her to move without at least saying good-bye.

It was sensible to ask Jack for help, even though I didn't want to get more involved with him. I knocked at his door but there was no answer and when I returned to my apartment, my phone was ringing. It was Abigail.

"You won't believe this." Her voice was light with relief. "Slade is in jail for attacking and killing a man in a bar. Even if he just gets manslaughter, he'll be in prison for at least seven years."

"You're lucky it wasn't you," I said. This confirmed my long held belief that Slade was just priming himself to kill.

"I know," she said. "That poor man he killed in the bar probably saved my life. I feel sorry for the man, but am so relieved, even though I'll be in the newspapers again. I've cracked a bottle of champagne. Come down and celebrate."

"I can't. I was about to call you. Madame A is gone, and I'm afraid something bad has happened to her."

"But why would you think that?" There was a note of impatience in her voice. "It's obvious she's gone to live with that Vladimir."

"And why would she go without telling me? She hadn't even met him last week. She's always suspicious of Russians she doesn't know."

"Well whatever, you're getting worked up over nothing. I'm sure she'll call in the next few days."

"You don't think I should call the police then?"

"You could, but they'll think you're a nutter. But getting back to Slade, isn't it amazing that I'm off the hook? I hope they send that SOB away for life. I packed up some things he left here and took them to his doorman. It's such a relief. I wish you would come down. And by the way, when are you coming to work?"

I took Abigail's advice and decided to wait until the next day to call the police. Then I would go to the rental office and find out if Madame A left a forwarding address or had spoken to some of the neighbors. Someone besides Tibor must have noticed the move. I was still sitting in my kitchen, unable to think clearly, when Ms. Springsmith appeared at my door.

"Christina, there you are. I have brought you something from Madame A who seems to have gone on vacation." She was without her dogs and seemed in a hurry.

"But her apartment is empty, even the huge bookcases." I lead her into the apartment past Tibor who was winding the cord to the vacuum and seemed astonished at all the fuss.

Ms. Springsmith looked around at the empty rooms; her hand went up to her mouth in distress. "Oh dear, could something have happened? We were not on speaking terms you know. Then last Monday, she came to my door, said she was going away on a short trip and that Vladimir, her husband's son or some such was coming the next day to move a few of her things. I assumed she had gone with him."

I was impatient. How could she not have seen more?

"What did she say to you?" I said.

Ms. Springsmith's face grew even redder and she grimaced, stuttering slightly. "She seemed a bit nervous, but I thought it was because she was rushed. And then we hadn't been friendly for some time."

She searched in her bag and pulled out a book wrapped clumsily in left over green Christmas paper. "She asked me to give you this. Said she wanted you to have a remembrance of her. Said it was Pushkin's poems or something of that sort. I must hurry. The dogs are waiting for me."

I stared at the book but didn't have the heart to take off the wrapping. Madame A had said it was a remembrance of her. People only did that when they were dying or going away forever.

I lay in bed listening to the stray cats screeching in the back garden. Their hideous arias were accompanied by raucous laughter and screams from drunks leaving the bar up the street. I closed my eyes, not to comforting darkness but to the huddled figures of Anna and Madame A being pushed down the hall, of Anna begging not to be taken away again.

Giving up on sleep, I paced around the kitchen trying to reassure myself. I could be imagining something sinister when it could all be perfectly innocent. There would be no reason for the neighbors to question the move. As Ms. Springsmith said, it seemed quite normal. Maybe Madame A would phone tomorrow. Maybe Zoe knew where she was. Maybe, maybe.

My mind strayed back to my neighbor's apartment. A vague indefinable thought began to take shape. In spite of the mess and clutter of years, Tibor had very little cleaning to do. Everything was swept and dusted, not a scrap of paper left on the floor.

It was the complete emptiness of the rooms, the thoroughness that seemed strange. A chilling realization swept over me. It was too neat, not the way someone who moved on short notice would leave a place. My stomach churned with fear. General Kosloff's words came back to me.

"When the Leather Coats want someone to vanish, they leave no traces, nothing. You always know it's them."

I could see him thrust out his hands to punctuate.

"*Chistka*, purging, everything clean."

Chapter 24

New York: 1970

MY APARTMENT, WHICH I had begun to regard as cozy, exuded a cold and unfamiliar air. The closed shutters on the back windows
seemed to be hiding some unknown menace in the back garden. I stood
shivering in my pajamas in the middle of the kitchen, thinking back to the
horrible images in the murder album, connected in some weird tangential
way to Madame A's disappearance. Kosloff had given me the album with
the cryptic remark. "It is time for you to have this."

When I opened the album the first time, I had been too shocked and
emotional to note any clues, and knew I must review it carefully using all
my skills as a researcher. I took it out of my handbag and sitting upright at
the kitchen table began to read.

At the top of the first page, handwritten in capitals was a title:

Page 1. BEFORE THE REVOLUTION 1916

An official photograph of Tsar Nicholas II and his family followed. It
was the identical photograph Madame A had kept on her shelf, but the
family had signed hers.

"Did you meet them?" I had asked, impressed with the personal
signatures.

"No, no, darling Christina, I never had the occasion to meet any of the Romanovs." She shook her head in sharp little movements. "I purchased this at Pasetti's Shop."

She had explained that well known photographers of the Royal Family like Hahn and Pasetti were permitted to sell copies of Romanov photographs to the public. These were stamped to signify official approval, but the family also personally signed and distributed these pictures to close friends.

There was no official stamp on Madame A's copy and I had asked if the Romanov signatures were real, thinking the picture might be valuable. She snatched it up and took it into her bedroom. Now I wondered if she had been telling the truth. Could she have met any of the royal family? And if so, why she would deny it?

There were no signatures or stamps on the first photograph dated 1916. Small precise handwriting identified each of the subjects, and their ages. Tsar Nicholas II, 48, sits among his daughters, the Grand Duchesses Olga, 20; Maria, 17; and Tatiana, 19. Anastasia, 15, has her arm around the Tsarevich Alexei, 12. Tsarina Alexandra, 44, stands directly behind him.

On the opposite page there was another heading in the same crabbed script.

SUMMARY

Here they are in 1916, still sheltered from the vicious uncaring world. Notice the subjects are well groomed, dressed in beautiful but simple clothes. They exude privilege and wealth. It will not last long.

This is a fairy tale picture, totally removed from the turmoil in the country. Russia has lost over one million men in the Great War. There are food shortages. Workers are starving. Strikes and unrest everywhere.

Page 2. ABDICATION AND IMPRISONMENT AT TSARSKOE SELO: March 1917

Small intimate snapshots of the Tsar and his family were inserted in a neat row with a description of each.

Photographs: Revolutionary guards pose outside the gates of Tsarskoe Selo; The Tsar happily shovels snow; Tsarevich Alexei looks wistfully through the locked palace gate. The Grand Duchesses, dressed in plain white blouses and dark skirts, heads shaved because of measles, laugh at the camera; Sad Tsarina in wheelchair takes the air.

I quickly leafed through more pages. There were many photographs of the Romanovs, but I sensed this collection was unique. These small snapshots were more intimate, taken and developed by family members who were caught up in the camera craze in the early 1900's.

In 1907 Kodak opened two shops in Petersburg, selling the Brownie Box Camera. The company sent staff to give operating instructions for the new cameras to each member of the Tsar's family. The film was in rolls, and amateurs could develop the negatives without a dark room. It was common knowledge that each member of the Romanov family possessed personal albums and pasted in photos almost every day, for every occasion.

SUMMARY

In March the Tsar abdicates, illegally passing over his son Tsarevich Alexei because of his illness, and hands the throne to his brother, Grand Duke Michael, who in turn abdicates. The Provisional Government takes over until elections can be held. The family is imprisoned in their palace at Tsarskoe Selo. Although it is humiliating, they still enjoy the creature comforts. They can still smile into the camera, but they are playing at being commoners to curry favor with their captors. Their dress has changed. No more elegant white dresses and hats. No more fancy uniforms with medals. There is a scramble among many of the Tsar's staff to abandon the family to save themselves. It is amusing how some of them sneak away. A shame the deserters were not caught on camera.

A few stay loyal like Anna Vyrubova, the Tsarina's dear friend. Vyrubova is hated by the Reds and is thought by staff to be endangering the family. She is persuaded to leave, in spite of the Tsarina's objections. Vyrubova had been a devoted follower of Rasputin, the healer of the Tsarevich. Her house near the Alexander Palace at Tsarskoe Selo was the secret meeting place for the family and the Holy One.

The Provisional Government attempts to get the Romanovs to England, but there is a delay because the children have contracted measles. It has become very dangerous for them. The Workers Soviets, controlled by the Bolsheviks, are hostile to the family. The Bolshevik press cries out for revenge. They blame the Tsar for food shortages, for losing the war. Can there be some way for the family to escape the country?

The album followed the same form throughout. First the title in capitals then photographs described in that same handwriting, and on the opposite page, the bizarre summaries. The notes, written in a glib breezy style, often only in phrases, seemed sinister. A faint revulsion filled me but I could not take my eyes from the pages.

Page 3. ON WAY TO TOBOLSK: July 31 Old Style. August 14 New Style

I knew that Lenin's government changed the older Russian calendar to the Julian calendar, moving it 13 days forward, but the Tsar continued to use the old style, as did the person creating the album. Could it have been someone in the Tsar's entourage who knew English?

Photographs: The Tsar and his children take a break, standing beside the train carrying them to Tobolsk in Siberia. They are innocent, smiling, and unaware of what awaits them. The Tsarina is missing from the snapshot. She knows the game, knows they are doomed.

SUMMARY

After the Bolshevik July uprising was quelled by government troops, Kerensky fears for the family's lives and orders them to leave Tsarskoe Selo, too close to Petersburg for safety. They pack what they can. The women sew jewels into their corsets and brassieres.

On July 31, their request for asylum in England is denied by the Tsar's cousin George V. Instead, they will be removed to Tobolsk, in Siberia and are very disappointed that it is not their palace Livadia in the Crimea.

The town, a backwater 200 miles from a railway station, is not yet under the influence of the Bolshevik Soviets. The citizens still revere the Tsar. Kerensky promises the family that they may return to their palace in a few months after the Constituent Assembly forms the new democratic government. He promises that their personal possessions stored at the palace will be safe. If he only knew.

I was overcome with the same sense of foreboding as when I first opened the album. It had taken a bizarre turn. This was not an ordinary photo album depicting happy family events, but documented their lives as prisoners.

Previously I had viewed the family as hazy, historical figures, but they became disturbingly real to me. I saw them with their small cameras, snapping each other in what they suspected might be the twilight of their lives. I heard their camera shutters click and recoiled at the real possibility they took snapshots of those planning to kill them.

The summaries, intimate but strangely removed, were in present tense as though the family were alive at the time of writing. Perhaps it was my imagination, but they now began to take on a sardonic, mocking tone, as though the creator of this macabre record was leering over my shoulder. My kitchen seemed a strange foreign place. I read on, pushed by fear.

Page 4. TOBOLSK: August to December, 1917

Photographs: The family, on the roof of the Governor's House, smile anxiously into the camera, hiding their fears, trying to cheer each other up. The Tsarina is absent. Refuses to play the game.

SUMMARY:

Tobolsk is not too uncomfortable for them. Its citizens are still ignorant of the fighting in Petersburg. Food is still plentiful. The family lives on the first floor of the house. In the early months they are allowed to walk escorted to church services. Now they are restricted to house grounds. The priest comes to them. They are devout; take comfort from their belief in God. Walks confined to small space between house and street. Hard, sad. Siberian winter sets in. They still believe they will be rescued. Guards, most from Tsarskoe Selo, not hostile. Once they even permit entry of visitors, men from outside who arrive with photographer.

Chapter 25

New York: 1970

I STOPPED, STARING at the kitchen door, listening to disturbing creaks from the hall. Why would the guards permit visitors accompanied by a photographer? Who were these men? I carefully went over the text, hoping to find some clue to their identity.

Page 5. REALITY August–December 1917

Photographs: Grand Duchess Olga, her face sad, pulls her brother Tsarevich Alexei round and round on sled in grey freezing cold, going nowhere. There is nowhere to go.

Small blurred pictures were pasted below, the subjects turned front, left and right, like mug shots of convicts. I had not figured out before what these photographs were. My Russian learned from Madame A was minimal, and the print was very faded and hard to read.

I placed the album directly under the kitchen light and drew my breath in shock. They were identity cards issued by the local Bolshevik government.

One card bore the face of Tsarevich Alexei, identified as Citizen Alexei Nikolaievich Romanov and the number 29-34-08 registered with the Cheka. The other with the number 29-34-09 belonged to one of his sisters, Grand

Duchess Anastasia Nikolaievna Romanova. My heart was thumping; I felt as though I knew them.

I tried to convince myself it was ludicrous that an old album covered in dust could cause such fear in me. The questions returned. Who had created this? Did Kosloff know? I could still see him that day at the restaurant, recovering from his ferocious laugh, wiping his eyes, and saying in his thick accent, 'Who remembers the past. Let him lose his eyes.'

The phrase now struck me as a warning. I looked at my watch; it was 3 a.m., and I was wide-awake. I got into bed and pulled the covers around me, unable to tear myself away.

SUMMARY

In October 1917, new commissars from Kerensky's government, Pankratov and his deputy Nikolsky, former prisoners in Tsarist jails, arrive to take charge of the Romanovs. Nikolsky resents family's privileged life. Says, with a hyena laugh, it is their turn to carry identity cards with a number. Humiliated by the commissars, they are forced to pose for mug shots and must carry the cards at all times, even though they are going nowhere.

Some of the guards turn hostile; write dirty words on swing, so children can't use it. They destroy the snow mountain built as a slide for the children by the family, soldiers who remain loyal and servants. If only that were all. There are no snapshots of the worse degradations. The situation grows worse, no money left for the family and servants. They owe every merchant in town. Messages are sent to the Provisional Government, asking for money, but there is no reply. Time stands still for them. They are forgotten in the chaos of revolution.

Kerensky has other things on his mind. He is dealing with the Great War, struggling to keep the army from deserting. There is lack of food and total disorder in the cities, and the Bolsheviks who control the Soviets are threatening to take power.

Kerensky foolishly uses the Soviet Red Guard to stop what he believes is a coup led by the White General Kornilov. He commits a major error by releasing many Bolsheviks from jail, and arming them. He continues to fight in the Great War, sends troops into battle and is defeated.

Confusion, disorder everywhere. Tsar and his family have opportunity to escape. There is help from outside, but alas, the rescue fails.

Page 6. BOLSHEVIKS TAKE OVER: October 25, 1917

Photographs: The new leaders Lenin and Trotsky harangue crowds from terrace of the former Petersburg home of the Tsar's mistress; crowds outside Government House in Tobolsk demonstrate in favor of the Bolsheviks; inside Government House the children and retainers sit down to lunch as though everything is normal.

SUMMARY

News travels slowly from Petersburg to Siberia. The prisoners do not learn for some time that the Bolshevik Revolution occurred on October 25 and Lenin is leader. The government is fast becoming a dictatorship; violence spreads. Use of terror is legalized to quell opposition.

The Romanovs' treatment grows unbearable. Guard changes to young radical troops sent from Petersburg Soviet. The family tries to befriend them but the troops are filled with hatred toward them. It is bewildering. Family's non-vintage wine maliciously dumped in river. Soviet committees form. All officers are ordered to remove shoulder straps, which indicate rank. The Tsar is ordered to remove his in an attempt to humiliate him. Rations are cut to those of common soldier. By all accounts the family does not complain.

Both Germans and Bolsheviks have renewed interest in the Romanovs for use as political pawns. Rescue plans by western allies and monarchists are in motion. Monarchists give precious objects and jewels to finance rescue mission. Rumors everywhere, that the Bogatyr will save the Tsar and his family. But no one seems to know the identity of this White agent. Perhaps only the Tsar knows.

I noted the mention of the Bogatyr, the only connection in all this to
Madame A.

Page 7. FINAL JOURNEY TO EKATERINBURG: April 1918

*Photographs: The new prison, Ipatiev House; Primitive carts called
Tarantass, wait to transport Tsar, Tsarina, Grand Duchess Maria and
aides to Ekaterinburg; Small snap of Prince Dolgorukov in better days.*

SUMMARY

*On 22 April Commissar Yakovlev arrives in Tobolsk with troops and cre-
dentials from the Central Executive Committee in Moscow. He orders that
the Tsar and the family come with him. The Commissar does not reveal their
destination, but is in a hurry to take the prisoners away from the competing
hostile Soviets of Omsk and Ekaterinburg. Both groups have arrived in
Tobolsk to take the Tsar in custody.*

*Tsarevich Alexei, bleeding internally from a fall, too ill to be moved. The
Tsarina Alexandra agonizes over leaving her son, but fears that the Tsar will
be forced to sign the treaty of Brest-Litovsk which Lenin has devised to end
Russia's part in WWI. The treaty gives away enormous amounts of territory.
The concessions to the Germans are humiliating for Russia. The Tsarina goes
with the Tsar, taking Maria and leaving the rest of the children.*

*On 26 April in early morning, four days after his arrival, Yakovlev, with
35 soldiers, takes Nicholas, Alexandra, and Maria away from Tobolsk.
They go overland, a hard journey bumping along in crude carts, with only a
straw mattress to soften the ride. They are put on a train at Tyumen. It goes
west toward Ekaterinburg, one stop, takes on another engine, then reverses
direction, travelling back through Tyumen towards Omsk. Yakovlev, warned
that Soviets from Omsk and Ekaterinburg are stalking them, stops train
outside of Omsk and goes alone into city to cable Moscow. Then the train reverses again to Ekaterinburg. He stands off a hostile crowd, and cables*

Moscow again. Then he gives in to the demands of the Ekaterinburg Soviet and hands over the prisoners.

Prince Dolgorukov removed to prison, never to be seen again. Buried. The Tsar, Tsarina, Grand Duchess Maria, and rest of staff are jailed in the Ipatiev House.

I could only imagine their terror at being separated, perhaps going to their deaths, never to see one another again. I tried to analyze Commissar Yakovlev's puzzling behavior. He was described by different sources as well spoken, educated, and so charming that many of the party believed he intended to rescue the family. His plan may have been to hand the family over to the Ekaterinburg Soviet in this roundabout way for political purposes. Or Lenin may have devised this ruse to convince those who paid ransom that he was sincere. There were other possibilities: Was Yakovlev taking the Tsar to Moscow to trial or to hand over to the Germans in exchange for a ransom already paid to Lenin? Or was he involved in the plans to rescue the Romanovs and put them into White hands? Kosloff had insisted there was a bribe paid for the family, as part of the plot to rescue them.

Then I stopped at something in the next paragraph.

Page 8. CHILDREN LEFT IN TOBOLSK: April 1918

Photographs: Colonel Koblinsky dismissed as head of guards; Rodionov, new commandant; Alexei recovering in bed with sisters, Olga, Tatiana and Anastasia, around him. Alexei and Olga on the train to Ekaterinburg, their last journey; Note the change in the photographs. Alexei looks thin, frail. There are no smiles for the camera on this last journey.

SUMMARY

Soon after the Tsar and Tsarina are taken to Ekaterinburg, an unofficial visitor comes to Tobolsk in the night to see the children. Secret visitor, very important. He makes them swear that they will follow his instructions.

*They must swear that if they ever see him again, they must pretend not to rec-
ognize him. It could mean their lives.*

The writer taunted me; not revealing the visitor's name. I conjectured
that there might be some connection between this secret visitor and the
unidentified men who were smuggled in to see the family in Tobolsk.

*Four weeks later Alexei recovers, and the remainder of the family travel to
Ekaterinburg. They undergo very harsh treatment, according to Baroness
Buxhoeveden, lady in waiting to the Tsarina, who accompanies them. No one
permitted to keep cabin doors closed. Sentries posted outside lavatories. When
they reach Ekaterinburg train station the children drag their luggage through
mud and rain, while the mob howls for their blood. Some retainers and aides
are sent to prison. Others are released and stay in the town. A few disappear
with the children inside the Ipatiev House.*

*Page 9. TOGETHER AGAIN AT IPATIEV HOUSE or 'THE
HOUSE OF SPECIAL PURPOSE', EKATERINBURG: July 1918*

*Photographs: Secret picture of house with fence built up to top floor, taken
after their arrival; Yurovsky, head of Ekaterinburg Cheka, mild looking
man with beard, but in reality a killer. Of course, everyone can be bribed.*

This was the last snapshot in the album. But marks on the next page
showed that a large photograph had been removed. Spooked, I sat upright.
Even though I had seen it before, the empty space was inexplicably
frightening.

Restless, I walked around the room as though reassuring myself that I
was in my apartment in New York and then returned to the album.

SUMMARY

*On July 4 Guard changes. Alexander Avdeyev, a fitter at a munitions fac-
tory, a drunkard and thief, is dismissed along with friends he hired from the
factory. Yurovsky and his men, some mercenaries from Latvia and prisoners*

of war who do not speak Russian, replace him. Who knows what really happened inside the house during those last days?

July 16–17 Middle of night. They are wakened, asked to dress, and called downstairs. Sounds of shooting are heard outside the house. ???

This is not what it seems. The Bolsheviks lie.

Eyewitnesses had stated that an announcement of the death of the Tsar was posted in Ekaterinburg. The poster also claimed that the Tsarina and the children had been moved to another place. Sometime later, the posters were torn down. A deliberate attempt to confuse and deceive the public?

I threw the album across the bed. I hated its irritating prose, educated, yet perversely childlike, tormenting me with questions. Who were the unauthorized family visitors? What had happened to them that night? Was this the truth about the family?

Madame A's apartment and the hall seemed filled with barely audible noises: of ghostly footsteps pacing back and forth, of hurried conversations and screams. Quaking with fear, I crept out in the hall, and listened against her door, but there was only silence.

Trembling, drawn against my will to the album I forced myself to read again the last two pages, which had terrified me at Abigail's in Quogue.

At the top was a quotation attributed to Chemerodov, the Tsar's valet, pleading with the guards.

"But they are innocent young girls. Please."

Below this was an O. It was drawn like a child's cartoon into a face with tears dropping out of the slit eyes. At one side in a bubble coming from the O's mouth were the words. *'Poor me, poor me'.*

Unreasonable terror clutched at me as I turned the page and lost focus for a few moments. Then it was as though the small precise handwriting opened, and I saw the reality lurking behind the last grim photos.

That day in July, it could have been any day in July; it is hot, very hot in the room at the Ipatiev House. The windows are painted over and shut tight. It is impossible to breathe. The girl feels like the captive of a malicious child, an insect in a jar, with holes poked in the top, barely enough air. Her body slippery with sweat, she waits. Soon they will knock and it will be her turn again. She thought the first time he might be kind, even save them, but then he called in the others, like a swarm. It doesn't matter what they do to her now. As soon as they touched her, she knew they were going to kill her, kill them all. They watch her now through the door with malicious black eyes. She tries to keep her concentration, not to have to use the toilet. The others never talk of it, but they know what the Leather Coats are doing. Her brother, eyes wet with tears, stares helplessly from the bed.

She feels alone, even though everyone is crammed together in two rooms. She looks at the icon over the bed. The others are praying, trusting to God, but she questions his mercy. If anyone lives through this, she hopes it will be her little brother. The Cheka are superstitious and have not touched him because of his illness but have made him watch. The eyes of the icon stare at her reproachfully. The knock comes. She makes herself small scuttling along at the bottom of the jar, shutting everything down, the humiliation, the pain, the terror, everything except the watching black eyes.

Chapter 26

New York: 1970

THE TERROR IN those last words held a strange immediacy and increased my growing fear that something terrible could have happened to Madame A.

I was haunted by the story of General Turev's niece Eugenia, who had remained in Moscow after the revolution and was arrested by the secret police. They stripped her and shut her into a dark filthy cell without heat, without food, without sanitary facilities. The guards would bring her out, covered in filth, to laugh at her condition. She went insane.

I heard the creak of the building door, and losing all control, rushed into the hall. It could be Madame A returning.

A hand came out of the darkness and gripped my arm like a vice. I could hear even breathing and feel the bulk next to me. I tried to scream, but another hand was clapped over my mouth. I was turned like a plaything to face my captor.

"Take it easy. You don't want to wake the neighbors," Jack said, taking his hand away from my mouth, but continuing to hold me.

I tried to hit him with my free arm. "You bastard. Why didn't you call out? I thought you were Madame A. She's gone, vanished with all her furniture. The *besy* have taken her away."

"The *besy*," he said slowly, "What exactly does that mean?" He picked up his suitcase with his free hand and steered me into the kitchen.

"The Russian Secret Police, the KGB." I stumbled over the words, embarrassed that I was in pajamas, knowing how crazy I sounded.

"Now hold on, aren't you being a little hysterical?"

In the light of the kitchen, still wearing his trench coat, he looked weary, pouches of fatigue hung under his eyes.

"Why is it," I raged, still angry at Abigail's indifference, "that no one seems concerned but me?"

He put his arms around me and sudden warmth slid through my icy body and stilled my heart. Dizzy, lightheaded, I stayed inside his embrace and pressed close to him, feeling his strength as I told him about Vladimir and Madame A's mysterious disappearance. "I think she's been kidnapped."

He moved away, and I self-consciously folded my hands over my low-cut pajama top.

"But why would anyone want to kidnap her?" He looked skeptical.

"I don't know." I told him what I knew, my voice shaking.

"Look. Don't worry. I'll do what I can. I'll have a look at her apartment. If she doesn't show up in twenty-four hours, we'll put out a missing person bulletin. I'll check out this Vladimir Antonov. I'm sure we'll hear from her in a couple of days. Try to get some sleep. I'll contact you when I have some news." He seemed preoccupied, cool toward me. I sensed he didn't believe me.

After he left I calmed down, thinking he was right and that I was imagining the worst. I cringed at my state of undress, my hysterical outburst. Even more humiliating was my obvious eagerness to stay in his arms. I was never at my best when we met, but it didn't matter. I had given up on men.

In spite of Jack's prediction, there was no word from Madame A in the next few days. Mrs. Vacek had seen men loading the truck, but didn't suspect anything and believed she must have gone to live with relatives. But the visit to the rental office reinforced my worst fears. The clerk, a plump blond woman eating a bagel with one hand and typing with the other, paused with a grimace of annoyance and grudgingly informed me that a dark man dressed in a suit with a heavy accent had paid Madame A's rent for two months. She couldn't give me his name or more description. He said she would not be returning. There was no forwarding address.

"Not returning?" I repeated the stark words, staring into the bored face of the clerk, hardly able to comprehend the meaning. I went back to my apartment and waited for the telephone to ring. Several times I heard people in the hall and eagerly opened my door expecting my neighbor to be there, beckoning me to breakfast, only to be disappointed.

There was no news from Jack, but I wasn't surprised. Even though he was running a check on Vladimir, he believed Madame A had gone to live with him, and that I was hysterical, a neurotic who imagined a kidnapping.

I had to take some action and phoned Kosloff convinced he might know something. His word *Chistka*, taunted me. I called the number over and over until finally a man answered and in a foreign voice said, "Do not call here. He's gone away." The line went dead.

At our last meeting Kosloff had mentioned that he sometimes could be reached at Petrushka's, a Russian restaurant on East 75th Street. He did occasional odd jobs for the owner Arkady in exchange for meals.

Chapter 27

New York: 1970

STRAINS OF RUSSIAN music floated over me as I approached
Petrushka's. Two men in peasant costumes sat inside the door playing the
melancholy tunes on balalaikas. The restaurant was decorated in café style,
warm and cozy with thick wooden tables and chairs and walls painted with
Russian peasant scenes.

Once I had suggested to Madame A that I treat her and Annushka to
dinner there, but she had visibly shuddered and shook her head.

"Thank you, but no. It is a dangerous place for émigrés. Some of my
friends patronize that place, but I am too old, too weak. It is full of spies.
The Leather Coats harass émigrés and force them to inform on their
friends. Yuri Petrovich Nemerov, our good friend, was followed home and
beaten to death with a hammer."

She waited for this to sink in and hissed. "The police said it was a robbery, but we knew better. I don't approve that Zoe goes there but she is
safe, always with Nicolae."

I presumed she was exaggerating since Kosloff, who was definitely
a White Russian frequented the place. Even though I suspected
something bad had happened to Madame A, I felt safe in going there.
After all, I wasn't a White Russian and had no idea what a KGB officer
would look like. My knowledge of agents came from novels and movies
and from my neighbor's descriptions dating from 1917, of the Chekists

who wore high boots and leather coats and carried Colt or Nagant revolvers.

"Today even though they dress differently, you would know," she would say darkly. "It is something about their carriage, their terrible eyes."

I found Kosloff, half hidden in shadows, at a small table in a far corner toward the toilets and the back entrance. He waved, a look of surprise on his face and motioned me over. When I reached the table he jumped to his feet, bowed stiffly, and kissed my hand.

"Christina, an honor. Are you meeting someone? I didn't know you frequented this place."

"I was looking for you."

He was not in uniform that evening, and wore an old threadbare dark suit from the thirties with wide lapels and large shoulder pads.

"I have been trying to call you for the last three days," I said.

"I do apologize. I have been out of circulation," he said in a low voice, looking around the restaurant. "What a coincidence that you found me. I am only here for tonight and must be discreet. But it would be a pleasure if you would join me for dinner."

He pulled out a chair and gestured extravagantly. The table was pushed against the wall, and we sat on either side of a half partition, looking out into room.

"I have this table for the evening, a favor for completing an electrical job for Arkady who always is very grateful. Out of necessity my talents as a saboteur, wiring explosives to blow up Red Army trains, have been put to different use."

His broad face crinkled into a smile. He motioned to the waiter, a thin spare man with a melancholy face.

"Yvegeny, bring us vodka. We'll order later." He turned to me, waiting for me to speak.

"I am so relieved I found you. I need to talk to you. Madame A is gone, her flat is empty," I said in a rush. "I know it sounds crazy, but I think she's been kidnapped."

His smile faded. "Are you telling me that Feodosia Petrovna Antonova has disappeared? What has happened to Annushka? I have been worried since I discovered Nicolae was involved."

"Anna died of a heart attack."

"Oh, dear little Annushka," he said, in a near sob.

"I tried to reach you. I thought Madame A might have got in touch with you," I was surprised that he hadn't heard the news from the émigré network.

"I apologize." He bowed from his shoulders. "But I must take precautions."

The vodka came on a tray with two small glasses. He reached eagerly for the carafe, poured two drinks, and knocked his back silently. I tried to do the same, but could drink only half. The fumes burned through my entire body, leaving me with a light disembodied feeling.

Tears dripped into his vodka glass. "Tell me, tell me. Everything about my poor Annushka Georgievna and Feodosia Petrovna."

Kosloff remained eerily still like the partisan fighter he once was, waiting for one of his explosives to go off, while I related the circumstances leading up to Anna's death and then Madame A's discovery of Vladimir Georgievich Antonov, and her disappearance.

Kosloff's normally dark yellowish skin had turned chalk white, and he quickly downed another drink.

The music grew louder to greet the arrival of eight burly men wearing shiny badly tailored suits. They sat in the front tables near the music and immediately began to toast each other, speaking in Russian and laughing loudly.

Kosloff watched them, his eyes squinting with hate. "KGB gorillas, always here," he growled. "They call themselves a fancy name, Foreign Counter Intelligence Directive, but they're only glorified thugs. Their job is to beat people up, kill them."

"Should we go?" I was alarmed. They were even more sinister than the picture Madame A had given me of commissars in leather coats and high boots.

"No, that would be suspicious. Until recent dangerous developments, I have been a regular at this table. They pay no attention to me. I'm just a handyman, too old and inconsequential for them to bother. They are unaware that I watch and know who among the émigrés works for them."

Yvegeny brought our dinner, but I didn't feel hungry.

"Eat," Kosloff commanded, "*Shchi,* cabbage soup and *pelmeni,* Georgian dumplings. They are delicious. You must eat."

"Madame A wouldn't just disappear and not tell me where she was going." I ate a spoonful of the soup, hoping the dizzy feeling from the fear and the vodka would go away.

He agreed. "It's not like Feodosia. Since Siberia, she is always very careful."

He concentrated on his meal, finishing with surprising speed.

"And I've never heard of this Vladimir Antonov." He tapped his mouth with his napkin.

"I remember what you said about the Russian secret police; that when they want someone to disappear, they do a clean job, not leaving a trace. Madame A's apartment was like that." I languished over my soup.

"This could be the case. I should have been more protective of her."

"But why? Would you know any reason why she might be in trouble?"

"When I met her in Siberia she seemed frightened of something more specific than the Red Army coming."

I was about to break in, but he stopped me, his memory flowing.

"As I mentioned before, I was a member of the resistance organization called the Brotherhood of St John of Tobolsk, formed to rescue the Tsar. I can't recall her exact words, but something Feodosia once said indicated she knew something, some dangerous secret about the Brotherhood. This was in 1919, but I believe her knowledge could be lethal, even now."

He was very upset about the Antonovas and perhaps had drunk too much vodka. The restaurant became noisier and more crowded as another group of very well dressed Russian men stood together at the bar with their backs to us. Four of them formed a wide circle and began to dance.

Kosloff's voice was barely audible, "I was not one of the inner circle of the Brotherhood, those who made the decisions. I did not know the identities of any members of this secret group nor that of the leader, the Bogatyr. Even those higher up in the organization did not know who he was. It was rumored that he had infiltrated the secret police and was an intimate of Lenin and Dzerzhinsky, head of the Cheka."

More men had joined the dance and the music and shouts grew louder. A few bottles crashed to the floor. I had to lean in close to hear Kosloff, who seemed oblivious, in a different sphere.

"Soon after I became involved with the Brotherhood, the plot to rescue the Romanov family from Ipatiev House failed. Someone betrayed us. The Cheka was able to identify the members of the inner circle by the Brotherhood symbol, a swastika tattooed on the inside of the arm. Since the use of it by the Nazis, it is no longer popular, but then it was a religious good luck sign." His laugh was harsh and dry. His mouth drew down in a half frown.

"Our network was compromised, and the Cheka arrested and killed the members of the inner circle, but never revealed their true identities. I do not know if anyone of them managed to escape, with the exception of the Bogatyr, or perhaps it was someone else posing as him."

"At this time, the White Army had taken Ekaterinburg and discovered the Tsar and his family had vanished from Ipatiev House."

He took another shot of vodka and lowered his head.

"It was after our entry into Ekaterinburg that I was ordered to kill two men involved in the disappearance of the family. I am sure the order was given by the Bogatyr."

"But why?" I said, declining more vodka.

"They were accused of being part of the execution squad, but they denied having anything to do with the Romanov murders. They claimed they possessed information the Brotherhood wanted to keep secret."

"Do you know the secret? Do you know what it was?" I was intrigued, although this seemed to have little to do with Madame A.

"No. Bribes were involved. But that would be only natural. Bribes were the only way to survive during the revolution. And we were not encouraged to ask questions, only to follow orders."

He kept his eyes on the dancing men as he spoke. Before continuing, he drew short labored breaths.

"I was a saboteur who wired bombs and blew up Bolshevik trains. After we mined the tracks we would escape on a sleigh drawn by hardy steppe ponies. It was an easy job to kill the two men. Both had escaped to Perm, still in Bolshevik control. I went undercover and hunted them down. Even though it was for the cause, I have never forgiven myself."

I didn't see any difference between bombing a train and killing the two men, but didn't point this out to Kosloff.

"One of the men in your custody had the photo album you loaned me."

Kosloff nodded. "He had stolen it, but even after interrogation did not reveal from whom or what location."

"So then, who finished the album? Surely not this man who took it."

"I don't know."

I sensed he knew more than he was telling me. "But why did you give it to me?"

"You are a researcher. I thought it might be of historical interest," he said in a sly manner.

"But is it the truth?" I persisted.

He shrugged his large shoulders, dismissing my question.

"I have it here." I reached into my bag.

"Keep it, if you wish. I was going to burn it," he said, looking up at the burst of noise. The front tables had been pushed back and more joined the dance circle, clapping one of the men in the middle.

Kosloff whispered, "They're dancing the *gopak*, very strenuous, lots of kneeling and jumping. Stalin once made Khrushchev who was very fat, dance it for him."

After Kosloff's story the dance seemed a macabre charade. The same hands that clapped and feet that stamped in a joyous dance, appeared heavy and menacing, more suited to beating and kicking people to death.

"What you told me about Madame A. Do you really believe her disappearance could be linked to something she knows from the past?" I asked again, thinking his imagination might be working over time.

"It is possible, very possible," he said, shrugging his shoulders. "I will try to find out what I can."

One of the men watched the circle and stamped his feet in time to the music. He moved closer to our table, turning slightly to stare at a younger well-dressed man. I saw his gray eyes, the snub-nosed profile, and the thick fingers working over worry beads. The sickening odor of his cologne wafted over me, and I shrank down in my chair. It was the man who had been watching me on the Quogue beach.

"My dear Christina, what is the matter? You look very ill." Kosloff looked alarmed.

"That man who has just turned toward us. I saw him on a Long Island beach. Do you think he could be following me?" I was barely able to get out the words.

Kosloff's large moustache twitched nervously. He whispered, "His name is Soso, the diminutive for Joseph, named in honor of Stalin. He's a Mingrelian from Georgia, like Beria, who once ran Stalin's secret police."

The lights dimmed to a romantic glow, and the music changed to a sensuous tango. Soso, clowning in a menacing way, slowly moving his hips, danced across the floor, stalking one of the well-dressed men who had stepped into the darkness. Soso locked him into an embrace, so tight that the man winced, and moved him in a slow erotic tango. Those watching laughed uproariously, but the dancing partner was stiff with terror. Soso pressed his entire body against the man, forcing him to bend back in a painful contortion. The hapless victim's face hung upside down before me, his coiffure spilling down at the sides. I jumped in shock at the white faced Nicolae, his eyes bulging with terror. Laughter surrounded me, making it all the more macabre. A dance of death.

The dance continued in the half lit room, and General Kosloff's eyes shot fire against his dark face, like flares lighting up a distant mountain.

"Stalin and Beria have been dead for years, but these goons still idolize and imitate them. Many who attended Stalin's dinners at his dacha in Kuntsevo were forced to dance a deux and then were taken away forever," he whispered. "I'll get you out the back way before he sees us. Soso is important. He has a hit squad working under him who only do big jobs."

The words 'big job' propelled me to my feet. Kosloff gripped my arm and pulled me down on the seat.

"Wait," he said, looking around. "Now, slowly, while he's got his back to us."

We moved quickly to the door. The noise of the men laughing and clapping followed. He waited until we were in the alley, then whispered,

"Do not come back here. These beasts take people back to Russia; sometimes convincing them it is for the best, sometimes by force. The poor fools die in the gulag, the labor camps. But Soso doesn't mind killing here if it suits him."

"But what about you? Aren't you in danger too?" We quickly crept through the alley packed with overflowing garbage cans.

"If they knew about my work I would be murdered, but they think I'm too old, a little crazy. I foster the rumor that I'm dying of cancer." He winked. "I am remarkably fit, but limp slightly because of a war wound."

"Why do you do this?" I liked the old general and was afraid for him.

He didn't answer until we found our way in the darkness past the high alley walls and were safely out to the main street.

"In the Fifties after the war, the Cement *besy*, my name for Stalin, gathered my people, the Kalmyk's, in the town square. They were herded into sealed boxcars without enough air, water, or food and dumped on barren land in the Arctic without shelter. Seventy-five thousand died, among them most of my relatives. I will never forget. Many monsters, still in charge were part of this mass murder. Others are living comfortably on pensions. I want them punished, and that monstrous regime destroyed."

He waited on guard while I raced for the corner and caught a cab. Still feeling the menace, I nervously looked out the back window. Kosloff was gone.

Chapter 28

New York: 1970

SOSO'S EROTIC TANGO with Nicolae spread like an ugly stain across my mind and refused to go away. Kosloff's claim that the thug was here from Russia on a 'big job' was frightening. I thought of going to the police but had no idea what I'd tell them.

I sat over a cup of coffee, brooding angrily over Jack's stubborn refusal to believe that something bad had happened to Madame A. I still had not heard from him in spite of his claim that he would handle everything. I was beginning to think he was incompetent, ignoring the fact that the longer my neighbor remained missing; the more likely harm might come to her. There was no point in waiting for him to find her. I would continue to investigate on my own.

I paced restlessly around the kitchen going over my neighbor's conversations, photographs, searching for any clue that might lead to her when the picture of the four Druzhina slowly surfaced from the back of my mind. I stopped in excitement. There was a fifth person in that photograph. Baron Egon Stocker, a plump young man with a mane of hair and luxuriant beard dressed in a white suit lounges back on his chair and observes, a sardonic look in his wide-spaced eyes.

It took a few moments before I realized with a shock that the baron was the only one in the Finland photograph definitely known to be still alive.

Two days later, on my way to the baron's apartment building on the Upper West Side, I went over what I knew about him. Stocker, worth millions, was a recluse and rarely left his apartment near Central Park. He was famous for his enormous collection of Russian art and often donated or loaned pieces to museums. A recent show at the Metropolitan Museum of Art had featured his icon collection.

His father was a Baltic nobleman and his mother, the American soap heiress Adele Whitlock. He cleverly used his connections in Russia and America, to amass his large fortune during the revolution. As I came out of Central Park, near the baron's building, I recalled Madame A's curious remarks about her friend.

"Rumors about the baron circulated throughout Petersburg; that he was an agent for the Whites or for the Bolsheviks, that he was a smuggler, or worse, a thief. No one knew what was true. I confess I have wondered where his true loyalties lay and still do not know. But once, I was amazed to see on his table a golden cross, several icons and Faberge eggs taken from Tsarskoe Selo after the Tsar and his family was sent to Tobolsk. I told no one."

The baron's grand building was surrounded with a large number of security guards. I was searched in the lobby and then escorted by two burly men to the elevator. Two more guards patrolled outside his apartment door. One of them, a huge muscled man with a thick impassive face ushered me into the paneled library.

The elderly baron wheeled into the room. He was clean-shaven; his luxuriant white hair brushed back like a lion's mane from handsome rather heavy features and he bore little resemblance to the young man in the Finland photograph.

"Miss Gartner, Baron Egon Stocker," he inclined his leonine head toward the tray on the table. "Please help yourself to some coffee."

"Thank you," I said, pouring from the Meissen pot into a matching cup.

His dark eyes studied me with suspicion. He nodded no to my offer to pour him a cup, keeping his hands under his blanket. It surprised me that he was without a nurse or attendant.

"I rarely see anyone since the accident." He looked down as though still puzzled that the pathetic sticks of legs under the soft blue cashmere blanket belonged to him.

I could understand his recurring surprise, for his upper torso was like an athlete's. His large shoulders and powerful looking arms bulged slightly in the paisley silk smoking jacket. His penetrating stare made me ill at ease, and I concentrated on the view from the library, which extended onto a penthouse garden overlooking Central Park, until he spoke.

"I agreed to see you only because Samuel, my oldest friend's son requested it." He was severe, disapproving. I had discovered that Sam Westerby's father and the baron were old friends and mustered up the courage to ask Sam to set up an appointment.

I blushed, thinking of the persuasive powers I had used on Sam. I had tried to be brisk and business like with my request, which he granted immediately. We ended up holding hands over a candlelit dinner at The Four Seasons. At the end of the evening, I had fallen into his embrace, perhaps promising more than I ever intended to deliver.

"Yes I know. It is very kind of you."

"In part I was curious. Samuel tells me you have some rather distressing news about an old acquaintance." He shifted restlessly in his wheelchair.

"It's Madame Feodosia Antonova. She's disappeared."

He took in his breath and his broad features seemed to shrivel in distress.

"Tell me what you know." He leaned forward in the wheelchair, listening carefully while I recounted everything that had occurred.

I told him about Anna's death after a heart operation and that Madame A had been very melancholy until she heard from the mysterious Vladimir.

"But isn't it logical that Annushka's death could be the reason for Feodosia's abrupt departure? She may have needed to get away from painful reminders. Are you sure that she has not gone to stay with this Vladimir or other friends?"

"I have been trying for over a week to find her. Her neighbor and friend Ms. Springsmith also believes there might be something wrong. I have filed a missing persons report and have tried to contact Zoe, her niece, but she doesn't answer her phone."

"Ah yes, Zoe, I did meet that charming girl some years ago. But I digress, this is very disturbing." After a few moments of silence, while he checked that his bodyguards were positioned on the terrace, he said, "I sensed from the first time we met that Feodosia Petrovna was never quite what she appeared to be, that she was hiding something. Perhaps it caught up with her even at this late period of her life."

He sat back in the wheelchair, musing in a sonorous voice, as he dipped into the past. "In 1917 when the Provisional Government was in power and we were briefly under the illusion that Russia would be a democracy, I was in business in Petersburg, buying works of art and other treasures from those anxious to leave Russia. You may have heard from my enemies that I bought the objects for low prices in rubles from those desperate to escape the revolution, and then shipped them abroad to sell them in dollars and sterling."

He stared fiercely at me. "You may think this was an unprincipled occupation, but those were desperate times. Many people needed help to convert their possessions into cash. In addition, looters, claiming to be revolutionaries, brought in goods taken from mansions they sacked and occupied. I flatter myself that by buying these precious objects, I saved them from destruction.

"I employed Feodosia to evaluate and catalogue icons and other works of art. She was an expert at spotting fake icons, and an attractive young woman, so intelligent, so charming." There was a wistful look in his eyes that suggested he had felt more than admiration for Madame A.

"Soon after the Bolsheviks came to power, I was forced to leave Russia. Malicious false stories about me circulated in Petersburg. I discovered my name was on the Cheka list of those to be arrested, in spite of the fact that I had donated my time and expertise assisting the Art Committee. When I fled, I was very concerned about Feodosia and the children and left her the keys to my office." His hands moved under the blanket wheeling the chair over to the windows, and he gazed at the park, seeming to study the trees.

"I did not know what happened to her and feared that she had been imprisoned, or worse, murdered. Then miraculously, she appeared here in my office in late 1921. She refused to tell me how she escaped," he said, coming back near my chair.

"She was still a charming woman, but it was obvious the revolution and the civil war had changed her as it did all of us. But more so Feodosia, I believe. Of course, I can only speculate, but even when she was struggling to stay alive in Petersburg, there was an openness and bravery about her." He slowly measured his words. "When she arrived here, she seemed fearful, secretive. It could have been related to her escape. I employed her again until my accident forced me into retirement."

I was surprised. Madame A never mentioned that she had worked for the baron in New York, but perhaps it just hadn't seemed important.

His smile was more like a grimace. "After my initial flight in 1918, my experiences with the Russians have run the gamut from a prosperous cordial relationship to this disaster. Strange, is it not?" He pointed to the limp forms under the blanket and sighed deeply. "I am lucky to have enough money to be cared for. Otherwise, I could be attached to a board with wheels, begging in the streets."

I shuddered and tried not to look at his legs. "Can you tell me what happened?" I leaned toward him.

His voice was hard, bitter. "In the first months after Lenin came to power, I was asked to continue on the Art Committee, cataloguing the confiscated possessions of the Tsar and the upper classes. It was not difficult in the confusion to smuggle out objects to the West. It was obvious that the Bolsheviks also needed money and the Art Committee sold some of the treasures directly. In the late 20's there were several auctions of these treasures held at Sotheby's and Christie's in England."

He nodded his head, large like an overripe melon, toward a table in front of me.

"I have kept this photograph to remind myself how deceitful and brutal some of those so called art experts were."

In the dark photograph, members of the Art Committee wearing odd hats and drab clothes, pose among a jumble of vases, furniture and paintings. A shadowy figure in a military uniform stands near the door, apart from the group. A large circle in heavy ink is drawn around him. I picked it up for a closer look, but his face was hidden in shadow.

"Who is that?" I asked, forgetting my inhibitions.

"A powerful commissar who appeared that fateful day the Cheka began to oversee the committee. During my last few weeks on the committee, I became aware that he was searching for an antiquity, called the Box of the Harpuiai. The Cheka also questioned committee members about an agent they were hunting down with the nom de revolution, *the Bogatyr.* They did not reveal his real name."

I slowly put down my coffee cup, rattling in its saucer. This was the same White agent, member of the Druzhina that Kosloff had described; the man who had ordered him to kill the Romanov guards; the man mentioned in the Count's obituary and in the 'murder album'.

The baron continued, "I was questioned several times by Cheka thugs about both the casket and the Bogatyr, but knew nothing. After my forced departure I settled here, but remained friends with some of the more enlightened in the new Soviet government. These friendships enabled me for a price to eventually return to Russia and conduct business."

He spoke in halting phrases, as though it pained him to continue. "Strange that over those eventful years, the Cheka questioning in 1918 had become a dim memory. Then in 1961, I received an unusual message from one of the Soviet's obscure government departments, requesting information relating to an ivory casket that disappeared around the time I left Russia. Of course, I couldn't tell them anything, but they didn't believe me."

He stopped for a moment, trying to control his rapid breaths, as though he were suffocating. "Shortly after this request, on my last trip to Moscow, I was arrested. During my ordeal in which the torturers injured my spine, they revealed more to me than I could to them. I discovered that a powerful commissar had been searching for this casket since 1918 and had kept me under observation all those years, believing I possessed the casket or knew where it was hidden. I am sure it is that man circled in the photograph."

"I also learned at great cost that something important was hidden in this casket. It was a *ukase* issued by the last Tsar."

"I thought it was a car accident," I said, appalled at this frightening story.

He shook his head. "It was my bad luck. The commissar had obtained false information about me by torturing some other poor soul."

"But what is a *ukase*?" I leaned toward him, unable to mask my curiosity. I couldn't imagine he had been crippled for this.

"It is a decree issued by the Tsar, which automatically becomes the law of the land. Of course, one would think this particular ukase would not be of any relevance so long after the revolution but I believe that it could be the key to some hidden treasure. But then, you must realize that only the Tsar's supporters would recognize the edict." His deep cough, a signal of his distress, rattled through his body.

"It must have seemed logical to the secret police that as a collector and dealer, I was hiding the casket. But I found it strange that the interrogator also was most curious about Feodosia and asked many questions. I told him all I knew, including that she was an expert on icons, but none of my information was incriminating. Why should it be? When I was of no use to him, I expected death, but to my surprise, I was released. Naturally, I assumed he was NKVD, the name then, for the Russian intelligence organization that questioned me. But having much time to reflect I think not. I have come to believe my interrogator in 1961 was this same powerful commissar from 1918 with his own agenda." He jerked his head toward the photograph I was holding. "I overheard his thugs call him the Raven."

"And you never saw your interrogator?" I asked. "How can you be sure it was this same man?"

"It was the same cultivated voice and the obsessive constant questioning about the casket and Feodosia that convinced me. I could not describe him. He was standing in the basement doorway, obscured by shadows, directing the interrogation. They blindfolded me and shut the door, perhaps to drown out my screams." His eyes closed, then snapped open in sudden alarm.

He recovered, and said in a hoarse voice, "Ironic, is it not, that I survived unscathed during Stalin's purges, but was tortured during Khrushchev's reign, the time of the great thaw."

"But the *ukase*, you think if it existed it was stored in this casket?" I persisted, suppressing the urge to flee from the room.

"Yes, that's my impression. If it has not been destroyed, it could be very valuable. I have kept quiet all these years, fearing for my safety. I tell you this now because Feodosia is missing."

"Maybe they questioned you about Madame A because she knew something about the casket." I said.

"It's more probable they only believed she had information simply because she worked for me."

"It's strange that they let you go," I said, shivering in spite of the warmth of the room.

"My theory is that either the official government got wind of my arrest and forced my release or my interrogator believed I would lead him to the casket," he said, forgetting his distress for a moment.

"Have you seen these?"

I opened my handbag and took out the press cuttings about Count Anatole Von Grubov.

He brought out his hand over the blanket and struggled to take the clippings. I stopped, my mouth open in horror. His fingers were twisted like corkscrews. He had no fingernails; in their place were black sores. His mutilated hand shook as he read the clippings. I heard his voice from a distance as I struggled to keep composed.

"So, Anatole is dead. He was a great friend of mine in the old days in Petersburg. I would not have been able to attend the funeral in any case," he said.

After he read the last article, he handed them back to me. "Now it is known that the casket which caused me so much pain still exists. Like me, I am sure poor Feodosia knows nothing. I hope she is spared suffering," he whispered confidentially, "They can never reach me now. I am safe here with my guards." His voice faltered as though he was not convinced.

I had a vague recollection of thanking the baron, and passing through his bodyguards. Then I found myself outside his building and running.

Perspiring and breathing hard, I stopped half way through the park, turning over in my mind the baron's story of a last secret message from the Tsar, hidden in a casket, and the Raven's search for it. There was no way he was lying about his interrogation. The bare trees hovered over me and through the wide bare circling branches I saw Madame A's face that morning I showed her the Von Grubov clippings. Her expression had been cold with terror.

Chapter 29

Rural Ohio: 2000

THE LID OF darkness closes over me and I pull the chain on the porch light, illuminating masses of insects lured to death by the heat and brightness. I remove another photograph, purchased from a former KGB officer, from its protective covering and examine it under the light. The prisoner's bearded face crawls with the dying insects. His white hair is wild, standing up in peaks; his strong features are swollen and crooked as though drawn by a cartoonist. He is propped in an awkward upright position and stares in bewilderment at the camera. Next to him a hand holds up the Russian newspaper Pravda. The picture has been damaged, and I can see only the month and year of the issue. This photo was snapped in the Lubyanka prison while I was drinking tea with Madame A in her kitchen.

January 1970: Moscow, Lubyanka, KGB Headquarters

Someone was calling his childhood name in the distance and he raised his face, basking in the golden sunshine. The fragrance of the grass and sea spilled over him. He was running in the fields near the villa.

"Steady old man." Kato, the guard, tried to still the prisoner's twisted arms and legs moving in a feeble imitation of running, as he helped him shuffle into the room. There was no sunlight. A florescent strip lit up the freezing windowless room of cement block. The guard propped his broken body on the floor against a concrete wall soaked with grotesque patterns of blood.

It was the first he had been outside his cell since the interrogations on his arrival in 1946. His mind was numbed by pain and hunger, but in his occasional flashes of lucidity, he held on to the fact that someone powerful was interested in keeping him alive.

"Wake up, old man!" Now this voice was closer, connected to the rich smell of tobacco, which filled him with longing. A trace of smoke lazily floated up from the battered table in front of him.

It came from a cigarette holder held between two long slender fingers. The soft white hands, with manicured nails were not like those of interrogators he previously had encountered. Now fully conscious the prisoner studied the signet ring on the man's right middle finger and when he raised his arm to smoke, saw the strange mark on the inside of his wrist.

He sniffed and inhaled greedily, unable to control his frantic yearning. The spicy slightly sweet aroma was unmistakable; Dunhill cigarettes had been the rage among his aristocratic friends who brought them back from London. The fragrant smell of tobacco stirred his memories.

Vivid images of his past floated in that delicious smoke. He was a dashing young officer fighting the Bolsheviks in the Civil War, escaping to Yugoslavia in 1921 after the defeat of the White Army. He was in command of his Cossack regiment in WWII, fighting with the Nazis to liberate Russia from the Bolshevik regime. He was surrendering to the Allies and forced to repatriate to the Soviet Union. The sweet aroma died and the insistent voice brought him to the present.

"Don't you know me?"

Now he was propped like a huge broken doll in an armchair and had a clear view of his interrogator who spoke in French.

Old, but well preserved, the man wore the insignia of a general, the only decoration on his severely tailored black military tunic. His iron gray hair, clipped short and combed straight off his forehead in 30's style, emphasized his striking features.

The prisoner eagerly sniffed the last wisp of smoke before his interrogator stubbed out his cigarette.

The general was speaking but the prisoner didn't hear him. He was occupied with studying the handsome face, the perfectly formed nose, the high forehead and cheekbones, the wide thin mouth with its cruel twist. The dark blue of his large intense eyes resembled the Byzantine icon of St. Vladimir that had belonged to the prisoner's mother.

The prisoner's shout, like an explosion, echoed in the room and down the corridor. The shock propelled him upright in spite of his crippled body.

"You." He tried to rise toward the general and fell back. "I believed you were dead." He stared in disbelief. Reeling, quivering sure he had at last gone mad. How could this be?

"I did die officially," The general said, shrugging his shoulders.

"Is it over?" The prisoner was moving his hands in agitation. "After all these years, have you come for me?" He was speaking haltingly in French, the language he had used before the revolution, and then stopped, looking apprehensively at the general, who nodded, indicating he could continue.

French, which he had inadvertently spoken on his first days in prison, had been the guards' justification for the crippling beatings. They called it the Tsarist language of their oppressors. His bones were flailed out of their sockets, his skin holding them like a sack. Merkulov, Beria's assistant head of the secret police, had personally conducted the brutal interrogations, the degrading anal examinations. He had begged for death.

There had been no medical treatment after the beatings. They were surprised and amused that he did not die.

"Perhaps you could think I have come for you." The general's thin mouth cupped in a mirthless smile.

"You work for them, the Leather Coats." The old man shouted, pointing a shaky finger. "You betrayed us." His voice weakened to a whisper.

"It was exciting, an irresistible power in deception. I had no time for Lenin's ideology, his flimsy excuse to become a new kind of Tsar, but I knew the Bolsheviks would take control of the government." The general picked up his Faberge jeweled lighter, took a cigarette from the gold case and lit up again.

The prisoner made involuntary moves toward the plume of smoke. He had the absurd notion that he could reach out and grab it.

"I thought it better to employ my special talents. I couldn't picture myself, a descendant of the great Khan and of Russian nobles, growing old like so many exiles in a shabby rented room, attending the same meetings, plotting endlessly. I chose to be here, even though my comrades are banal murderous scum." The general sighed, lifting his eyes toward heaven like the saint in the icon.

The prisoner raised his head defiantly, showing traces of the once proud army commander. "You knew I was here. You let them do this. You were like a brother." The big skeletal man rolled his eyes back and howled his grief like a wounded animal.

"You must calm down. That sounds rather like bourgeois slander."

The interrogator smiled at his feeble joke and glanced down at the papers on his desk; the motion seemed to ignite a deep anger.

"I saved you from hanging, you traitor." His voice was hoarse, rasping. "Did you forget you fought for the Nazis, against me, against your own country? When they brought you and your filthy troops here, I wanted to save you, but did not dare release you. Stalin was watching, so I hid you away, stored you forever like a living corpse." He took a long draw on his cigarette.

The prisoner flinched at the words and stared in disbelief at this man, his friend who had ordered his torture. He shook his head to rid himself of the echoes of his men's screams.

"You are the betrayer. I have discovered that you lied to me." The general stopped his rant and raised his eyes toward the sumptuous rooms above the basement, the smoke coiling around him.

"You will be rewarded if you cooperate."

"But I know nothing of the outside world since the end of the war. I don't even know if Stalin still lives." He felt an uneasy stirring, a combination of fear and hope.

"Ah, but you have withheld important information from our past." Then his voice had become soft, as though reading a fairy story to a child.

"As you are aware, in the new world order designed by Lenin and his Central Committee, stealing from the rich was encouraged by the regime. Many priceless works of art were stolen and removed from Russia during the confusion and struggle of attempting to make everyone equal. Even our great leader Lenin was held up by thieves on his way to headquarters and his papers and money stolen."

His laugh was dry, mocking. "But you are the vilest of all thieves. You know why I have come for you."

The prisoner fought to keep still, his craving for the tobacco gone. A terrible coldness, like a sliver of ice, pierced his body. He hadn't dreamed it would be this. How could this devil know? He twisted his head back and forth, to deny.

"Let's talk about one objet d'art. You must remember. It is extremely rare, the only one of its kind. This exquisite antique once belonged to Helena, the Emperor Constantine's beloved mother, and was brought to Russia during the last days of the Byzantine Empire." The general stubbed out his cigarette and rose from his chair. Thin but muscular, he paced back and forth behind it as though lecturing to a class.

"In the Eighteenth Century it became the property of Count Anatole von Grubov's family. Recently, I have discovered that in early 1918 the Count fled Russia without the precious object which he had given to the late Tsar Nicholas II. I have information that the Tsar passed it on through his aide Prince Dolgorokuv to a member of the Brotherhood.

"As you know from your own experience, this was one of many ineffectual organizations plotting the Tsar's escape. After the Brotherhood's abysmal failure and the Tsar's murder, the treasure vanished. I have been searching for it for thirty years."

He stopped pacing and faced the prisoner directly. "I had become convinced that in spite of years of strenuous effort I would never find it, this key to complete power over Russia. Then Anatole in his desire for recognition gave this indiscreet interview to a *New York Times* reporter."

In a triumphant gesture, he waved the clipping toward the prisoner and began reading in Russian. The old man closed his eyes, trying to shut out the words.

When the general finished, he came around to the side of the chair and whispered, "Listen to me. I have discovered who was in possession of this objet d'art. You must confirm what I believe to be the truth. You must reveal where it is hidden."

The prisoner remained silent even after the questions repeatedly cracked over him. He struggled to drive away the vivid image of the casket, but it crowded everything else out of his mind.

The general stopped and offered him a cigarette.

He wanted it, could not help himself and grasped it tightly while his interrogator clicked his lighter. With great effort the old man raised it to his lips and the heady taste and smell of tobacco engulfed him.

He drew slowly on the cigarette wanting it to last forever, to carry him away with the memories. The door opened and in the stream of light, a man with a camera strode quickly toward him. The general moved behind the chair and held up a newspaper next to his face. The photographer stood a few inches in front of him and pointed the camera. There was a blinding flash, then another, and he saw only white for a few moments. A sinking despair overcame him. They would use the photograph.

"We will send one of these photographs to your family." His tormenter faced him.

Did his family know he was still alive? He had never dared hope or let himself think of that possibility until now. But he knew the man was lying. They all lie. The cigarette had lost its flavor. He dropped it on the floor.

When he repeated for the last time that he knew nothing, he was looking up at two beefy men with bored expressions. Pain began.

He heard another person speaking. Was it his voice? Was he thinking the words running through his head or was he saying them aloud? He often spoke his thoughts aloud in his cell and the guards would yell at him to shut up. It was always a surprise that he could not tell the difference. Sweat poured off him with the exertion. Now he was sitting before a table, in front of paper, a pen placed in his crippled hand. Through a veil of blood he scrawled his signature..

He heard his disembodied voice say, "It was all so long ago. I know nothing of what happened since. Will I be released?"

The general rose triumphantly, picked up a luxurious sable cape embroidered on one edge with his family crest and draped it around his elegant Savile Row tailored uniform.

"I will set you free. After all, death is freedom."

He did not beg for his life as they dragged him out of the chair. Instead he shouted at the retreating figure, *"Besy,* God will not forgive you."

The general turned to face him for the last time. *"Besy,"* he said in a soft voice, nodding his head in agreement. "An apt description. I am one of those bestial creatures. How else could I have survived unless I became like them? Goodbye, old friend."

The old man became conscious in his last moments and found that he was dangling from a wall, hooked by his ribs like a slab of meat. He made one futile effort to free himself as he felt life drip slowly away. Pale figures, half human winged creatures, pressed down on him, spinning faster and faster.

Chapter 30

New York: 1970

I TRIED TO concentrate on the map directing Ms. Springsmith from East 82nd Street to New Jersey but the discoveries of the last few days distracted me.

Both Kosloff and the baron claimed Madame A had changed, and became secretive, frightened after her escape from Russia. The baron's story and mounting circumstantial evidence led me to believe her disappearance could be linked to this lost casket.

Ms. Springsmith turned onto the Garden State Parkway. We were heading to the Jersey Shore to find Sergei. It had occurred to me that Madame A might have contacted her son and I had asked Ms. Springsmith for help. Madame A had given her Sergei's address some time ago, but she had never had reason to use it.

"I'll take you," she said, "I am devastated that I didn't try to question Feodosia Petrovna when she came to my door that day. It is quite possible that Sergei may know what happened to her. Perhaps she's even staying with him." I felt heartened by her words.

But when she picked me up early that morning in her Mercedes she seemed anxious, unlike her usual confident self. "I've left the dogs behind. The back seat is not safe for them," she said, handing me the map.

We turned off the highway into a gas station to ask an elderly man at the pumps for directions. He hooked his thumbs into his bib overalls. His tanned sparse features wrinkled in distaste.

"The Seabreeze, that's where those hippies have moved in. They're ruining the town."

We drove into Seaside Heights, once a popular middle class resort now in decline, passing old faded hotels with peeling paint and dirty broken windows, their crumbling porches occupied by vacant looking people swaying back and forth on rockers or crouched in doorways. The shabby little shops and neon signs with letters missing marred the seaside landscape of soft golden sand and dark blue of the ocean.

I searched past the wooden rickety cottages for some redeeming features, but saw only a vast wasteland of low flat buildings delineated by the unflinching blue of the sky. I had envisioned Sergei on a windswept unspoiled beach, living in a modern artist's studio, with huge canvases awaiting his brushes.

Ms. Springsmith had snapped up her waxed jacket, a dismayed look altering her usual cheery features.

"I knew it wasn't a garden spot, but isn't this quite terrible?"

Her grimace betrayed an uneasiness that I felt.

Our mood became even darker as we pulled up to the battered looking Seabreeze Hotel; its original sign had disintegrated, replaced with one handwritten in crude letters on cardboard. Three rickety steps led to the winding porch. An old refrigerator and various other rusted appliances occupied places where lovers once sat in painted wicker chairs.

Many of the windows were boarded and the hotel seemed deserted, a silence falling over it that made us both whisper as we crept along like intruders. Another crudely lettered sign, 'Followers of Josephus', was nailed to the corner of the porch.

We both jumped as the large door to the hotel crashed opened, and a young girl clad in a long black robe stood in the doorway. Three other girls in their teens and dressed in long ragged robes surrounded her. The girl's white face was colored with several purple bruises. She looked at us with wide frightened eyes.

"Josephus ain't here," she said with a country twang.

I stepped forward, and she retreated inside the doorway. She was heavily pregnant.

"Maybe you can help us. We are looking for Sergei Antonov. It's an emergency." I said.

The girl thought for a moment, twisting a lock of her long blonde hair, then said, "Yeah, the old Russian was here, but I don't know now."

"Does he live in the hotel?" I said.

She pointed around the corner to a set of stairs and then quickly slammed the door.

My heart pounded with each step as we climbed the rickety stairs. A ragged figure suddenly appeared on the landing; it was too late for us to retreat. I was sure he was a drifter, rifling Sergei's apartment. As he came closer, I saw that his eyes were vague and crazed, as though he might be strung out on dope. His gray hair was long and matted, grown together with his beard, and he resembled a mutant grasshopper, dressed in black pants, a loose shirt, and sandals. He didn't speak and stared out with cunning from the canopy of hair. Ms. Springsmith and I stood very still, hanging on to each other in panic.

He stopped when he saw us, crouched down, and raised his arms over his face, babbling something in Russian. Shocked, I realized the pathetic figure could be Sergei. Overcoming my dread, I moved closer, feeling faint from the odor of unwashed flesh.

"Are you Sergei Georgievich Antonov?" I raised my voice, deliberately using his patronym in the Russian custom, hoping to get his attention.

He brought his arms down.

"Da, Yes." With a sinking heart, I realized Madame A had deceived me. This creature was not in any way like her description of her handsome artistic son, nor did he bear any resemblance to his photographs.

How cruel his experiences must have been. His fear and inner agony had somehow distorted his body, pulling his features sideways, enlarging the nose, bending him over, forcing his arms to hang near the ground. No wonder Madame A preferred his old photographs.

"Are you from Maman?" His voice was high, and childish, with the perfect English of an educated foreigner.

"Yes, I'm Christina Gartner, a friend. Your mother asked me to help you." I took a discreet step away from him.

"This is Ms. Springsmith, another friend of your mother's," I said.

But there was no greeting from her.

"Are you ok?" I whispered.

She nodded weakly, her face a white blob.

I turned back to Sergei, still on the landing floor. He was staring up at me, "Your Maman has gone away and did not leave me her new address. Do you know where she is?"

He shook his head violently, his hair like wet seaweed.

"No, no, are they coming for me too? Poor Maman."

He cowered lower to the floor and began to weep.

"We need your help. Do you know someone named Vladimir?" I said, trying to keep calm in spite of the scene in front of me. He stopped weeping; rubbing his eyes like a child, and looked up again confusion registering in the blank eyes.

"I don't know. A man came asking for me last week. Josephus said he was nice, gave money, but I knew he was a Leather Coat. They always pretend to be nice. But I know better. They lie. Maman always told me the Leather Coats kill. I hid underneath the house." He pointed to a crawl space below. "Josephus said this Coat offered him money to find me, but he didn't tell where I was hiding. Then the Leather Coat went away. He said he would come back, that he wouldn't give up looking for me." His voice ended in a high unearthly wail.

"What did he look like? Did Josephus tell you?" My chest throbbed, and I couldn't help looking over my shoulder.

"Josephus said the man was big, dressed in a suit. And there was another man waiting in a car. He didn't see his face."

Sergei hid his head. I froze for a moment, unable to continue. Could it be Soso looking for Sergei? Ms. Springsmith made a strangled noise. She was gripping the stair railing, her face white and strained.

Sergei seemed so frightened that I couldn't bring myself to tell him that his sister was dead and that his mother had disappeared. Instead, I took a hundred dollars from my bag.

"Your Maman asked me to give you this while she is away. Don't let anyone take it from you. I'll send you more soon."

"Ah, now I can continue with my holy work." His face brightened. Suddenly rational, he took the money and placed it in a plastic blue woman's handbag he must have picked up in the trash.

He stood up and leaned towards me. His stench was overpowering.

"I must hide from the Leather Coat."

"Yes, you must hide from everyone except me, your mother's friend, Christina Gartner," I looked directly into his face.

Before I could ask how I could find him, he repeated almost to himself, "I will tell Josephus. Only Christina Gartner, Maman's friend, must know my hiding place." He slipped past us and scuttled off down the stairs, so quickly it was impossible for either of us to stop him.

Ms. Springsmith threw up over the upstairs railing and collapsed on the small porch near Sergei's door. I hurried to help her up.

"So sorry." She staggered, trying to regain her balance, and hung on to the stair rail. "I'm all right now. Just such a shock. Oh look, he's left his door unlocked."

Through the open door, decorated walls blazed with color, their brilliant gold and red shapes arranged, like icons, with great artistry. The room resembled a Russian Orthodox Church with an *iconostasis* fronting the altar. We walked hesitantly into the room. Ms. Springsmith shrieked and backed out to the landing. I stood for moments in a kind of paralysis, unable to comprehend what was in front of me. With a sudden jolt I realized that these were not icons, but pictures constructed from parts of women's bodies cut from porno magazines. Faces of heavily made up women pouted over the top of enormous breasts, the nipples showing through black net. Others, with expressions of terror, were joined up to different lower halves in lingerie, some with legs wide open. All of the subjects were bleeding with red paint. Votive candles were arranged in front of them, as though circling an altar. The entire room was a macabre temple to the violent desecration of women.

"Beastly, beastly," Ms. Springsmith moaned from outside, "I want to go now."

Feeling faint from the stench and the scene in the room, I pulled my jacket around me like a shield to keep from touching anything and forced myself to look around. The remainder of the room held a small cot, a plastic chair, table and work stand. Stacks of porno magazines, photographs of murder atrocities and the more mundane scissors, paste and cans of paint lay all around. Sickened by Sergei's ghastly shrine I questioned if he ever could have been a child of promise, a genius. Perhaps Abigail had been right that Madame A lied about most things.

Ms. Springsmith's normally flushed face was chalk colored and her hands were shaking after throwing up again in the hotel yard with the Josephus followers watching, but she insisted on driving. Eyes locked on the road, she sped quickly through the town and onto the highway. Scenes from the room crawled through my mind; the contrast between Sergei's perversion and his innocent childlike behavior was bewildering.

"Why would anyone be after Sergei," I broke the tense silence, "He seems harmless even though he's mentally ill."

"Who knows?" Ms. Springsmith snapped, "None of it makes sense, including that weird bunch of people, the Followers of Josephus. Have you ever heard of them?"

"No." I remembered the fear in the girl's eyes when she answered the door.

"I am sorry I ever got involved. I wonder who that man looking for Sergei could be, the one he called the Leather Coat?" Her eyes never left the highway. I knew that she was shocked and disgusted by Sergei and his iconic porno, but it was only later, after the evil things happened, that I realized she was terror stricken by Sergei's description of the man who had come looking for him.

"These people Sergei called Leather Coats could have something to do with Madame A's disappearance," I said.

"Let's not talk about it now. I must concentrate on getting us back." Ms. Springsmith had lost all her 'jolly hockey stick' cheerfulness. Dazed by what we had seen, we sped the rest of the way in silence. I gazed anxiously at the speedometer, but said nothing.

As we were nearing the Upper East Side, she said, her voice odd and wavering. "You know that book Feodosia Petrovna asked me to give you, the one by Pushkin. May I see it?"

"Of course, I'll bring it over tomorrow," I said, trying to calm her, although I was really shaken myself.

Ms. Springsmith squealed the brakes, slowing down as we pulled into our street. A couple came out of my building, and I strained to see them in the darkness. The man had his arm close around the woman, and pulled her to his chest in a passionate embrace. The light from the street lamp exposed them as they walked arm in arm. I felt a tug at my heart. It was Jack and Zoe, Madame A's niece.

Chapter 31

New York: 1970

CRUSHED AND HURT by their embrace, I opened my apartment door. Fear slid through my body like a melting ice cube when I saw the note. I quickly tore open the envelope.

Christina, I tried to reach you today. I have begun an investigation into Madame A's disappearance. There are a few leads in the case but nothing to report. Will be in touch.
—Jack

Tears came to my eyes. He believed me, but any relationship was over.

I was awake most of the night. The image of Jack and Zoe passionately kissing under the streetlight only added to my distress at the terrible events of the past few days. I felt betrayed, abandoned like the scabby stray cats in the back garden. He must love her. But how could he love someone like her? I saw myself, lying naked, passion spent, looking up at the kitchen table. What a ridiculous figure, so unlike myself. I knew they were laughing at me. It was mortifying. Although I wasn't a radical bra burner, I had written papers on women's rights, yet I seemed to persist in getting involved with men who degraded me. I wanted to retreat into some hiding place, like the hollowed out sycamore tree on the farm. But this wasn't about me. An elderly Russian émigré, my friend had been kidnapped.

The next morning I knew what I had to do. I quickly retrieved Madame A's envelope from my boot and opened it. The contents, a notarized letter giving me power of attorney, the number 292408 and a small brass key, meant nothing to me. But then I recalled how upset she had been that day. She had asked me to keep it secret, especially from Ms. Springsmith.

I thought over Ms. Springsmith's odd behavior yesterday and her request to see the book of Pushkin poems Madame A had given me.

Why did she want to look at this? I picked up the book from my bedside stand and took off the loose Christmas wrapping. The cover read Пушкин. I opened to the first page, also written in Cyrillic. Ms. Springsmith had denied that she knew Russian. She claimed Madame A told her it was a book of Pushkin's poems, but I believed she was lying, that she had unwrapped the book and read some of it before giving it to me.

I threw on some clothes and went over to Ms. Springsmith's, but the shutters on the large windows were closed and no one answered the door. After a short walk I returned and impulsively phoned Jack, and then Zoe, but was not surprised when neither picked up. A sudden image of them together made me slam down the receiver. The bastard wasn't searching for my neighbor. More likely, he was still in bed with Zoe.

I sat near the telephone in a kind of limbo, waiting for some news of Madame A. Nightmarish images, as though snapped by a deranged photographer, flashed before me. The Georgian thug with his worry beads clicking. The baron's twisted body. Sergei, eyes wild with fear, peering out from his pornographic temple.

It was impossible to reconcile the early photographs of the handsome young Sergei with this ruin of a man. I was not surprised that Madame A had hidden him away all these years, but wondered if she knew that he was living with the weird Followers of Josephus. I tried to bring some sense to what had happened yesterday. The episode seemed divorced from reality. After all, I had no evidence that anyone was looking for Sergei except for his own claims and he was obviously mentally ill.

I puttered around the kitchen. A sense of impending of danger crept over me like poison gas seeping through the door and the walls. I brewed another pot of coffee and tried to control my fear by using a scholarly approach, attempting to place all that I knew about Madame A's kidnapping in some logical order when someone knocked.

Trembling, I stared through the peephole straight into Zoe's black eyes.

My first impulse was to tell her to go away, but thinking she might know something about her aunt, I reluctantly opened the door.

She was dressed in chic black, her dark eyes and pale face surrounded by a black fur hat. She looked beautiful, which made me hate her all the more. I didn't invite her in.

"I have been trying to reach you," I said in my nastiest voice. "Do you know where your aunt has gone? She disappeared without leaving an address, and I am really worried. I assumed you were out of town when you didn't answer your phone. I've filed a missing person's report."

She struggled to be civil. "Jack Reilly told me about poor Auntie. He has been comforting me."

More than just comforting, I thought, infused with hatred.

Zoë's large eyes narrowed in dislike. "What did she tell you?"

When I explained what I knew about Vladimir, she didn't seem surprised.

"Jack said the police have not been able to contact this Vladimir. Did you know him?" I said.

She shook her head, fidgeting, touching her hat and her bag.

"I've already told Jack that it is possible Georgi had a son by this second wife, but I had not heard of it." She leaned toward me over the transom.

"But I must ask you. Did my aunt leave anything with you? Anything at all? Please tell me. It is terribly important." Her face had lost that haughty look.

I shook my head.

Her voice held a note of urgency. "She told me once that she would need me if Anna died, that there was something, a secret she had kept, that there was something of value. I must know."

I put on a bland innocent expression and said nothing.

Trembling, she raised her voice. "You must know something about it. You've been to see that idiot Sergei. Why? You tell me why!"

"I thought he might have some idea where his mother had gone, but he didn't. I also gave the poor man some money to live on until she returns," I finally said.

"What business is it of yours?" Zoe shouted.

"You couldn't really care. He's in bad shape. You've never done anything for him."

"No, he was embarrassing. At first, when I came here he was still almost sane, but as the years went by he became impossible."

"So you wrote him off," I said in disgust.

"Yes, but now it is very important that I find him. He's gone into hiding since you've been to see him. I think you know where he is."

"I'm afraid I can't help you."

Her voice became a harsh whisper, "You stupid bitch. You're in danger. Don't you understand? Stay out of this or they'll kill you."

She left, slamming the hall door. The noise shot through me. She knew I had been to see Sergei. Her panic infected me and I rushed to put the envelope back in my boot. I sat shivering, confused, when the phone rang.

It was Samuel inviting me out to dinner. The sound of his voice, from the real world was reassuring. He apologized for the last minute invitation, but had just returned from a business trip to Chicago and wanted to see me. I eagerly accepted, realizing I couldn't sit here for days waiting for news or for someone to kill me. When Sam picked me up, I slipped the Pushkin book in my handbag, thinking Ms. Springsmith might be home later.

We went to a small Italian place in the West Village, and sat in a cozy wooden booth at the back of the restaurant. I reached across the table and touched his cheek, so happy that he had called. He was everything a woman should want. "Thanks. I needed to get out. I've been sitting by the phone all day waiting for news. It was nice of you to call." I didn't mention how frightened I was.

After we ordered salad and pizza, I took a sip of wine and relaxed a little in the friendly atmosphere. Nothing seemed so bad or irresolvable at this moment.

I had been ill at ease with Sam the first few times we met, but our evenings were becoming more frequent, and I liked it. I knew he was serious about me and I was fond of him. We had slipped into a comfortable relationship, almost like friends. I was grateful for his solid presence that night.

"Any news from the police?" Sam asked.

"No, it's been very frustrating. They haven't been much help. And I haven't been able get in touch with anyone else." I was thinking of Jack's desertion. "Even Ms. Springsmith wasn't home this afternoon. You remember the neighbor with the dogs. Yesterday she drove me to the Jersey Shore to see Madame A's son, Sergei, in case she had contacted him."

"What did he have to say?"

"He didn't know anything about his mother's disappearance. The man is a mental wreck, and really needs help."

I didn't go into detail. Sergei and his iconic porno seemed too embarrassing and unreal to discuss in a restaurant, and Samuel might think I was suggesting erotic scenarios for later.

He tried to reassure me. "It seems unlikely that anyone would want to harm a little old lady. You said yourself that she was harmless."

"I know." I remembered her volcanic shudders when she spoke of the Leather Coats.

"I still think she'll turn up, probably just forgot to notify you," he said as the pizza arrived. He put a slice on my plate. I picked off a piece of pepperoni.

"I'm really grateful to you for getting me in to see the baron. He did know Madame A well and is very upset that she's disappeared. He told me what happened to him in Russia. What a tragedy." The baron's gnarled hands like bent twigs appeared before me and I lost my appetite.

"So you know it wasn't an accident. He was a vigorous man, loved the ladies. My father says he is very bitter about his situation, can't adjust. It is curious because he was friendly with the Soviet regime. The baron told my father his jailers asked a lot of questions about the restoration of the Romanovs, which he couldn't answer. You probably noticed he has bodyguards and everyone who visits him is carefully screened. He's still afraid of being murdered. What a way to live."

We changed the subject then to Slade's trial coming up in a month. It had been reported that he was refused bail.

"Abigail is so relieved. But she'll have to testify since she was his last girl friend; at least the last one we know is alive," Sam said.

"If Abigail's lucky, he'll get life," I said,

On the way home in the taxi I snuggled against Sam, feeling safe, deep in thought, and something Sergei said came back to me. At the time I had been so shocked at his appearance that his words hadn't registered. It had been a curious statement. He said he always hid from the police. Then he said, 'The Blood Stiller warns me.' Was he hearing voices or was this someone he knew?

Samuel interrupted, "Shall I come in with you?"

"Thanks for the evening. But no, I have to stop in to see Ms. Springsmith tonight." I kissed him rather absently, not realizing it would be the last time I would see him, and got out of the car. I hurried along the empty street toward Ms. Springsmith's house constantly looking over my shoulder into the dark.

Slow drips from a drainpipe, like blood from a wound, fed my fear. The roar of a motorcycle speeding down the street momentarily broke the silence. As I approached the house, my mood lifted. Drawing room lights glimmered through the drawn curtains, and strains of 'Swan Lake' flowed out to the street. She must be having a party I thought as I climbed the steps. Her front door was ajar. I called out and then walked in.

The music was accompanied by someone screaming.

Chapter 32

Rural Ohio: 2000

I SINK DOWN on the porch into the darkness, into nothingness, to escape the pictures, seeping out through the print of the newspaper cuttings I reviewed today, but they catch me up, and cause me to whimper small animal sounds of terror. The dog's ears go up at this sound and he slants his large shaggy head, watching me uneasily.

The newspaper reports of the murders are collected now and filed in the proper place. I have noted in the folder that the articles are filled with lies of omission concerning the details. According to the police, the motive was burglary. The killers were never found. To spare the public, the descriptions of the bodies are sanitized and bear only a small resemblance to the carnage I found that night.

Quogue, NY: 1970

I came out of the darkness, sweating, shivering on Abigail's bed in her house in Quogue. Faint strains of Swan Lake rolled about in my head. The rose pattern on the bedroom wallpaper seemed unnaturally large.

Abigail's face mingled with the roses.

"It's Ok. You've had a nightmare. You've been unconscious for three days."

I sat up, surprised to be here, wearing one of her filmy nightgowns. "How did I get here?"

"We left my loft three days ago. I thought it was best to get you out of town. You've been on those pills and out of it since you left the hospital. Wonder if they would help me lose weight. If I'm out cold, I can't eat."

"But what about the gallery?"

"Don't worry." She gave me a sympathetic almost frightened look.

Then it came to me. I shook so violently that Abigail had to take the glass of water she had given me. I am walking through the open door; figures hang like puppets; the smell of burnt flesh and fur; Ms. Springsmith's face, one side curiously like the pulp of crushed melon; no place to walk. The screams had been mine.

Hot tears ran down my face.

"Steady," Abigail said, taking my hand.

She had dropped by my place after her date and found the street crowded with police, and Ms. Springsmith's house cordoned off. When she rang my doorbell, she found more police. Someone had broken into my apartment and the Vacek's upstairs had called them. I was taken to the emergency room at New York Hospital and treated for shock.

I remembered vaguely then that two policemen had visited me in the hospital. They had asked me a lot of questions, but mainly wanted to know where I had been that evening, and what I was doing at Springsmith's house.

I couldn't stop trembling and huddled in the blanket, covering my head for the comforting darkness. "I'm all right," I told her, even though it wasn't true.

Abigail left the room for a moment to set out some soup and bread and returned to help me to the kitchen. I took one look and fell in a faint. I heard myself say, "Sorry." as she helped me up, handed me another pill and a glass of water. I slept again, thankful to sink into blankness.

Then Abigail was shaking me gently.

"Jack Reilly is here."

Before I could make a protest, he was standing in the doorway.

I couldn't bear to look at him and broke into sobs.

He came over to the bed and put his arms around me pulling me hard against his chest. I wanted to stay there forever.

"No need to ask how you're doing," He took some tissues from the nightstand and gently wiped my face.

I couldn't speak; just wanted him to continue to hold me.

He moved away when Abigail brought in coffee. She poured, handed each of us a cup and left again. He put my rattling cup and saucer on the table.

"I know how bad this has been for you." He sat close to me. "I know you're still in shock. But I need your help. You have to snap out of it. We think the same thugs who killed Ms. Springsmith, her butler and dogs, also broke into your apartment."

"What? How can that be?" I said, finding it hard to catch my breath.

"There is nothing definite yet, but preliminary evidence suggests these crimes could be connected to Madame A's disappearance. But we haven't found a trace of her and haven't been able to locate Vladimir Antonov. I've assigned two more detectives to the case."

"Oh great, now you believe me. Ms. Springsmith and her butler had to die first." I started to cry again.

He ignored my tears and spoke slowly, thinking aloud, "The motive wasn't robbery in either case. They were looking for something, maybe information from Springsmith. She could have told the killers you were in possession of what they wanted, and they searched your flat. Do you have any idea what they could have been hunting?"

I shook my head. "But if she told them something was in my apartment, why would they kill her?"

He dropped his sympathetic pose, and let out a short laugh.

"Why not? What would be the point in keeping her alive? You saw what they did. They're pros, only interested in doing the job. They wouldn't want witnesses. First, they knifed the butler to scare Springsmith, and then went after her dogs." He stopped for a moment, and then said, almost as an afterthought. "No one tortures like someone trained by the Russians."

"Russians, how do you know they were Russian?" I was dizzy with horror. The roses on the wallpaper merged into huge blobs of red, and

Soso's face rose before me. I staggered to my feet to escape, but he grabbed me and sat me back down.

"Christina, you need to tell me everything."

"All I know is what I told you about Vladimir Antonov. Madame A planned to meet him before she decided to move in with him and his family. She seemed so happy. It was a solution to her problems. These murders have nothing to do with me or my friendship with her."

He said nothing for a moment, but softened the grip on my arm. "When was the last time you saw Ms. Springsmith alive?"

The question, like a slap, jerked me back to the smell, the horrible scene. I took a deep breath and tried to stop my mouth from quivering.

"We drove to visit Sergei, Madame A's son, thinking Madame A might have contacted him. He didn't know anything. In the end, we didn't tell him that she might have been kidnapped or that his sister was dead because he is not very well. He said someone had come looking for him, but he wasn't very coherent. I gave the poor man some money to hold him over."

"Where were you earlier on the night of the murders?" He still held my arm as though to comfort me.

"I told the police all this at the hospital." I protested weakly.

"Tell me again," he said.

"I had dinner with Samuel Westerby."

There was a slight look of surprise on his face, as though it was hard for him to believe anyone would be interested in me.

"Why were you at Springsmith's house that evening?" His tone implied that I had something to do with her murder.

"I had tried to get in touch with her all day, but she didn't answer her telephone or the door. She had asked me to drop by, so I decided to walk over after Samuel brought me home." I began to weep again.

"That's it?" He let go of my arm.

Wiping my eyes, I nodded. There was no point in mentioning Zoë's visit and her warnings because he was sleeping with her and wouldn't believe me. The picture of their long embrace under the streetlight somehow kept me from telling him about the envelope, or the book of Pushkin's poetry, nebulous clues that he would think I imagined.

"If you're not telling me the truth, they could kill you too."

He got up from the edge of the bed.

"Don't leave the house. We've got a watch on outside."

"Am I a prisoner?" I wiped my eyes.

"For your own good. You saw what happened to Springsmith."

He leaned down and patted my shoulder. He spoke to Abigail in the kitchen. Then I heard the door shut and his car pull out of the drive.

I lay back on the bed and tried to compose myself, to think. He said I was in danger, guarded by the police. I rose from the bed, swaying with weakness and grabbed my handbag resting on the chair next to the bed.

"What are you doing? You should be in bed." Abigail was standing at the door.

"Just checking on my credit cards," I said, noticing my boots lined up underneath the chair.

"I made sure you had your handbag."

"Thanks Ab. Thanks for everything."

After she left the room, I rushed over and felt inside the right boot. The envelope was still there.

For a moment I stood at the window watching the storm break. Branches on the huge trees blew and crashed together and rain blasted the side of the house.

That day when I knocked on Ms. Springsmith's door and all was dark, the killers were inside, torturing her. For an instant, I felt soft innocent fur, a cold nose, and my heart seized up with quick stabbing pains. Right then I should have packed up and taken the next plane back to the farm in Ohio.

Instead I reached in my handbag and found the book Madame A had left for me and tore off the green wrapping. There was still a faint hope she had left a message, some clue for me, and I could help her.

Chapter 33

Rural Ohio: 2000

THE EARLY MORNING light streams past the forest through the
open door of the cabin, pouring over me like liquid gold. I am holding the
Pushkin book, bound in dark red leather, faded by time. The dog paces, and
brushes against me, anxious for the morning walk to patrol the boundaries
of the farm. But I linger, tracing the title tooled in gold. It takes me back to
that day at Abigail's house on Long Island when I first opened its cover and
began to discover Madame A's true past and the secrets she was hiding.

Quogue, NY: 1970

I sat motionless in Abigail's cheery bedroom in the fading afternoon light.
The newspaper report of Ms. Springsmith's murder glared at me from the
bed stand. A strange incessant quivering overwhelmed me. I crushed the
newspaper as if to drive away the images and threw it in the bin.

I stared at the book in my lap, still not daring to open it; aware that it
was probably the last object Madame A had touched before she disappeared. The small bit of Russian I learned from her enabled me to
translate the title 'Pushkin', her favorite Russian poet. I could see her at the
breakfast table, surrounded by her photographs; her sapphire eyes glinting

like sharp stones behind her reading glasses, murmuring the poet's lines, *'We live without power of law; like flocks of ravens they come and sweep over the land.'*

I opened the first page, mystified that it was in Russian. What would be the purpose of giving me a book I couldn't read? I flipped through more pages, and the book seemingly by its own volition, sprawled open toward its middle as though the binding had been damaged.

A photograph fell out. It was Madame A's favorite of the group in Finland. *The Druzhina* was written underneath the picture, and her words echoed in the room.

"This was not the last time I would see my *Druzhina*. Our lives would intertwine during the terrible days that followed. Each one of them would come at crucial times to save the children and me. But then greed and hunger for power separated us. They all were murdered."

'Christina, remember your promise.' was scrawled in heavy pencil over the Cyrillic print of that page. I was startled at this direct plea for help. Yellow frayed sheaves of notes in English were pasted over the original pages of the book.

After Annushka's death, I remembered hearing her late at night rustling and tearing papers. She knew she was in danger, wrote this message, ripped out these pages from her journal, and hid them in the book.

The introduction was dated Harbin, 1921.

At the end of 1916 I began writing this journal in English even though it is not my first language. Originally intended as an exercise, it has become a record of my life when the Russia I knew was beginning its descent into darkness. The enemy is closing in and my end may be near. I continue writing in the belief that those who interrogate me will be ignorant of the English language. We have lost the cause for now, but not, I believe, forever. This is a testament of truth about me, a small conspirator in a great effort. I hope that after I am gone this will survive. Feodosia Petrovna Antonova.

Madame A's notes began two days after Rasputin's murder.

December 20, 1916: Rasputin Murdered

Georgi brought me the terrible news. He rushed into the drawing room and sank into a chair, not removing his cloak, hardly able to form the words. Yesterday Rasputin's body surfaced on the Malaya Nevka River near Great Petrovsky Bridge. His hands were frozen in a raised position, his last attempt to untie the ropes that bound him. I knew this could only mean the Holy One was still alive when the murderers threw him into the icy river. This was proof of his great powers. As his frozen body began to thaw, believers in his holiness collected the bloody black water to drink or to keep as a relic of worship.

Georgi had heard that two of the murderers were from the Royal family, Grand Duke Dimitri Romanov and Prince Felix Yusupov, married to the Tsar's niece. The others were Vladimir Purishkevich, Lieutenant Sukhotin and Dr. Stanislaus Lazavert, who poisoned the cakes offered to the Holy One.

That evening Rasputin was lured to the Yusupov Palace on the pretext of meeting Princess Irina, Yusupov's wife, who was away in the Crimea. He was poisoned with potassium cyanide, shot several times, beaten and kicked and thrown into a hole in the ice. Some believe he will come back from the dead.

The description was straight out of a schlock horror movie, but still I was not prepared for the next entry.

I feel nothing but grief, terrible grief at the Master's death, so brutal. Rasputin, a great healer who had never harmed anyone, suffered greatly. I regret that I was not there to collect his holy blood, dripping like tears from his body. Early this morning I rushed to the Holy One's apartment to retrieve the photographs and other objects that would identify me. The Tsar's secret police surround the apartment, waiting to arrest any of the Holy One's followers who might appear, but I knew the Okhrana agents still would be sleeping off their vodka from last night. Hung over, bleary eyed, bundled up against the cold, the agent I had bribed cursed violently before letting me enter the apartment.

These words conjured up Madame A as though she had walked out of an old Russian newsreel.

She wears a dark hooded fur cloak and rushes out of a grand apartment building on the Neva and steps into a waiting *troika*. Her piquant features with high cheekbones and slanted sapphire eyes are slightly blurred with grief and fear. The air is sharp and cold, accented by the acrid smell of coal fires, and as the rising sun spreads a pale blue light over the white landscape and classical buildings, she pulls the hood closer to disguise her face and commands the *troika* to stop at 64 *Ulitsa Gorokhovvaya*. Her dark cloak swings as she hurries to the back entrance of Apartment 20, and presses her body against the wall to avoid being seen until the door opens.

I rubbed my eyes disconcerted at the image, so vivid that it seemed I could reach out and touch her. It was crazy, but I sensed it was somehow related to the weird erotic visions I had experienced. Perhaps they were induced, so I eventually would believe. Transfixed, I eagerly read on.

I could not stop weeping as I rushed to the room where he had brought me for my initiation, my entry into his aura. It contains only a bed. I lay down on the bed, looking up at the cross hanging on the wall above and became faint with desire, remembering how the Holy One held my body tightly between his two legs before we came together. My desire for him was holy and our couplings were spiritual acts, not earthly love.

I dropped the book as if it was a bomb tossed on my lap. Wild images rushed through my head. She was not a casual acquaintance of Rasputin, but had some intense ritualistic sexual relationship with him. Shaken, I picked up the book that had landed near the door.

When I believed I was unobserved by the guards, I hurried to his bedroom and opened the heavy drawer in the chest and took the photographs from the small shelf. I quickly gathered my clothes and other possessions, which could be used as evidence against me. I do not believe anyone knows.

When I returned home, Georgi was still in his dressing gown pacing the room. His face was distorted into a stranger's by rage and fear; he shouted at me to stay away from Rasputin's apartment. I know he is right. It is dangerous. He has heard that the police are attempting to incriminate someone other than the Romanov relatives in the Holy One's death. Thank God, Georgi does not know my secrets or why I returned to the apartment.

I stopped for a moment, taking this in. She had returned to the apartment to remove any traces of her intimate relationship with Rasputin. What were her secrets? I wondered if they were in the photographs she retrieved from the monk's cupboard.

The next journal entry was a day later.

Dec. 21, 1916

Rasputin was buried today in secrecy at Tsarskoe Selo beneath the aisle of a new church built by Anna Vyrubova, the Tsarina's friend and a disciple of the Holy One. Devout followers, including the Royal family attended the Orthodox service. The Tsarina placed an icon signed by his disciples on his chest. There will be no more visits to Vyrubova's house near the Alexander Palace to meet with the family. As his favored one I always accompanied Rasputin to these secret meetings. On our last visit, the Tsarina seemed undone, ready to collapse.

Many of the Romanov relatives and conservatives in the government celebrate Rasputin's savage murder while I mourn the Holy One and believe even more in his powers as the Blood Stiller.

A cold chill passed through me as I recalled Madame A's description of the shamans who possessed the ancient power to stop the flow of blood. She had truly believed Rasputin was a blood stiller and she attended the secret burial of the monk, restricted to the Tsarina's inner circle. This could only mean she was not a mere acquaintance of the royal family, but an intimate friend. Why would she deny that she knew the Romanovs? And what exactly did it mean that she was Rasputin's favored one? I believed this had more significance than the sexual relationship with him.

March 2, 1917

Revolution. Chaos in the city. The Tsar has abdicated and is held prisoner with his family in Alexander Palace at Tsarskoe Selo. The Provisional Government, composed of members of the last Duma and led by Prince Lvov, is in charge until the elections for a Constituent Assembly. Everyone is full of hope for a free democratic Russia, but I live in fear they will discover some trace of me in the Holy One's apartment.

March 15, 1917

Drunken soldiers removed Rasputin's body from his grave at Tsarskoe Selo. I watched as they desecrated his corpse and burned his remains nearby at Pargolovo Forest. They were like devils, tearing up the grave, throwing his bones, carrying his skull to the fire. As the smoke and flames grew, they began running, screaming in terror away from the fire. In spite of the violations to his body The Master's power lives on. Stunned by the savagery, I ran into the forest and was pierced by the light shining through the birches. I was overcome. His rapture filled me with his power. I must never reveal it.

What could she mean? Did she see some kind of vision in the forest? It was a strange religious fervor, puzzling for someone like Madame A. I squirmed, remembering my weird vision in front of Bloomingdale's window and went back to the notes.

March 30, 1917

I hurried past a crowd listening to speeches, idle hostile soldiers who had deserted from the front, hanging out in doorways eating and spitting out the husks of sunflower seeds. I managed to find a troika and reached the bridge near Ulitsa Millionya. Peter had sent a message to meet him there.

I felt the same heart stopping, a sharp pain in my chest when I saw him striding toward me. He was disguised in dark shabby clothes and a cap to hide his features. The hostile Soviet Military Committees had dismissed the officers of the Tsar's elite guard. Peter barely escaped from the gates of Tsarskoe Selo with his life. He swept me into his arms.

I could hear Madame A as we sat at the breakfast table. "Both Peter and Dimitri joked that they were in love with me." She had glanced at me in a sly way. Perhaps then she had wanted to tell me that Peter Von Krantz was her lover, had wanted to tell me all her secrets, but did not know if she could trust me.

As we walked toward his family's deserted mansion where we once danced together and fell in love, Peter told me the war is lost, the army is finished, that all discipline is gone with this weak new government. The troops only want to get home to grab their promised share of land. The Germans soon will be marching through the streets.

The mansion on the Moika is boarded up and looks shabby and neglected. Like others, it will soon be occupied by a citizens committee or looted by the mobs that roam the streets. Peter tore away the boards nailed across a window in the back near the servants' entrance and we wandered like intruders through the cold rooms. In the silence of the abandoned house, he lifted me onto the bed. We did not take off our clothes. We knew it was dangerous to be there. There was a passionate urgency to our love making as though it might be the last time. We lay, not speaking, listening to shouts and gun shots and crowds singing the Marseillaise. My tears fall on the page. I may never see him again.

Peter has changed; his face is drawn and pale. He is on the run for killing a member of the Soviet Military Committee. The commissar had ordered his men to execute two of Peter's fellow officers. Peter said that before they killed Sasha and Niki, they carved pictures of medals into their chests and nailed their epaulets to their shoulders.

Hardly able to breathe, I asked if they were hunting him. He said that they soon would discover he was the killer. Gripping my shoulders tightly, his eyes dark with emotion, he said he was convinced we must fight, that we cannot appease or negotiate with the revolutionaries.

At the bridge he wrapped me inside his cloak, holding me close keeping me safe for a few moments. He would not tell me where he is going.

I record his exact words just before we parted.

"We have not given up the Tsar. We have organized to rescue him and to end the revolution. There will be an uprising. Our allies, who have agents in the country, have sworn to help us." He begged me to join him.

I paced the floor, the terrible scenes from Ms. Springsmith's still winding through my head. I wondered bleakly if this would be Madame A's fate if we didn't find her. The journal gave up many of her personal secrets, but none of the facts seemed connected to her disappearance. I sat down and continued reading.

April 10 1917

I received a message from Peter that he is safe and try to bury my anxiety in the wild parties we attend almost every night. As members of the Intelligentsia and the Kadet Party we mingle with poets, artists, musicians, officials, ex-tsarist officers, and even high-ranking commissars from the Soviet. There is much drinking and use of cocaine while everyone argues about what Russia will become. I do not think the country will come to much if these parties continue.

At Count V on Grubov's, where everyone of influence goes, I discovered to my surprise and delight that Dimitri was present. I am so happy that he is safe for the moment. Nadya Martinova, my husband's latest young mistress, arrived with an entourage of revolutionaries. With guns in holsters, they swaggered around in leather coats and high boots, aping gangsters from American movies. They seemed harmless, ridiculous in their play-acting, but Dimitri warned me they are dangerous killers, and they spy on everyone; no one is safe from them. I suddenly panicked that I have left something in Rasputin's apartment and that they have found it and know about me. I watched their faces for any sign of this.

Nadya Martinova is beautiful and loves the attention. The revolutionaries have taken her up as a kind of mascot, which irritates and frightens Georgi. There has been gossip about his relationship with the girl because she is so very young. Everyone knows that Georgi has connections and favors Nadya's father with government contracts. Georgi moved over and took her arm, leading her away from them.

"So that's the bastard's payment. A little whore. Why don't you leave him?" Dimitri said in a derisive tone. "The children," I said.

When I stopped reading, the sun had set, and I quickly put on the bedroom lights and drew the curtain against the darkness. Abigail passed my room, flicking on the hall lights on her way to the kitchen. I returned to the journal and the noises from the kitchen faded.

April 12, 1917

The night air was very damp. The thaw had begun. I glided over the luxurious leather seat, feeling a sense of unreality riding in an automobile confiscated from the Tsar's garage. The chauffeur was a stranger. He did not speak.

Georgi had begged me not to go, said it would end in our deaths, that I am the mother of two children and should take care of them. But I told him I only had promised to meet Peter, nothing more. I ran from the house to the waiting auto. As it made its way forward, my stomach constricted with fear and I desperately longed to be home with Sergei and Annushka. I did not even know my destination and was afraid to ask.

We crossed Troitskiy Most and the streetlights again went off, leaving only the faint glimmer from the Winter Palace. A crowd was gathering as we approached Troitskiy Ploschad. Many of them held torches and banners announcing that Lev Trotsky, one of the famous revolutionary leaders, would be speaking in the square. The combined smell of burning fires and piles of uncollected garbage on the streets crept through the windows like some approaching menace.

The driver swerved to keep from hitting those who marched into the street and cursed when they began to throw mud and rocks at the auto. Suddenly we jerked to a stop, surrounded by a frightening crowd shouting obscenities, believing there was a hated Romanov inside. A figure appeared out of the darkness, squashed against the window. A passing torch lit up his face smeared with dirt. His features were swollen and misshapen from disease and alcohol. He shouted at me, pounding on the window. I became lost in his bloodshot eyes, their broken veins like streams of blood. His violent pounding went on, forcing me to look again. I cried out in fear and pity. He was pounding with stumps; all that remained of his arms, screaming for others to join him. I closed my eyes in panic and sank back.

Trotsky's arrival saved us. The crowd forgot us, rushing into the square, emptying the road. The auto moved ahead. The silent driver looked back, his eyes deep set in a narrow face like a skull, to see that I had not fainted. The journey ended on Ulitsa Kuibysheva, at a large house next to the now confiscated mansion of the ballerina, Mathilde Kseshinskaya, former mistress of the Tsar.

I was ordered out of the car and pushed along by the driver through the basement entrance, once used by the servants. I fought the urge to run away as he commanded me to follow him up the rickety stairs, reeking of urine, to the second floor. He was taking me to the enemy. He stopped in front of a heavy oak door. I stood trembling, faint with terror as he pushed against the door. It swung back, crashing against the wall. I cried out in surprise. The Druzhina were waiting for me.

Chapter 34

Quogue, NY: 1970

ABIGAIL'S KNOCK DREW me back to the present, but
Madame A's last entry lingered with me.

> *I told them I could do little to help them, but they insisted that I belonged to
> them, and always would be one of the Druzhina. They said I would be
> needed in the future. I consented to join them because I loved them. I was sure
> we would be arrested and shot, but Dimitri laughed aloud at my worries.
> They were gentle with the needle, but when it pricked my skin, drawing the
> heart of Buddha, I fainted.*

"Chris," Abigail called out opening the door, her face soft with concern, "I saw your light. Do you want some dinner?"

"Thanks Ab, but I think I'll just climb into bed."

As soon as she closed the door, I settled in, pulling the rose patterned
bedcover around me, pleased that Abigail had put me in her old childhood
room with paintings of horses and dogs, away from the one that had
haunted me with the sad ghosts of her dead cousin. I turned on the reading
light by the bed, and plunged back into the notes.

April 16, 1917

Fear, like a cage encloses me, blighting my life. It separates me from everyone. I smell it through the urine and decaying trash on the backstairs leading to the meeting place, and sense the sinister people who loiter in the yard are waiting to find us out.

I am now a member of the cell. Even if I had refused, my association with Andrei, Dimitri, and Peter would compromise me. In my calmer moments I wonder what they know about me. Are any of my secrets with the Holy One safe?

April 20, 1917

We met at the Astoria Hotel, always filled with army officers and their wives. I passed on the message, enclosed in a book of Pushkin's poems; terrified that one of Lenin's agents will find me out. Sergei and Annushka were with me as cover on the pretext of having tea in the large reception room downstairs.

We walked out to the statue of Peter the Great at the water's edge near the admiralty, and Peter recited lines from Pushkin's poem, 'The Bronze Horseman', depicting the great flood of 1824. The children were delighted. My only emotion was relief that no one had followed us.

April 24, 1917

A sense of dread always overcomes me when the car arrives. I am dressed to be obscure, a revolutionary in a white blouse, black skirt, and boots. My hair is drawn up in a severe bun. Dimitri thinks this espionage costume suits me. It is spring, but the air is still freezing. I have stopped wearing my fur cloak as it has proven to be dangerous. On my last trip one of the men in the yard grabbed at me, saying I was an impostor, that no one of the people would own a coat like that.

I always am silent during the journey, concentrating my energy on surviving the trip up the back stairs, perplexed at what I am doing. It is insane to be part of this, to risk my life. All I have done is deliver messages in Petersburg. But I know there is more. The Druzhina claim there is a mission.

I am a prisoner in a hostile alien land as I stumble in the near darkness past sinister looking men in ill-fitting uniforms, carrying guns. They look savage, their white teeth gleaming out from dirty faces. I heard that yesterday they lined up a group of officers, traitors to the revolution and shot them, near the Moika Canal.

I stopped, and scrambled toward the foot of the bed and grabbed the photograph. Now I understood the intimacy, the implied secrecy in the faces of the four. The Druzhina was a spy ring. It was obvious that they were the leaders, the inner circle of the Brotherhood organization Kosloff had described.

Chapter 35

Quogue: 1970

I TURNED TO the day the photograph was taken, sensing that the journal was leading me to a dangerous secret Madame A had kept buried for years.

August 5, 1917 Finland

Peter, Dimitri, and Andrei have arrived at the dacha. They are secretive about their movements and report only through Andrei who channels the information to the Bogatyr. After the meeting we four ride out through a path in the forest, the Druzhina together; would it be for the last time?

There was another entry with the same date.

August 5, 1917 Finland

Is it wartime and the possibility that if I am caught the revolutionaries will show no mercy that has led to my wantonness, my madness? Today, Peter met me in the forest, its graceful white birches sheltering us from the late morning heat. He has a beautiful face, like an angel in a Rublev icon. As though coming in for the kill, he viciously lifted my skirts; my legs trembled around him as he forced me against the tree. He stifled my cries of wild passion with his hand pressed against my mouth. Afterward, we walked among the birches in the forest until I, devastated by his act of possession, could stop shaking.

He did not tell me he loved me, but said, "I will not live without you. Whatever happens I will come back for you. I will save you."

It was so very different when Dimitri made love to me the next morning in the small boathouse. He was slow, gentle, sensuous, and even though there was a chance that we would be discovered, we stayed together talking, laughing in the afternoon heat. I reached up and touched his thin face. He looked like an ascetic, a saint. His light eyes burned through me. We are soul mates.

I have rationalized my reckless immoral behavior. I have become a different person because of the uncertainty and violence of the times and often wonder if my two lovers know or if Georgi suspects that I am unfaithful. I desperately want us all to stay together. I have loved them both since I was a child; they are a part of me. I will not choose between them.

At the table we behaved decorously and talked of the war, the mounting casualties, and what we will do when we return to Petersburg. There still may be hope for the Provisional Government. Kerensky was made premier on July 21. He straddles both sides and is also a leading figure in the Soviet. They have told me that Lenin, the leader of the Bolsheviks, is in hiding from the government near here. He is accused of being a spy, and taking money from the Germans. We know he is a dangerous man although most of the people are unaware of his power.

The next morning before sunrise the Druzhina left on their mission.

August 10, 1917

Kerensky is trying to appease the Workers Soviets. They are controlled by Lenin who has escaped arrest. The Soviets demand the death of the Tsar.

On July 31 the Tsar and family were removed from Tsarskoe Selo to Tobolsk in Siberia by order of Kerensky, who claimed it was for their safety. The family is being held in the Governor's Palace.

It is agreed that it will be easier to free the Romanovs in this Siberian backwater where the people are still loyal to the Tsar. I have not received my assignment for this mission, but the order is that I am central to the plan.

October 10, 1917

Andrei has been arrested along with General Kornilov and his staff after their march on Petersburg to destroy the Bolsheviks. Kerensky stopped the action by arming the Bolsheviks and releasing Trotsky and other revolutionaries from prison, further diluting his power. I learned today Andrei and the general have been moved from the Metropol Hotel to Bhykov Monastery. I wonder if I ever will see my dear Andrusha again.

November 1917

Lenin and his Bolsheviks have taken over the government. On October 25 they seized control of the telegraph, the army barracks, and the police station. They overran the Winter Palace and arrested the members of the Provisional Government. The Bolsheviks are still a minority party, but act with decisiveness, and have gained support among the crowds on the street. There is an ominous calm.

December 1917

Georgi vanished some days ago. The last time I saw him, he claimed he has information that is dangerous, that everything has gone wrong, and that the Bolsheviks will kill him if they discover what he knows.

Supplies of food and fuel are scarce in Petersburg. The trains are crowded with people travelling out to the country to barter clothes, jewelry, and small objets d'art for necessities. People stand on street corners trying to sell all their possessions for a stick of firewood or a piece of bread.

I continue to work for Baron Stocker, cataloguing the art treasures. He has a connection in the government who allows him double rations, which he shares with us. Every day I hurry through the streets to the baron's office near Nevsky Prospect, risking my life. It seems strange in a civilized city like Petersburg to have gangs of soldiers and workers riding around in auto-mobiles confiscated from the wealthy, shooting off guns in the streets. People seem bemused, unaware, not quite believing in the danger. Ordinary pedes-trians out doing errands often are killed by stray bullets. And now it seems more dangerous when it is becoming evident that the shootings have become deliberate.

The baron is not himself. He has visibly aged since being accused of smuggling by the more radical art committee members. He is planning his escape and has hidden away precious objects, roubles and foreign money to take with him. He leaves money with me and warns me that Red Guards are searching the houses of formers, aristocrats, bourgeoisie and the intelligentsia, considered traitors to the people.

December 1917

I have heard nothing from the Druzhina. Dimitri and Peter have left the city for unknown destinations. Andrei is in prison. I am alone now with the chil-dren and wonder how we will survive.

As instructed I went to the meeting place, the bench near Pushkin's statue and was approached by a man cleaning the streets. He swept a paper over to me. My heart pounding, I waited until he was far down the path, and then picked it up from underneath the bench. It was a list stolen from the Bolshevik headquarters to be passed on to the cell.

I hid in a doorway in a small street near St Isaac's Cathedral. With shaking hands, I opened to the first page with 'To Be Approved' at the top. The list was precise, in alphabetical order with addresses the Bolsheviks had obtained from the Petersburg telephone directory.

On the last page Lenin had written, 'For the Archive'. I had heard that Lenin writes this phrase on death sentences. It is an evil joke and means that his cold-blooded orders will be buried forever in the archive. I read back over the pages, recognizing names of friends, and acquaintances and then a strange numbness gripped me; my blood stopped flowing. I saw my own name and address.

I fled with the children that night. As we scurried through the dimly lit streets, we came upon a dead woman lying on the pavement; her clothes had been stolen in the night. Annushka sobbed at the sight. Sergei's eyes widened in horror at the dead horse lying near the canal, huge chunks of its flesh hacked out for food.

Both Sergei and Annushka are without a spark of life, like ancient little people from a folk tale. Sergei will not speak. Annushka says that he is too filled with grief. He told her that the dead horses and the naked bleeding woman were always in front of him, would not go away. I ask her to plead with him to speak, but he remains silent.

We still are hiding in the baron's office. He has fled with what money and jewels he could, and left the key for me. Those who looted his warehouse have not bothered to return.

It is freezing and there is no firewood left. We sit bundled up around a small fire burning the last chair in the office. I dream of escaping, that Peter or Dimitri will come to save us, even though the Cheka is hunting them.

I stopped, motionless, listening. There was a faint click of shoes on the outside porch near my window, coming closer. Jack said he had men guarding the house, but I feared they would be no match for the killers. I held my breath. The sound of steps continued. I pushed up against the window and looked out in the darkness. I began to breath again. The

moonlight illuminated a tree branch tapping against the window. I hurried
back to the journal.

January 1918

*My hand trembles as I write. We are escaping by train to Omsk, now one of
the White strongholds in Siberia, travelling with forged papers.*

*Our last days in Petersburg were terror stricken. Gregori, our old servant,
risked his life to warn me that the Leather Coats were coming for us. In despair, I had bundled up the children and was waiting until dark to flee from
our shelter into the streets. I heard heavy boots on the stairs. And the knock
came. Trembling, a thick knot of fear in my stomach, I opened the door to
find a young commissar dressed in a leather coat.*

*We were arrested and taken stumbling through the streets in the darkness,
avoiding a wild drunken troop of Red Guards and were hurried into the
back of a horse drawn wagon. I tried to calm the children, holding both of
them.*

*To my surprise we were quickly ushered out of the wagon at Nicholaevsky
Station and escorted to a private railway car. A rough looking Bolshevik
commissar handed me papers, which listed us as dependents of one Victor
Matsev, an important member of the new government. We settled into the car,
dazed and puzzled by the reprieve. I could only think one of the Druzhina
had saved us.*

*Two men in Red Army uniforms guarded the car and provided us with food
and water. They watched us with curiosity, and only one of them spoke to us,
warning us to stay in the carriage. As the train jerked into motion I was ignorant of our exact destination, but knew we were going to Siberia. We
crossed the Urals and arrived in Tyumen yesterday. The guard informed me
that we were on the train to Omsk, the White stronghold. All trains were
delayed and we stalled on the track.*

One of the guards told us that the resistance had blown up a train. I tried to quell my rising hope when I heard rumors that the Bogatyr led the saboteurs. The White resistance regards the spy as a savior. His exploits have, in the Russian way, already become legend.

Two days later at sunset, the train crawled forward and I waited with halted breath, in fear that it would stop, and we would be pulled off. But it chugged on, moving faster, giving off sparks and smoke. Then it seemed to fly, bellowing through a white landscape. The sound of the wheels on tracks was soothing and the car was luxurious, a temporary haven. I bathed the children and then myself for the first time in days. They were exhausted and fell asleep almost immediately.

That night the door opened and he was there, holding me. "You are safe now, out of it all." He had saved us. I knew he would come.

He said the war to overthrow the Bolsheviks had begun. The Druzhina were meeting in Tobolsk where the Tsar and his family were prisoners. I said, "You are the Bogatyr." He smiled and did not deny it. I knew it was true.

"Take down your hair," he said, as he unbuttoned my gown. He handled me as though I were a precious object, and might break at his touch. Then he was rougher, more insistent. The train let out a mournful cry as it plunged into the wildness of Siberia.

The next morning when I woke, he was gone.

The bedroom faded and in that moment I was on the train rushing through Siberia with Madame A and her lover. Who was he? Did he rescue her from Petersburg?

Omsk 1918

Very crowded here, a struggle to find somewhere to live. Even the city's large solemn looking administration buildings are packed with refugees. We are in rented quarters, part of an old crumbling mansion in the best part of this Siberian city with an elderly couple, the Shumatovs. There is a government of sorts, but the city is filled with idlers and fake soldiers, wearing phony insignia and strutting about the cafes. Speculators buy supplies meant for the White Army from corrupt officials and sell them at high prices to the Reds, making fortunes.

People believe this is the last of their days and want to live while they can. Like the others I grab at happiness, living with my lover in the midst of terrible uncertainty.

April–March 1918

Civil War has begun in earnest. The Bolsheviks have removed the Tsar to Ipatiev House in Ekaterinburg. the Cheka have named it the House of Special Purpose. It is ominous; something must happen soon. I wait anxiously for news.

July 30, 1918

The combined Czech and White army force have captured Ekaterinburg and discovered that the Tsar and his family have vanished from Ipatiev House. Terrible evidence inside the cellar suggests they had been massacred just days before the Whites took the town. Both the local government and the army are searching the area, but no bodies have been found. There are rumors the family has been taken to Perm. Peter returned only for one night and warned me not to believe anything I hear. He told me there had been a failed uprising in Moscow, involving the British agents O'Reilly and Lockhart. Now that he is gone, I have no contact with the Druzhina. I can only hope the Brotherhood rescued all or some of the family.

November 18 1918

I work on Admiral Kolchak's staff, writing, and translating messages to the White army in the South and to the Allies who, since the Great War ended, have tentatively helped the White cause.

General Turev offered the children and me a place on his train, a luxurious travelling hotel with heat, light and good food.

We now advance in luxury, safe with the troops. For miles there is nothing but flat plain, the only towns clustered around the railroad stations. Refugees, carrying all their possessions, walk or ride on horses, carts, or oxen, following the tracks. Sometimes entire villages are fleeing; a frightened rag-tag group of school children, farmers, former nobility, and families of soldiers looking for a safe place, but they find nothing. I think of all the abandoned houses in Russia, the tables left with food; the samovar still boiling.

There was a break in the page. The next entry was scribbled hurriedly and appears to have been pasted in after the others had been written.

Early morning I stand outside in the snow and wait as the sun rises. I open my arms to the light and the Holy One's aura surrounds me and penetrates me as he did when alive. And I know his power and skill remain within me. The Master's Skill, Z …

The rest of the page was ripped out. What was this? My skin crawled, thinking of her standing in the snow, raising her arms in some occult ceremony. What did she mean by penetrated by his aura? I knew Rasputin was the master. And the Z? Could she have written *Zagovarivatt' Krov*, the skill to stop the flow of blood?

Chapter 36

New York: 1970

THE NEXT MORNING Ab and I were sitting in the sunroom in silence, drinking coffee. The sun was shining, coaxing out the green buds on trees pressing up against the windows, but the scene of the murders hung oppressively over the cheery room. Abigail began to wave her legs up and down in some new exercise, breaking the silence.

"Do you think you're over the shock? The doctors said it would take a few days. You seem miles away."

"I think so. Thanks for taking me away and putting up with my hysterics."

"I can't imagine what it was like when you found the bodies." She crossed her legs, holding them in a pretzel position.

Abigail could have no idea of what I saw in that room. The newspapers had carried the stories every day, but their descriptions were a faint sanitized version of the images that haunted me.

Ab pointed to the newspaper she had been reading earlier.

"Ms. Springsmith, her butler and the dogs will be buried in England at the ancestral home, Springsmith Hall in Leicestershire, East Midlands. Even the Queen is attending the funeral. She must have been very important in English society."

"I guess. But that didn't stop her from being murdered."

Abigail jumped up and peeked out the front window.

"I don't see anyone, but I suppose they're out there guarding the house,"

She came over to me and held my hands. "You're shaking. I know it's scary to have your life threatened, but I think the police are just being extra careful. Don't worry, nothing can happen to you here."

I wasn't so sure. The smell of burning flesh assaulted me; the trees outside looked artificial, like a stage setting. Abigail sat down in the wicker chair beside me, her long red nails clicking on her coffee cup.

"The police are only interested in you because you knew Ms. Springsmith and found the bodies. You know, I am beginning to think you might be right, that the old lady has been kidnapped, but it couldn't involve you. You were a total stranger to her until three months ago. And look, when they check everything, you'll be free to go back to Soho with me. I'm sure it will turn out right."

I stifled the impulse to confide in Abigail. In the light of day, the journal seemed the result of an overworked imagination and read more like a sensational novel than the truth. She would laugh if I told her that Madame A had been a disciple of Rasputin and a spy during the revolution. I still had no solid clues to her disappearance and was beginning to doubt I would find anything in her notes.

Distraught and frightened, I had made a decision. "Ab, I'm sorry, but as soon as I find out what happened to Madame A, I am going back to Ohio for awhile. I have to get away from this." I tried to hold back tears.

Then I told her that my trip with Ms. Springsmith to see Sergei might have put me in danger. I explained that Sergei was mentally unstable, and described, somewhat inadequately, his pornographic icons.

"You mean he has porno on his walls?" Her dark eyes became even larger with fascination.

"He called it his work, but it was terrible, frightening. Ms. Springsmith seemed really scared. It seemed to me she was repelled by Sergei's walls, but even more upset by his story of the men who came looking for him."

"It's good that they're investigating everyone," Abigail said. "Don't worry, it means they'll probably still find your neighbor alive. Anyway, I wish you wouldn't leave New York. I'll miss you." She jumped out of her chair. "Come on. Let's have some breakfast."

I followed her into the kitchen and sat at the table drinking orange juice. Abigail pushed up the sleeves of her cashmere sweater, and slapped some bacon into a frying pan, simultaneously throwing slices of bread into the toaster with the efficiency of a short order cook.

"So," she said, hands on her lean hips, "that cop is your neighbor, le sauvage noble. I saw him standing in the hallway of your apartment that night after they'd taken you to hospital. I had a better look at him here. What a hunk. I can't believe you barely mentioned him."

The bacon sizzled, and she gave it a poke with her fork.

"The name fits. He certainly doesn't have that all American boy look," she reflected, turning the bacon. She expertly cracked four eggs over the skillet. "I'd say rugged and exciting. And good in bed." She sighed like a schoolgirl, pushing her long glossy hair out of her eyes.

"He's not my type," I said.

"He believes you're his. Didn't you notice the way he looked at you?" she said, poised with the turner over the eggs.

"You're imagining that. And he's a cop. He's antagonistic toward me. I don't like him." I pictured him with Zoe.

Exasperated, she stabbed at the bacon. "You don't have to like him. There's something different, sexy about him, almost dangerous. Just let me know if you really aren't interested." She seemed to have completely forgotten her experience with Slade.

In one deft movement she placed the filled plates, toast, and cutlery on the table. I hadn't told the truth. Not liking him was too tame. My feelings for Jack were more like a boiling cauldron, an odd mixture of hatred, and desire. He entered my thoughts far more frequently than I wanted.

"This is delicious," I said, managing to clean my plate. "You could have been a cook."

"All on account of my nanny who lied on her resume. She was a former short order cook at a truck stop who studied French in her spare time. She told my parents she was a graduate of the Sorbonne. Instead of French she taught me the art of slinging hash, on the off chance I would need a second career. Oh, someone's out there."

She took her plate to the counter and went to the door.

"Christina," she said, coming back into the room. Jack was behind her, and didn't let her finish the sentence.

"You have to come with me."

I jumped up from the chair in panic. I hadn't expected him to return so soon.

"What makes you think you can give me orders? Do you have a warrant?" I remembered that phrase from a police drama I'd seen on TV.

"No, I prefer that you cooperate now that I'm in charge of the case."

"That certainly gives me confidence." I was bitter and disgusted. He could have done something earlier to find Madame A.

He moved a few steps closer to me. His voice was hard, urgent.

"Listen to me. There are definite links between Madame A's disappearance, Ms. Springsmith's murder, and the break in at your apartment. At this point in the investigation, you're a suspect and a witness. You need to tell me everything you know about this."

"There is nothing to tell."

"I can take you in and arrange police protection at the station or you come with me. You're safer with me." He came even closer, shutting out the light from the window. His black turtleneck, and leather jacket gave him a sinister look. His warm embraces were a distant memory, as though he had been a person I dreamed up out of need.

"A suspect. That's ridiculous. Why don't you catch the real murderers? I tried to get you to investigate Madame A's disappearance, but you were too engrossed with your affair with Zoe. That was more important than a kidnapping or murder. And Zoe was obviously too involved with you to even answer her telephone or check on her aunt."

He jerked his head back in surprise, his narrow eyed look reminding me of Slade's, and I realized with a spasm of fear that I may have gone too far.

He ignored my reference to Zoe. "Why not you as a suspect? A society bitch who appears in Women's Wear Daily isn't exempt from the law." I flinched as though he'd hit me.

His voice was mocking. "Didn't you think I'd run a check on you? Now pack up. We're going back to the city."

I still didn't move.

He took a notebook from his jacket pocket.

"We recovered this little black book at Ms. Springsmith's, something the killers overlooked. She managed to hide it under one of the dog beds," he said.

The picture of Ms. Springsmith's slow tortuous crawl to hide the notebook blotted everything out for a moment.

"She kept an intriguing list of Russian names and addresses, including Antonova's son Sergei; an interesting émigré circle." He flipped through the notebook. "Many of them seem to be old friends of our missing neighbor and might know something. We want to interview Sergei. My officers report that he has disappeared from his apartment. Do you know where he is?"

I shook my head, unable to speak.

"Maybe he'll talk to you. It's important. Hurry up." He was cold, officious, his eyes dark, without any reflection.

Abigail, shocked into silence, watched from the doorway, her face a picture of astonishment. She helped me gather up some clothes and waved from the drive.

"See you at the gallery," she yelled.

He drove his MG top down, an unlikely car for a cop, in the fast lane of the expressway.

"Wouldn't it make more sense to take Zoe with you?" I shouted into the cold wind, my braids flying as he wove dangerously between lanes, horns honking in our wake.

"After all, she's Madame A's niece and speaks Russian and is your lover. I saw you coming out of the apartment building with her," I yelled, and then wanted to take back the words, floating in the rush of air past the car. As if I cared about their affair.

"Let's keep her out of this," he said in a menacing tone, which meant he was still sleeping with her.

I hoped I made him uncomfortable, but it was difficult to read what he was thinking behind those aviator sunglasses. He looked more official and physically intimidating, looming in the seat beside me.

"Who are you? I know nothing about you. Oh sure, you flashed some kind of ID at me, but that could be anything." My voice faded. I burned at his treatment, but was afraid to further antagonize him. I had seen the worst consequences of physical violence, far more brutal and sickening that I could ever have imagined.

He looked over at me and with one hand took out his ID and slapped it on the seat between us. The photo seemed genuine. There were the words NYPD special liaison and some other abbreviations, but I was too preoccupied by the speed of the car to figure these out. He stepped harder on the accelerator, and the landscape fuzzed together, then altered again to branches reeling above me as the car swerved off the road. I screamed.

Chapter 37

New York: 1970

I SAT IN furious embarrassed silence somewhere off the Long Island Expressway at Sal's Diner. I picked at my salad and tried to avoid staring at the jagged scar on Jack's wrist as he munched on a large hamburger and fries. The nauseous smell of grease and fried onions wafted over me. A piece of lettuce stuck in my throat.

"Relax. There's nothing you can do about your neighbor at the moment." He grinned, obviously amused at my hysterics when he had abruptly turned off the highway. "This is my first intake of calories today. I was at work early this morning at the murder scene."

Maybe he thought he was witty. How could he grin? It was grisly, so unfeeling. He had no respect for anyone.

"Don't you worry about cholesterol?" I stabbed at another small bit of lettuce, and then put down my fork.

He raised one eyebrow over the sunglasses and grinned again before taking another bite. It was maddening. I shifted uncomfortably on the large leather booth facing the windows and studied the diner's gleaming Art Deco interior.

A middle-aged waitress with orange hair bustled toward the tables. Her sad dark eyes would study her order pad, and then take the plates three or four at a time from the wide opening in the wall behind the counter. She looked over and smiled at us as though we were an ideal happy couple.

The parking lot was nearly empty, with only three cars looking match-box size in its cavernous space. It was early afternoon, but the sky was dark and overcast, threatening a spring storm. Dot turned on the neon sign; its garish flashes of red and blue blinked over the lot like an ominous warning. Jack removed his sunglasses and watched out the window as if the killers were lurking out there along the highway.

The waitress leaned over the counter chatting with a gray haired stocky man in coveralls. He took out some coins and played one of the shiny chrome jukeboxes, placed like small shrines at intervals along the counter. Heads cocked, they both listened dreamily, while Dot swayed a little to the strains of *Bobby McGee*. I wondered if they were in love and met somewhere after the diner closed. Or maybe they played out their melancholy idyll forever like the forlorn isolated figures in a Hopper painting.

As Janis Joplin wailed loneliness and abandonment, I saw my face, distorted, in different pieces, reflected in the jukeboxes. I covered my eyes in tiredness. How had this happened? I was sitting in a diner with a virtual stranger with whom I had had sex and he cared nothing about me. I was a witness to those unspeakably brutal murders. My neighbor had vanished. I was a fugitive, on the run; I couldn't even contact my dad. Finally, I took my hands away. He was watching me, but didn't say a word, just continued to demolish his hamburger.

"Do you think Madame A is dead?" I was close to tears.

"It's a possibility." He was deadpan.

"What do you mean?"

"The Springsmith murder. Definitely a wet job."

He wasn't grinning now. I felt woozy. The polished chrome on the pie case glared. Ms. Springsmith crushed face passed before me. Black points were gathering in front of my eyes.

I shuddered. "You really think it's the KGB?"

"Their intelligence unit operates here under cover of the UN. They have diplomatic immunity."

"Like the Leather Coats, the Cheka?" I said, "Madame A is still frightened of them."

"Same organization, new name. The Russian Security services have gone through several names since the revolution: the Cheka, the OGPU, the NKVD, and now KGB. They also have numerous uncomplimentary nicknames, like the Organs. Older émigrés still call them the Leather Coats." He picked up his fork to eat his fries.

By now I was reasonably sure what wet job meant, and wasn't up to hearing a clinical explanation.

"But how would you know that it was the KGB?" I said. Jack finished his fries without answering, scooping up tons of ketchup with his fork to accompany them. "And why would they be interested in Ms. Springsmith? It all seems so far-fetched." I hoped he would say something to reassure me.

"Maybe not Ms. Springsmith herself," he said slowly, looking up from his plate, "but something they thought she was hiding. The same could be true of Madame A. We just don't know yet."

He wiped ketchup from his mouth leaving red stains on the paper napkin. My stomach lurched.

"Good thing you weren't in your apartment," he said, a serious look replacing his grin, "I want you to think back to the last time you were with the old lady. Are you sure you can't remember anything that might be important to the case?"

I shook my head and moved farther away from him on the sticky leather seat, feeling guilty at withholding my small bit of information. I wanted out, away from him, from everything.

He shoved his empty plate to the side and took another small notebook from his pocket, studied it for a moment, then stared as though he could see through me. "So far we know that Ms. Springsmith was an informant in that weird world of Russian émigré politics. Several émigré organizations delude themselves into thinking they can overthrow the Russian government, but they can't even agree on what form of government should replace it. The monarchist Double Eagle is the most organized and serious of these groups. Springsmith probably needed to belong to this fantasy world to juice up her life. We know she attended their meetings with General Turev."

"Ms. Springsmith was involved with the Monarchists? But she's English."

"Her father, Lord Reginald Springsmith, was a British agent during the Russian Revolution, working with the Whites to overthrow the Bolshevik government. He wrote a couple of books about his adventures in Siberia, *With the Brotherhood* and *Agent for the Whites*," Jack said, flipping to a page in the notebook. "We found them on her bookshelf. Have you heard of them?"

I shook my head in astonishment.

"The man fancied himself an adventurer, a swashbuckler," he said with scorn. "A lot of upper class amateurs played the spy game then; most were not very effective. Violet Springsmith had strong ties to the Double Eagle through her father."

I leaned back in the booth, remembering Ms. Springsmith's hearty denial that she spoke Russian and her preoccupation with what she called Madame A's treasures. Could her father have told her something about Madame A?

"This Double Eagle group at first struck me as passé, full of aging generals, countesses, crazy monarchists, crackpots." He turned the page, reading over his notes and stopped to light a cigarette while Dot poured coffee in the thick white mug. "But I changed my mind after reading current files. Lenin and Stalin did take the Monarchists very seriously."

He mused, "Even now under Brezhnev, the ruling Politburo believes that émigrés are a threat to the Soviet Union. A healthy amount of paranoia seems to exist among the exiles. Certain émigrés claim they are under constant surveillance. Our files show that from the 20's to the present, important members of the Double Eagle have been killed on the streets of Paris and New York, often in hit and run accidents. Some have been kidnapped or lured back to Russian to be tortured into confession and then executed. One exception is the influential member of the Double Eagle who recently died peacefully in bed. At least we think so."

"You must mean Count Von Grubov." I remembered the look of terror on Madame A's face; her violent reaction to the obituary and accompanying articles.

"There are others besides the Count in Springsmith's notebook. A General Turev and his son, Paul are also listed. Have you heard of them?"

"I was invited to General Turev's for Russian Easter. He's a very cultured, civilized man, devoted to the Antonovas. His son Paul lives and works in Paris for the organization. Madame A trusted the general implicitly. She told me he had checked on Vladimir Antonov."

Jack seemed skeptical "Turev's our first stop."

I tried to assert myself, but my voice trembled. "I want to go to my apartment first."

"I don't think so," he said.

"I have a right to check on my things. I'm not a prisoner." My voice rose. The waitress and her friend glanced at us.

"Ok, ok," he conceded, "But it's not a good idea."

I started out of my seat, but he sat back in the booth and flicking a match, lit up another cigarette. His dark eyes had changed to a golden soft light, and he looked less threatening, but I had hardened toward him. And that violent scar and his mocking grin got on my nerves. I waved my hands to get rid of the smoke. He ignored me. Finally I snapped, "The smoke will probably kill me before the murderers can."

He stared at me with narrowed eyes and puffed harder, releasing billows. He could have been an entry in Guinness for the record in rudeness. He finished the cigarette without speaking and then stubbed it out in the ashtray.

I was beginning to completely hate him when he leaned across the table and captured my hands with his. They were very large and warm and sent a thrill of pleasure through me.

"Look, there seems to be no reason the Bolshie's, the KGB, if it is them, should be interested in a little old lady, even if she is an émigré. There is the Cold War. They have other problems, like missiles, deployment of troops, to worry about. It could be she's too busy settling in with this Vladimir to call you," he said, still holding my hands.

"Have you managed to find out anything at all?"

"I have men searching the files and out looking for info on Antonov, but so far, no luck. That could change any time. We have some leads. The old lady is a refugee from the revolution and Springsmith had that Russian connection. It's just an idea. But her disappearance and the murders might be linked to something in her past." He had come to the same conclusion without any of the clues I had discovered.

"My contact works in the agency archives and is doing some research for me. We were in high school together, then Fordham. She was persuaded to help."

He smiled. I knew she had to be an old girlfriend, still falling over herself to please him. He was so arrogant, wanting me to know I was one of many conquests. I tried to pull away, but he gripped my hands tighter.

"It's a long shot and it will take time. She's searching for material from the early 1900's, but it's tough finding anything from that period. The US was in its infancy in intelligence gathering, and there wasn't even an official agency until 1947. Before that, any intelligence work was informal, handled by the Treasury and State Departments, and referred to as the Hidden Hand. Dramatic, huh?" He laughed.

"Many of those old files were destroyed or are hidden in other sections of the archives, not easy to trace. A lot of the information she's found so far is irrelevant since most of Madame A's contemporaries died of old age or were killed in the revolution and civil war."

He took his hands away but his warmth lingered, leaving me with regret.

He put his matches in his pocket. "But since General Turev is still alive, someone else from that period of the revolution could be involved."

He jumped to his feet and paid the check.

"If we hurry we can pick up your clothes and get to Turev's this afternoon. What is it?" he said, seeing me hesitate.

With the true interrogator's instinct he sensed I was about to tell him something. But I changed my mind, thinking Madame A's journal couldn't really have been what the killers were after. Her notes were intriguing, but surely not relevant. And I didn't think it would have changed anything if I had brought the Pushkin book to Ms. Springsmith. A sharp sliver of light from the shiny chrome jukebox stabbed at me, and I closed my eyes. When I rang her doorbell that fateful afternoon and there was no answer, they were torturing her then.

Chapter 38

Rural Ohio: 2000

BEFORE I BEGIN my night vigil on the porch, I review General Turev's account of his capture by the Bolsheviks and subsequent escape to the South of Russia. It is riddled with clever half-truths; a competent device to disguise lies. However, the incidents were so long ago that no one would discover his falsehoods unless they had been on the railroad car when he was arrested. I have gone through the pages, with the appropriately named magic marker, savagely underlying the lies. And then packed the papers in the metal box to be taken with other materials to the lock up storage on the outskirts of Columbus. I turn off the porch light and in the dark, even nature seems deceitful. The once benevolent trees take on grotesque shapes with wild hair like bogeymen, like the killers who stalked me. I did not know what lay in wait for me when Jack drove me back to New York.

New York 1970

Jack left the expressway, crossing the 59th Street Bridge. Its seven story pylons were blanketed by dark billows of cloud. Jack pulled off and put the top up on the MG, continuing uptown to 82nd Street. We arrived at my apartment around four in the afternoon, and raced for the building through the breaking storm. I hurried through the hall, past my neighbor's silent empty apartment, and quickly opened the door to mine. I stepped back, struggling to breathe.

A terrifying collage of pieces of my belongings swirled around me. My apartment had not only been searched; it had been vandalized. The sink and toilet were filled with human feces. Smashed furniture, clothing torn by knives, food, fragments of glass and dishes were left in mounds in the middle of the room. Blood was smeared on the walls and dripped over piles of my clothes.

My legs became heavy clubs and the soft buzzing in my ears grew louder, like a chainsaw. I felt Jack behind me, his arms supporting me. He carried me up the stairs to his apartment.

He told me later that the blood on the walls was the same type as Ms. Springsmith's, and that the human tissue removed by police had been identified as hers. The killers had bundled her, still alive, over to my apartment, while they searched, obviously not finding what they wanted.

He placed me on his sofa, where I sat like a zombie unable to move. He rubbed my hands as though I had frostbite and forced me to drink a shot of whiskey. Then he gently laid me on his bed, covered me with a blanket and closed the door behind him. I heard him going down the stairs.

Random thoughts drifted in and out of my mind. It was impossible ever to live in my apartment again. I felt weak, helpless against these killers. He came back into the room with some of my clothes stuffed into a large Bloomingdale's shopping bag.

"I have to get you out of here. No one must know where you are," he said.

I nodded weakly, the prod of fear at his words forcing me to sit up.

Now I did believe him and numbly followed his directions, knowing that only he could protect me. When I had recovered enough to use the telephone, I contacted Abigail to tell her I was going back to Ohio and asked her to let Samuel Westerby know.

"Where are you? You don't sound right." she said.

"I'm fine," I said, "I won't be gone too long."

Then I called my Dad and explained that I was going on vacation with Abigail and would visit him when I returned. I gave them both a number where Jack said I could be reached.

The storm had ended but left damp gloomy air like a dirty sponge over the city as we crossed 59th Street on the Upper West Side to General Turev's. His old manservant, wearing a blouson over baggy pants like a Russian peasant, stepped outside his apartment to greet us. He was hostile and unimpressed with Jack's credentials.

"Who are you? What do you want?" He gripped a broom with a heavy handle like a weapon.

"We are here to see General Turev," Jack said.

"I do not know the location of the *Vozhd*. He left yesterday. Maybe for Paris," he said.

I stepped from behind Jack, and the old man leaning forward, recognized me. "Oh, it's you Miss. You're the friend of Madame Feodosia Petrovna Antonova." His fierce expression dissolved into a smile, and he leaned the broom against the wall.

"Please, you've got to help. Madame Antonova has disappeared. We need to speak with General Turev. It may save his life," I said.

He paused, giving Jack another suspicious look.

"The leader has gone to his officers' headquarters. A terrible tragedy has occurred. He is not himself," he said.

The old general's Cossack headquarters was in Hell's Kitchen, at 9th Avenue and 52nd Street. We parked near Murphy's Bar; its green cloverleaf neon sign followed us across the street and through the door to a rundown tenement.

The light bulb in the dingy hall was gone, and we climbed the uneven stairs in semi-darkness. I heard a thud and claws scraping across the landing. A rat scurried away in front of us. I stifled a scream, but we kept on going.

When we reached the top of the stairs, lights went out under the door of the apartment, plunging us into complete blackness.

"Get behind me." Jack kept his arm around me for a moment, then reached for his gun and knocked. "Police," he said. "Open the door."

A tiny stream of light came from the peephole, and he held up his badge.

The door opened and we stared into the barrel of a pistol, held by a man in a costume drama outfit that I recognized as a Cossack uniform from old photographs of Madame A's brother Andrei.

The man brought us slowly into the kitchen, bare with cracked walls and worn lino, and furnished sparsely with a cheap plastic table and chairs. It was spotlessly clean, like a military barracks, with uniforms hanging on hooks, a samovar, and a bottle of vodka on the table. Someone lay in bed in a room off the kitchen.

"Stay where you are."

The Cossack giving the order was a huge man with a curling moustache. Two others, also in full military dress joined him, holding drawn swords. Even Jack started with surprise at this spectacle. The three former soldiers were huge with slanted piercing eyes in dark wrinkled faces. They were in their seventies, but very fit, a ferocious body guard.

General Turev had told me at the Easter celebration that he hand-picked his Cossacks and after the defeat of the White Army had brought his younger men to New York.

"What do you want?" The man in charge growled in a Russian accent.

"Is General Turev here? I need to speak with him. It concerns Madame Antonova," Jack said, holding up his badge.

"Ruslan," The man lying in the bed called out, "Put down the pistol. Let them come in."

Then he issued a command in Russian and the men sprang to attention.

Ruslan didn't look happy as he lowered the pistol and motioned us into the bedroom.

General Turev, wearing an old fashioned nightshirt, struggled to sit up in bed, his aide arranging pillows behind him. Since I last saw him, his debonair manner had vanished and he had become a frail old man. The patch on his blind eye was gone, exposing a sore looking pink hole. His hands shook as he struggled to bring the blanket up to his chest.

"Security Division." Jack leaned forward to show his badge.

"I know about people like you," Turev said in disgust, turning his head away to the wall filled with icons, a multitude of black eyes looking down on us.

"My son. They've killed my Paul in Paris. It was made to look like a hit and run." His voice sounded far away. The old man nodded to himself, as if confirming the dreadful fact. "My dear Paul was coming out of organization headquarters. An automobile drove up on the sidewalk and ran him down. No witnesses."

He gestured to Jack and said, "It makes no sense for the police to investigate. That's how the KGB operates. It's *Chernaya Robata*, Black Work."

"I'm very sorry," I said, holding his fragile, paper-thin hand, remembering he had spoken with affection and pride about his only son, scheduled to take over the Double Eagle.

"How do you know that?" Jack said, taking out his notebook.

"When Vladimir Antonov contacted Feodosia Petrovna she requested that I check on him, although she believed he was genuine. I put my Cossacks to work and discovered too late that there is no Vladimir."

No Vladimir. The reality behind those words stung me with surprise, like stepping on a bee with my bare foot.

"You can trust no one," Turev said in a low broken voice, looking directly at me. Was he trying to tell me something? I let go of his hand.

"Are you sure about this?" Jack said.

"We located Georgi Antonov's widow Nadya. Since then, I've been in hiding. I warned Springsmith and my son, but it was too late, too late." He shook, covering his face with his hands.

Jack continued to take notes, ignoring the old man's distress.

"Why did you warn Ms. Springsmith?" he said.

"Violet's father, Sir Reginald, and I were companions in the civil war. He organized safe houses and networks for the White movement. Violet always was sympathetic to the cause."

Turev's tears were gone. He sat up straight in bed, his voice growing stronger, "We were prepared for the coup. It is the right time. It is extremely sad, but sacrifices must be made to achieve our objective."

"So what did Springsmith do for you?" Jack persisted.

"Violet kept a watch on those who visited Feodosia and Annushka. We were particularly interested in the niece Zoe and her boyfriend, Nicolae."

"And what was your particular interest?" Jack sat down on the chair next to the bed.

"Our organization was approached by Nicolae, acting as a messenger for someone inside the Kremlin." Turev stopped to swallow some pills with a glass of water, brought by one of the Cossacks who darted venomous glances at Jack.

"Thank you Ruslan," Turev said, still swallowing with difficulty as though the words stuck in his throat. "This source informed us that the extreme level of discontent in the Soviet Union would make it possible to take over. There is much unrest, particularly in the mountainous areas of the Caucasus. I had no doubt that Russia was ripe for a coup and that someone with great power inside the government offered to support us in the takeover. As the *Vozhd*, the new leader, I was destined to be in control of our country."

This sounded to me like the delusional ravings of an old man unbalanced by grief.

"Nicolae claimed we would be contacted on how and where to obtain funding and the all important legitimacy for our rule. We believed him to some extent, but didn't completely trust him. There always remained with us the slight suspicion it could be a trap, that Nicolae could be an agent provocateur," he said, stopping for a moment to find the right words. "It was a simple task to receive this support. I was asked only to spread the rumor among émigré circles that I was acquainted with this Vladimir Antonov. That was all. I did nothing wrong." His voice was pleading.

"I followed these instructions as it seemed of little consequence for great rewards. In the beginning, I believed Vladimir did exist, but even when I discovered there was no Vladimir, it didn't seem important. I had no idea that Feodosia Petrovna would be harmed or poor dear Violet. And now my Paul," he said, his voice shaking with emotion. His body seemed to shrink under the bedclothes.

"What convinced you that Nicolae's approach was genuine?" Jack raised his head from his notebook.

Turev clutched at his blanket, his voice barely audible. "Believe me, I know how they work. Those directing this operation possessed knowledge that could only have come from a fellow officer or friend in contact with me during the civil war. They knew secret details of the Brotherhood and had access to sensitive material known only to certain members of Kolchak's Siberian government."

I was stunned. Had Turev had been part of the Brotherhood? Madame A had mentioned him in her journal, but not in that connection.

"Tell us about the Brotherhood, about what happened in your past."

He held his hands to his chest, struggling to breathe, his memories revived. "In 1918 during the civil war when I was commanding troops under General Kolchak, our train was ambushed, and we were captured by the Reds. My dear wife was with me on that train."

His voice was choked with the memory.

"They held my gentle Marousia in a room next to my interrogation room. I could hear her screams. They beat me with rifle butts, and I lost my eye. When I came near to death, I agreed to work for them to save myself and told them everything they wanted. They killed Marousia. I don't know why they released me." He held his hands over his face.

"I know it was a long time ago, but can you remember anything about those who questioned you," Jack said.

Turev's words came out tortuously as though his body still remembered, "I am sure he was an important Bolshevik, a political commissar. He conducted his interrogation from behind a screen so I never saw him. He spoke with a muffled voice, but I could detect from the wording of the questions that he was cultured, from the upper class."

A tremor ran through him. "The interrogator was mainly interested in finding out about espionage networks. My confessions were beaten out of me. I said anything they wanted and may have been responsible for betraying agents involved in a mission to rescue the Romanovs. But at that time I knew the operation had failed, and that the agents and the members of the Romanov family had been captured in Perm.

"Our intelligence had reported that two of our men disguised as beggars were on the return trip to Omsk when they were captured. At least that is what we thought. I do not know what happened to them, but it was highly probable that they were murdered. Feodosia was ignorant of my part in betraying Marousia and the Brotherhood."

I looked away, repelled by his confession. He stopped again to catch his breath, and then seemed to recall something.

"I never thought this was important until now, but my interrogator wanted information on Feodosia, where she had gone when she left my train. He seemed obsessed. He questioned me about the casket called the Box of the Harpuiai and tried to torture me into revealing its location. It was all in vain because I didn't even know if it still existed. It was rumored to have disappeared along with the Romanovs.

"In exchange for my freedom I agreed to search for the casket among my fellow members of the Brotherhood and to report to them on White Army intelligence. Not long after that I fled south and escaped to the West. I never discovered anything about the casket. Then information concerning it came to light recently with the death of Count Von Grubov."

"You read the articles on Count Anatole?" Jack said.

"Yes, of course, all the émigrés did. It was very encouraging to know that it existed. We believed that finding this casket and its contents would be most important to our cause. You must realize the approach from the important contact inside the Kremlin seemed genuine to all of us in the organization." He raised his arm in a weak gesture.

"And you knew that you might be putting the Antonovas in danger, that Madame A might know something about this casket?" Jack said.

"I never imagined that my contacts would commit these monstrous acts. It seemed perfectly all right to say that Vladimir existed. It was only to be for a few days, until they could talk with Feodosia. Now it is all over. With my son dead, there is no one dedicated enough to lead the Monarchists to victory. They planned to use us and then destroy us. I will not lead us back into Russia. Our plans are dead. There will be no coup."

He broke into heaving sobs.

"Are you telling me you let them take the old lady?" Jack said.

"They said they only would ask a few questions of her. It was for the cause. I didn't know, I didn't know," he said.

"Where can we find Georgi's widow?" Jack went on quietly, ignoring the sobs.

He caught his breath and finally was able to answer. "She worked as a cleaner in an apartment building on 79th and Park, but could have moved on by now."

"Enough." The Cossack commanded, pointing the gun at us.

Jack stared at Turev.

"I could put you under arrest as an accessory to kidnapping and murder, but assume you won't leave here. Call them off."

General Turev issued a command in Russian and we were escorted to the door.

As we quickly walked across the street to the car, 'There is no Vladimir' echoed in my head.

Chapter 39

New York: 1970

JACK DROVE UPTOWN, crossing 57th Street and heading north on Park Avenue. We were silent in the car, engrossed in our own thoughts. What I suspected was true; there was no Vladimir. The émigrés I had thought so charming had hidden ruthless plotters and aided the killers. I longed to escape this crazy nightmare, to be home safely sitting down to dinner with my father or taking a walk in the fields.

But in spite of growing evidence to the contrary, I hadn't given up the possibility that Madame A was still alive. After all, how reliable was Turev? We parked on 79th Street in front of a monumental brick building, decorated in faux French style, like Turev, an aging courtier covering a multitude of sins.

We found Nadya Martinova Antonova, Georgi's widow, in the dark dank basement. A thin woman in her sixties, she wore a faded cotton dress and men's work boots and was finishing up her workday, squeezing dirty mops into a large drain.

Startled at seeing us, she held out the mop in an ineffectual attempt to fend us off.

"Who are you? What do you want? Get out of here." she said, her voice high with fear.

Jack showed his badge and told her about Madame A's disappearance and Ms. Springsmith's death, explaining that they might be connected.

"I read about the murders." A violent shudder went through her body as she placed the mop in the large sink along the wall.

"We would like to ask you a few questions." Jack said.

Nadya's mottled legs gave way like bowling pins. Jack helped her up from the floor and led her over to a stool. She sat down heavily and took a swig of vodka from the bottle she dug out of her dress pocket.

"How did you find me?" She lifted the bottle again, and took another drink, her mouth working.

"General Turev," Jack said.

"I beg of you. Please go. They will kill me too."

"Why do you say that? What do you know? Who are they?" I broke in.

"Just talk to me a few minutes, and I'll give you enough to get away permanently." Jack's voice grew gentle and persuasive..

He sat down on a large wooden crate, facing her. I found a broken chair near the sink, which held me precariously.

She shrugged, her mood becoming fatalistic.

"What does it matter if I talk to you? I'm a dead woman anyway. And if the Leather Coats don't kill me, I can use the money. I am moving on after today. In the end they will find me, just as they did Georgi, but I prefer death to being sent to one of their camps. You can see I'm desperate."

Swaying on the stool, she raised her eyes, pleading to Jack.

"I can see that," Jack said, "How did General Turev locate you?"

"One of his Cossacks was once a customer, very vigorous for his age and now just a friend. Some time ago, I had a small business." She studied the mop dripping in the sink, and then looked at us defiantly. "I wasn't always like this."

She reached in her dress pocket and brought out a photograph.

"Would you ever guess that this beautiful woman was me, Nadya Martinova Antonova?"

She slid from the stool, lurched over under the hanging light bulb and held up the grainy photo. Her hand was rough and grimy, the fingernails broken and filled with dirt.

Her voice grew tearful, filled with longing. "My hair was the color of ripened wheat. I needed no ornaments, only my beautiful skin and hair, my fine figure. You can see. I show this to everyone. I was fifteen years old then, but already a mature woman, a beauty."

She handed us the creased photograph with pride. Posing in a ball gown, she is extraordinarily beautiful, her fine features framed by lustrous blonde hair. Her large dark eyes gaze up at a bushy haired man with wire-framed glasses, dressed in military uniform.

"Is that Trotsky? Can it be?" I asked, hardly believing it, remembering a photograph of the revolutionary I'd seen in an old book.

"Oh yes, that is the great orator, the Commissar of the Red Army, favored to rule after Lenin. He was like all the rest, appreciating great beauty. He was very masculine and attractive. It was all that power. After Lenin's death, Stalin ran him out of Russia and then had him assassinated in Mexico with an ice pick. So sad," she said and then brightening, continued on about herself.

"As a young girl during the early period of the revolution, I was the darling of the Bolsheviks, the favorite of Trotsky."

I could see faint traces of her former beauty that must have captivated Trotsky, but it was as though time had crumpled her, like the photograph, wrinkling her face, fading her eyes to dullness. A scarf covered what was left of her hair, bleached and coarse.

"Everyone on the left had friends among the poets and writers of the day. I met Georgi at one of the poet Mayakovsky's parties. We all felt that a new day was dawning. When the Bolsheviks took over, I had great hopes." Her voice became shrill. "But even my intimate friendships with the Bolshevik commissars couldn't save my father."

"So you left Russia about this time?"

"Yes, after they murdered my father I decided to go with Georgi. I had no one. We were both on the posted list to be arrested. There was no reason to stay unless one had a death wish."

When Jack asked if she had a son named Vladimir, she threw back her head and laughed wildly, showing gaps in her teeth.

"There is no Vladimir. You ask the same question as Turev. It is so amusing. Georgi and I were fond of each other, but it wasn't a passionate sexual relationship. But why do you ask this silly question?"

"So General Turev is telling the truth," Jack said.

"Perhaps about some things." She abruptly turned, waving her thin arm at the mop and buckets. "I do not think I deserve this life. Many of my fellow countrymen did far more horrible deeds than I to escape, but the so-called respectable Russian community will have nothing to do with me."

She spat with contempt and slumped back on the stool.

"The general does not care what happens to me. He is a cold bastard. I will tell you all I know." She squinted, turning her large dark eyes into little points of hate. "People believe I took advantage, ran off with Georgi and left Feodosia and the children at the mercy of the Bolsheviks. But I was a mere child. One should ask what Feodosia Petrovna was up to in Petersburg. There were many rumors. And then what was the behavior of the so respectable Feodosia and others in Omsk and Harbin?"

"You obviously did nothing to discourage Georgi from leaving her," I said.

"Believe me, Feodosia and Georgi were living apart. In the same house but apart. All the émigrés ignore the rumors of Feodosia's affairs. Why is she such a favorite? Believe me; she was definitely not interested in Georgi."

The drink had affected her and she spoke quickly, "Georgi was involved in many businesses with Rasputin, mostly government contracts and mining rights. For a time after the revolution he continued to do well in some business deals with my father, Alexander Martinov. He was a lawyer and a prominent member of the Cadets, one of the liberal political parties destroyed by the Bolsheviks." She stopped for a moment, coughing heavily.

"But then Georgi became so very frightened of something. I begged him to tell me, but he refused. We fled across Siberia and then on to the US and Princeton. Georgi had a colleague at the university who knew his work as an eminent geologist. This acquaintance helped him get a full professorship with a good salary. We married here, after his divorce from Feodosia. I thought I would be safe for the rest of my life."

Her cough sounded loose and tubercular. The dim basement, a large square room with tiny windows overlooking the street, was cold and damp; beads of water covered the cement walls.

"I suppose my story after all these years isn't very interesting. Just some old slut banging on about former glories." She lowered her head, not looking at us.

"Please go on," Jack said.

"Georgi's wretched family turned up and nothing was the same."

"When was this?" He raised his head from his notebook.

"I don't remember the exact day. It was March I think, 1921. We had been living in our lovely home since 1919 and entertaining among the best society."

Jack's intent gaze made her pause.

"Of course," she said nervously, glancing at me for some imagined support, "I did exaggerate my place in Russian society, but that's what they wanted to hear. It was more exciting to be Countess Nadya than plain old Nadya. I wasn't the only Russian who pretended to be an aristocrat."

She sniffed and looked at her photo again.

"So the family turned up," Jack said, bringing her back.

"Yes, I was out shopping for a cocktail party we were giving for Georgi's colleagues that evening. Can you imagine, looking at me now that I had cocktail parties?"

She cackled from deep in her lungs.

"That day when I returned, they were standing in the drawing room in front of Georgi. It was a complete shock. We had no idea they had been able to escape. They were like ghosts; the strange sickly boy, Feodosia, thin and pale, even less attractive than she had been, and the sullen fat little bitch Annushka."

Her voice was rough with anger.

"It was true they had suffered, but I didn't care. I was ready for a fight. They weren't going to ruin my life."

"What happened?" I was desperate to know.

She shrugged her shoulders, still mystified.

"A fight wasn't necessary. Georgi was hysterical, almost incoherent. All I could make out from his shouts was something like. 'How could you get mixed up with murderers! It was bad enough that they forced me, implicated me.' He went berserk, shouting, 'That's not my son.' Feodosia kept arguing that it definitely was Sergei, but that he had been very ill and emotionally scarred by what happened to them in Russia.

"Georgi wouldn't listen to reason. He behaved like a man insane, ran to his desk, wrote out a check and screamed at her to get out. Even I thought that was cruel to the children. After all, he was their father. Both of them were sobbing and Feodosia was in a daze. They went quietly." She shook her head as if she still didn't quite believe it all.

"After that visit, Georgi was never the same. He told me he knew something that could lead to his murder. I begged him to tell me what it was, but he wouldn't. Believe me, he wasn't evil; he was just a coward. He had everything to live for. I was still beautiful. He was a very distinguished scientist. He became a haunted crazy man."

"Did he ever see Madame Antonova and the children again?" Jack took out his cigarettes and offered her one. He was gentle, good at getting her to talk in spite of her suspicion and fear.

"Thank you," she said. He lit it for her and she took a long draw before answering, "No, Georgi said he never wanted to see them again. He called them ghosts from the past, said they were not really alive anymore. This would have been perfect for me except that …"

She stopped, puffing rapidly on her cigarette, her face contorted with pain.

"In the following months, he became worse, paranoid, acted strangely and could no longer do his job. A year later he quit, and we moved to a farm in Putnam County in upstate New York. He insisted on keeping our location secret. Soon after, he completely lost his mind. He began to see and talk to ghosts, ranting about how he should never have become involved and that Feodosia had brought a curse on them all. Before he died he spoke in a panic about photographs he must destroy, whispering over and over that he never should have taken them.

"He was alone in the barn feeding the cows one cold winter evening when I heard the shot. I called the emergency number, but it was too late. He died from a bullet in the head. There was a pile of ashes on the floor beside him. He had burned the photographs."

"And you believe he took his own life," Jack said.

She murmured almost to herself, "Maybe, maybe not."

"Do you know anything about those photographs?" I thought of Georgi searching his photography room in a panic before fleeing.

"Only when he mentioned them to me just before his death, but I recall when we had escaped the Bolsheviks and arrived in Tyumen, in Siberia, he left me alone for some days and travelled with his camera to Tobolsk. When he returned he destroyed his camera and all his equipment. It was very strange and he never explained," she said.

"You can probably guess the farm had never been my idea. I am sure he only wanted to hide there," she said, suddenly changing the subject. "It didn't bring much when I sold it and moved here. That was all another life ago." She laughed, her face contorted grotesquely.

"Did anyone from the Russian community contact you recently?" Jack said.

"General Turev, because he wanted information. I told you I was friendly with one of his Cossacks, a former customer. That is how he located me. He wanted to know, just like you, about our phantom son Vladimir."

Although she laughed again in that strange uproarious way, a wistful look briefly passed over her face, as though perhaps she wished Vladimir had existed. At least she would have someone.

"I must go." She got up quickly, tossing the cigarette butt into the sink. "Georgi's crazy ravings had the ring of truth. They will be after me, even though I know nothing. I've told you everything and nothing."

She disappeared into the broom closet. In a few minutes, she emerged in an old black dress, her bleached straw like hair piled up high, and her work boots exchanged for black stiletto heels.

Jack helped her with her moth eaten fake fur jacket.

"Can we give you a lift somewhere?" he said.

"You can drop me at the Tunnel. I'm no longer on the game, have not been for many years, but have friends, my only friends there. They will hide me." Her look of fear had returned.

Jack handed her money and escorted her to the car. Nadya squeezed in beside me on the seat meant for one, humming a tune under her breath. She said nothing more as Jack crossed 79th. Street and drove down 9th Avenue to the Holland Tunnel, a pick up place for prostitutes. Two of her friends were already trolling in the cold night air. She left the car without saying goodbye and stood by the road, aging, shabby, solitary but in a defiant pose.

Chapter 40

New York: 1970

BEFORE WE DROVE into the tunnel, Nadya suddenly turned and waved. I thought how cruel fate had been to her. She was terrified when she apparently had nothing to hide, and seemed totally ignorant of Georgi's intrigues.

Nadya still was puzzled by his actions long ago in Siberia. He risked their lives, delaying their escape to travel to Tobolsk. He had believed that his dangerous secret was safely hidden in the past until Madame A and the children showed up at his home. This had to mean they knew what he was hiding.

"She's a real crazy," Jack said, lighting a cigarette as we drove through the tunnel away from the city. I recoiled at his cruel description of her. She was not crazy, only frightened.

"I hope she's safe," I said, sorry for her.

We emerged from the tunnel in New Jersey speeding along the Pulaski Highway. Jack fell silent, and I stayed close to him, our bodies slightly touching. Beyond the lighted highway, a vast wasteland of industrial spillage spread for miles. Huge storage barrels leaked chemicals and old machinery sprouted from the poisonous ground.

Nadya's wild laughter, her phrase, 'No Vladimir' seemed to come at me through the car window. My hopeful picture of Madame A sitting in

Vladimir's garden in a Chekhovian setting was replaced with an ugly vision of her buried in a place like this.

"Where are we going?" I said, trying to keep the nervousness out of my voice.

"To a motel, one we use to hide witnesses."

He seemed to have no feeling at all for me. He slowed the car and pulled over the road barrier into a vacant lot filled with skeletons of abandoned cars. But then he took my hand in a clumsy way and stared out the window, studying the bleak terrain.

"There is something I should tell you. It could have nothing to do with Madame A's case because it is highly improbable that the Bolshie's would go to all the trouble. There is no reason why the KGB, if it is them, should be interested in a little old lady, even if she is an émigré."

"What is it?" I said, suddenly wary.

"Our watchers reported that an unidentified body wrapped in sheets was taken from an ambulance and placed on an unscheduled Aeroflot flight to Moscow. Flight list had no name; only that the passenger was a visitor, a relative of someone in the Politburo going home for an emergency operation."

"Well then, why do you think this woman could be her?"

"It was different from the usual KGB operation. No one in surveillance reports any agents leaving the Russian Embassy. All personnel intact as far as we know. And there is something else. Our source inside their embassy says officials know nothing about this."

Oil tanks loomed in the field like malevolent animals, and a melting gaseous smell filled the car. I choked on the stench.

"They have taken her back to Russia," I cried, tears welling up in my eyes. Now I believed the same killers who tortured Ms. Springsmith and trashed my apartment had kidnapped Madame A. And it seemed possible that I would be next.

"Hold on." He put his arm around me. "We don't know that. This flight occurred a week after she disappeared. It could be someone else. She could be busy settling in with this Vladimir. We both know now that General Turev and Nadya Antonova are capable of lying if it suits them.

Truth does not seem to come naturally to these people. We'll keep looking for this Vladimir."

After a long pause he said, "Are you sure you've told me everything you remember?"

I nodded, not able to lie out loud. I was tempted to tell him everything, including what I had found in the Pushkin book. But some part of me resisted. He had looked at me as though I were a crazy woman when I claimed Madame A had been taken away by the *besy*. He would probably laugh at what I considered evidence.

I often have wondered what really made me keep these nebulous clues to myself. Perhaps it was Jack's forceful insistence that made me hesitate. I have never been an impulsive person. In fact, one of the few rash acts in my life had been marrying Lawrence, and it had ended in disaster.

Jack crashed into my thoughts. He had moved away from me and turned in the seat to face me, his mood had changed.

"You're not telling me all you know. I could arrest you on a number of charges: withholding evidence, impeding investigation, even accessory to Springsmith's murder," he said. "We might have been on the trail earlier."

In the growing darkness, I looked out at the rusting iron machinery in this barren place, where victims were shoved into abandoned autos, and crushed into oblivion by a huge car wrecker. Would he tell me to get out here, in the middle of nowhere? There was nowhere for me to run or hide. Fear made me belligerent.

"I don't know anything more. If I did, why would I tell you? After all, you and Zoe were together. So are you and Zoe still lovers?"

What I said hadn't made any sense and was tied up with my confused feelings toward him. He pulled out onto the highway, the car bumping over debris, and stepped on the accelerator, driving in hostile silence.

An hour later, he dumped me into a shabby motel room along Route One. The sign Old Homestead Inn with several letters missing blinked ominously. He was furious, complaining that my overnight bag brought from Quogue was heavy.

"It must be all those vitamins and beauty products you use," he said in disgust.

"I can't stay here," I said, choking on the combined odor of floral room deodorant and roach spray that pervaded the room.

Maybe it was the sickening smell, but I was really afraid now, and lost my composure, and began to cry silently.

"You have no choice," he said, then seeing my tears, suddenly relented. "Don't worry. It's clean and safe. Relax, I'll get some food."

I wiped my eyes.

"So are we hiding?" I tried to keep the catch of panic from my voice, hoping somehow it wasn't true.

"You are, and you'll cooperate if you have any sense. You've got to trust me. I'll be in the next room. Don't lock this door." He pointed to one separating the rooms.

The door closed and I stood motionless, staring at it for a few minutes. The room, clean in that superficial motel way, was cold and grim, with old grey curtains drawn unevenly over the one small window. A bed, chair, small table, and bed lamp were the only furnishings. Alarming red brown stains ran down the walls, and deep cracks in the linoleum suggested violence rather than ordinary wear. The place breathed fear.

I moved slowly as though my feet were stuck in wet cement and sank to the chair. Traffic noise from the nearby highway roared through my head. I don't know how long I sat there until Jack returned.

"I brought you a salad and some hot coffee." He put the dishes down on the table.

"Thanks," I said, grateful that it wasn't a hamburger. I was relieved that he no longer seemed angry, but found his sudden shifts in mood bewildering.

"See you tomorrow. Knock if you need anything."

Don't go, don't go, I begged silently as he shut the door.

I forced myself to eat the salad and drink the hot coffee and tried to calm down, telling myself this hiding and living in fear could not last long. After I finished eating, I went into the bathroom for a shower, careful to lock the door. It turned out to be surprisingly clean, although there were no extras, just a thin towel, soap, and a cup wrapped in plastic. I unwrapped the tiny piece of soap and turned on the shower.

As the warm water flowed over me, a picture of the Raven, the baron's interrogator, this phantom figure from the past, began to form. I imagined him, tall, slender, with great secret power, standing in front of me, his cigarette smoke swirling, hiding his face.

A vague impression rising like the steam from the shower permeated my consciousness and took form. The secret police interrogations of Turev and the baron, although decades apart, were strikingly similar. I realized with a shock that the Raven could have interrogated them both. It seemed crazy, but was it possible he was still alive?

Chapter 41

Rural Ohio: 2000

I FLICK OFF the porch light and reflect on how the prisoner's confession set the Raven's deadly search in motion. I know now what Madame A meant by the betrayals. Her words hang in the night air, whisper over the ruined cornstalks. I continue to concentrate on preparing the files and return to the dossier on the Bolshevik agent, the Raven.

Moscow 1970: Lubyanka

The general carried his old friend's confession in his briefcase and swooped in triumph through the elegant marbled halls, his cape flying, the heels of his soft leather boots clicking on the polished parquet floors.

Nikita, his new driver in his early thirties, stood at attention, holding open the door to the customized black Volga. An expression of fear crossed Nikita's face as this man known only to him as Sir stepped inside.

Settling in the back seat the general pushed open the curtain and curled his thin lips in distaste at the grimy windows of the *Detskiy Mir* Department Store. Against his wishes The Children's World Department Store, the largest toy store in Russia had been built in 1957 across the square from KGB headquarters. It was close enough for the privileged children picking out toys to hear the faint screams of the tortured floating across the square from the Kennel, the basement of the *Lubyanka*.

The store's location had been chosen to honor Felix Dzerzhinsky, the founder of the Cheka, who chaired the commission on children's welfare. The general had pointed out that this was in bad taste, to no avail. Iron Felix's organization often imprisoned or executed parents and left orphans roaming the streets scavenging for food. Later, the government began imprisoning children of political enemies at the age of ten and extended the death penalty to twelve year olds. Death and the children, he thought in disgust, tapping lightly on the glass that separated him from Nikita.

The car rushed past the enormous six-meter statue of Iron Felix, his old comrade, preserved in bronze in the long leather coat of the Bolshevik police. This was another lapse in artistic judgment for which he couldn't forgive the Communist regime. In spite of strenuous effort, he had failed to influence the mediocre taste of those in power. He took some comfort that the Art Nouveau exterior of the *Lubyanka*, a left over from the pre-revolutionary past, possessed some style.

As the car sped through the Moscow streets slushy with snow he settled back into the large seat, flicked on the light and studied the *Times* newspaper clippings and his old friend's confession.

His nest, his name for the Volga, was furnished with a large console from where he controlled his network. Always restless he spent much of his time working in the comfortable back seat while the Volga roamed Moscow like a migratory bird, casting its shadow on the empty streets.

It was an advantage to have lived so long and to know and remember everything. Few left on earth knew his real name or the identities he had used in the past. And it was possible no one alive was aware that the large dark Volga's, their doors opening like huge beaks to swallow people, taking them away forever, were called 'Ravens', after him. In the early twenties, a hapless driver, too full of jokes to survive, had contributed his nom de revolution, Raven, to that sinister Soviet vocabulary.

Leaning forward the Raven opened the refrigerator filled with western luxuries, which his driver picked up daily from the Bureau of Special Passes, a store reserved for the Communist elite. He selected a bottle of mineral water and gulped it down. Interrogations always made him thirsty, but fortunately not for alcohol. Most of the Politburo, including Brezhnev and much of the Russian population were embalmed with vodka. Drinking was a way of life for many Russians and for the ordinary citizen, a momentary escape from poverty and a humdrum existence. His abstinence from alcohol was one of the reasons he had survived Stalin's purges and had become the director of a powerful secret network.

His power had come gradually, like an underground spring slowly seeping, then flooding the land. Before the revolution he had spied for the Okhrana, the Tsar's secret police, his cover secure because of his position in society. In the early years of Bolshevik rule and Civil War, he became a double agent, working for both the Whites and the Reds and then exclusively for the Cheka. From that time he also had begun to operate secretly, outside the structure set up by Lenin and Stalin.

It was true that he had luck. He had escaped Stalin's purges in the thirties by faking his death and creating a new identity. First hiding in Mongolia and China, and then later the Caucasus, he moved in the gangster underworld, slowly strengthening his intelligence network.

His minions were young Chechens, Ossetians and other tribal peoples from the Caucasus. Forcibly removed from their lands by Stalin, these ethnic groups hated the Russians and were easy to manipulate. And of course, he paid them well from profits in the black markets.

Then he studiously had cultivated his friendship and influence with Yuri Andropov, Chief of the KGB, and had been appointed a member of the Collegium, the ruling body that controlled all government decisions. He smiled with satisfaction at the hierarchy he had created. Andropov and his KGB controlled Brezhnev while he had built a secret power base under the KGB chief's nose.

Over these years his men had infiltrated every department of Russian intelligence and were waiting for his orders. His heart pounded as he looked again at this confession, major intelligence needed for the mission's success. The casket soon would be in his hands, but he must temper his excitement and wait for the right moment for the call to action.

In the short time since he had become aware of the casket's existence, he had activated his clandestine personnel in Department Four of Foreign Intelligence. Known as The First Chief Directive, it was charged with the task of infiltrating Russian émigré organizations. Then he had resurrected the illegals. His spies had been placed years ago in western countries and lived undercover, assuming normal lives as citizens.

His last command would be issued to Department V, the high security section which prepared plans for assassination and sabotage in the event of war. But in this extreme case, Department V would be turned against the Politburo of the Soviet Union, eliminating all the members.

"Now we have entered life in death," he murmured, looking out at Moscow's silent streets piled with dirty snow, hiding the bodies of the homeless who had frozen to death. There was none of the chaos of the revolution or the brutal purges of Stalin; it was a society standing still, awaiting death. It had become obvious to him that no one believed any longer in the Soviet Union's march toward a Socialist paradise; and the trickle of KGB officers defecting to the West had become a gusher.

At a recent meeting of the KGB *eminence grise*, the Collegium, Andropov had asked why people always wanted to defect to the West and why western agents did not want to come to Russia. He looked bewildered, more like a retired professor than someone who wielded the power of life and death over the citizens of the Soviet Union.

The Raven knew Andropov was out of touch as the Collegium formalized plans to offer defectors a tempting lifestyle. It was obvious they would fail. Who would want to come live here?

Corruption was even more rampant than before. The average person stood in line for hours every day for food. There was nothing to buy and nothing to sell unless obtained on the black market, which he controlled. He thought of the country as a dead animal, with those in the power structure like parasites gnawing away at the insides. The organ would soon disintegrate and the country would be plunged into violence and anarchy, ready for him to step in.

Snapping a small switch, he ordered the driver down Ulitsa Prechistenka. Disgusted by the change of street names to honor dubious Bolshevik heroes, he persisted in using those from his youth.

The driver nodded nervously, looking away from the rear view mirror, alarmed that the car had skidded wildly on the slush and he was forced to swing the wheel back to steady it.

But the Raven was not aware of Nikita's mistake. One of his old family palaces, confiscated in early years by the Soviet state loomed in front of him. He signaled the driver to stop near the entrance. Nikita opened the door and he stepped out at the gate, oblivious to the freezing slush creeping around his boots.

He stared at the pastel yellow mansion, remembering a party given for him by his parents when he had joined his regiment.

For a brief moment he saw her, as she was that night at the party. It was still painful to remember. She had possessed incomparable grace and intelligence, conformed to his exacting ideal. He had fallen hopelessly in love; he had thought it was forever. Now there was barely a glimmer of recognition of what loving her had been like. After her betrayal, only anger and hatred remained, festering. He quelled his sudden impulse to step inside the mansion to recapture that moment, knowing he would be depressed at the faded grandeur. Over the years the neglected mansion, now some government office, had lost its beauty. Its elaborate, but peeling, shutters closed it off from the world. It had fallen into ruin.

He climbed into the car, quickly closing the curtain, and as they drove to the Arbat district, the liveliest part of Moscow, he reflected on his search for the Tsar's casket. It had begun in 1918 in the civil war during his interrogation of a White Russian officer. The tortured man had spouted information about the casket, the Box of the Harpuiai. It was completely irrelevant to the intelligence the Cheka were seeking, but it confirmed certain rumors he had heard, and had sent him on a quest, which became an obsession.

In the last few years, reconciled to his failure to find the box, he had planned to defect, to abscond with highly classified files, and spend his last days in Western luxury.

Then fate intervened with the recent newspaper clippings, which corroborated other evidence that the casket still existed and presented him with a more exciting alternative than defection. Tomorrow he would meet with his agent, groomed for the mission and give the orders.

His lips twitched in a smile. It was ironic that with all the high tech equipment and armaments that governments possessed, his new regime would be built on a secret treasure hidden long ago, out of the reach of even the most efficient modern intelligence agencies.

This new intelligence was not exclusive to him. Before this was over there would have to be interrogations and then, the inevitable *Chistka*, the cleansing or purging of those who know. It was his strict policy to eliminate anyone who recognized him from the past or who could have any knowledge of his mission. He never veered from this rule. *"Chistka,"* he whispered. It was a beautiful word, even the sound of it made everything pure. Finally, he would have his revenge on her.

He pushed a button and spoke softly, giving the order. Then to his own bewilderment, he was overcome with sadness and collapsed into the far corner of the seat, thinking of his last sight of his old friend.

Chapter 42

New Jersey: 1970

COULD THE RAVEN be alive or was it just my imagination that conjured him? The picture stayed with me after I turned off the shower. I quickly dried off with the threadbare towel, put on my flannel pajamas taken from my apartment, a reminder of when life was normal, and climbed into the bed with the Pushkin book. It was hard to concentrate with the picture of the Raven floating in my head and I could not help glancing at the door and listening for footsteps outside. Jack was in the room next door protecting me, so I tried to get a grip on myself and collect my disparate thoughts.

In spite of any danger I was determined to press on until I discovered what had happened to Madame A. I had given her my word to help Sergei when the time came, and she trusted me. At the moment, my only recourse was to return to the book.

When Jack had arrived unexpectedly in Quogue, I had stopped reading at the point when Sergei became ill. It skipped to the next year. The traffic roar grew faint as I began to read.

June 12, 1919

Sergei is sleeping now and I write again, if only to myself, to try to fill the deep silence. I watch the long path in front of the house and wait for the doctor, for Peter or Dimitri or Andrei. Annushka and I and poor dear

Sergei have been living here for weeks. The house, an elegant wooden villa, built by a mining millionaire seems set apart, untouched by the war and the world of violence that we have left. The paint on the wooden house, once a subtle blue, is cracked and fading adding a romantic charm. There is a small domed turret at the very top of the house with a little walk, so that one can see for miles across the flat plain. I climb the stairs to the tower in the morning and at dusk to avoid the Siberian heat, and watch the winding dusty road that leads to the deserted small village some miles away.

Annushka wanders through the thick and overgrown garden that hides us from the rare passer-by. She is grave, hardly speaks, and spends many hours sitting beside Sergei's bed. She insists that Sergei is still sad because of the poor woman and the horse and that there is nothing we can do to make him happy again. I refuse to believe her. What can a child know?

When Sergei fell ill, we were forced to leave the luxury of the train, the good food, and the victory celebrations. It wasn't concern over Sergei that has led us here, but worries that he would spread the disease to others in the train, although Dr. Ushakov was not certain that it was typhus, which is killing people by the thousands. It cannot be that, although I don't know what his illness is. I have kept the children free from lice that cause the disease. Before I left the train, I received the medicine from the courier. It was most important. Peter brought us here and said he would return, but weeks have passed.

The next entry, undated, was scrawled, untidy, although I still recognized Madame A's handwriting.

It is too late, too late. My heart is broken. We struggle to dig the grave. Poor Annushka does not weep. She watches me uneasily. She blames me, suspects me, something she overheard.

I stared at the stained walls of the motel room. Could this mean her son was dead?

Annushka is angry, but what could I do? I had to take the poor child in. My dear brother Andrei came to us dressed in rags carrying the boy who was bleeding heavily from a wound. The boy is tall, emaciated, with even features and blue eyes. Andrei claimed he found him by the road. I tended to his wounds, bathed him, put him to bed. Andrei said only that he was caught in the middle of battle, but I knew. Annushka was very unhappy. I admonished her, said we should try to help others.

The boy doesn't seem to see anything around him. Whatever has happened to him has made him an empty husk. In spite of my sorrow, I am overjoyed at seeing my dearest brother; that he survived. He would not say where he was going and asked me to keep his visit secret. There is crisis; the Red Army has advanced across the Urals and the Whites are in retreat. Andrei then revealed my true mission and commanded me to help the cause. This was what the Druzhina had planned when they asked me to join them, when they marked me with the heart of Buddha. I am distraught and beg him to tell me who knows my secret. I have told no one.

What the Druzhina ask of me is very dangerous. I do not think it is coincidence, an accident of fate, as Andrei claims, but I must obey, fulfill my part in the mission. Annushka horrified, refused. It was only after Andrei warned that our lives would be in danger that I agreed, although I don't understand everything. Andrei has lost all contact with Peter who did not return. I fear the worst.

Andrei arranged for our return to Omsk. I am back at Kolchak's headquarters. Many dispatches sent to allies to try to counter Red advance. There is panic everywhere. I live in constant fear that Annushka will speak, but everyone who knew the children has fled farther East to Vladivostok. I have grown to love the boy. He speaks little but smiles often and depends on me. Andrei ordered me never to question him. It is too dangerous.

My dear brother and the children now know everything. It is all for the Brotherhood.

I stopped, mystified, trying to construct meaning from her words. Could it be that Madame A's son died, and another boy was brought to her, and she had managed to save his life? I heard heavy footsteps outside my motel window and a murmur of conversation. I listened closely. They were speaking Russian. Two large shadows loomed on the wall. I clutched the book and dropped down on the floor behind the bed, holding my breath, Ms. Springsmith's torture flashing through my mind. There was the sound of someone running, breathing hard and then the muffled explosive noise of gunshots.

Jack burst into the room and found me crouched on the floor.

"Are you all right?" He helped me to my feet.

"Yes," I said, staggering, hardly able to stand, "Who was it? Were they after me?" I knew the answer.

He nodded, breathing hard. "I think I wounded two of them. They won't be back tonight, but we have to move you tomorrow."

Then, as though the action had released some feeling in him, he held me gently. I curled up like a child beside him on the bed. When he drew me to him, the thrill, the sweetness was unbearable. I could not locate where I was as he moved over me. And then I was standing at the end of the quarry in hot sun. I felt a wild rush as I dived, stepping away into free fall, whirling with ecstasy into space. My body felt him, like the touch of wind and I opened my legs in wild astonishment, as I plunged into the deep. He was with me, carrying me along on the wind on the long slide down. I abandoned myself.

Chapter 43

Ohio: 2000

BEYOND THE CABIN I hear a rustle in the dry leaves and grip the shotgun waiting for the predator to step into the clearing, but there is nothing. From the dense forest the distant cry of a wolf pierces the air. The dog whimpers and paces the porch.

The howl of loneliness stabs at me, bringing back my loss. Sometimes I remember only how I gazed upon Jack, my lover, momentarily shutting out all that happened afterward. I look out at the clear sky, at the moon gleaming through the branches of bare trees and try to picture him, to remember his exact words, although I remind myself that memory turns words into what we want to believe. Did he say, 'I love you? I'll come for you'? My desperate unaccountable love for a man I hardly knew began in those few moments. Its intensity surpassed anything I could have imagined and still, after all these years, distorts my vision of him.

New Jersey: 1970

Jack stayed with me that night in the motel room, and I slept intertwined with his body. Sometime before morning I dreamed one picture, like a flash photo. A lone man is trudging in the snow on the vast Siberian Plain. I watch warily, not knowing his intentions. I struggle to see his face.

When I woke Jack was gone. I showered and dressed and hurried to the motel diner next door. It was empty. Because of past experience I couldn't help worrying that he had abandoned me. The lone waitress, a plump young girl with a round cheerful face, showed me to a booth beside the window. Her long skirt and white blouse were designed along with the plastic wagon wheels decorating the entrance to create the pioneer atmosphere.

I wondered miserably if my fate was to spend my life in motel rooms, eating in places like the fake homestead restaurant. Finding little on the menu that appealed, I looked out at the car park and saw Jack with his arm around a pretty dark haired woman. They were engrossed in an intent conversation. She was wearing a fashionable suit and high heels. Feeling ugly and unkempt in my jeans and braided hair, I shrank back in the booth, hoping they hadn't seen me. He looked toward the restaurant, sensing he was being watched. Before I turned away, I saw him laugh.

When he joined me at the table, he leaned over and kissed me. A rush of love and relief that he had not deserted me swept over me like a jet stream, making me quite dizzy.

"Was that the person shooting last night?" I asked, knowing it wasn't her.

"No," he laughed, as though the gunshots were nothing. "I don't know who they were. I'm still checking."

I moved closer to him for comfort.

He said, "That was Sarah, my friend from archives. She dropped off some information faxed from DC before driving on to work. But the files are so old, it's practically useless."

He held up an official looking folder. "Not much here, a few profiles. She's still digging around. What remains of intelligence from the early 1900's is totally unorganized. There is one interesting thing, but let's order breakfast first."

He put the folder on the seat, motioned the round-faced waitress over, and ordered the combination, pancakes, sausages, and eggs. She said they had no yoghurt or fresh fruit, so I drank my coffee and ate a piece of toast. Jack concentrated on his food in silence while I stared out at the parking strip in front of the motel where the killers had stalked my room. This

morning the place seemed less menacing. A woman and her two small children sat down in the next booth and for a moment, it all seemed normal. I
thought about the last time anything had seemed normal.

After he finished eating Jack took out some old discolored papers
from the file. "This report seems irrelevant, but was so odd I thought I'd
show it to you, just in case you might remember something Madame A
said."

Sidney Reilly, a British agent in Russia during the revolution had written this report.

"Reilly, called the Ace of Spies, was famous in intelligence circles. We
know from reliable sources that he was involved in a number of missions to
overthrow the Bolsheviks and put the Tsar back on the throne," Jack said,
watching me while I read the report, dated September 1919.

*At the time of the reported execution of the Tsar and his family, July 16–17
1918, one of the leaders of the Cheka circulated the legend that the entire
family had been murdered. This story was so pervasive and convincing that
the majority of the Russian population, the émigrés and the remainder of the
Romanov family believed it, with the exception of the Dowager Empress
Marie, mother of Nicholas II. Only three agents were aware that this legend
had been devised as part of the plot to save the family.*

*The legend eventually may have become the truth. With the exception of pre-
tenders, none of the Tsar's family has appeared after that night. Concurrently
the Bolsheviks also put out the story that some of the Romanovs survived.
Before the Romanovs vanished the Bolsheviks were using them as pawns in
negotiations with the Germans and Allies. Lenin secretly was given large
amounts in ransom to enable rescuers to save the family.*

*The Bolshevik government took great pleasure in deceiving and confusing their
enemies; it became the policy of the state to lie. None of their reports can be
believed.*

I handed the paper back to him thinking maybe only the creator of the
macabre murder album had known what occurred that night in Ipatiev house.

"The Cheka spy who created this legend is mentioned only briefly and then not by his real name, only his nom de revolution. Can you believe it's the Raven, the same man who interrogated Turev? There isn't much in the files about him. The few notes reveal that his real identity is not known, that he might have been an intelligence officer who worked for the Okhrana as an agent provocateur before the revolution. He then switched loyalties to the Cheka during the civil war."

"Can it be? We know he was some kind of commissar, but what is an agent provocateur?" I asked, my pulse racing at this new information.

"The Okhrana perfected this role. These agents played both sides, and often instigated operations against the Tsar's government to incriminate and jail revolutionaries who became involved in their plots," he said.

"After the Bolshevik takeover their secret police, the Cheka, adopted this same technique and employed many former Okhrana agents. Even Stalin is suspected of working for the Okhrana in his early years as a revolutionary. If this is true, this Raven worked with both Lenin and Stalin in the early days."

He shuffled through the pile of papers while the waitress brought more coffee. "There's one report that the Raven disappeared after the civil war, maybe in one of Stalin's purges. He could have had many identities."

He paused and drank some coffee then flicked a match with his thumb and lit up a cigarette. "I thought Madame A might have mentioned this man to you."

"No, I only heard of him when I spoke to the baron and we interviewed Turev," I said.

"In the past year we have had indications that someone in the upper echelons of Soviet intelligence wants to defect, but on his own terms. It's highly unusual. The man seems to have real power and access to highly secret channels, but we have no name. We are searching archives, but it's highly improbable that this man is the Raven.

"Stories circulated that the Romanov family was alive in late 1918 and this Raven could have decided to capitalize on them, taking money from the monarchists on the pretext of conducting a search for the family. Regardless of what happened then, the accepted story is that the

Tsar and his family were murdered in the early morning of July 17, 1918."

I said nothing more, but was now convinced of one chilling fact; the Raven was alive.

Chapter 44

New Jersey: 1970

JACK PAID THE check and waited for me at the cashier's desk. "Are you ok? You look a little pale," he said, his face unusually soft with concern. "I know you're scared. Don't worry, we're moving to another place."

"I'm used to being scared now. I was just thinking about that report from the old archives," I said.

Actually, I had been agonizing about how stupid I had been last night, to leave myself so open to hurt.

Jack drove farther into New Jersey and pulled up at the Excelsior Motel, a bleak stucco building with water stains like rusty tears running down its side. I could see it would not live up to its name.

"This is it," he said, and then noting my expression, gave me a hug. "It's not so bad."

When he returned to my room after checking in, he locked the door and pulled me close, removing my jacket, my sweater and jeans, my bra and panties in a very efficient manner. I stood before him, naked, vulnerable.

"Take down your hair." His voice was rough.

As I slowly unwound my braids, I pictured Madame A on the train taking down her hair for her mystery lover. Then we were on the bed and as he moved across me, I closed my eyes in the pulsating warmth and again

I was on the edge of the quarry, only this time I was falling, not diving, and I rolled over and over with him, landing in some vast unknown territory.

Hungry for each other, we continued our passionate affair hardly leaving the room, for several days that seemed to merge into one. I had surrendered unconditionally. My past memories were laid waste, and Lawrence seemed hardly to have existed. All I knew or wanted was Jack.

The last day he leaned over me and said he had been away too long and had to go to his office to check in.

"Where is your office? Do you have to go into Manhattan?" I sat up.

He didn't answer me. While he was getting dressed, he said it was too dangerous for me to go out, even to the motel restaurant. Before he left he brought me a thermos of coffee and sandwiches. I hated being shut up in the room, but was too proud to ask him to take me with him.

After he closed the door I sat forlornly behind the closed curtains, feeling helpless, waiting even though he hadn't said when he would return. It was cool outside, but the small room with poor ventilation seemed like a prison cell. The air-conditioner ran constantly, and had begun clanking as though about to break down. In the rackety noise, I imagined I heard, whispered over and over, *Chernaya Robata*, 'black work', the sinister words the KGB used for murder. This phrase became mixed up with strains of the tango and the image of Soso slowing dancing toward me.

This was unbearable. I was scaring myself. I had to control my mind. I hurried to the bathroom and splashed cold water on my face to wash it all away. Then I poured a cup of coffee from the thermos and opened the Pushkin book. There were longer intervals of time between the journal entries and they were written in a hurry, the pages torn and some not even dated.

September 1919

Omsk. Have returned with the children and am again working at the Stavka, Kolchak's headquarters. Panic and confusion everywhere. When I left because of Sergei's illness, the White Armies had advanced toward Kazan and Moscow, past Ekaterinburg and Perm across the Urals, but at the end of July the Red

Army had crossed the Urals, driving the Whites back. Many here have already fled east to Vladivostok, knowing the end is coming.

Madame Timireva, Admiral Kolchak's mistress, found us a room in an old rundown hotel. I am devoted to her. There is little heat and we carry water from a pump in the courtyard, but we are lucky to have the place to ourselves. The children stay alone during the day, and in the evenings I try to occupy them with lessons. The boy is recovering, although he shouts out in his sleep and cries.

I have heard through headquarters that General Turev, retreating on his train near Perm, was captured along with his wife. No news since.

A General Kosloff, head of a secret intelligence unit, has arrived with bad news. He reported directly to Admiral Kolchak that the Reds are advancing upon us at 27 miles per day. His agents have intelligence that members of the Brotherhood have been captured and murdered by the Cheka who always arrive ahead of the Red troops to arrest any White sympathizers. I often am overcome with grief and have to force myself to work.

Kosloff claims he was in Ekaterinburg and Perm when the Whites took control and discovered that the Romanovs had vanished. Tells a strange story; there were several plots to rescue the Tsar and his family, and that one attempt might have been successful. He hints that an agent posing as a guard infiltrated Ipatiev House, and bribes, a great amount of gold, were given to the soldiers.

Kosloff heard the family were taken to Perm by the Whites and hidden there until someone betrayed them. He has no way of knowing if any of them escaped. He will not say more. Kosloff is very friendly and realizing I am worried about loved ones, tries to comfort me, but I am suspicious that he would confide in me. What could he want? He looks at me as though he wants to speak about something. I ignore this; no one can be trusted.

October 1919

It is a miracle. My brother Andrei survived and is here. He fears Dimitri is dead, murdered by a Cheka agent. They discovered he was the leader of the resistance, the Bogatyr. I grieve for him and feel I did not value his love. I close my eyes remembering how he had come to me on the train and made love to me. He saved us.

Andrei does not know what has happened to Peter. He was not at the meeting place. He says there is a traitor among us and I must not trust anyone, even dear friends. He brought the secret to me. I now know everything. If the Cheka discover that I am hiding it, they will hunt us down and kill the children and me. They destroy anyone who knows. Sometimes I close my eyes and see the graceful carved figures of the Harpies, with their wild hair, half human, ready to claw me to death.

On the stained motel wall, I seemed to see weird shadows of the Harpies dancing, clawing the air and recalled the description of the casket in the Von Grubov newspaper article. Now I knew.

The object of beauty that terrified Madame A was the Box of the Harpuiai, supposedly lost since the revolution. The casket was in her possession while she was in Siberia.

Chapter 45

New Jersey: 1970

I HURRIED TO the window to check the parking lot, empty except
for the manager's car, went to the bathroom and again splashed cold water
over my face, but it did nothing to calm my growing fear. I turned back to
the Pushkin book, knowing there was more to this story.

November 1919

> *We are evacuating Omsk and travelling with Admiral Kolchak's staff.
> Kosloff's scouts report the Red Army will be here in two days. I want to flee
> with the children and my burden, but Admiral Kolchak refuses to leave until
> the very end. I cannot abandon the admiral and Madame Timireva, my dear
> friend.*

> *Russia's Gold Reserve has been packed in seven railway cars. I think it is
> dangerous to travel with the gold bars, said to be worth millions, but the ad-
> miral believes it still gives his government power and is a bargaining chip.
> Kosloff, who is going with us, brings us furs and provisions. He knows there
> will be a shortage of fuel on the way. I have prepared the children for the long
> journey, but the boy is unaware, still in a trance.*

We left only hours before the Red Army entered the city. Have been busy drafting messages and receiving them. Kosloff sometimes stays with the children. I forbid them to look out the train windows and have drawn the blinds. For alongside the rails, on the trakt, of the great Siberian way, thousands of refugees flee east through several feet of snow. Some reach out to us, beseeching us. It is horrifying to witness such suffering and not be able to help. In the snow and cold, remnants of the army, families, children, some on sleds, some walking, move past the window in waves, like subjects in a moving picture of hell, blood the only color in the stark landscape of suffering. Huge black birds perch along the way, watching indifferently.

December 1919

Czechs have put our train on the down line that has been clogged for weeks. We have no fuel, and there is hostility toward us at the stations brought on because the Kolchak government did not pay the stationmasters. We have not moved for six weeks. Fear and hopelessness pervades. Drunken, frightened men, brawling and debauched, dressing in women's clothes, unspeakable acts in front of everyone. We hide in the cabin. Kosloff and I play chess with the children.

Kolchak and Timireva rarely emerge from their cabin, but conduct themselves with dignity. I once entered their carriage to give him a message. The door was open. They were unaware of me. I glimpsed them lying side by side, and saw her reach up, caressing his face. The gesture of love and devotion saddens me. We send pleading telegrams, messages to the Czechs, the Allies, General Janin, but no answers.

Admiral Kolchak has been arrested, and we have been moved to one second class carriage going to Irkutsk. I still send messages, hoping to get through to the Allies.

February 1920

Czech soldiers warned us that it would be disaster to stay with the admiral. We have been on the run since the Irkutsk government captured Kolchak's train. Today I learned the admiral has been executed. Madame Timireva is still at Irkutsk. Since I fled the Kolchak train, I keep the shabby bag holding my dangerous secret under my dress and covered with my shawl and fur cloak. We now wait in the icy cold of Nizhne Vdinsk station, crowded with other desperate refugees fleeing east. There have been no trains for days. I write to keep sane.

Late February 1920

While waiting at Nizhne Vdinsk for the train to Harbin, we were captured by a Red Army unit, and herded with others away from the station into town and down a dark cellar in the police station. After two women, wife and daughter of a local merchant were led up the stairs, I heard pleading, then gunshots. The children huddled against me in the freezing cold, but then were taken from me screaming. I prayed that they would be spared. I was in terror that the Cheka knew all about me.

Light blinded me as they pushed me up the stairs. Someone was calling to me. I felt myself falling.

These notes were ripped and pasted in haphazardly as though Madame A had only a few moments before the book would be discovered.

Peter looked down at me. He was dressed like a commissar in leather coat and high shining boots. He kissed me gently and anticipating my question told me the children were resting in the next room. We were safe. Filled with a wild joy and relief. I thought I never would see him again. I threw myself into his arms. He said he had convinced the Cheka that jailing or killing him was detrimental to their cause.

He had known of our location for some time because he had been working with the Brotherhood. Then his face seemed covered in shadow and he whispered that the Cheka had arrested all those involved in the plot, just as Kosloff had told me.

I asked if the others could be alive. He said he had little hope, that the police were merciless with traitors. Interrogations were brutal. The prisoners would reveal all, even my part in the plot. His words seemed like a threat. He claimed that he had avoided suspicion. They had let him go.

Andrei had told me there was a traitor, to trust no one. In a moment that broke my heart, I sensed Peter was lying to me.

I couldn't believe he was guilty of betraying the Druzhina. We were his friends from childhood. But when I looked up at his beautiful face, I knew that it was true.

I asked him what would happen to us. He smiled and said we would return to Petersburg and would live with him. He said I would be protected.

I realized with horror that the children and I were his prisoners and that if he tired of me he would have us arrested. Destroy us. I couldn't let him see that the attraction I once felt for him had turned to fear and hatred. It is obvious he doesn't know about Andrei's visits or that I have the precious object in my possession. I am terrified that he will recognize the boy who cowers and trembles when he comes near, and will not look at him. I explain that he is very ill and keep him in bed. If only Dimitri were still alive, he would save us.

The traffic noise faded and I seemed in another place and time as I read over her words, soaked in panic, crazy with fear. Peter, her friend from childhood, her lover, was the traitor. There was no date for the next entry.

Must try not to show my revulsion when my captor wants to make love, do not know if he is convinced I still love him. His beautiful face now seems mocking, a mask of hatred. He works for them, the secret police, the torturers. We are with him in his headquarters and at night hear screams from the jail next door. I am exhausted with worry that Annushka will reveal accidentally what she knows. She was so happy at first to see her Uncle Peter, but I have warned her. It is a terrible burden for a young girl.

I have made progress with the boy using my healing skills. He is uncomprehending of much around him. His appearance is slightly different from my son's, but I have convinced Peter that the boy is Sergei and the changes in him are a result of illness

Last night Peter caressed me and said that I had betrayed him with Dimitri and that I was a deceitful whore. He had known from the beginning that Dimitri was the Bogatyr, and mockingly recited the verse about the Bogatyr, one I knew from childhood.

'He fixed a tempered arrow,
And drew his silken bow-strings;
He shot at Nightingale the Robber
Putting out his right eye from its socket
Nightingale fell to the damp earth.'

His embrace became a vise, but I would not give him the pleasure of crying out. He said it is all reversed from our childhood fantasies. The Bogatyr has fallen to the damp earth and he the Nightingale lives on. His next words left me shivering.

"I could not use Nightingale as a nom de revolution. It sounds too tame, does not resonate with the proletariat. I chose a more sinister bird, The Raven."

I put the book down, trying to absorb these last incredible notes. Peter von Krantz, her lover, was the Raven. Her terror seemed to leap from the page. He could take her back to Moscow and put her on trial as a spy, shut her away in prison, kill her.

The Raven put us under guard on a train to the East, telling me he would soon come for us. I hid the objects with Annushka and the boy. The landscape from the train window became a blur in my terror. We are now across the Russian border, in Harbin, Manchuria. Russians have lived here for many years, and it is like stepping back in the past, into a part of

Petersburg. The guard who accompanied us on the train has fled to Shanghai, and mercifully I am free of him, the Raven. Must get away from him forever.

We have been here some months, but have no money to get to Vladivostok and escape from him. Each day I wake sick with panic that he will come.

Tomorrow I meet with a man connected to Chang Tso-lin, the warlord who rules Manchuria. This man is also an acquaintance of Ataman Semenov who has agreed to get me a pass to Japan and has written me an introduction.

I met my Chinese employer at the Hotel Moderne. He was dressed in silken robes and had a long drooping moustache and fingernails like knives. He is called the Mandarin, and is notorious for badly treating the Russian women who work for him. I do not care, am determined to do what he wishes, anything to get away.

Harbin, Manchuria 1921

The Raven traced me to the Hotel Moderne, where I often meet clients. He has many aliases, and presently goes by Victor Matsev. As we sat drinking wine, I trying my best to look bright and happy, he suddenly laughed uproariously and said he had killed Dimitri, that he was a fool. He said sarcastically that it was for the cause. I lowered my head, and gripped my sides, thinking my body would fall apart with grief. It seemed a miracle when Kosloff suddenly appeared at our table, surprised and delighted that I had survived. He knows something is wrong and wants to help me, but it is too late.

The Raven has ordered us to be ready to leave for Petersburg within the next few days. I must escape tonight to Vladivostok. The Mandarin has entertainment houses here in Harbin and in Vladivostok, employing Russian woman as prostitutes. I needed to work two months for passage to Vladivostok, but he said I would be worn out too soon and not worth much. He bargained with me for our lives.

It was dear little Annushka that he wanted, accepted in payment for our escape. Her screams echoing down the hall when they took her will haunt me forever. Is survival like this better than death? It was one night, but then there are all those other nights when she cries out with pain. Even though we are safe, still she wakes, pleading for me to save her. These are the choices one has to make. There is stillness in her eyes as though she is dead. When she was carried back from the Mandarin's rooms she said, 'You let them do this, hurt me to save him.' She pointed at the boy, who cowered in the corner.

'No Annushka,' I said. 'It was for you to escape.'

Vladivostok

As we sailed from the harbor, Annushka was very ill, and using my skills I was able to stop the bleeding. There was no comfort. I could not rest. I desperately wanted to kill myself by jumping overboard, but the children would have been left without anyone to care for them. I learned that the Raven searched for us for weeks in Harbin. After that, he disappeared from my life. There were rumors that he was shot down in Siberia by a desperate White officer. All of the Druzhina are gone, down that long corridor of death that was Siberia.

The journal ended on this grim note, although I suspected there was more that she chose to withhold from the reader. I believed the journal was the truth. This was the worst of the secrets that Madame A carried with her. A shiver of revulsion passed through me. A ten-year-old child was forced to submit to the cruel sexual needs of the Mandarin to save her family and to protect some valuable secret. Poor Anna managed in some ways to rise above what happened to her. I now understood why she had been so fearful, angry and cold to everyone and why Madame A tried so hard to placate her. Her wailing cries as she left her apartment for the last time now took on a more sinister meaning.

The motel was deadly quiet. Frazzled, edgy, I started at the sound of the key turning in my lock and the door opening and looked behind me. Jack came into the room looking apologetic.

"Where have you been?" My shriek hung in the air over the sound of the air-conditioning.

"Sit down," he said, moving me toward the edge of the bed.

"Nadya Antonova is dead. Her body was dumped near the tunnel entrance. She was strangled with her own net stocking. Her colleagues," he smiled grimly, "couldn't identify the car or the driver."

Chapter 46

New Jersey–New York: 1970

I SANK INTO melancholy at the news of Nadya's death, remembering her sad face breaking into a smile as she waved at me. It seemed to lend inevitability to my own murder. Jack put his arms around me, and reading my thoughts said it was unlikely her murder was connected with the case, but I wasn't convinced.

"I hate this place. I want to go home."

"Get ready. We're getting out for a while," he said.

My mood lifted. For the first time in weeks, I was doing something normal, having dinner with someone in a restaurant. To others at the surrounding tables we must have looked like an ordinary young couple. But I knew I was living on the edge. I had washed my hair and pulled it up in a chignon, put on my one good sweater and my jeans. Jack wore his black leather jacket and a dark blue sweater. No one could see the gun that bulged slightly from the shoulder holster under his jacket. He did not look like a cop and I tried to forget everything but being here with him.

"This is great," I said, taking a sip of wine. We were sitting at Sloppy Louie's across from the fish market and New York's old seaport. The restaurant with its crooked floors and rickety chairs and tables covered with red checked tablecloths was crowded for a Tuesday night.

From our cozy table Jack continued to watch the car, parked across the street underneath the black steel girders of an abandoned highway.

He turned to look at me. "You needed a break. Hiding out in a motel room is no fun."

"How do you know I'm safe here?"

"Don't for sure, but they wouldn't think you'd leave the hideout to eat at Sloppy Louie's."

"Hm. Probably," I said, with a twinge of fear.

"I want to apologize for treating you badly." His voice was hesitant; he didn't like apologizing.

"I know I've been hard on you. In spite of everything I liked you from the first." He looked a bit embarrassed.

I had the outrageous thought that he might be keeping me in custody not only to protect me, but also because he cared for me.

"You had a strange way of showing your affection," I said.

"It's just that I didn't expect you to be the way you are."

"What do you mean?"

"The reports led me to believe you were some spoiled society bitch."

"I guess you could think that." I couldn't keep the anger out of my voice. I knew he had information on me, but I burned with resentment at this mention of reports.

"And it isn't true. You seem wholesome, a little old-fashioned." His apologetic grin was irresistible.

"Thanks a lot. You probably think I preserve my own vegetables on the weekends."

He ignored this and took my hand; it felt lost in his large grip.

"I fought liking you, knowing that there was no future in it."

"I understand." I sank back into my chair. "You're against forming a relationship with a divorcee."

"It's not that." He stared out at the street. "Since I returned from Nam, I've been a mess, a disaster with women."

"You seem to be doing ok with Zoe." My voice was tinged with sarcasm.

"We weren't into anything long term. I'm strictly a loner."

"Don't you have family?" I was beginning to feel sorry for him.

"My parents were emigrants. They died when I was two. My two older brothers raised me. We lived in Hell's Kitchen in the Irish community. Both of my brothers were cops, good cops, but they wanted something better for me. So off I went, no argument, to college, helped by a football scholarship, but law school was postponed by Vietnam. I was drafted before the lottery."

"Oh, I see," I said, surprised that he had opened up to me.

"No, you really don't see." He stopped for a moment while the waiter took our order.

A dark look passed over his face. "Too many things happened. Too many innocents were killed. I saw guys fry their brains on dope. I was one of them. And when I came back, both my brothers, the only family I had, were gone. Cal was ill before I left and died of cancer while I was in Nam. Jimmy was shot by a crack head."

I wanted to say something sympathetic, but couldn't think of anything that didn't sound stupid. He was wrapped up in his story, living all the bitterness again.

He took a drink of his wine. "I didn't go to law school, but got clean and joined the force." He hadn't mentioned alcohol, and I thought again of the night he accosted me in the hall and used the excuse that he was drunk.

"Why didn't you go back to law school?"

He shrugged his shoulders, "Real reason? I couldn't do without violence. I could beat up sleaze bags, dealers. Only you know that."

I have never been good at hiding my feelings and drew back with a look of horror.

"Sorry, I shouldn't have gone on about this," he said.

"No, it's ok. I wanted to hear it. I want to know everything about you."

"You know, you're the first woman who's interested me for a long time," he said.

I didn't know what to say, wondering if he really meant it.

"I have tried to figure out what it is about you. You are beautiful in a way." His eyes studied me.

"Thank you," I said, not sure if that was really a compliment.

"But it's your honesty, and your belief in people, that they will do the right thing that I love. It is a rare quality, missing in my world." His face softened and for once did not seem so intent, so watchful.

I had never thought of myself in this way, and had believed I was naïve rather than so honest.

The waiter brought our dinner of soft-shelled crab, salad, and fries. I was grateful for the interruption. We ate in silence and when we finished, he sat back, took a match from his pocket, flicked it into flame with his thumbnail and lit a cigarette. There was something disturbing in the expert way he flicked the match.

"How did you end up married to Digby? It doesn't figure."

"Do you know Lawrence?" I was stunned, put off guard by his question and stared around the room at the other tables for a moment.

"No, only what I read in the gossip columns and in the reports. But how did you get into that situation? Files don't tell me that." He was looking at me with narrowed eyes, coldly sizing me up again.

"I wonder now myself. It all seems so far away, unlikely," I said, knowing I sounded nervous. "It wasn't all bad. At least I met Abigail, who is really a good friend."

He laughed. "She has almost as bad taste in men as you."

I could feel myself blushing, the red creeping up my neck. He must know everything about me, and my friends. Now that I had slept with him, he knew the intimate part of me too.

"Lawrence and I are from the same part of the state. He was taking some summer courses at the university. I met him in a bookshop."

"But to marry a guy like that without knowing it. Or did you know?"

I hated his questions, which seemed to imply there was something wrong with me.

"I'd rather not talk about it." I added lamely, "We were happy together for a while." I felt hot, a little sick.

I stammered on, unable to stop myself, "It was pretty awful for me after the divorce. I was very unhappy when I moved into the apartment building. That part of my life seems remote and trivial compared to the horrible things that have happened." My voice choked.

He reached over and patted me on the shoulder. "Let's go."

I rose, still angry at his prying questions. Even though Lawrence meant nothing to me now, it was none of his business.

"Sorry I upset you," he said.

"When will this be over? I really only care about Madame A. Now that we think she's gone for good, this just seems dangerous. I never expected to be hiding out in motels forever. Are you any closer to finding the killers?" I stood by the table, shivering, the fear returning.

"We'll be making arrests soon," he said as he paid the check. "It's important that we get in touch with Sergei. He may be in real danger. We'll start early tomorrow."

We walked quickly across the dark street to the car.

"Do you know what Sergei is like?" I said.

"Yah, we did a sweep on him after contacting the local police."

I persisted. "He has mental problems and should be treated gently. Madame A claimed it was the trauma from his experiences during the revolution."

"The local police did mention he was a nut case. They lost track of him. Our men have been searching for days, but can't find a trace of the old man."

"Sergei told me a man had been looking for him, and that he was going to hide." I was relieved that he couldn't see my face in the dark.

"Did he say where?" He opened the car door for me, all the while looking around.

"No, he didn't," I said.

"We tried that freak, Josephus aka Nelson, head of the cult, but no luck. All this mumbo jumbo about Nelson being born in Tibet and having healing powers is pure crap," he said.

On the way back to the motel, my mind was on Sergei. It seemed unfair to tell Jack that Sergei might not be Madame A's son.

As we walked slowly into the motel, I didn't even flinch when Jack took out his gun and surveyed the area. Nothing was normal in my life. When we reached my room, he went in first. Then he returned from inside the door and I was back in his arms.

Chapter 47

Rural Ohio: 2000

I SIT MOTIONLESS on the porch, and try to recapture being with Jack, to feel again the fierce heat. I see myself spread on the grass after my free fall into his arms. The sun pins me to the ground, penetrates my body, spreads it into the earth and fills me with an unbearable intense pleasure. For moments the feeling obliterates all I know about him.

'*Crazy for Loving You*', the phrase from the Patsy Cline song that my dad would sometimes play in the evenings, meanders to me from out in the fields. It fills me with regret and sorrow.

New Jersey: 1970

While Jack slept, I gently traced the scars on his body which he first claimed were football injuries, but tonight when he undressed and saw me staring had said vaguely they were something that happened in Vietnam. I knew he didn't want to talk about them. They zigzagged across his wide muscled back and down his legs and arms, like deep lightning strikes of pain. Although he could have received them from some terrible torture in Vietnam, the thick scar tissue seemed older, like ruins from another time. My last thought before drifting off to sleep was that the scars had come from some violent place alien to me.

Just before I awoke, the same strange dream flickered before me, like an old movie. A man is walking in vast fields of snow. He is dressed in bundles of clothes, his face obscured.

It was late morning when I reached across the bed to Jack and found he was gone. He had left a note on his pillow with orders not to leave the motel and to meet him in the restaurant for lunch.

As the hot water of the shower gushed down on me, the images of Jack and last night faded, replaced by Nadya's crumpled face, mouth open in a wild despairing laugh. I quickly turned off the tap, shivering in spite of the water temperature. Jack had said that Nadya could have been strangled by one of her old customers, her death unrelated to Ms. Springsmith's. I wasn't convinced of this. She said she hadn't been working as a prostitute for years.

Still shivering as I attempted to dry off with the threadbare towel, my thoughts turned to the last terrified entries in the journal describing a frantic Madame A, fleeing Harbin with the children and the casket.

Madame A had believed that the other members of the Druzhina were dead. I pulled on my Levis and a sweater. Could she have discovered the Raven her old lover and enemy was alive before she was taken? The thought made my heart pound.

I finished braiding my hair, put on some lipstick and walked to the restaurant. My heart lifted when I saw him waiting. He came around the table and kissed me, and I knew this was not a casual affair; I was so in love with him I ached inside. This seemed the perfect time for me to tell him everything, to unburden myself, but the words caught in my throat,

After we ordered sandwiches and coffee, he said, "I have more information which shows our investigation is going in the right direction. We found Nicolae Stravsky holed up in Turev's apartment," he said, as though he had expected it.

"General Turev's? I can't believe it."

"Yeah, Turev was lying when he said it was all over. He still thinks Nicolae can help his organization. The old general is a sick man, but can't be trusted and has been checked into a hospital under guard. Nicolae, our KGB man about town, is being held for questioning. At first, he asked for diplomatic immunity, but changed his mind and now wants to defect. Says his life is in danger. That sack of shit, I'd like to be in charge of the interrogation." Jack's eyes turned hard and black, like lumps of coal. His face shut down, expressionless.

"Did you find any of the other men involved?" I said, flinching at his words.

"We're working on it." He stopped when the waitress brought the sandwiches and coffee. He picked up his sandwich, and then put it down.

"Zoe discovered her father was alive when Nicolae gave her the recent photograph of him in prison. She was lured back to Russia in hopes of seeing him. Her father's name was Andrei, but the family often called him Andrusha."

I dropped my cup, splattering coffee across the table. "You can't mean Madame A's brother is alive? He was killed in the late thirties after the civil war. At least Madame A told me so. I am sure she believed he was dead."

The waitress came to wipe the table. "Thanks," I said still stunned.

Then I said, slowly "Nicolae kidnapped Madame A."

"Not the actual kidnapping. He planned it and Zoe helped him set it up. She was told she could rescue her father if she helped them. Whoever ordered the kidnapping promised not to hurt Madame A and Anna."

"But how could Zoe believe these people?" I said.

"She wanted to. She wanted to see her father again."

I remembered her loud argument with Madame A. Although the shouting had been mainly in Russian, Madame A's phrase in English had been clear, insisting that the photograph was a fake. But then later perhaps she examined it more closely and realized that it was of her brother Andrei.

"Nicolae must know everything," I said.

"He claims his orders were issued from someone outside his department, more powerful than the KGB. He was paid to keep quiet."

"Then Zoë's father really is still alive," I said, to confirm this astonishing fact.

"There was proof that Andrei was still in prison in January of this year when his photograph was sent to Zoe. Look at this." he said, taking a photograph from his pocket. I stared at it, wondering if Zoe had given it to him.

An old crippled man with a long matted white beard and hair blinks at the camera in bewilderment. He is not recognizable as the young Andrusha in Madame A's photographs. Next to Andrei, a hand holds up a copy of Pravda with the date January 1970. I could see the man's shadow in the background.

I looked closely at his hand and noticed a curious mark at the edge of the wrist.

"We have info that Andrei was executed shortly after this photograph was taken."

"And Zoe didn't know this?" I said, stating the obvious.

He shook his head, genuinely sorry.

"How terrible and sad," I felt that to some degree I had misjudged her. Then suddenly I remembered, my mind racing,

"March," I said, "two months later. That's just after the Count's obituary along with the article about his art collection appeared in the *Times*. Wait, I have them here."

I took the clippings out of my handbag.

"Madame A was very upset by this article quoting from an interview the Count gave in December 1969 before he died. Now it seems obvious she was frightened of something mentioned in the newspaper because ..." I stopped.

"What?" He leaned toward me.

"Oh, I don't know." My stomach fluttered. I couldn't bring myself to tell him what I'd discovered in the Pushkin book nor anything else I knew about the case. I knew he would be angry.

"Let me see that." He quickly read the newspaper cutting.

"Did she ever mention this casket?" His eyes stared into mine.

"No." My voice shook, even though I wasn't technically lying. It was only through reading her journal that I knew about the casket.

"The timing of Andrei's or Andrusha's photograph and his execution interests me. It has to be connected to something in the articles. It couldn't be a coincidence. Why now? The man had been held in prison since 1945."

"And until Zoe showed her the photograph Madame A had thought he had been killed years ago, and didn't believe her," I said, staring at the photograph, imagining Madame A's shock.

"Sergei is the only one left of the family. We have to find him before Nicolae's thugs get to him. He might know something about the casket that could lead to Madame A." I couldn't look at him.

"We'll check out this morning," he said.

I said, "I'm sorry about Zoe. I know you cared about her."

"Hell yes. She was drugged and wheeled onto an Aeroflot plane. Who knows what will happen to her after the interrogation? But I told you we were never serious. She always was in love with Nicolae."

"And was he in love with her?"

"He's told interrogators that he had an affair with her to gain her confidence, get her to do what he wanted."

Shivering at his description of Zoë's fate, a series of unwanted images wound past me. Zoe dragged by two brutal looking men into a car, then given a shot, gagged and wrapped in sheets and sent to Moscow to end her life in a cellar. I stood up from the table leaving my sandwich untouched.

"I'm not very hungry. I'll get ready to leave."

I regretted not telling him everything as soon as he came over and gave me a big hug, leaving me weak with desire.

Back in the room I packed up, putting the book back in my large handbag, and then sat on the edge of the bed trying to think clearly. I felt compelled to continue this search until I found out exactly what had happened to Madame A. She was the one person who mattered in this whole mess, besides Jack.

And Jack. I was uneasy at how much I loved him. It was a little scary that every part of my past had been devastated, wiped out by this wild feeling. My passion for him, acted out in motel rooms, in danger seemed slightly fantastic, unreal. I couldn't visualize our having a home, family, regular jobs, a normal existence. Yet I was desperately in love; he had saved my life, and I knew I was safe with him.

I decided to brave his anger, and tell him what I had discovered about Madame A's kidnapping and hand everything over to him. I took the Pushkin book from my handbag and walked over to his room. The door was ajar. He had his back to me. With that tenderness borne of love, I noticed how thick and powerful his neck and shoulders were and remembered how gentle he could be. I started toward him, to throw my arms around him and froze.

He was talking on the phone. In Russian.

I strained to remember the Russian that Madame A had taught me. I understood only one phrase. *'Ona verit mne'*, she trusts me.

Chapter 48

Rural Ohio: 2000

"ONA VERIT MNE." She trusts me. I say the phrase aloud, still bitter at that long ago betrayal. I repeat it to the flawless blue sky as I walk the boundary of the farm, dry leaves crunching underfoot. The dog's black fur with ruff is growing thick and shaggy for the coming winter. He lopes along in glee at freedom from the cabin. Belonging to no one, the dog was sitting on the cabin porch when I arrived here, as though he knew I was coming.

Surrounded on all sides by a great forest, the cabin sits in a small curve of a large crown of a hill. The road to the farm, which faces south, is invisible even in winter to anyone approaching. Reduced to a track, it is barely passable.

This is a place for last stands. Dad had told me that the hill was a natural fort, so the Indians had chosen it for one of their larger villages. According to legend, Spybuck a Shawnee had refused to be moved farther west and held off the settlers for days in an attempt to protect the spirits in the Indian burial ground. When the settlers eventually overran the place, no trace of him could be found. There is a story that Spybuck's ghost still wanders this land with the spirits. I instinctively retreated here to the safety of my childhood after I received the threatening e-mail messages.

When I walked into a real estate office in Columbus that Saturday and asked to see property in this area, it seemed too coincidental, more like a miracle that the cabin was on the market. The realtor, a tall thin man dressed in his golfing clothes, had just stopped by to check his mail. His tanned angular face wrinkled in surprise when I said I was interested and was willing to pay the asking price. He explained that the Safford property had been in constant litigation for well over a hundred years, and the house had not been lived in since 1962 when Miss Adelaide Safford died. Her distant relatives agreed to sell the homestead to pay the legal costs incurred over the years Miss Safford had fought to keep it.

It was as if the land and Miss Safford, an old friend from my childhood, had responded to my need.

I saw a lot of Miss Safford after my grandmother died. In days after the corn and wheat harvest, Dad and I often would drive out to visit her. He would park the pickup halfway up the lane and we would walk the path to preserve the truck. It would kill the shocks, he always said.

Miss Safford, a tall thin figure, gray hair neatly piled on top of her head, would come out on her porch, her shotgun aimed straight at us, her dogs howling from the yard. Dad would raise his arm and yell, "It's me Addy."

As we made our way gingerly through the snarling pack of hound dogs, I could see her welcoming grin, like a cut through her fine chiseled features. She always wore a long black dress, leather lace up boots and sometimes when the weather was bad, a long coat and a large brimmed felt hat. I thought of her as spry and someone to be reckoned with

By the time we reached the porch, she would have placed a jug of homemade whiskey and some apple cider for me on a rugged looking plank table. We would drink out of fine crystal goblets, remnants of her family fortune. After a few glasses the two of them would loosen up and tell me again the stories of what they called the old times of Spybuck, and of the first Christina, my ancestor.

Then I would wait hours at Miss Safford's while my dad went hunting. I was never bored. There was plenty to read. Miss Safford had shelves lined with books and always told me to help myself. From the porch I would stare hard into the forest of maple, pine, and oak and sometimes thought I glimpsed, like wisps of smoke weaving through the trees, the faint trace of the ghosts of Christina and Spybuck, and the lost Indians walking next to the house through their graveyard, now an abandoned corn field.

Now in the daylight I see movement through the red and gold of the trees, and am on my guard. Sun prickles the back of my neck, and a cold queasy feeling ripples through me. I wonder if the implied threat on email means they are here, hiding in the forest.

I search the ground for footprints and look over the boundary of trees, beyond which the prairie grass begins, but there is nothing; maybe it is the ghosts. Much of the prairie, once hunting ground for Indians, has been cultivated into huge farms with grain silos piercing the sky. I think now of the story of the first Christina who was captured by Shawnees from an outpost not far from this farm. As a prisoner she was brought to this place, and then carried off to the Falls near Lake Erie and sold to a Shawnee who had lost his wife.

During that autumn's harvest she was sent to the fields with the other women to pick corn. She had walked slowly to the edge of the field, and disappeared into the trees. Fleeing through the forest, she travelled two hundred miles to the settlement, following the river, once hiding from a party of braves under an overturned canoe, and in hollowed out trees. When the small bit of food she had smuggled was gone, she scavenged for berries and stole a piece of raccoon cooking on an Indian campfire, but was near death when she reached the settlement. The scene runs past me, just the way Dad and Miss Adelaide told it.

"They found her lying face down in the snow just outside the fort. She was a brave woman," Dad would say.

"You have that same blood." Miss Adelaide would look at me with grey frostlike eyes. "I can see it in you, the same coolness in danger."

Her description of me as courageous always amused and perplexed me. I thought of myself as timid, a coward. But her words came to my rescue when I realized I too was a captive.

Heading back toward the cabin, I recall that as terrified as I was of the stranger who called himself Jack, a part of me was operating like that Christina from long ago.

New Jersey: 1970

'Ona verit mne.' She trusts me. The phrase ran over and over in my mind as I sat on the bed behind the locked door. Sickened by his cruel deception, I rushed to the bathroom and threw up.

With a jolt I remembered that after we had made love, I had traced the scars on his body and asked him what had happened. He had refused to answer, then said Vietnam, but there was something evasive in his voice. He was lying about the scars, about everything. Who was he? He was not Jack Reilly. To me he had become the Savage. He was one of them.

The phone calls he had told me to make to my friends and my father had made it easy for him to take me away. I moved in a daze toward the nightstand and picked up the telephone. There was no dial tone. I thought of running out, of calling the police, but I knew he would stop me. There was nowhere to turn for help.

Trembling, holding back tears, I checked that the Pushkin book, the murder album and the envelope were still in my handbag. He might have searched my things while I was out of the room, but I always took the three sources of evidence with me. It was certain that if he had found them, he would have murdered me. He will murder me. My mind was racing.

"Christina," He called to me from outside the door. The purple carpet seemed to jump up in my face. I swayed, faint with terror.

I flung open the door.

"What's wrong?" he said, putting his arm around me.

I let him touch me, even though I was repelled.

"I might have the flu. I feel a little sick," I said.

He moved away, staring at me.

"Do you think we can try to find Sergei today? Do you feel well enough? If we get to him, I'm sure he'll talk to you."

"I'll try," I said, wanting to shrink away.

The ride in the car was torture. I was rigid, silent and then realizing I might appear suspicious, broke into nervous chatter. Scenes of Ms. Springsmith's death popped up before me as I glanced at the powerful bulge of his arm muscles, the gun in his holster.

Once we turned off the highway into suburban streets, and I watched people doing safe ordinary things like going to work, taking kids to school, walking a dog. I wanted to roll down the window and cry out for help.

He stopped for gas and I went to the bathroom, searching for the payphone, but when I found it, he was there waiting, watching. Still, he didn't suspect I had found him out. He thought I was naïve, and I decided in some vague jumbled way, to try to continue on as though I knew nothing. In the end, I was saved by his false impression of me.

I have tried many times to recall exactly the events that followed to include in my personal file in the archive, but I can't remember what I said to him. I have found in my research that memory is often inaccurate, too influenced by feeling.

I do recall the constant throbbing in my head. The Savage had to stop the car more than once along the highway while I vomited. After that, he seemed to give up looking for Sergei that day and pulled into a Holiday Inn, jerking hard on the hand brake. I sensed his impatience and disappointment as he quickly registered and led me to the room.

I lay flat on the bed in my clothes, hoping he wouldn't touch me. An air of menace surrounded him as he leaned over me and asked, "How are you feeling?" Behind this pretense of concern, I knew he didn't care. He wanted to kill me; he only needed me alive to find Sergei.

"Will you be ok by yourself? I have to go into headquarters." He couldn't hide his irritation and didn't offer to call a doctor.

"Yes, I'll be fine," I turned away from him gripped by nausea.

When I heard the door close and the heavy tread of his footsteps down the hall, tears of relief streaked down my cheeks. Feeling faint, I staggered from the bed and tried the door, but he had somehow locked it from the outside. The telephone on the nightstand had been disconnected. I rushed to the window and squinted through one of the slats of the venetian blind to the parking lot. The car was gone.

Panic seized me and I pounded on the door and shouted, but no one came. The place seemed deserted. He had asked for a room farthest from the office so no one would hear my screams. That thought propelled me into action.

I clutched my boot ready to break the window, when a key turned in the lock.

"Maid service." A small woman in a headscarf wearing a white smock opened the door and stood outside with her cleaning cart.

"That's fine," I said. "I was just going out."

Taking only my jacket and handbag, I raced to the emergency exit at the back of the motel and slipped into the growing darkness.

Then I was running in a wilderness of vacant lots high with weeds. Huge vats with garbage from businesses fronting the highway filled these waste disposal sites. I tore my jeans climbing the barbed wire fences separating the properties. In the grimy twilight, I stumbled across potholes and fell face down into an enormous moving pile of trash. Startled rats scrambled out in front of me, brushing against me. I stifled my screams, struggled up, and using all my strength, ran on until I felt it was safe to go back to the highway.

I surfaced several blocks down from the motel at a bus stop sheltered by the roof of a diner. I tried to clean off the dirt and the smears from my fall while I waited in the shadow of the building, knowing he might have returned and be out looking for me.

When the bus to Manhattan arrived the driver didn't seem to notice that I was filthy and trembling. I sank into a seat near the front of the bus, empty except for a boy and girl in their teens engrossed in one another who sat toward the back. Crouching down in my seat, I turned my face away from the window until we passed the motel, and then scoured the highway in the fading light. It was not long before I spotted a car rental and getting off at the next stop, ran back along the highway verge, the traffic roaring by, throwing up dirt and debris in my face. When I reached the rental office, I murmured a silent thanks to Abigail who had picked up my bag from the hospital the night of Ms. Springsmith's murder.

The two girls at the desk were polishing their nails and hardly noticed my dirty face and torn clothes. They stopped grooming to fill out the papers, take the cash and hand me the keys to a nondescript black Ford. I drove madly, not caring where I was going until I found a rest area, locked the door, and slept for a few hours. I woke with a start, was sick again and moved to another spot, like a fugitive. For the moment, I had escaped.

Chapter 49

New Jersey: 1970

THE SAVAGE'S ARMS, which once held me with tenderness, were
around me and when his strong hands moved toward my neck, I screamed,
and woke with a start in half darkness, not knowing where I was. Relief
flooded through me when I felt the cold steering wheel of the car against
my arm. Shivering from the cold air, I started the engine and moved on.

I checked my watch. It was 7 a.m. the sun was still low in the sky, and
I drove fast along the highway in the midst of growing traffic, passing muf-
fler repair shops, used car lots, fast food restaurants, until I saw a White
Castle restaurant and stopped. From the car I looked into the windows of
the fake medieval fortress and watched the sleepy waitress turning on the
lights and making coffee, putting out the napkins and salt and pepper. I was
alone, and there would be no knight in shining armor to rescue me. With
shaking hands I locked the car and went in to get some coffee.

In the restroom I tried to clean up from my fall in the vacant lot. I
splashed water on my face and studied my reflection in the mirror. Was this
real? I seemed removed from this stranger, my hair wild, dirt smearing my
face, my eyes wide with terror and bewilderment, like a fugitive posing for a
mug shot. I went back to the car, drank my coffee to warm up and switched
on the engine, then switched it off. A sudden urge overcame me to drive
away from the danger. It would be easy to turn onto a road that caught
Route 40 and drive west toward home, toward safety. In my highly

emotional state, I saw myself, safely living on a farm, cooking breakfast for one of the young farmers I had met at a Grange dance.

On the road again I watched out the back mirror and sped toward Route 40 West, but when I reached the junction, the vision of Madame A the night I met her rose in front of me, her face lighting up with pleasure as her little crooked hands grasped the cup of herb tea. Her words, 'How lovely, to try something new,' filled the car. I screeched on the brakes, turned around and headed back to the Garden State Parkway and Seaside Heights. Even though Jack might kill me, I was going to the Seabreeze Hotel to speak to Josephus, my only thought to rescue Sergei and escape from them. The Savage had sent Soso and his thugs to find Sergei. My God, this killer who called himself Jack was their boss.

The betrayal again hit me hard, as though I had slammed into a wall. Sickened by his deception, my mind was clear, running past the horror of his murders, like a cold wilderness stream. The revelation came as I floored the accelerator and the roadside; the cars in the next lane became a blur. He had made love to me only because he needed me to find Sergei and then the casket. After that, he planned to kill us both.

Apprehension seized me as I pulled into the drive of the Seabreeze Hotel. The abandoned frigs, rusted out cars and debris on the lawn seemed to have proliferated into a jungle since my last visit. From the open windows and noise, it appeared that more people had joined the cult.

In the yard, a young woman dressed in a long black shift, her brown hair dangling to her waist was leading four small children in a game of ring around the roses. She stopped and hurried toward me, her clear brown eyes looking me over.

"Are thee here to see the leader, Josephus?" The use of thee startled me. Jack had sarcastically called it cult talk.

"Yes, Yes I am. I need his help."

With the children running behind, we walked through a path littered with toys, papers, old nappies and candy wrappers. If I could believe Jack, Josephus' real name was Richard Nelson. He claimed to have been born in a Tibetan monastery, and raised by monks, but in fact, he was the son of a prosperous factory owner and had grown up in Short Hills, New Jersey.

Before he became Josephus, Nelson had done time for manslaughter and a series of petty crimes. A rape charge had been dismissed.

When we reached the porch the girl turned, her plain features clouded with worry.

"Please wait here," she said and went inside.

A high whiny voice floated out the door. "Who's out there?"

After some irritated mumbling, a man in his early forties stepped out. He had thick childish features in contrast to his tall lanky body. His hair was very blond and cut short. He was surprisingly clean and wore a dark suit, white shirt, and black tie. A whiff of the air from inside the house, a mixture of unwashed bodies, incense, and marijuana swept over me, and I involuntarily stepped back.

"I am Josephus. Peace to thee sister." His eyes, an arresting cobalt blue, stared in suspicion, while his large knuckled hands drew together as though praying.

"Thank you. Peace to you," I said awkwardly, forcing myself to go closer.

"I'm Christina Gartner, Sergei Antonov's friend, his mother's friend. I'm sure you have heard of his mother, Madame Feodosia Petrovna Antonova."

He frowned.

I went on nervously, "I was here to see Sergei a few weeks ago. He is in great danger, and I know that he is hiding. He told me I could reach him through you. It is urgent I speak with him."

Behind Nelson, a group of women and children pressed themselves against the inside of the screen door, staring at me.

The screen door slapped against the frame and a girl, who looked about thirteen, came out. Her faded shift was open at the front and a tiny baby hung onto her right breast. She had a plump face, rounded in innocence, a baby herself.

"What does she want?" she asked anxiously in a southern accent.

"Not about thee, Dorcas. Go back inside," he ordered.

He winked at me as though the two of us were in complicity, but his eyes were blank.

I shivered. He was disgusting.

"You ain't working for the pigs?" His eyes narrowed in suspicion.

"No, I need to find Sergei. It's urgent."

"The pig cops always hassle us. We were sent here with special messages, special powers. We harm no one," he whined.

"What do you mean? What powers?" I said, a sick feeling rising in my stomach again.

"The healing old Antonov can do. The holiness of it all. When I first set up in the hotel and met the old Russian, I thought he had a screw loose. But he can heal; even stop the blood flowing from a cut. I've seen him do it. He works miracles. I've been trying to get him on TV. He is a little crazy, but he speaks the universal truths. And our purpose was revealed through him."

"What is that purpose?" I asked, trying not to show disgust. He leered at me suggestively before answering.

"Old Antonov's one cool dude. Through his words and deeds he reveals the secrets of the next world to us."

In spite of the leer, he spoke with some conviction. I wondered just how much of this Josephus believed and how much he merely used to enslave his credulous cult members, who appeared to be a harem of underage girls.

"He is no longer known as old Antonov. He is the Blood Stiller. His gifts for healing, and prophecies were learned from the peasants of the old Russia." Sergei the Blood Stiller? I was shocked, and mystified, and guessed this healing bit could be Nelson's con game to bilk money from the seriously ill.

Josephus cut in, "We've set up a healing center, and have many pilgrims coming to us to be cured. We ask for nothing in return, but do accept donations." He waited expectantly.

"Maybe you should come another time," he said, turning away.

"I do not want to harm him. I only want to help. Please, it may mean his life. Can I contribute to your healing center?" I dug frantically in my bag until I found my wallet and gave him fifty dollars.

He relented, partly because of the bribe, but I guessed he also figured that without Sergei, he would have to find another leader for his cult.

"Do you have ID?" he said, with a self-important air.

I handed him my driver's license. He examined it carefully, looked at me, handed it back and went inside, scattering the spectators like flies away from the screen door. He returned with a grubby piece of paper.

"I had orders to tell only you," he said. I glanced around the side of the porch and saw the two Harleys, with strange wolf heads inscribed on a decal fastened to the handlebars. Josephus noticed my look of alarm.

"Those guys landed here this morning." He drew himself up with pride.

"Said they'd heard about me, wanted to join up for the good of mankind. They're downtown at the coffee shop. I told them that the cult was growing fast and there were new rules; a fee for joining, and the women are off limits. The women are only for me, the leader. I instill them with the spirit." His grin was lewd, repulsive.

This cult seemed an eerie return to the world of Rasputin and the Khlysts. I turned so that he couldn't see my look of disgust. It was frightening to think that Josephus might have adopted Khlyst practices in an even more perverse way. The girls seemed cowed and scared and two who were peering out the screen door were pregnant. What did go on in that house?

"Be careful." I said, "Don't tell anyone I've been here." I tried not to run to the car.

When I was safely on the road, my mind turned back to Sergei, the Blood Stiller. Did he really work miracles and heal or was he just a profitable fraud set up for Nelson?

Chapter 50

New Jersey: 1970

HARRIED BY THE sight of the wolf heads on those Harleys, I forced myself to slow down. The vision of what they would do to Josephus was horrifying.

Rewinds of the past flashed in my head. I had been so mired in self-pity that I ignored all the danger signs. Madame A telling me Jack had just moved in two weeks before me; his trips out of town; Jack deliberately seducing me. Why hadn't I questioned that no other policemen were around?

And even more chilling, Abigail had said he was in my apartment, ahead of the regular police, the night of Ms. Springsmith's murder. And then Nadya. There could only be one conclusion. My mind dropped into a black pool, and I went off the road, the car bumping along the verge in the grass. I managed to stop the car and sat drawn up on the seat, breathing hard before I willed myself to push on.

The gory list tormented me until ahead against the dark sky loomed the untidy pile of Asbury Park. Its amusement park rides and arcade games occupied a ramshackle boardwalk beside the sea and sky, both dark and scummy, like piles of dirty laundry. It was too early in the season for many tourists, and the beach, a brown sheet of emptiness, was foreboding as though waiting to be scrawled with some terrifying act. I parked near the boardwalk and walked quickly toward the arcades, the wind throwing stinging grains of sand in my face. Gulls circled above, shrieking, their wings flapping.

I searched for the funhouse and, startled by an enormous mechanical fat lady in front of the gaudily painted entrance, tripped over the uneven floor. She laughed and shook maliciously as the cars ran in and out of the tunnel, oblivious to the absence of passengers.

A strongly built middle-aged man with a shaved head, operating the engine stepped out of the shadows. "I'm Joshua, Praise be to God." A wide smile, showing missing gaps in his teeth, lit his pleasant weather beaten face. Tattoos covered his arms up to his t-shirt. One of the Baby Jesus and the Virgin Mary was incongruously drawn next to a naked woman named Nadine.

Polite in that glazed over manner like the girls in the cult, he carefully read the note and led me down a narrow stairway underneath the funhouse. Huge gears clanged together, pushing the cars along, creating a terrible din. We entered a small tool room, which had to be Sergei's hideout. His collections of bottle caps, paper clips, and lurid magazine pictures were heaped in piles along the wall. A faint odor of dead fish permeated the room.

Joshua jerked his head slightly toward the large stack of boxes and whispered, "The old fellow ain't been so good lately. Says this room is too cramped, reminds him of the past, of death. He goes out to walk sometimes, just to get fresh air, even though Josephus says it's risky. Can't figure out why. He has this amazing healing power and is our leader, but it's not to do evil. Why would anyone want to harm someone like him?"

He left on this plaintive, indignant note.

Sergei was nowhere in sight. I looked at my watch. It was already late morning, which made me even more desperate. I sat down on the only chair unnerved by the reverberations of the fat lady's laugh, and the clang of the cars from above. The Savage was on my trail at this moment. I had to be patient, to be careful not to scare Sergei, but we had to hurry, to get out of here and hide somewhere.

I looked at my watch again, and continued to wait in the hot stuffy room, with deafening noise overhead. I mulled over why Madame A had chosen me. I had thought it was because she trusted me, but in reality it may have been that I was available and just plain gullible. Before I came

along she must have considered confiding her secrets to Ms. Springsmith or
Zoe, but she hadn't really trusted them. It was now clear that anyone with a
slight connection to this casket risked death.

There was a scuffle and a slight scratching in the corner. Sergei appeared from behind a pile of boxes, his arresting lovely blue eyes staring at
me through his tangled hair, and when he saw I was alone he crept out. As I
moved toward him, his smell overwhelmed me, and I regretted that one of
the cult tenets didn't specify taking baths. It was no wonder he wasn't encouraged to go out. He was dressed in the medieval looking black robe of
the cult and resembled a patriarch who'd been living in a cave for a hundred
years. I had promised Madame A that I would help him, but it was not going to be pleasant.

"Sergei Georgievich," I yelled over the clanging. "Josephus told me
where to find you. I'm Christina Gartner, the friend of your Maman. I visited
you about a month ago and gave you some money. Do you remember me?"

He nodded, but didn't seem sure.

He backed into the corner, threatening to return to his haven behind
the boxes.

"Sergei, you must come with me now. The Leather Coats know where
you are. They are coming to kill you."

He started, jerking like a cornered animal. His eyes grew very large, the
pupils dilated. "Yes, yes, they will kill me."

He was gulping for air. At least he had sense enough to know he was
in danger.

In confusion he ran about the room, picking up bits of his collection
and putting them in a plastic garbage bag. The fat lady's laugh rang out ur-
gently above us.

"My collections, must not leave my collections," he murmured.

As he turned again to pick up more papers, he dropped a small object
on the floor. I leaned over to pick it up and saw that it was an icon on a
chain. I gave to him and he placed it in his bag.

I led him up the stairs away from the clanging cars, the laughing fat
lady and out to the car.

In spite of all the documentation in my possession, Sergei's true identity still remains a mystery. But I was not thinking of that as we drove away

from the amusement park. All I knew was that he could hold the key to finding the casket. But if he did know something, would he remember in his present state?

As I drove I occasionally glanced at him. He was thin and although hunched over, fairly tall. The graying beard and hair and the way he was dressed would have frightened anyone, but I had discovered he was very timid and afraid, always afraid.

"Josephus calls you the Blood Stiller," I said.

"Yes, Da," he nodded, speaking in his high childish voice. "Maman taught me when I was ill."

The hairs stood up on the back of my neck. I swerved nearly driving off the road.

"No one knows the healing but me and Maman. Everyone else is dead." I felt sorry for him and couldn't break the news about his family now.

"Does Josephus know any of your secrets?" I probed.

He shook his head vigorously.

"Are you friends with Josephus?"

"He is kind to me," he said slowly, "The women took care of me when Hasim left and I was alone." The old soldier had told Madame A he no longer watched over the one designated by blood. I wondered what the words meant. Could that be Sergei?

I studied the face of this eccentric man, searching in vain for some resemblance to Madame A's old photographs. It was still hard for me to accept that he was a replacement for her son. But it seemed to me that she had not been deliberately deceiving me about Sergei's condition. Sharp as she was about everything else, her view of Sergei remained the same as when they escaped from Harbin and arrived in the United States.

I guessed that she placed him in that hotel apartment after his reputed breakdown, and Hasim, like a family retainer, looked after him until recently ordered away by someone. I believed it was Turev. As the years passed, and there seemed no chance of returning to Russia, she was forced to leave him in the rotting hotel, hoping the killers would never find him. When Madame A realized that there was imminent danger, she had depended on me to help. I was trapped into knowing too much, too deeply involved to extricate myself. My own survival was bound up with Sergei's.

He sat rigid in the seat beside me, his large bony hands clutching the seat as though afraid to move.

Frantic that I was being followed, I pulled off the main highway and onto a secondary road. We had started out late, and by now the Savage would be searching for us.

"Don't worry," I said, trying to soothe him and to keep the panic out of my voice, "I'll take care of you. Your Maman would wish it."

He flinched and a look of sadness came over him as though he sensed that Anna and Madame A were gone, and that Hasim was never coming back. He knew he was alone in the world except for me, and that there were men who wanted to kill him.

Chapter 51

Rural Pennsylvania: 1970

I NEEDED TIME to persuade Sergei to trust me. My nerves jangling, I turned again onto a secondary road, and after driving for what seemed forever, found a Hertz rental car office in a small shopping mall. I parked the car, locked the door and told Sergei to wait while I rented a brown Chevrolet and then ducked into a small gift shop and bought a canvas bag. I rushed back to pick up a dazed Sergei and his belongings, and abandoned the first rental car at the mall. Knowing Jack would be on our trail, I sped off onto a country road, and drove miles desperately looking for a place to stay the night.

The Beaver Creek Motel was set back off the road next to a creek that reeked of sewage. A restaurant stood at the entrance with several trucks parked nearby. Farther on toward the creek ten wooden cabins were hidden among weeping willows.

Leaving Sergei in the car, I checked in, paying cash, giving the name of Anna Smith. The middle-aged woman in hair curlers did not ask for identification

"Cabin 5, check out tomorrow at noon." She took the cash without looking up.

I stopped at the diner and bought some coffee, eggs, and toast served up in cardboard cartons and carried it all back to the cabin, one room with two single beds.

Sergei's smell was almost too much for me, but dismissing the idea of trying to persuade him to bathe, I sipped my coffee and watched him, trying to figure out what to say. He ate quickly using the plastic knife and fork with excellent, refined table manners.

After he finished I said, "We're both hiding, on the run from the Leather Coats. They are murderers."

He twisted and wrung his long bony hands but said nothing, staring out the window of the cabin. Again I said his mother had asked me to help him, tried everything to get him to talk to me, but he did not respond, in fact, didn't seem to hear me.

Desperate to wake him from his trance, I took the murder album from my bag and held it out to him.

He grabbed it from me with shaking hands, and leafed through the photographs, murmuring as he turned the pages.

"Once men came. One man took pictures, many pictures." He continued to look through the album, humming contentedly.

"Sergei, where were you when the man took the photographs?"

In the long silence that followed, I could hear birds softly settling in the trees for the night. Then he said, "In the house. We were together in the house."

"Did you know the man who took the photographs?"

He shook his head. "But I did see him again. He was shouting."

"Where did you see him again?"

"When we came here from Harbin. He shouted at me and Annushka and at Maman." His lips quivered.

I got up and paced the room with excitement, remembering Nadya's story. When Madame A and the children had shown up at Georgi's home in Princeton, he had shouted that Sergei was not his son and ordered them out.

Sergei seemed to be talking to himself. "Long ago, in that bad time, there were two men. They fought over me. One died there. Then a man came and took me away." He closed his eyes. "They were the Druzhina, the outriders of the Bogatyr in the story Maman always told me. The Bogatyr, Ilya Muromets, the Cossack, had come to save me."

To my amazement, he turned his face upward and in a melodious sing-song voice, chanted in Russian. When he finished he said, "I slept a very long time. Maman helped me to wake up."

He seemed to be growing more amenable and trusting so I showed him the contents of the envelope.

"I was given this number and key by your Maman," I said.

His eyes lit up, and he quickly opened the album to the page with the mug shots, the ID photos of the Tsarevich and his sister, Anastasia.

"Sergei, who are you?"

He wouldn't answer me.

"I think you know about this casket, The Box of the Harpuiai. It was brought from Russia by your mother and contains important papers. We must find it. Do you know where it is?"

My intention was to go to the police and even though I would sound like a crackpot, ask for protection. I planned to tell them that someone was trying to steal Sergei's property. It was a risk because the police could be working for the Savage Jack.

"No, it means death. Maman said they would kill for it."

"Sergei, you must help me. Where did your Maman hide the casket?"

He stared off into space, thinking hard. "I don't know. Don't remember."

Then slowly as though sleepwalking, he picked up his large garbage bag and rooted through his possessions, finally bringing out the small icon.

"Maman gave this to me a long time ago. She told me a story. I remember now."

The icon was a nativity scene featuring the Holy Family in a cave.

"Maman told me the casket is hidden at the place where the Savior was born. It is secret," he whispered, holding his finger to his lips like a child.

He repeated that sentence several times, like a chant he had been required to memorize.

I found it hard to think over his chanting. Surely Madame A couldn't have meant a cave or the real Bethlehem. The casket had to be somewhere in this country, where Madame A could have travelled. And from some obscure nook in my mind, came Ms. Springsmith's haughty comment.

"Feodosia goes to a friend for a few days twice a year. It's one of those nondescript midwestern states, all much the same in mediocrity, possibly Ohio, Pennsylvania, or Iowa."

"Sergei, I know where it is," I said, interrupting his chant.

He stopped, slightly disconcerted, then his eyes lit up.

"Does anyone else know?" I asked again.

His face darkened. "Only Maman, Annushka and me. The others died."

I wanted to ask him what had happened to him during the revolution, and so many other questions, but he seemed to go off in some reverie and closed his eyes. It was as though this brush with reality was too much for him.

"Why don't you lie down," I said.

And he did, covering his head completely with the blanket.

I sat up all night, listening to the screams and crashing bottles of a Hells Angels party in the cabin next door, the sounds escalating my fear that Jack had found the abandoned car and was on our trail.

Perhaps it was the combination of seeing the murder album after so many years and the noise from the wild party that awakened Sergei to his violent past. He sat up and began to speak. It was a strange incoherent narrative that didn't have much to do with our predicament, but I recorded his words as accurately as I could without disturbing him.

I dozed off and was awakened by sun slicing through cracks in the blind. Sergei was sitting up, watching me suspiciously.

I told him to wait inside while I crept past the cabin next door to the diner to buy breakfast, stealing through the parking lot filled with all the motorcycles from last night's party, unaware of the Harley with the Death's Head hidden among them. We ate quickly and then headed toward Bethlehem.

Chapter 52

Bethlehem, Pennsylvania: 1970

WE DROVE INTO Bethlehem, Pennsylvania. Its vast steel factories loomed over the landscape like dark prehistoric creatures. Sergei had remembered the name of the Bank of the Nativity, located on the outskirts of the town. The bank's restored colonial building stood in immaculate grounds surrounded by huge oak trees planted before the Revolutionary War. First founded by German farmers, who settled in the valley in the 1740's, it was a small anachronism, refusing to be swallowed up as a branch by the larger banks. Its existence depended mainly on the farm families in the area who had remained loyal. I could only marvel at Madame A's ingenuity.

"Can I help you?" Mr. Muhlenburg, the bank manager said in a cold unfriendly voice. He was a staid young man in a dark suit, with pale blue eyes that regarded us suspiciously as though we had come to rob the bank.

We had rushed into the bank just as it opened, and he, the guard, and the young woman teller were sitting down to coffee and doughnuts. He had been startled and unhappy at being interrupted by an odd looking pair, one of whom seemed to have stepped out from a medieval tableau. He glanced at Sergei, unwashed in his black robe, his long hair and beard and turned away for a moment to hide his distaste. Even though I had managed to take a shower, I was not looking my best after a night sitting up in the room in the same clothes.

Before he could dismiss us I produced the safety deposit box number, 29-34-08, the key, and the signed paper giving me power of attorney over Madame A's affairs. He then asked for proof of identity and checked my driver's license thoroughly.

"This is a deposit box with specific instructions," he said, ushering us into his paneled office. He unlocked a file cabinet beside his desk and removed a slim folder, opened the cover and carefully read the top paper, then looked up in surprise.

"There are some special requirements, very unusual."

He pursed his lips in disapproval, as he read from the paper. "If Madame Feodosia Petrovna Antonova, the depositor," he pronounced the name slowly, almost in distaste at its foreignness, "is not present, and if the person accompanying you is one Sergei Georgievich Antonov, he must be identified by a permanent mark on the inside of his wrist." His voice trailed off in disbelief.

I was equally incredulous at the request. It seemed incongruous in this formal office, but Madame A must have included this strange provision in case something happened to her.

Sergei understood and slowly pushed up the sleeve of his black robe, placing his left arm, which shook violently, on the desk. Mr. Muhlenburg and I looked down.

We both drew back in shock. On the inside of his wrist, just below his hand, barely discernible, was a swastika tattoo.

Sergei said, "It is the heart of Buddha."

Unlike the startled banker, I knew this swastika had nothing to do with the Nazis. It was the secret sign of the Brotherhood.

"That's it." The banker moved quickly away from Sergei toward the door, and we followed him to an enormous vault, its steel door opened by combination. Sergei grimaced with fear as we stepped in.

"Is this a prison? Are we going to be locked up?" he asked in a tremulous voice

"No, no, it's a bank vault," I whispered. "This is where you will find the casket."

Mr. Muhlenburg went deep into the vault and brought out a large safety deposit box. He placed it on the shiny mahogany table and pointed to a brass bell at its side.

"Ring when you are finished," he said and left quickly.

I took out the key, hurriedly opened the deposit box and drew out the contents.

"This can't be it," I stared in disappointment at a battered biscuit tin labeled Huntley and Palmer's. Batches of old pens were stored inside.

Sergei cleared away the pens from the top layer of the tin. He removed the layer and lifted out the Box of the Harpuiai. It was exquisitely beautiful. The miniature carved scenes decorating the ivory casket brought to life the episodes from the Greek myth of Jason and the Golden Fleece. It was exactly as described in the newspaper article about the Count.

"It's yours," I said, unable to take my eyes from it, "Your Maman wanted you to have it."

Something inside rattled as he slowly turned the casket. A look of terror contorted his face as he examined each carved panel and stopped at the scene of the Harpies tormenting blind Phineas. One of the terrible creatures was facing front, staring directly at us.

With a shaking finger, Sergei pressed its wing tip and the box sprung open.

"Papa, Papa," he cried out in a loud high voice.

He seemed unable to move, so I examined the hiding place within the lid and found a thick folded vellum paper. The rattle had been caused by rolls of old camera film. Sergei remained transfixed, still staring at the casket.

"Sergei," I said gently, "We must leave here now. Should I keep all of these things for you until we're safe?"

He looked up. "Yes, I never want to see any of it."

I put the sealed paper, which was thick and expensive and well preserved and the rolls of film in my handbag. Then I closed the lid of the casket, carefully placed it inside the biscuit tin, and put it into the canvas bag I had brought from the car.

I rang for Mr. Muhlenburg, and as calmly as I could, said we would not need the deposit box any longer.

As we left, I said to the mystified bank manager, "Someone may come asking about us. Please don't tell them anything."

I drove frantically out of town, risking a speeding ticket. As we turned onto a small dirt road and then another, going deeper into the countryside, I glanced over at Sergei. He had pulled up his black cowl and had withdrawn into it.

I was still astonished at the strange events that had occurred since I found him. His tattoo and knowledge of the casket came from a mysterious past. I wasn't sure there was a logical explanation for it all, but I sensed there was some other secret involved, something more dangerous than the casket. Who was this strange man who had replaced Madame A's son? That was my last rational thought that day. Two motorcycles sped out of the small country lane, followed by a large black car.

Rural Ohio: 2000

I couldn't save Sergei. His death was reported as accidental in the newspaper articles that I am about to file in the archive. To comfort myself, I lean back on the porch step, letting the cold autumn air caress me, but it does not ease my pain.

Rural Pennsylvania: 1970

The car pulled in front of us, forcing me to slam on the brakes. Sergei's constant muttering turned to a wild shriek. I looked out of the car window. Jack and three men I recognized from Petrushka's were coming toward us.

Soso smashed in the window, unlocked the car door and pulled me out.

"Go ahead, kill us you bastard." I screamed at Jack, at the same time realizing that I didn't mean this.

"Let her go." he ordered Soso.

He stepped toward me, and I flinched, backing away.

"Look, what's wrong with you? Calm down. Why did you leave the motel?" He seemed genuinely puzzled.

"Because I know you're going to torture and kill us, just like poor Ms. Springsmith." I was still screaming, but wanted him to take me in his arms, to tell me that it was all a mistake.

He didn't look directly at me and didn't deny my accusations. I tried to keep my voice on an even keel, but it rose to a hysterical pitch. Sergei, terrified, had jumped out of his seat and was attempting to hide on the opposite side of the car.

"That's stupid," Jack said. Soso and the other two thugs stood watching impassively.

"Is it, is it?" I screamed, backing away.

"Christina, I'm not going to hurt you."

He pulled me hard against him, holding me as I struggled.

"I heard you speaking Russian on the phone back at the hotel. You're working for them, you bastard." I said between breaths.

Shocked, he let me go and stepped back, then seemed to recover.

"Yes, I should have told you." His voice was rough, the accent more pronounced.

"Did poor Madame A discover this before you took her away?" I was sobbing.

"No," he said.

I sensed he wasn't going to kill me immediately and tried to calm myself, to think.

"I know it looks suspicious but in these last weeks I have been working on my own. I had an argument with my superior, and don't trust him. There was a disagreement over whether this was just a burglary and missing person or something more important. You've got to believe me."

Rural Ohio: 2000

I still desperately want to believe him. A phantom, he appears before me on the step of the cabin porch, pleading with me. I think of his words, his last glance at me. What did he say? I love you. I am coming back for you. I try to keep this in mind as the next scenes hurl past me, and he changes into a cold murderer.

Rural Pennsylvania: 1970

His accent was foreign, Russian. "We have to take Sergei in for questioning."

Everything moved quickly in front of me, unreal, horrifying.

"Run Sergei!" I remembered shouting, but Soso grabbed him and threw him down on the road.

They pushed a syringe into him, while he lay shrieking, his legs wriggling like a helpless insect. Pulling away from Jack, I raced up and down looking frantically for a car, but the country road was empty.

I pleaded with Jack, did everything he asked. I gave them the Box of the Harpuiai in the canvas bag, but that didn't save Sergei. He was in another world when they bundled him into the car.

Rural Ohio: 2000

There is no documentation for what passed between Jack and me, for the look in his eyes as he held the gun to my head. I can only describe his haunted expression, his indecision. As I've noted, memory is unreliable.

Rural Pennsylvania: 1970

I interpreted his last full gaze at me as one of love before he ordered me into a clump of bushes off the road out of the sight of the others. He shot twice into the air. A dull unbearable pain slowly spread through my skull, and I dropped into a black void.

Chapter 53

Rural Ohio: 2000

IT IS EARLY afternoon, and the sky is darkening over the clearing, growing black and swollen in the north above the forest, about to burst with snow.

I stopped at a small country market this morning and the woman with a woodcut face behind the counter said, "We're in for a big one. And before Thanksgiving."

I was disguised as an ordinary shopper, dressed in a good pair of slacks. I nodded in commiseration.

Most of the trees look spindly, bare of leaves with only tall green pines left as sentinels over the forest. The cold has forced me inside the cabin. Each day I build the fire in the iron stove in the kitchen, risking the chance that they will see the smoke. In the dim light I read the newspaper clippings that pertain to this part of my story. They are arranged by date and subject, and preserved digitally, but I have the need to see the genuine article. The cold meaning behind the date of one newspaper clipping dated May 7, 1970, forces me to move closer to the stove. They interrogated Sergei for two weeks.

From the edge of the forest the wolf howls, this time louder, more insistent. The dog raises his head, his long furry ears upright, and pads to the door. His pale eyes seem to look at me with sadness, as though apologizing for leaving me alone.

I close the door after him, and notice a slip of paper had slid out of the pile of clippings to the floor. I pick it up, puzzled that it had been placed with the newspaper cuttings. This is uncharacteristic of me. I have always been fastidious with my records and papers. I am apprehensive because I don't recognize at first that it is my handwriting, feverish, hurried in pencil on the back of an old shopping list. There is no date, but the paper is as yellowed as the newspaper cuttings.

My hands shake so violently that the print weaves. My notes are of Sergei's incoherent ravings recorded in the middle of the night in the motel shack while the Hells Angels' party raged in the next cabin.

Sergei in a dreamlike state comes back to me as I read my record of his words.

"Fairy Tale," he murmurs, smiling at the pictures of the Romanov family before their captivity. "It ends." He nods his head up and down like a child.

He stares at the photographs of the Romanov children left in Tobolsk after the family had been separated.

"The Bogatyr came. Told secrets. Enemies, traitors everywhere. Must never tell, never recognize him. It will mean death. He will rescue us."

He flips quickly to the page with the drawings describing the last day at Ipatiev House in Ekaterinburg. "Hot, no air, windows shut, can't breathe. Bad men here. Noise, blood everywhere. I see him, the Bogatyr. Everything black."

I stop reading my notes, trying to make sense of these mad ravings and conclude Sergei could be describing the murders of the Romanovs. Could he have been told the story or did he witness what occurred in Ipatiev House the night of July 16? He said the Bogatyr would save him. I know that Dimitri was the Bogatyr. I wonder if he did rescue anyone from Ipatiev House. It would have been difficult with the number of fanatical Bolsheviks and Cheka agents guarding the house. There had been several rescue attempts but according to historians, they all appeared to have failed.

I get up and feed the fire, then return to Sergei's words, incoherent with fright.

"Light comes. I see again. I hide in snow, cold. Two men, one I know. The Bogatyr has come for me. Never use real name. They shout and fight each other. The Bogatyr knocks the man down and walks toward where I hide. I see the enemy's hateful face. He shoots. The Bogatyr falls down. His blood looks black on the snow."

Sergei raises his fist. "Beat, beat. He beats the Bogatyr's face with his gun. Nothing left. Papers in pocket. Enemy's step crunches, crunches in the snow past me to his horse."

I remember how he jumped up and paced the room, his eyes even more wild with fear, how he pounded furiously on the cabin door as though to break free before collapsing into a stupor.

I put the paper down, thinking that though his words correspond to other circumstantial evidence; objectively they could be the delusions of a crazy old man.

I am suspicious that this evidence leads me to one conclusion about Sergei's identity. I put on the kettle to make coffee and search out the kitchen window, my new sentry post. There is no sign of the dog. Waiting for the kettle to boil, I try to make sense of Sergei's words as the scenes roll by:

I see the two spies, Dimitri, the Bogatyr and Peter, the Raven, Madame A's lovers, standing in a snowy field in Siberia. They are meeting after the Romanov family's hiding place was uncovered in Perm, after the rescue attempt failed. Dimitri, knowing that Peter has betrayed them, has hidden Sergei.

Dimitri accuses Peter of treachery. Their faces are red and angry as they argue violently and fight to the death. Peter loses the fight and falls to the ground, but rises up and shoots Dimitri as he turns his back. Then he beats Dimitri's face so that he could not be identified, takes his papers and buries the body in snow.

Sergei watches, hiding behind bushes in terror, until Andrei, Madame A's brother comes at the appointed meeting time and rescues him. Sergei is suffering from his wounds when Andrei takes him to Madame A. A few months later when the Whites face certain defeat, Andrei orders her to hide the Box of the Harpuiai and the boy. Could that be the true story?

The dog scratches at the door and I let him in, eager for his companionship. His coat has become even shaggier in the past weeks and he is distant to me, as though he has another life out in the forest. He gobbles the piece of pork I saved for him, but turns away when I reach down to pet him. I have begun to suspect he is not a dog, but a wolf, an impostor.

Chapter 54

New York: 1970

"AN IMPOSTOR! YOUR noble savage turned out to be an im-
poster," Abigail said. "In a way, it's kind of exciting, that is if he weren't a
murderer. Do you suppose he went back to Russia, if he is Russian that is?"

"I don't know." I thought of my nights with him and wondered where
he was, if he was still alive. I was too grief stricken and agonized to confess
he had been my lover.

We were in the huge drawing room of Abigail's Park Avenue apartment, another property left to her by Auntie Beatrice. Abigail never used
the place and was thinking of putting it on the market. In the meantime, she
had decided, after picking me up at the gas station in Pennsylvania that it
was the safest place for me. A week passed before I was able to face what
had happened that day.

I came to, lying in a clump of bushes out of sight of the road. My head
throbbed. A huge bump protruded from my forehead where Jack had hit
me, and blood streamed down over my face. Holding my head, I staggered
to the edge of the road looking for help, but it was deserted.

Terrified that they would return I ran, stumbling along the dusty road,
for what seemed like miles until I came to an Esso gas station. A mechanic
dressed in coveralls, his face smeared in grease, saw me collapse and rushed
out to carry me inside. He brought several bundles of wet paper towels to
help stop the blood. He wanted to call an ambulance, but I said I was all

right. Then I rang Abigail, relieved to hear the excited cackle of her voice. The mechanic took the phone and gave her directions, then put his jacket down on a bench in his office and helped me lie down.

I cowered on the bench in a fetal position in the dingy office, holding the wet towels to my head, hardly believing I had escaped death. At some point, I realized the thugs had made an enormous mistake. They only had been interested in the casket and had ignored my handbag. It had been twisted around my arm when Jack hit me, and I had carried it with me along the road. With my free hand, I opened it and found the ukase and the old rolls of film from the casket. I was sure Jack would soon be aware that the Tsar's last order was gone. I shook all over, even though it was sweltering in the small office.

The mechanic stopped his grease job several times to check on me. He brought me more cold wet towels and a drink of water. He again offered to call an ambulance, but I refused.

"Thanks, you're very kind. My friend will be here soon," I said, feeling dizzy. I leaned back and closed my eyes. I don't know how many hours passed before Abigail came running into the office. I heard her thanking the man.

"What in the world are you doing here? I thought you were on vacation," she said as she and the mechanic helped me into the car.

"Ab help me, they're going to kill me."

Although curious by nature, she didn't press me for details at first, but raced back to New York, had my head stitched up at her doctor's, reported the abandoned cars as stolen, and took me back to her apartment. The doctor said I had a concussion and should rest quietly for a few days.

In spite of the pain and blurred vision, I managed to tell her what I needed to about Jack and Sergei and the casket, and how worried I was about Sergei. Although she didn't quite believe it all, she tipped off the police anonymously from a pay phone. But I knew it was too late.

"It's bad manners for me to say I told you so, but Sam and I were right about your neighbors." She went on, thinking aloud. "So that day when you left Quogue, this Jack was just posing as a policeman?"

"Yes, he deceived me." I did not want to go into how easy it had been.

"But how did he do that? I thought he had policemen watching the house."

I shuddered picturing those men. "They were his men, the killers."

"And you discovered Madame A is dead?" Ab sat down in a chair opposite me.

"Jack told me when he was pointing a gun at me, just before he knocked me out. He said she died of heart failure the day after they took her away, but I can't be certain he was telling the truth. And there wasn't a Vladimir Antonov. He was just a ruse created with Turev's help to get Madame A to go along quietly until it was too late." I could imagine her terror when she realized it wasn't Vladimir, but the killers who had come for her.

"And the murders were all because of this casket; the Box of the Harpuiai that Madame A brought from Russia and hid all these years?"

"Yes," I said.

"That's strange. She probably could have sold that casket long ago for a lot of money and been rid of it."

"It wasn't that simple. I don't think it was hers exactly. She was keeping it for Sergei. The worst was that anyone who had knowledge of this casket was in danger," I said.

"And Violet Springsmith? Did he?" Abigail was agitated and frightened.

"What other conclusion can I come to?" I choked out the words, still not wanting that to be true.

"He must have been there when she was tortured and murdered." There was a strange tremor in her voice. "I remember now. I saw him that night at your apartment and just assumed he was on the case. When I knocked at your door, he answered with a startled expression. I noticed he had blood on his shoes."

She was silent for a long time and then trying to shake off that image said, "But tell me. Why is this casket so important? It sounds incredible to me. What could something found in an antique box matter now? It must be some kind of scam."

"The killers work for someone plotting to take over the Russian government." I didn't tell her I was convinced he was a spy called The Raven, who had been searching for this casket since it disappeared in 1918. She would think I was permanently damaged from the knock on the head.

"The Russians used Turev and his émigré organization, the Double Eagle, a ruthless bunch who also planned to stage a coup, to try to locate the casket. They believed I passed some knowledge of it to Ms. Springsmith. Jack knew that I could lead them to Sergei who could find and open the casket." I said.

She was skeptical and I didn't blame her.

"I don't really know the truth. You could be right. It might be a scam, but it is important enough for them to kill," I said, thinking how the émigré circle had fooled me, how Madame A had seduced me into their web.

I stayed hidden in the apartment. Jack and his killers would discover the ukase was not in the casket and certainly come after me.

Two weeks later Abigail came in with the *New York Times*, holding it out in front of her as though it were on fire.

May 7 1970

CULT OF BLOOD STILLER IN MASS SUICIDE

Members of the Cult of the Blood Stiller were found dead by police yesterday in the Seabreeze Hotel in Seaside Heights, New Jersey. The group dressed in black robes, lay on the large kitchen floor with the gas oven on and the doors and windows sealed. Police found a note declaring the members would all meet in heaven, and are treating it as a mass suicide. The list of the dead included one Sergei Antonov, 66, and Josephus, aka Richard Nelson, 45, both of that address. One other male has not yet been identified. The police spokesman said the others found were teenage girls and children. Their names have not been released.

The article stated that the cult claimed to have the power to heal the sick and had recently opened a healing center. The leader Richard Nelson had been under investigation for sexual abuse of minors. It concluded with neighbors' claims that strange ceremonies and orgies had taken place at the hotel. Abigail looked at me, her large eyes incredulous.

"Honestly Chris," she protested, "You don't think this was all to cover up Sergei's murder?" I nodded unable to speak; fear filled my stomach up to my throat. I felt sick. There had been nothing I could do.

"These people are dead serious," she said gravely, unaware of her pun.

After a few moments of contemplation, she asked, "What was this Blood Stiller cult?"

"I think Nelson got the idea from Sergei. He and Sergei lived in the same hotel." The throbbing pain in my head returned.

I explained what I knew about the ancient healing arts of the shaman in Siberia and how Rasputin supposedly used this skill of stopping the flow of blood to help the Tsarevich Alexei who suffered from hemophilia.

"And you think Sergei was not Madame A's son, but someone she brought with her from Russia?" Abigail sat up straight on the silk damask couch.

"Yes, although he never claimed to be anyone other than Madame A's son."

"But what does Sergei have to do with the healing? It all seems so hokey," she said.

"Rasputin was murdered in 1916, but Madame A was his disciple who learned and practiced his secret healing skills, and Sergei did call himself the Blood Stiller," I said, thinking aloud. Then it came to me, an idea so weird that it sent a shudder through my body. Could Sergei have learned the art of stopping the flow of blood from Rasputin or Madame A and healed himself?

Chapter 55

Ohio: 2000

IN 1989 LONG after I went into hiding, several newspapers reported that the bones of the Romanov family and servants were found in the woods near Ekaterinburg. In 1992 after much controversy, samples of the bones were sent to Forensic Science Service at Aldermaston England for DNA tests that confirmed that these bones were those of the royal family.

There were questions concerning the validity of the DNA tests, that the evidence was contaminated, perhaps even tampered with. It was argued that the tested bones were taken from graves of other Romanovs. All the same, I was relieved. A burden was lifted from my shoulders. Sergei may have been an impostor, but it seemed certain he was not the Tsarevich.

In 1998, the day after Yeltsin's inauguration as President, the newly discovered bones were buried in St Petersburg, in the Cathedral of SS Peter and Paul at a service which most of the remaining Romanovs and Yeltsin attended. This burial seemed to settle questions about the murders. But, having learned from the émigrés, I know the Russian government can never be believed.

An unsettling disbelief filled me when it was reported that the bones of two Romanovs were missing. One of them was the Tsarevich.

New York: 1970

I stayed on in the apartment for some weeks after Sergei's death, seeing no one except Abigail and her trustworthy housekeeper Mercedes, who had been with the family for years. Abigail remained at her Soho place so she wouldn't be connected to the apartment still in her aunt's name. I can't remember what I did those days, but think I mainly stared out the window, watching both sides of the street.

One night toward the end of my stay, Abigail came in with a large pizza and a message.

"A General Kosloff came to the gallery today. He asked for you. I pretended, of course, that I knew nothing, that I thought you were still on vacation."

Fear shot through me.

"What did he look like?" I said.

"Elderly Russian with a bald head, great moustache, stocky figure, looked a bit oriental around the eyes. He was dressed in a shabby uniform and was wearing a cape. He was very tense, and constantly looked out the window at the street."

That could only be Kosloff. How had he known to contact Abigail?

"Do you want to see him?"

"Yes." I was sick again and couldn't eat the pizza. Fear had permanently unsettled my stomach.

I took the risk of meeting Kosloff at the Metropolitan Museum, a short walk from the Park Avenue apartment. He strode in without his cape, wearing a threadbare tunic and khaki trousers and carefully looked around the room before bowing and kissing my hand.

"Miss Christina, I am so relieved that you are all right."

"How did you know to contact me through Miss Townsend?"

"I have sources. When I heard rumors, I thought your beautiful friend might know where you are hiding."

"She brought me the message right away because I am leaving today." I wondered what rumors he had heard.

"Good," he said, looking around anxiously. The gallery, filled with medieval altarpieces was empty this morning.

"You know that Madame A is dead and that they took Sergei and the casket and killed him." My voice sounded hollow in the empty room.

He nodded. "There was no way to help her. She became involved long ago, before I met her. It seems after all these years someone discovered her deadly secret."

"Did you know anything about Sergei's connection to the casket?" I said.

"It was a surprise to me."

I had the feeling he wasn't telling the truth.

"Wasn't it Perm in Siberia where one of the men you shot had the photograph album?"

"They begged for their lives, claimed they had not taken part in any executions, but had been assigned by a secret agent to protect someone. I didn't believe them because the album, which they had stolen, was the only evidence they had. They pleaded with me, swore it belonged to the boy." He stopped abruptly. "There is no point in discussing this further."

Then he said, "I heard about recent activity last week while repairing electric wires at Petrushka's. It is very dangerous there. Soso's men are hanging around, believing there is no evidence against them. But my dear Christina, I am here for another reason. A so-called government man will contact your friend, Miss Townsend to arrange a meeting with you. My advice is to talk to no one. There is no one you can trust. Flee, go into hiding. Change your name."

"Do you know the man who calls himself Jack Reilly?" I said.

He emphatically shook his head. I didn't believe him. "But I have heard that he is working for someone who has great plans, who needs the Tsar's casket."

"Do you mean General Turev?"

He laughed scornfully. "No, he is inconsequential, a poseur. He is not in control of the operation."

"How many of the émigrés know what's going on?"

He didn't answer my question, and then lowered his voice, "I have heard that there is someone, a Bolshevik agent from the past, a former White officer who betrayed us. I believe the Raven is still alive and searching for the casket."

Before he left he asked if I found anything in the casket.

"No," I lied, wondering what he knew about me. I had become like the émigrés. I trusted no one.

As I hurried back to Abigail's apartment, I heard running steps behind me. Kosloff caught my arm, panting from exertion, and said, "The real Jack Reilly was killed in Vietnam."

The pavement seemed to move around me like a tidal wave as the full realization of Jack's deceit flooded over me. I ran back to the apartment.

That was the last time I ever saw Kosloff, but I did take his advice and left New York that night, going into my own Siberian exile. I knew that Jack was an agent for the Raven and that the Raven masterminded the plot from Moscow. Facts later confirmed it.

I never discovered who Kosloff was really working for, but learned later that he managed to survive until one night in 1977 when he came out of hiding and ventured to Petrushka's. On his way home a mugger killed him in the street. The murderer used a hammer, Soso's favorite weapon. His murder occurred shortly after Brezhnev razed Ipatiev House to the ground, erasing all evidence. Yeltsin, then Regional First Secretary in Ekaterinburg, was in charge of the demolition.

I kept returning to Kosloff's part in the Brotherhood plot and have always wondered if he had been told the Raven was the traitor. Perhaps he had been given the traitor's real name, but had never seen him. This would explain his failure to recognize the Raven disguised as Victor Matsev with Madame A at the Hotel Moderne in Harbin.

I had no doubt the killers intended *Chistka*, the deathly KGB cleansing Kosloff spoke of, to anyone who knew about the casket. I changed my location for a second time after Kosloff's death.

Chapter 56

Rural Ohio: 2000

THE TEMPERATURE HAS dropped below freezing, bringing a stillness to the landscape broken only by the flapping of the crows perching on the broken fence. I stuff the stove with wood and look around at my last hiding place. The cabin is much the same as when I hibernated here during my childhood illnesses.

One winter when I came down with measles, Miss Adelaide bundled me up and placed my bed where it is now by the stove in the kitchen. She read to me to protect my eyes, concocted a strange kind of poultice to relieve itching, and cooked my favorite dishes. Miss Adelaide was never motherly, but was my greatest friend. When I entered high school and spent more time in town, I was surprised to discover that people thought she was a little crazy, in spite of the fact that she was so smart and had gone East to a fancy college. She once showed me a picture of her fiancé who had been killed in World War I. After receiving notice of his death, she had moved out here and only went to town for provisions.

"There seemed no point," she had said.

Still thinking of Miss Adelaide and wondering why I hadn't done this before, I go to the fireplace in the living room and pull out the loose bricks in the chimneypiece. Beneath the crumbling bricks and dirt, I find two of her crystal goblets wrapped in newspaper, and the photograph of her fiancé in army uniform.

I believe she would approve of my taking her name and identity when I went into hiding. After all, she had been a virtual recluse for years and was forgotten in this area. No close relatives remained alive. She would say it made sense.

My identity and location have remained a secret since I left New York. Abigail had been prescient. I did become a research librarian, and lost myself in a suburb of Columbus, leading a solitary life, friendly but not close to neighbors, conducting research for history professors and doctoral candidates. I worked alone and with the advent of the Internet, most of the research was done in my home. Word got around the university that I was fastidious and extremely accurate, and I was in great demand.

Soon after I settled in, I began collecting material for the archive, which gradually took over my life. Perhaps my solitary childhood had prepared me for this near monastic existence: obsessing over events that occurred years ago, studying documents and personal accounts, attempting to solve the mysteries which had forced me into hiding.

Over the years Abigail has been my only contact from my former life. She continues to be a steadfast friend, accepting my claim that my life is in danger, but remaining incredulous about much of the story. She comforted and helped me through my pregnancy, attending to all the practical details.

The nausea that gripped me when I discovered Jack's betrayal may have been fear at the onset, but it continued for weeks. Eight months after I went underground I gave birth to a daughter. I named her Katya Ivanovna; the nearest I could come to her father's identity. Abigail hid me at one of her family houses in Michigan and was present when I travelled to New York to give birth. Shortly after, she took Katya away.

I try to be objective, to think of my pregnancy as a mistake, a trivial incident, but the feeling of grief over my lost child seems to grow with the years. The image of the miraculous curve of her tiny head against my breast remains with me.

The only traces I have of Katya are the few photographs that Ab sent over the years to a post office address in Indiana. I look at them with longing and reluctantly file them away.

But now I keep the recent photograph of her close to me in my jacket pocket. Katya, her skis stuck upright in the snow, stands against the background of majestic mountain peaks. She has my blond hair, but her face is angular with high cheekbones, the dark eyes slanted. The face laughing back at me is his. My heart breaks when I look at her and think of how I loved him once.

The fire crackles, rendering the stove incandescent. After I eat my soup I try to feed the dog, who disdains my food after his long sojourns in the woods. His ears prick at the distant howling and he looks at me, imploring. I let him go.

Warmth steals over me as I spread the remains of the archive around me on the bed, reflecting on how slowly new information came in the first years after I went into exile. The original files mainly consist of my own collection of evidence, émigrés' private papers, books, and personal reminiscences.

My research has progressed rapidly since 1991 after the downfall of the Communists and thirty years after General Turev believed that Russia was ready for a change in government. I imagine the joy the émigrés now long dead would have felt and picture them slightly dazed, wearing their turn of the century clothes, travelling back to their old haunts.

That year of the downfall I began an email correspondence with someone named Boris, who claimed to have access to KGB files and was willing to sell information. Boris was acquainted with a Columbia University professor named Kutsevnov, for whom I had done extensive research. I had never met the professor, but his introduction to Boris provided me with an invaluable source.

Among the many other documents Boris made available to me in 1994 were official papers and photographs scanned from an old KGB dossier on Madame A. The documents were all in Russian, but that did not matter. I had become fluent in the language over the years.

The short note in the file on Madame A states:

Feodosia Petrovna Antonova: Counter-revolutionary spy. Deserted Soviet Union in 1921. Died in 1970 of a heart attack while returning to the Soviet Union.

I remember a phrase used ironically in the murder album, 'pictures do not lie', as I arrange the four photographs in chronological order.

The first still shocks me. Madame A, wearing a long white robe, kneels before Rasputin. This snapshot from 1916 is faded and even with the magnifying glass it is difficult to make out what is going on, but I assume this is a significant moment in a Khlyst ceremony, perhaps one of a series of pictures that she managed to keep from the Okhrana after Rasputin's murder.

I place the remaining three in a row. Tsarevich Alexei posing alone, Tsarskoe Selo, 1916, Madame A with Sergei, Finland, July 1917, Madame A and the boy who was Sergei's replacement, Omsk 1918.

The boys in the photographs are blond, rather tall, and thin with even features, and greatly resemble each other. Madame A had recorded in her journal that the change of identities was an accident, purely coincidental, but I am not convinced and have returned to the notes from that time period. She had written that medicine arrived for Sergei just before she and the children left for the mansion outside Omsk. Could the medicine proved to have been fatal, to have caused an accident, making the exchange less of a coincidence?

The last snapshot from Madame A's file, dated *Caucasus 1970*, pictures a close-up of a grave. The headstone reads *Feodosia Petrovna Antonova*. Again, doubt creeps in concerning the authenticity of this photograph. Her constant refrain, 'the Bolsheviks lie', echoes within me. It is possible that her bones are buried in a crushed car in the wastelands of New Jersey.

Next I turn to the brief notes on Peter Von Krantz, aka The Raven, that accompany three photographs sent by Boris in 1994 before his messages disappeared from my computer screen.

Serbsky Institute.
Patient, Peter Von Krantz, 80, Nom de revolution The Raven. Arrested 1978 for espionage. Active role in counter intelligence during the revolution and civil war. In later years, foreign intelligence advisor. In good physical condition, but diagnosed as mentally unstable, suffers from 'creeping schizophrenia'. Committed for treatment, 1977.

The first photograph of Lenin was snapped in 1918 soon after the Bolsheviks took power. A man with a circle drawn round him stands in the background behind Zinoviev, Stalin, and Trotsky. I focus the magnifying glass on the obscure figure. It is the Raven.

There are two more recent photographs taken by a professional using a zoom lens. In the first an elderly man in a dark military tunic and high leather boots is being helped, nearly carried from a large black car. The second shows the man and his helpers entering the building. He seems to falter or struggle at the open door. It is difficult to ascertain if he is being aided or taken prisoner. Both photographs are dated Moscow, March 8, 1977.

Moscow: March 8, 1977

It is cold and bleak; a dense fog covers Moscow's streets. The Raven is not surprised. He has been expecting them for the past seven years. He keeps his dignity and does not protest as they stop the car. He says nothing when one of the Leather Coats crawls in beside him, his tiny eyes studying the instrument panel in front of him with amazement. The other thug rides beside his driver, Nikita, and orders him to speed to Ulitsa Prechistenka.

Flashes of the Lupukhin, Smirnov and Dolgorukov Mansions appear outside the car window, his last glimpse of scenes of wonderful parties before the revolution. For an instant he is flooded with the memory of Feodosia whom he loved and lost. Abruptly the mansions give way to a high wall. The car pulls up to a gate, manned by guards, and after getting permission, continues down the long drive of the Serbsky Psychiatric Institute.

He has sent many of his enemies to the Serbsky in recent years. It is a new way of punishing dissidents and other troublemakers, with drugs and shock treatment. Far more subtle than the Gulag for ridding the state of enemies, it is a favorite of Andropov because it is less subject to protests from the international community.

The Raven has known for some time that he was betrayed by one of his own, someone as clever and treacherous as he. The Box of the Harpuiai and its contents have eluded him. The Tsar's last edict would have given legitimacy and power to a new Russian government under his rule. It is too late for him, but the ukase is still out there, waiting for the designated one. Long ago he made contingency plans.

His thoughts end in a fight for breath as they jerk him unceremoniously out of the car and drag him toward the door. He struggles at the last, but it is futile.

Chapter 57

Rural Ohio: 2000

FOR TWO DAYS a light snow like down feathers has been floating aimlessly and melting on the ground so I risked another trip to the lockup. I left early this morning after loading the cases of the archive and took the back roads, travelling slowly, until I reached Mount Sterling. I turned onto Route 56 and finally I71, passing the road sign for the turn off to the Digby place. Lawrence had sold the Digby Company and all the land fifteen years ago and moved to a villa in Morocco, where he entertained a series of willing boys. By that time Pinky had been discarded. I saw myself as I was then, and cringed at my self-pity over the break up which now seems so insignificant compared to all that has happened.

The beautiful Digby homestead has been torn down, and the land is now covered with an upmarket housing development that runs near to I71. The landscape of my childhood has disappeared, leaving me like an exile in a foreign place. I turned onto 670 and followed the signs to Easton Town Center, skirting to its east and parked near the storage building to unload the heavy metal cases. The storage unit is located in a solid new building, which will keep the archive safe until Katya finds it.

I returned early this afternoon, satisfied that only one steel case remains in the bedroom of the cabin. It contains the last, the most important parts of the archive.

I warm myself by the stove in the kitchen and watch the snow, now falling in thick white curtains. From the special waterproof folder, I remove the contents of the Box of the Harpuiai, the reason I have been forced to hide all these years.

After I disappeared from life as I knew it, I waited a couple of months, ensuring I was safe before having prints developed from old rolls of negatives hidden in the casket since the revolution. I hesitated before opening the packet from the camera shop, half fearing scenes like Kosloff's picture of decapitated enemy heads or of atrocities featuring the Tsar and his family. At first glance the photographs seemed to be of banal receipts and book keeping records. It was only on further examination that I realized they could be my death sentence.

As I line these up before me, an unsettling sick feeling of deep anger and fear overcomes me when I think of the torture and murders committed in the hunt for these documents.

The first print shows a deed to the gold mining districts of Nertchinsk and Altai, owned by the Tsar and left to the Brotherhood. The next details the name of the Swiss Bank, Pictet & Cie and an account number for his heir 29-34-08. The last one depicts a swastika identified as the Sign of the Brotherhood.

The significance of these documents was not clear until I examined the next photograph. Even now I gasp at the enormity of the secret. It shows receipts and shipping documents for a vast load of gold bullion, secretly moved out of Russia in 1916 by order of the Tsar.

According to the record shown on the prints, this hoard of gold from the mining fields of the Altai, was moved by train to Archangel and loaded onto the ships Tsarevich, Poltava, and Slavos. The shipping logs and registration trace the arrival of the gold to Le Havre, the port of entry in France, then on to a train to Geneva and its final destination, a vault in Pictet & Cie. This vast fortune, now worth billions of dollars, with power to ignite a revolution still lies in wait in the dark cool vault.

Two photographs are placed with these documents; the first dated June 10, 1916 shows four young men dressed in heavy coats and seaman's hats posing on a dock in front of a ship called the Poltava. Still shocked, I recognize Peter, Dimitri, Andrei and Sir Reginald Springsmith, all named at the bottom of photograph. I can only think this is the mission, to remove the Tsar's gold to a secret place, the mission Madame A was so terrified of exposing.

The last photograph is dated 1918 Tobolsk, and I know these are the unknown visitors to the Romanov family mentioned in the murder album. The subjects, identified in the picture are: The Tsar and his family, Peter, Dimitri, Andrei, and Sir Reginald Springsmith, Ms. Springsmith's father.

I use the magnifying glass to examine again the small marks that appear on the bottom right corner of each print, like some flaw in the negatives. I have determined that they are the Russian initials, G.A. For Georgi Antonov?

Georgi took these photographs on his trip to Tobolsk just before he and Nadya escaped from Russia. The prints he burned before his death must have been his forbidden copies, his claim to the fortune. Perhaps this was why he became so frightened when Madame A and the children arrived at his home. He saw that Sergei was not his son, but a dangerous replacement. Georgi realized his life was in danger, that there were others who knew he had copies of the photographs.

I let the dog in for the night. He shakes his thick fur, wet with snow, leaving puddles by the door, and settles down near the hot stove. I turn to the most significant part of my archive, the Tsar's Last Ukase. I unfold the thick vellum with the engraved Double Eagle, the Imperial Crest at the head. In the shadows of the red glow of the stove, I see the Tsar in his study in Tobolsk, about to be taken to his death. I am there, a prisoner in the room with him that day, 25 April 1918. I hear the scratch of his elegant onyx pen and feel his shame and anguish for all his failures. But, now the enemy has come. He shuts out his regrets and the commotion in the courtyard to stay focused. In these last moments before they seize him, he must write his final ukase.

My son Tsarevich Alexei will survive and God willing, the family will be protected. The Tsarevich has never officially abdicated. He is The Tsar of all the Russias. To aid him or any of my heirs in the return to the throne, I order that the bearer of this edict will receive all monies and title to lands currently held on deposit in the bank Pictet & Cie in Geneva, Switzerland.

Tsar Nicholas II.

Then he picks up the Box of the Harpuiai, turns it until he stops at the Harpy's face, presses its wing tip to open the casket, and places the ukase inside. His shadow fades from the glowing stove, and it occurs to me that the Tsar assumed that his son would be saved soon after he issued this ukase. Could the Tsar's heir really have been Sergei? Or was he used in some elaborate hoax to get money from the Swiss bank? There are so many lies. It is impossible to get at the truth.

Chapter 58

Rural Ohio and Columbus: 2000

THE DOG WATCHES me with pale, dispassionate eyes as I drive away. The metal case containing the last files and my computer hard disc rest on the seat beside me. Before the first frost while the ground was soft, I had walked into the forest and dug a deep hole. This morning I buried my computer, filling its grave with the dirt I had left in a pile beside it. The jeep bumps and skids on the snow as I turn onto the country lane. It is glass slippery, but I press on the accelerator, panicked over the last message on the computer.

I am coming for you. I have assumed the nom de revolution of the Bogatyr. Is it not ironic?

The group photograph that followed this message held me in a paralysis of fear and conjecture. It could be true, but it was too late. I did not have time to check on this photograph and placed it in with the last files in hopes that Katya will discover its significance.

I drive like a mad person, sliding onto the highway, my mind racing back to 1996, when Yeltsin with the support of the oligarchs was re-elected in Russia. I foolishly began to feel safe. It seemed obvious from the information that Boris was sending me that all who knew of the casket had either been murdered or died of old age. Although reclusiveness had become a natural way of life, there had seemed no need for me to hide any longer, so I began planning a trip to New York to see Abigail, and to find Katya. I also wanted to visit my father's grave. I had seen him only once for a few hours before going into hiding and had tried to explain what had happened, but he didn't believe me.

It has always been my habit to closely follow events in Russia, subscribing to many news sources. Shortly after Yeltsin became president, the Russian government began to sell off their assets and the age of privatization began. A group of businessmen, backed by mafia and with cooperation from the government gained control of deliberately undervalued government owned businesses, and natural resources and became billionaires. They formed a coterie around Yeltsin. Russia had become a dangerous place, like the Wild West; assassinations by Russian mafia and private security firms filled the newspapers, along with stories of conspicuous consumption by the nouveau riche.

It was March 11, 1996. I had made my plane reservation to New York and was examining a photograph of Yeltsin surrounded by his aides and supporters.

The highway seems to fly up in my face, and I jerk reflexively as that moment of terror returns. Like a Grimm's character, revived like a *besy* from some dark underworld, the man I knew as Jack, my lover was standing slightly to the left of Yeltsin. I picked up the telephone and cancelled my reservation to New York.

Over the next four years with frantic obsession, I used all my expertise as a researcher to be certain that what I had discovered was not the result of a solitary overworked imagination. I collected and studied countless photographs of Yeltsin and his aides, of the oligarchs, of the grand parties. Was the man in the photograph Jack? Was he still alive?

The same man appeared frequently but always as an obscure figure in the background of Yeltsin's coterie. His hair had thinned and he had grown heavier and looked far more Russian than I remembered, but even in the blurred photo I seemed to see the same intentness in his glance. At last he broke away from the shadows and I enlarged this picture from the background of Yeltsin's group. He was boarding a private jet with a much younger blonde woman. His piercing gaze was still there, but his features were thicker and more brutal. I went over articles many times, but never discovered his alias even when he posed with a group of oligarchs, owners of the Siberian gold and nickel mining production fields. I believe he has many identities.

At the beginning of this year, Putin succeeded Yeltsin as President, and news reports suggested the new leader had fallen out with the oligarchs, his benefactors. Sources quoted the new president stating that in the future the oligarchs would not figure as a class in Russia.

News and magazine articles questioning the legality of purchases of Russia's natural resources appeared in Russian and foreign news media. One from the *Economist* was titled, *Who Owns Russia's Natural Resources?* Several of the oligarchs, some of whom were planning to run for office in Russia's next elections, were threatened with arrest for not paying taxes and for fraud. The man I believed was Jack vanished from the newspapers and magazines.

It is snowing heavily now and the traffic on I71 has slowed. The jeep crawls toward Easton Town Center. The windscreen wipers move frantically, like the pounding in my head as I think of the consequences of my foolish mistake.

Disturbed and mystified by the oligarch's sudden disappearance from the news, I requested Boris to hunt for information on Jack Reilly.

There was one last message from Boris, the word 'No' before he signed off forever. Soon after this, the sinister emails began which caused me to flee to the cabin.

The snowplows are out, and the traffic begins to move. Finally I turn into the parking lot of the storage building.

All the while one terrifying thought remains in my mind. Jack is alive. He is the predator hunting me down to steal the ukase in a murderous bid to usurp power.

Chapter 59

Columbus and Rural Ohio: 2000

THE LAST OF the archive rests in the lock-up and both keys have been posted to the care of Collins and Chuter, a law firm in New York. I try to control the fear that grips me when I think of the internet message and this last photograph. But I can do nothing about that now. Whatever happens, I am determined that Jack will never seize the gold for his own evil purpose.

The treasure and the archive over which I have labored for the past thirty years will go to Katya. I am confident I am not putting her in danger. They are ignorant of her existence and there is nothing to trace her to me.

This strange legacy is all I have to leave to her, but she will know my story. She will know that I gave her away to save her. Perhaps she will even forgive me and realize how much I missed watching her grow up. We are both casualties of the past.

Now that the archive is hidden away, I feel enormous relief, but also emptiness, a sense of loss. Even though it is still snowing hard, I put off returning to the cabin and drive into the Easton Town Center, park the car and walk into a well-groomed colonial village theme park, its luxurious shops and restaurants built on lawns and separated by small street corners.

I cross in front of a square decorated for Christmas with wreaths, candles and small white lights, and wander like the ghost of Spybuck, through an alien landscape of shops, studying clothes, furniture, and china, luxuries of modern life that are of no use to me.

It is near noon and I stop at the Cheesecake Factory and order a sandwich. Four women and a little girl of two sit down next to me, fluttering cheerfully around the table like small colorful birds. Dressed in attractive casual sportswear endemic to the Midwest, they are all related, four generations. The oldest, the great grandmother, a tiny lively woman, sits beside the little girl, picture perfect with beautiful rosy skin and dark curls popping up all over her head. I look at them with envy. They have gone on with life, but I have remained with the ghosts, wandering in the past with Madame A and the émigrés, with Miss Safford and the dispossessed Indians.

"Are you all right?" One of the women, with short dark hair, sharp brown eyes, and a turned up nose, looks at me with concern.

"Thank you, I'm fine," I say in surprise. I had thought I was invisible to them. I eat quickly and nod to them as I leave.

On the way back to the cabin, I stop at a supermarket and on impulse, buy an expensive bottle of champagne. My thoughts turn to the Jack I once loved. I remember his arms around me. He had refused to kill me even though it might have meant his own life. I crazily still long for him to say it was all a mistake.

It is nearing dark and snowing hard as I pull up beside the cabin. The dog is gone for good this time. I hear the howling from the pack farther away. I have known for some time that he is a wolf, but did not want to admit it.

I feed the fire and dry off from the snow before making the last preparations. I place rolls of old negatives I found in Miss Adelaide's closet, and a piece of thick paper from one of her books on the floor in front of me and light a match to them. It is difficult and I wait impatiently for them to catch and then stamp out the blaze, leaving a small residue, enough to fake the contents of the casket. Then, I foolishly open the bottle of champagne and set it on the kitchen table beside Miss Adelaide's crystal goblets. Resuming my vigil from the bed I stare out the kitchen window, at the falling snow and wait for him, the shotgun in my lap.

In the pale morning light a dark shadow appears against the white landscape near the lane and advances toward the cabin. A heavy thud shoots through my chest as though my heart is bursting, and I am falling into the dream. A man is walking in the snow. He is heavily clad, bundled up so I cannot see his face. Before in the dream I thought it was Siberia, but the snow is outside my cabin. Before in the dream, he is always trudging in the distance so it is hard to know where he is going. But now I realize he always has been coming for me.

Note: In 1914 at the beginning of WWI, St. Petersburg was changed to Petrograd because of anti-German feeling, to Leningrad in 1924 after the death of Lenin, and back to St. Petersburg in 1991 after the fall of the Soviet Union. St. Petersburg or Petersburg is used throughout the novel, reflecting what the public called the city at that time.

Biographies of Historical Figures

Anna Anderson (1896–1984)

Pretender to the Russian throne. Anderson claimed to be Grand Duchess Anastasia, daughter of Tsar Nicholas II. In 1938 her supporters filed a suit in the German courts to prove that she was the Tsar's daughter and heir, survivor of the massacre in Ipatiev House. In 1970, the court ruled that there was not enough evidence to prove that she was the Grand Duchess. She married American professor Jack Manahan in 1969 and settled in Charlottesville, Virginia where she died of pneumonia. She was buried at Castle Seeon Germany. DNA testing in 1994 seemed to prove that Anderson was not Grand Duchess Anastasia.

Yuri Andropov (1914–1984)

Leader of the Soviet Union from 1982 to 1984. He was head of the KGB, Russia's State Security Service from 1967 to 1982 and known for his ruthlessness in putting down the Hungarian uprising in 1956, and for the brutality of his agents. He died of ill health in Moscow and was buried in the Kremlin wall.

Lavrenty Beria (1899–1953)

Chief of Soviet Security and Secret Police, NKVD during World War II. Deputy Premier of USSR from 1946 to 1953. During Stalin's purge (1937–38) he and his organization tortured and killed many of the dictator's political enemies. After Stalin's death in March 1953, he made a grab for power but was arrested by a group lead by Khrushchev, Molotov and Malenkov. He was executed, cremated and buried in an unmarked grave in a forest near Moscow.

Dr. Evgeny Botkin (1865–1918)

Personal physician to Tsar Nicholas II and his family. He followed the Romanovs into exile and was imprisoned with them in Ipatiev House. His personal effects were found at the Four Brothers Mine near Ekaterinburg, which indicated he had been murdered with the family.

Leonid Brezhnev (1906–1982)

Leader of the Soviet Union. General Secretary of the Central Committee of the Communist Party of the Soviet Union from 1964 until his death. He succeeded Khrushchev and ruled over a period of economic stagnation. He died of a heart attack and was buried in the Kremlin Wall.

Baroness Sophie Buxhoeveden (1883–1956)

Lady-in-Waiting to Tsarina Alexandra of Russia. She followed the Romanovs to prison in Tobolsk, but was not permitted to join them in Ipatiev House in Ekaterinburg. She was released from prison by the Bolsheviks, and escaped across Siberia to Denmark. Later, she refused to support Anna Anderson's claim to be the Grand Duchess Anastasia. She died in England in a grace and favor apartment granted by George V.

Marshall Chang Tso-lin: (1875–1928)

Powerful warlord who ruled Manchuria from 1916 to 1928. Known as the 'Old Marshall', he was allied with Japan and supported the restoration of China's Qing Dynasty. He was killed near Shenyang by a bomb planted under his train by a Japanese Kwantung army officer.

Prince Vasily Dolgorukov (1868–1918)

Marshal of the Imperial Court and aide to Tsar Nicholas II. He followed the Tsar and his family into exile and prison in Tsarskoe Selo and Tobolsk, but was not permitted to join them at Ipatiev House in Ekaterinburg. He was arrested in April 1918, imprisoned and shot in the woods on the outskirts of Ekaterinburg on July 10. He was buried after the White Army recaptured the town.

Felix Dzerzhinsky (1877–1926)

First head of the Cheka, the Bolshevik secret police established in 1917. He organized the reign of terror to keep the Bolsheviks in power. Known as 'Iron Felix' for the Cheka's merciless torture and mass executions without trial, he died of a heart attack in Moscow and was buried in the Kremlin Wall.

Captain Radola Gadja (1892–1948)

Leader of the Czech regiments in Siberia. He was promoted to Major General in the White Army, but was dismissed by Admiral Kolchak in 1919. He was involved in a failed coup against Kolchak and fled to Europe. After WWII, he was jailed for being a Fascist sympathizer and died in poverty in Prague.

George V King of England (1865–1936)

Grandson of Queen Victoria and first cousin of Tsar Nicholas II. He succeeded his father Edward VII in 1910. After the Russian Revolution, he refused asylum to the Tsar and his family because he feared greater political unrest from the socialists in Britain. He died of ill health and was succeeded by his son Edward VI.

General Maurice Janin (1862–1946)

French Commander of Allied Forces in Siberia during the Russian Civil War. He guaranteed the safety of Admiral Kolchak, head of the White Siberian Government, then ordered the Czech Legion to arrest the Admiral and hand him over to the Social Revolutionary government at Irkutsk. The Admiral was tried and executed. As a result, Janin was relieved of his command, ordered to return to France and demoted. He died in France shortly after the end of WWII.

Alexander Kerensky (1881–1970)

Prime Minister of the Russian Provisional Government from July 21, 1917 to November 8 1917. After the October Bolshevik Revolution, he escaped through Finland to London and then France where he actively opposed the

Bolshevik regime. During the Russian Civil War he opposed both the Reds and the Whites. At the beginning of WWII he moved to the United States. He died in New York and was buried in Putney Vale Cemetery in London after the Russian Orthodox Church in New York refused him burial.

Nikita Khrushchev (1894–1971)

Leader of the Soviet Union from 1953 to 1964 during the Cold War. He is known for his denunciation of Stalin's purge in his famous Secret Speech. He supported the early Soviet space program and attempted agricultural reforms. His reign at the height of the Cold War resulted in the erection of the Berlin Wall in 1961 and the Cuban Missile Crisis in 1962. He was removed from power in 1964 by party colleagues and succeeded by Leonid Brezhnev. He died of a heart attack in Moscow. He was denied a state funeral and burial in the Kremlin Wall. He was buried in the Novodevichy Cemetery in Moscow.

Admiral Alexander Kolchak (1874–1920)

Supreme Ruler of The White Siberian Government in Omsk from 1918 to 1920. Previously he was a Polar explorer and Commander of the Black Sea Fleet in 1916. He retreated by train from the Red Army advance to Omsk with his government and followers, including his mistress Mme. Timireva. During the retreat he was arrested by the Czech Legion on the order of General Janin and handed over to the Social Revolutionary government in Irkutsk. He was shot and his body pushed under the ice of the Ushakovka River.

General Lavr Kornilov (1870–1918)

Commander in Chief of the Provisional Government Army. In September 1917 he led the Third Army Corps in an attempt to get rid of Lenin and the Bolshevik Soviets and to place Petrograd under martial law. Kerensky, fearing a military coup, dismissed Kornilov and his officers, and imprisoned them in Bhykov Monastery. Kornilov and his men escaped to the Don District, where he became Military Commander of the White Volunteer Army. He was killed by a Red Army shell landing on his headquarters near Ekaterinodar and buried there. The Bolsheviks retook the town, dug up his body, dragged it through the streets and burned it on a rubbish dump in the main square of the town.

Mathilde Kschessinskaya (1872–1971)

Mistress of the future Tsar Nicholas II. A Prima Ballerina, she was the subject of gossip for conducting simultaneous affairs with the Tsar's cousins, Grand Dukes Sergei Mikhailovich and Andrei Vladimirovich, giving birth to a son Vladimir in 1902. She fled to France after the revolution and married Grand Duke Andrei, possible father to her son. In 1929 she opened a ballet school in Paris and taught the famous ballerinas, Dame Margot Fonteyn and Dame Alicia Markova. She died in Paris, eight months short of her 100th birthday and was buried in St. Genevieve des Bois, the Russian cemetery in Paris.

Vladimir Lenin, born Vladimir Ilyich Ulyanov (1870–1924)

Leader of the October Revolution in 1917. He became the head of the Bolshevik Russian government from 1922 to 1924. Once in power, he began to confiscate all private property, and also ended Russia's part in WWI. He founded the Cheka and instituted the Red Terror to eliminate opposition and consolidate power. He died after a third stroke at his estate at Gorki, outside Moscow, was embalmed and placed on exhibition in Lenin's Mausoleum in Moscow on January 27, 1924 where he remains today.

Vsevolod Merkulov (1895–1953)

Head of NKGB, state security from February to July 1941, and from April 1943 to March 1946. He worked for Beria, head of the Russian secret police. After Stalin's death, he was arrested and executed by firing squad along with Beria and five others. The bodies were cremated and buried in an unknown location near Moscow.

General Evgeny Miller (1867–1939)

Chairman of the Russian All-Military Union, an active anti-communist organization, from 1930–1937. He was Commander of the White Army in Northern Russian during the civil war and after the White defeat, settled in France. He was kidnapped in France by Russian agents, drugged and placed in a steamer trunk on a Russian ship to Moscow. He was tortured in the Lubyanka by the secret police and shot nineteen months later.

Vladimir Purishkevich (1870–1920)

A monarchist politician known for his part in the 1916 assassination of Rasputin in an attempt to save the monarchy. In 1917 he fled to Southern Russia, which was still controlled by the White Army. He died from typhus in Novorossiysk.

Vladimir Putin (1952)

Current President of Russia. A KGB officer for sixteen years, he became Acting President after Yeltsin's resignation in 1999 and then Prime Minister. He was President from 2000 to 2012. After a change in election laws, he ran for a third term in 2012 and was re-elected President for a six-year term.

Lieutenant Sidney George Reilly MC, Born Georgi Rosenblum (1873–1925)

Russian-born secret agent for British intelligence, known as the Ace of Spies. He was deeply involved in espionage during the Russian Revolution and Civil War and attempted to overthrow the Bolshevik regime in 1918. A master of deception, he may have been a model for James Bond. In September 1925, Russian agents lured him over the Finnish border to the Soviet Union on the pretext of contacting a member of The Trust, a fraudulent anti-communist group. He was interrogated in Lubyanka prison and executed in a forest near Moscow. Rumors circulated that he was alive and had become an advisor to Russian intelligence.

Grand Duke Dmitri Pavlovich Romanov (1891–1941)

First cousin to Tsar Nicholas II. He participated in the murder of Rasputin and as punishment was banished to the WWI Persian Front. He escaped from the Bolsheviks to London with British help and lived mainly in France. He suffered from tuberculosis and died in a sanatorium in Davos, Switzerland. Rumors circulated that the Bolsheviks had murdered him.

Ataman Gregory Semenov (1890–1946)

Commander-in-chief of the Chita Military District in the Trans Baikal region. Known for his brutality, he controlled the railways in the region and held up trains and extracted bribes for permitting supplies for Kolchak's forces to pass through his territory. After the White defeat in Siberia, Kolchak passed command of the eastern territory to him, and he continued to fight the Bolsheviks until 1921 He eventually settled in Manchuria, worked with Japanese intelligence, lead the exiled Russian and Cossacks in the area and was employed by Puyi, the last Manchu Emperor of China. In September 1945 during the Soviet invasion of Manchuria, he was captured by Soviet paratroopers and taken to Moscow. He was charged with counterrevolutionary activities, and executed by hanging.

Lieutenant General Andrei Shkuro (1887–1947)

Commander of the First Cossack Division in the White Army. He went into exile in 1920 in Serbia and France. During WWII, he organized a unit of anti-Soviet Cossacks, White émigrés and Soviet prisoners to fight with Nazi Germany to free Russia from Communism. At the end of the war, he surrendered to the British, was forcibly repatriated to Russia and executed by hanging.

Nicolas Sokolov (1882–1924)

Appointed January 1919 by Admiral Kolchak, head of The White Siberian Government, to investigate the assassination of the Romanovs. When the Red Army recaptured Ekaterinburg, Sokolov fled to France with the physical evidence he had collected. In 1924, he published his seven volume 'The Judicial Enquiry into the Assassination of the Russian Imperial Family', which concluded that the Romanovs had been murdered in Ipatiev House and their bodies burned to ashes. He died in Sabres, France shortly after publication of his work.

Joseph Stalin, born Iosif Dzhugashvili (1878–1953)

All-powerful Dictator of the Soviet Union from 6 May 1941 to 1953. He was General Secretary of the Central Committee from 1922 to 1953 and led the Soviet Union during WWII. He was a member of the Bolshevik party and took part in the Bolshevik revolution of 1917. As General Secretary, he consolidated power after the death of Lenin in 1924 and thereafter ruled by fear. He forced Russia to become an industrialized country and began an agricultural program, which resulted in famine in 1932–1933. During his repressive regime, millions of people were sent to the Gulag. During the Great Purge (1937–38) he eliminated his enemies and old Bolsheviks who were major figures of the revolution on the pretext of rooting out enemies of the government. Thousands were executed. Officially Stalin died four days after a massive stroke, but rumors abound that he might have been murdered by warfarin, a tasteless rat poison possibly added to his wine by Beria or Khrushchev. His body was embalmed and exhibited in Lenin's tomb. On 31 October 1961 it was removed from the mausoleum and buried in the Kremlin Wall.

Mme. Anna Timireva (1893–1975)

Admiral Kolchak's mistress. She was the wife of Navy officer Sergei Timiryov, a friend and subordinate of Kolchak's. She divorced in 1918, joined Kolchak in Siberia and travelled with the Admiral during the Siberian government's retreat from the Red Army. She accompanied him to prison at Irkutsk after his arrest by the local Social Revolutionary government. After his execution, she was released, but was hounded by authorities and imprisoned seven times. In 1950, she was released and worked as a set designer for the Rybinsk Theater. During the Khrushchev thaw, she was given a small pension and played bit parts in movies until her death.

Leon Trotsky, born Lev Bronstein (1879–1940)

People's Commissar of Military and Naval Affairs. He was the founder and first leader of the Red Army and a major figure in the Bolshevik victory in the Russian Civil War. A member of the first Politburo, and effective rival to Stalin, he was removed from power in 1927 and deported from the Soviet Union in 1929. While in exile in Mexico, he actively opposed Stalin and was assassinated with an ice pick by Ramon Mercador, a Soviet agent.

Mme. Anna Vyrubova (July 16 1884–July 20, 1964)

Best friend and constant companion of Tsarina Alexandra. A religious mystic, she became a devotee of Rasputin when he supposedly saved her life after she was severely injured in a railroad accident. Her small house outside the gates of Alexander Palace at Tsarskoe Selo became the secret meeting place of Rasputin and Tsarina Alexandra because these visits outside the palace grounds were not entered in official court records. After Rasputin's murder she was moved into the palace for safety, but then was arrested by Kerensky's government and imprisoned at the Peter and Paul Fortress. She was released and escaped to Finland in 1920. She became a nun and died in Helsinki.

Vasily Yakovlev, born Konstantin Mâčin (1885 to 1938)

Appointed by the Central Executive Committee of the Bolsheviks to transfer Tsar Nicholas II and his family from Tobolsk to Omsk. He was then ordered to divert the train to Ekaterinburg. There he handed the prisoners over to the local Soviet. He was arrested and executed in 1938 during Stalin's Purge.

Yakov Yurovsky (1878–1938)

Commandant of Ipatiev House, Member of Ural Regional Soviet and Cheka, Bolshevik secret police. Yurovsky was in charge of the Cheka squad who murdered Tsar Nicholas II, his family and retainers on night of July 16/17 1918. He died in Moscow of a peptic ulcer.

Prince Felix Yusupov (1887–1967)

Known for taking part in Rasputin's murder in the Yusupov Moika Palace in St Petersburg. The prince, from one of the wealthiest families in Russia, was married to Princess Irina Romanova, niece of Tsar Nicholas II. After the murder, Yusupov was not prosecuted but placed under house arrest at his estate outside St. Petersburg. He escaped the Bolsheviks, wrote two books about the murder and died in France in 1967. He was buried in St. Genevieve des Bois cemetery in Paris.

The Blood Archive, Book 2 of The Russian Trilogy, continues the story of the mysterious Romanov archive, destined to change the course of history. Worth billions, the archive holds startling and previously undisclosed evidence linked to the intriguing mystery surrounding the 1918 murders of the Romanov family.

An oligarch and ex-KGB spy, a brutal killer, is relentless in his hunt for the secret documents. The heroine, Katya Marston, a spoiled English woman, is forced to team up with Roo Yoder, a down to earth Midwestern deputy sheriff, in search of the archive. Sensing that they are in peril, but unaware that they are on the killer's hit list, the mismatched couple race from London, to New York, rural Ohio and the French Alps in search of the treasure.

An intriguing question lies at the heart of this intricate action packed novel: Did one of the Tsar's children survive the Romanov murders in 1918?

Look for The Blood Archive, Book 2
at your favorite online retailers.

About the Author

Judith Windeler who writes under the name Minerva Taylor is an American living in London. She spent ten years researching primary source material on Russia's Revolutionary and Stalinist Periods. Judith lived in New York City for thirteen years, and met many Russian émigrés, including her White Russian neighbor, a mother with two children abandoned by her husband, who escaped on her own from the 1917 Revolution through Siberia. Daily breakfasts and frequent other meetings with her émigré neighbor and her friends provided material and inspiration for these fast moving historically accurate novels.

The author has written three novels and two entertaining and educational children's books. Previously she was extensively published on three continents as a freelance writer.

CPSIA information can be obtained at www.ICGtesting.com
Printed in the USA
BVOW08s0739161016

465165BV00001B/58/P